LOVE C

Liberty was trembling by the time Judah's mouth settled on hers. He drew her body tightly against his, and her blood flamed with desire. The evening sounds of the swamp faded as he whispered her name in a passionate voice.

"Not what I had in mind when I promised you a wedding night," he told her, looking deeply into her eyes. "I must say, we do seem to make love in the most unusual places."

"You aren't . . . you wouldn't be considering . . . not here in the open?"

"I believe that is exactly what I have in mind. When I am near you, all I can think about is taking you to me. I want you, Liberty. I will always want you."

Her heart cried out, wanting to hear him speak of love, not want. Already her body was reacting to his touch.

"I feel we are the only two people on earth, Liberty. It seems if I wanted to, I could reach up and pluck the stars right out of the sky."

She wondered what thought he was trying to convey to her. It didn't matter. She had never known such happiness. For the first time in her life, she felt as if she really belonged to someone. She was Judah's wife, and there was such comfort in that thought. She dared not ask if he loved her—for the moment it was enough to know he desired her. . . .

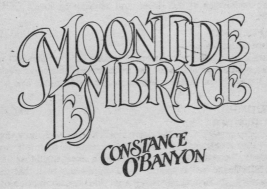

MOONTIDE EMBRACE

CONSTANCE O'BANYON

ZEBRA BOOKS
KENSINGTON PUBLISHING CORP.

ZEBRA BOOKS

are published by

Kensington Publishing Corp.
475 Park Avenue South
New York, NY 10016

First printing: October, 1987

Printed in the United States of America

DEDICATION

This is for you, Karen and Gerald Gee. How far we have traveled together—how many unforgetable memories we shared. Amid tears and laughter we faced our growing years and survived only because we had each other. I would do it all again if I had the two of you beside me.

In loving memory of David Joe Gee. You touched our lives so briefly, but left an imprint that will endure. I believe we are better, and more tolerant, for having known you.

To my friend, Phil Cease, from the Great American Shoe Store. Thank you for your wonderful sense of humor that allowed me to make a pirate out of you.

Moon Tide

Moon Tide rising impels frothy waves upon the shore.
Cannons break the silence like the thunder of
impending war.

You tantalized and seduced my love, oh deceiving
devil moon.
In your golden light of splendor you hide the
promise of forthcoming doom.

The canvas spread to catch the wind as my love sails
to sea.
Moon Tide you are triumphant, for he loves duty
more than me.

Constance O'Banyon

Part One

Betrayal

Chapter One

Outside Boston Harbor, 1811

A heavy fog hung in the air, making it impossible to see more than fifty feet ahead. With her captain at the helm, the *Winged Victory* was running smoothly over the choppy sea. She was a twenty-eight-gun frigate with a long keel that produced a finer line than that of most frigates, and made her ride lower in the water. Her undercut hull was built for swiftness, adding several knots to her speed. Her three masts supported yards of white canvas that now billowed in the wind.

Judah Slaughter, her captain, stared through the fog. A worried frown creased his brow, and he wondered how much longer he would be able to keep the *Winged Victory* afloat. There was precious little money coming from the coastal trade. His cargo from Boston to South Carolina was usually furniture and household goods. The return cargo was always raw material—cotton, timber, or sugar cane. After paying the crew's wages, there was hardly enough money left to buy supplies for the next voyage.

The first mate, Philippe Cease, a man of medium height, with soft blue eyes and a ready smile, made his way up the quarter-deck. Approaching his young captain, he stopped at his side, and both men stared into the fog, trying to catch the first sight of the Boston shoreline.

Judah Slaughter stood with his legs widespread, while the wind ruffled his golden, shoulder-length hair. His white linen shirt, with its crisscrossed ties, was open at the throat revealing the golden hair on his broad chest. Judah was a handsome rogue. His face was deeply tanned; his turquoise blue eyes were penetrating and seeking, almost overwhelming to any person he chose to intimidate.

Philippe knew his young captain was a powerful force that invoked confidence from the crew members of the *Winged Victory*. Without question they followed his orders to a man.

Judah caught the smile that curved the rough plane of his first mate's face. "Is it visions of gold that hold your attention, my friend, or were you thinking that you are only hours away from home?"

"Neither. I was just thinking that there are very few men who have a gut feeling for the sea, even fewer who have a deep kinship with it—men who use the seven seas to their best advantage, and feel the slapping of the waves in some innermost part of their brains. In all my life I have known only three men who had that God-given ability. Your papa was one of them, and you are another."

Judah smiled at the compliment. "Who was the third?"

Philippe grinned, and his blue eyes danced. "With all due modesty, I must admit it is none other than I." A teasing light sparkled in his eyes. "And to think my mother wanted me to be a cobbler, and make shoes. Had I followed her advice, I would have missed sailing with your father and yourself, and some of the greatest adventures of my life."

Judah felt proud that Philippe should compare him to his father, for Philippe had stood by him when he was nothing more than a young, floundering youth learning to be a man. Judah had never known his own father, who had died when Judah was but an infant. It was Philippe

12

who had served his father, taking the young Slaughter under his wing and teaching him about the sea.

"With you, I am reminded of your papa. When you issue an order, you never raise your voice in anger, yet your men would follow you into hell. Your papa would be proud of you."

The *Winged Victory* had always been a privately owned vessel. It had once belonged to Judah's father—it now belonged to Judah. Daniel Slaughter had won many sea battles when he had used the ship in the Revolutionary War. He had sailed her as a privateer, to help the American cause, and he had been a hero, decorated for bravery by President Washington himself.

But he had been killed in a sea battle involving the Barbary pirates. That fact burned in Judah's heart. He hoped one day to face those pirates and gain some amount of satisfaction.

At Judah's mother's request, Philippe had taken over the *Winged Victory,* and had enlisted her in trade for several years. But very little money had come from the venture. The ship had fallen on hard times, and was placed in dry dock until Judah was old enough to take her out and make her seaworthy again.

Judah looked at his first mate. "I have learned much from you, Philippe. You took a half-grown lad, and made a sea captain out of him. Do not think I am not aware of the times you stood at my side, quietly showing me the right way to carry out a deed. Most of what I am, I owe to you, my friend."

Philippe clapped Judah on the back in a rare show of affection. Always when the crew was about, Philippe treated his captain with professional respect. "I owe it to your papa to look after you, so I stood in his place and taught you the things he would want you to know. I guess you could say I borrowed the joy that would have been his in watching you develop into a fine captain." Phi-

13

lippe's eyes danced with mischief. "Of course, I never got around to teaching you about women . . . but I believe you were born knowing about them."

Judah laughed. "Not so, my friend. I find myself in a quandary where the fair sex are concerned. I admit to being at a loss when it comes to having an intelligent conversation with them. Besides my mother, I find very few who have a serious thought in their heads."

"What about your pretty songbird, Adriane Pierce?"

"Adriane does not have to be intelligent. She has other attributes to her credit."

"Such as?"

Judah smiled. "She has a lovely voice."

"Ah, yes, I have heard her sing. She does indeed have a lovely voice," Philippe agreed.

Judah thought of Adriane. He had met her one night when he'd attended one of her performances at the Blue Rose Theater in Boston. Her face was lovely, and her voice sweet. He had been surprised when she had allowed him to call on her, and his puzzlement had deepened when she'd begun to favor him over older, wealthier men. She had now been his mistress for two years.

The watchman broke into his thoughts, yelling down from the crow's-nest. "Land ho! Boston Harbor dead ahead."

Judah knew these waters as well as any man, knew where to look for sand bars and shallows. Bringing the *Winged Victory* about so her sails caught the billowing wind, he headed her nose into the horizon and home port.

A heady wind dipped out of the angry, gray sky and slammed frothy waves against the *Winged Victory*, which was riding high in the channel since her cargo had been unloaded and placed in warehouses along India Wharf.

14

Judah, draped in a black cape, turned his face to the wind, tasting the salty mist that wet his lips. His turquoise blue eyes moved past the channel, choked with sailing vessels, to the shops, the numerous inns, and the brick warehouses that cluttered the waterfront.

Since Boston was located on a peninsula, the city was almost like an island, and it was quickly becoming a major harbor, in spite of the fact that many American ships were being challenged by British, as well as the French fleets. Rumblings of war were in the air. America was waiting, holding her breath. She had enemies—powerful enemies. Aside from the English and French that tormented the American shipping trade, there were the Barbary pirates to contend with. The pirates controlled the Mediterranean, and demanded tribute from any vessel within her waters. It did not matter that a peace treaty had been signed between America and the Barbary States in 1805. For several years now the Pasha of Tripoli had renewed his piratic attacks, taking American ships and enslaving both the passengers and crew, sometimes even women and children.

Judah knew in his heart that one day he would do battle with the Barbary pirates, and avenge his father's death. His most fervent wish was that he might stand face-to-face with Abdul Ismar, the man who had struck his father down.

The dark mood left Judah and a smile curved his lips as he caught sight of a lone carriage rattling down India Street, the horses straining against the wind. After being at sea for the last month, he welcomed the thought of a few hours of pleasure with Adriane.

Judah waved to his crew and, with a chuckle, charged each of them not to waste their first night ashore on the pleasure of women and demon rum.

Adriane poured wine into the delicate glass, then handed it to Judah. Her heart was beating wildly as he lifted the glass to his lips and took a sip, his eyes moving down her body. Even though she was five years his senior, she found him to be the most exciting man she had ever known.

He reached out and pulled her onto his lap, and she melted against him, trying to analyze her feelings. Why did Judah Slaughter have the ability to turn her bones to molten lava? She had known many men who desired her. What was so special about him?

He twisted a red curl around his finger and gently pulled her face closer to his. Shivers of delight raced through her as his lips touched her mouth. "Can you stay long?" she questioned breathlessly.

"No. Just the night."

Disappointment clouded her eyes. "But why? I have missed you. I had hoped we could—"

His mouth covered hers to silence her. When she was breathless from his kiss, he raised his head and smiled down at her. "We must make the best of the time we have," he whispered.

Still hurt that he was not going to spend more time with her, Adriane drew back. "Why can you not stay a day or two?"

"My mother has sent word that she wants to see me. I must leave early in the morning."

"Will you be back before you sail again?"

He toyed with the bow on her gown. "I don't know."

Adriane sighed heavily and laid her head against his broad chest. She had realized long ago that she would never hold the smallest part of Judah's heart. She would have to be content with the knowledge that, at the moment, he desired her. She was wise enough to realize his craving for her would wane in time, and she would have to let him go. Already she could read discontent in

16

his eyes.

As his lips moved down her arched neck, Adriane ran her fingers through his golden hair. She must not think of tomorrow and the agony of parting from Judah. Tonight he belonged to her, and her alone.

Judah called to his mother as she waited on the steps of her modest, red brick house, and Gabrielle Slaughter's eyes softened when they rested on her son's handsome face. Joy sung in her heart as he strode toward her, his black boots clicking on the cobblestone walkway.

When he reached her side, Judah picked her up and hugged her tightly. "You are looking wonderful as always. I believe you live life in reverse and grow younger with the passing of time, Mother," he said, placing her on her feet and beaming down at her.

A soft smile curved Gabrielle's lips, but her eyes were clouded. "Welcome home, my son," she said with a heavy French accent. "You always know what to say to make me feel good about myself."

Judah did not miss the troubled expression on her face as she led him into the sitting room. "Is anything the matter?" he asked. Like his father before him, Judah spoke with a definite Boston accent.

"We will speak of it later," Gabrielle responded as Nelda came in carrying a tea tray. The maid beamed a welcome to Judah. "I made your favorite butter cake," she announced proudly.

"You spoil me, Nelda."

The white-haired maid giggled. "I suspect all women spoil you, Master Judah," she declared.

When Nelda departed, Judah's attention returned to his mother. Even though the bloom of youth was no longer on her cheeks, and the curls that softly fanned out across her forehead were sprinkled with gray, she was still a lovely woman. There was an elegance about her, an air of superior breeding. She came from a proud old French family which had settled in New Orleans over a hundred years earlier.

Gabrielle motioned for Judah to sit beside her near the warm fireplace. After pouring him a cup of steaming tea and placing a plate of cakes within his reach, she met his inquiring glance. "What is your news, Mother? Are you troubled about something? You are not ill, are you?"

Soft firelight fell on Gabrielle's face, disguising the worried frown that curved her lips downward as she watched his face expectantly. "I have received a letter from my father. He has asked that I come to Bend of the River Plantation and bring you with me. He says he is . . . ill, but that it is not of a serious nature. Can you imagine the joy that filled my heart when I read his letter asking me to come home after all these years?"

Judah looked at her through lowered lashes. "I find it strange that you would be enthusiastic about the prospects of visiting your father when for so long he has turned his back on you. I, for one, have no intention of going to New Orleans to see a man who has, until now, ignored my existence."

Linking her arm through Judah's, Gabrielle Slaughter snuggled closer to him for warmth. "I know it is difficult for you to understand a man like my father. He is proud and stubborn." She smiled. "Sometimes you remind me of him."

Judah stared at the fire, lost in thought. His grandfather lived on a plantation outside New Orleans, and according to his mother, ruled it with an iron fist. "Philippe tells me I am much like my own father," he said with feeling. "I have no desire to emulate a man who has so cruelly turned my mother away from his door."

Gabrielle's eyes took on a wistful look. "It is a pity that your father didn't live to see what a fine son he had in you." Her eyes misted. "He would have been so proud of you today."

Judah clasped her cold hand in his. Even though her husband had been dead for many years, Gabrielle still mourned his passing. Daniel Slaughter had not been a wealthy man, since he had enlisted the *Winged Victory* in the defense of his country, rather than turning to piracy as many other American shipowners had. All he had to leave his wife and son was his good name, the modest Tudor cottage, a small income from property left to him by his father, and of course the *Winged Victory.*

"Will you come with me, Judah? Will you visit my father at Bend of the River?"

Judah picked up the wool coverlet that was folded over the back of the settee, and placed it across his mother's lap. "Have you asked yourself why my grandfather would issue an invitation to you after all these years? You will never make me believe he is sorry for how he treated you in the past and wants to make amends." His eyes showed the skepticism he was feeling.

Gabrielle studied her son's face, trying to see him through the eyes of the many young ladies who flirted outrageously with him. To people who did not know him, Judah might appear somewhat arrogant and overconfident. To Gabrielle, he had always been a loving and dutiful son.

There had been many lonely days for Gabrielle since Daniel had been killed. She sighed, remembering the lonely nights she had lain awake aching for her husband. All the medals, the letters of praise from a grateful country had brought little solace to her widow's bed. The one bright spot in her life had been her son. Judah had the same blond handsomeness as her dead husband, but his deep turquoise eyes came from Gabrielle's own father.

Yes, she thought, there had been difficult times in the past, but she had stubbornly persevered for her son's sake. Judah was a son any mother would be proud of. His manners were polished, and he was a handsome rogue — this he had also inherited from his father.

Her hand moved up to brush against his cheek. "I know how much it will wound your pride to take me 'to Bend of the River, but it would mean so much to me to have you with me."

Judah's eyes softened. "I always find it hard to say no to you." His lips curled in a smile, then hardened into a firm line. "But do not ask more of me than I can give, Mother."

She shrugged her shoulders. "I suppose I could go alone. . . ."

Judah drew in a deep breath, knowing his mother had won. He would never allow her to face her father without him at her side. "When would you like to leave?" he asked, admitting defeat.

Her smile was bright. Then she touched her lips to his cheek. "I believe good things will come from this visit. As you know, my father is wealthy beyond anything you can imagine. Perhaps I can persuade him to give you the money to make the needed repairs on the *Winged Victory*."

"No, that is the one thing you must not do, Mother. I will never take money from a man who denied my existence and swore that you married beneath you when you wed my father. I want nothing from him."

"But you will go with me?"

"If it is your wish."

She laid her head against his broad shoulder. "You are a good son, Judah."

"I can only imagine how you must have twisted my father around your little finger. I myself can never resist your pleas."

"No, no. It was always the other way around. Your father could charm the birds from the trees when he

20

wanted to. You are a rake, and have your father's glib tongue. If you can so easily charm me, do you not think you must be devastating to the inexperienced young ladies of your acquaintance?"

His laughter was warm. "How can I answer such a question without appearing to be an egotistical fool?"

Gabrielle laughed softly. "No need to answer, you scoundrel. I have had any number of young ladies inquiring as to when the *Winged Victory* would put into port. It is my belief that you could pick and choose a bride from among Boston's finest families."

"I believe you are deliberately trying to flatter me, Mother. Could it be that you are trying to lure me into a marriage with someone of your choosing."

Gabrielle laughed merrily. "I leave the choosing of a bride to you, Judah." A mischievous light sparkled in her eyes. "Still, I would not say no to Abby Munsinger. She is a lovely young lady."

"Her feet are too large, her ankles too thin."

Gabrielle pretended shocked surprise. "How would you know about her ankles?"

He smiled. "I notice the small details."

"And Carrie Lundigan?"

"I cannot abide her twittering laugh."

"Sissy Dewitt?"

"Too skinny. Did anyone ever tell you that you are a meddlesome woman, Mother?"

"On occasion," she replied, undaunted in her quest. "How about Maggie Dewitt?"

"Too stout." Judah held up his hand. "Can we not talk about something else? Tell me more about the letter from your father."

Gabrielle Slaughter removed the crumpled letter from her pocket and lovingly pressed the wrinkles out before replacing it in the envelope. "I could not believe it when the letter came. After all these years, I was sure my father

21

would never consent to see me again. Imagine him changing his mind."

Judah clamped his jaw together tightly so he would not be tempted to express his own views on his grandfather's belated invitation—belated by twenty-five years. Judah thought of the man as an unfeeling bastard who still wanted his own way. Seeing the wistfulness in his mother's eyes, he knew it was best to let her put her own interpretation on the letter.

"I know what you are thinking, Judah, but you are wrong."

He smiled down at the tiny woman who had been his whole world for so much of his young life. She had kept them going despite impossible odds, and now she never complained when he was at sea for months at a time, but welcomed him joyously when he returned. "What am I thinking, Mother?"

"You are thinking that I should have thrown this invitation back in my father's face, but you do not know him as I do. I always knew the day would come when he would want to see you, so he could judge for himself how you had turned out. He has no family other than his younger brother's son, Sebastian. He is an old man, and wants to see his only grandson. I will be proud to present you to him. I believe he will find you are a credit to the Montesquieu name."

Judah's reaction was swift. His turquoise eyes blazed, and his chin set in a stubborn line. "I bear the name Slaughter, as did my father," he reminded her with a slight sting to his words. "I will never apologize for a name that is as old and as prestigious as Montesquieu. Why should I be concerned about whether or not I measure up to your father's idea of what a gentleman should be? If my father was not good enough for him, then neither am I."

Gabrielle felt tears well up in her eyes. "No one could have been prouder of your father's name than I. Daniel

22

was a hero, and died a hero's death. I have letters from Thomas Jefferson and John Adams praising his heroism." Gabrielle dabbed at her eyes before continuing. "When I met your father in France, the summer we were married, he was acting as an emissary for the Continental Congress. He was a good man, an honorable man. I loved him well. You must always be proud that he was a hero."

"A hero . . . but dead nonetheless," Judah said bitterly. "Your father disinherited you for marrying him, since he felt you had married beneath you, and in all these years he has returned your letters unopened and has refused to communicate with you in any way. Why are you not suspicious about why he wants to see you now?"

"It is as I said. He wants to meet you. He is an old man, and wants to make peace before he dies. I have heard that he made his nephew, Sebastian, his heir when he became displeased with me."

Judah laced his fingers together. "I see that you have kept up with your family. I wonder how you accomplished that?"

His mother returned his smile. "My girlhood friend, Minette, lives in New Orleans, and we communicate each Christmas. She always keeps me informed on local happenings."

Judah glanced down at the envelope on his mother's lap. "Just what does the letter say?"

"It simply states that I am to bring you to New Orleans. There we will be met and transported to Bend of the River Plantation. Your grandfather was always one to issue orders. He expects everyone to submit to his command. It is his way," she said apologetically. "If one loves Father, one overlooks his domination."

It was hard for Judah to feel charitable toward a man who had broken his mother's heart and had left her alone and floundering after her husband had died. He was thoughtful for a moment while he worked the details out in his mind. "I will have the *Winged Victory* outfitted tomorrow. I have always considered testing the trade in the Spanish Territories. I suppose now is as good a time as any. While I take you to see your father, Philippe can sail on to the Spanish coast. He will then return to New Orleans and wait until you are ready to leave. Is this satisfactory with you?"

Her eyes sparkled happily. "Oh, yes. That is very satisfactory with me."

Judah had no intention of remaining at Bend of the River Plantation one day longer than was necessary. A feeling of dread passed over his heart, for he had the strangest feeling that he would soon be stepping back into his mother's past and there would be no place for him there.

Chapter Two

Louisiana, 1811

It was a swamp world of strange undisturbed beauty, a land of struggle and survival—a majestic wilderness. Great oaks were draped with cloaks of gray Spanish moss. Willow trees dipped leafy branches in the mirror-bright water, while the mighty cypress trees stood like ghostly sentinels, guarding against man's intrusion into this paradise.

Overhead, a heron glided on the soft morning breeze. Below it, the lazy bayou sheltered a multitude of wildlife before it emptied into the Mississippi River. One of the swamp's wayward sons, an alligator, eased through the green blanket of wild hyacinths and disappeared from sight.

Suddenly a small skiff skimmed over the bayou, breaking the halcyon silence. A family of nutria scurried to the water's edge. Large turtles, sunning themselves on cypress logs, occasionally plopped into the bayou. As the skiff bumped against the mossy bank, the lone occupant, a young girl, stepped agilely ashore and secured the boat to a sun-rotted log.

At fifteen years of age, Liberty Boudreaux was as much a part of this land as the white-tailed deer that now darted through the blackberry thicket to approach her, unafraid. She was a frequent visitor and was welcomed by all the small animals that called the swamp home.

The skirt of her gray homespun gown was tucked inside her waistband, revealing muddy, knee-high brown boots. Her golden hair was plaited into a single braid that hung over one shoulder. Liberty was a child of the earth, attuned to every aspect of nature.

The white-tailed deer nudged the young girl's hand, and was rewarded by the sound of laughter. The girl reached into her pocket, then offered the large animal a handful of grain. Other animals, smaller ones, began to timidly poke their heads from the underbrush. A venturesome swamp rabbit hopped across Liberty's boot and was offered a soft pat and a plump carrot.

As Liberty dropped down onto a carpet of soft lilacs, she was immediately surrounded by her strange entourage. In this swampy isolated world, the girl was not lonely, for she had her animal friends. This was where she always came when her own world offered her only neglect and heartache.

There was joy in Liberty's heart as she breathed in the exotic fragrance of the numerous flowering plants that dotted the landscape. This wilderness could be harsh and dangerous to anyone unfamiliar with its hazards—but not to Liberty. She knew every inch of this swamp, knew where the pools of quicksand were located. They could swallow a man without leaving a trace of him. She always avoided the poisonous snakes that lay in wait for the unaware, and she had a great respect for the alligators that ruled the swamp kingdom.

Liberty also knew where Zippora, the old black woman, lived with her simple-minded grandson, Reuben. Liberty avoided the old woman most of all, for it was said that she was a witch and practiced voodoo. That fact did not seem to stop many fashionable young ladies from flocking to Zippora when she went into New Orleans to sell her love potions, gris-gris, and good-luck charms. The old woman was quite the rage among the more prominent women of New Orleans.

It was rumored that Zippora had been very beautiful in her youth. She was said to have been a slave until her young master fell in love with her and set her free. Liberty doubted this to be true. Liberty's mother believed that Zippora herself had circulated the story so she would appear tragically romantic to the young ladies of quality.

When Liberty was in the swamps she would often see Zippora and her young grandson from a distance. Liberty and the old woman had an unspoken agreement; they never invaded each other's privacy. Liberty certainly had no intention of even nearing Zippora's territory. No one ever crossed Zippora's land.

Suddenly the soft peaceful sounds of the swamp were disturbed by the sounds of man's intrusion. Voices were raised in anger, and there was no mistaking the sound of the whiplash that filled the stillness. The small animals scurried into dense undergrowth, while the fleeter deer bounded into the air and disappeared down a grassy slope.

Liberty stood up slowly and moved toward the sound. Keeping in the shadow of the willow trees, she made her way to the place where the red cypress-stained swamp water forked and emptied into the Mississippi River. She cautiously parted the willow branches and held her breath as she watched the two men struggling with a young boy. It took her only seconds to see that the boy was Zippora's grandson. The poor child was frightened out of his wits, and was making fearful whimpering sounds.

Liberty had no trouble recognizing the two as slavers that sailed the Mississippi River looking for runaways. Everyone knew they were residents of Barataria, the haven for Jean Lafitte's cutthroats and pirates. Liberty's soft lips curled in disgust as her anger boiled. When one of the men raised his whip and applied it to the young black boy's back, she didn't stop to weigh the consequences, but

27

ran to the river's edge and bounded onto the swamp boat.

Before the startled slavers could react, she had jerked the whip from one of them and had tossed it onto the riverbank. "How dare you do this!" she cried, bending to gather the sobbing young boy in her arms. "I am appalled that you would torture a child. My father will hear of this, and you will regret your folly."

The man who had been wielding the whip now turned his attention on Liberty. "Mayhap I just trade the boy for you, little girl." Grinning, he showed chipped and blackened teeth. He smelled of the sweat that dripped down his face and onto his shirt, plastering the material to his body.

The second man reached out and grabbed Liberty's braid, jerking her face up to his. "Who would your pa be, that you should want to threaten us with him?"

Now Liberty could see the folly of her actions. She knew she had placed herself in real danger. These men were unscrupulous, with no regard or respect for human life. They ran a black-market slave ring, and wouldn't think twice about harming her. Nevertheless, her eyes sparkled with anger. "My father is Louis Boudreaux, and he will see you dead if you do not release me at once."

Loud laughter came from both men. "I know about Monsieur Boudreaux. You can't be the daughter of such a fine gentleman. You look like nothing more than a poor little swamp rat."

The young boy had been all but forgotten, and Liberty surreptitiously watched him crawl over the side of the boat, drop into the water, and swim around the bend of the river, toward the bayou. She was glad he, at least, had escaped the two men.

Tears of pain brightened her eyes as the slaver applied pressure to her hair. "Allow me to introduce myself to you, little girl. I'm Sidney, and this here's my brother, Frank. There ain't no need for last names."

The man called Frank flicked his tongue out and allowed his eyes to feast hungrily on the delicate young girl. "Bet she'd be a tender young thing, Sidney. We found ourselves a prize today. Suppose we take her home with us, mayhap fatten her up a bit."

"Yeh, she's a mighty spicy piece at that," his brother added, running his filthy hands down the front of her gown and pinching her firm young breasts until she cried out in pain.

Liberty swung wide and caught the man hard across the face. He only laughed and picked her up in his arms. She shuddered in disgust when he stepped out of the boat. Then she quaked with fear, realizing what the two men had in mind for her, knowing there was no one about to come to her rescue.

Sidney carried her up the grassy bank and out of sight of the river. Tossing her onto the ground, he quickly straddled her, while pinning her arms above her head. "Me and my brother will both have us a time with you, little swamp rat."

Grabbing Liberty's chin in a viselike grip, Sidney made her look at him. He was crude and filthy — she could feel the bile rising up in her throat. Defiant blue eyes challenged him. Liberty knew she had to try to save herself. Even though she struggled with all her might, he only laughed at her puny efforts. Angry and frightened, Liberty spit in the man's face.

"Damn you," he swore, striking a forceful blow that brought blood to her lips and almost made her lose consciousness.

Liberty's head was swimming, and she felt as if the ground tilted up and hit her in the face.

"Have at her, Sidney; then I'll take me a turn," Frank said, dropping down and grasping Liberty's arms. "She ain't a bad looker, and I like 'em young."

Liberty knew it would do no good to plead for her

freedom. These men were past reasoning. She fixed her eyes on a moss-covered tree limb, trying to resign herself to her fate, but a tear slid down her cheek as she remembered that today was her birthday and no one in her family had remembered. Since she was about to be ravished by two slimy creatures who would probably kill her afterward, Liberty prayed for a quick death.

She felt the man's hands slip under her gown, and she gritted her teeth to keep from crying out. Closing her eyes, she tried to blot out the sight of his ugly face. It was so quiet; hardly a sound could be heard above the two men's labored breathing. It was as if time had been suspended and the whole swamp world was watching and waiting to see what would happen to the young girl.

Suddenly the sound of a bullwhip crackled through the air, shattering the stillness. Sidney leaped to his feet, while his brother stared in disbelief at the tall black woman who wielded the whip like an avenging angel, or perhaps a devil.

"Back away from the girl, white man," Zippora said in a deadly calm voice — a voice laced with a heavy French accent.

"Who are you?" Frank asked, releasing Liberty and standing up beside his brother.

A sudden gust of wind swirled about Zippora, and her dark eyes blazed with a strange yellow light. "I am one who will horsewhip you if you do not do as I say."

Sidney advanced a step toward the old woman. "Ain't no threat coming from you gonna scare me off. I don't care if you are an old woman. I'll tear your head off and feed it to the 'gators."

"You had better take my threat as real, white man." The whip slashed through the air and caught Sidney across the cheek. Swearing in pain, he reached up to find blood flowing from a deep gash. "I'll kill you for that," he swore angrily.

30

By this time Liberty had gained her footing and was backing away. Again the whip snaked through the air, this time wrapping around the neck of the second brother. Zippora yanked on the handle and toppled the man to the ground, where he twisted and gasped for breath.

"I predict your death," Zippora said softly. "I see your boat sinking in the river. I hope you can swim against the current."

Sidney watched his brother unwind the whip from around his neck before he blurted out. "I know who you are! You're that damned witch, Zippora."

"That is so. My grandson you met earlier," she answered, nodding to the young black boy who had come up to stand beside Liberty.

Frank stood on shaky legs, and his eyes bulged out in fear. "We been cursed, Sidney. This here's the voodoo woman. We're as good as dead!"

"Shut up, you fool," his brother commanded, backing toward the boat while keeping an eye on the old woman. "We didn't mean no harm, ma'am. We was just funning with the boy."

"Were you also funning with the white girl?" Zippora asked, pointing a bony finger at both men.

"What should you care about a white girl?" Frank questioned, as his back came up against a tree that was blocking his exit.

Zippora's eyes rested momentarily on Liberty and seemed to soften. "I care about this white girl," she said, tossing the whip down. "Go. You have already incurred my wrath. Do not force me to send the raven to pluck your eyes from your dead bodies."

It took no time at all for the two brothers to scamper around the bend to be lost from sight. Liberty drew in a deep sigh of relief, until her gaze met the yellow eyes of Zippora. The fright she'd felt when she'd thought the two men were gong to ravish her was a puny feeling compared to her fear of this woman.

"I will . . . just be going, too," Liberty said, taking a step backward, trying to remember where she had secured her skiff.

Zippora shook her head. "You will come with me so I can tend your wound and mend your gown. Then you will be free to go to your home, Liberty Boudreaux."

Liberty eyed Zippora, ready to take flight if the woman should come too near. Apprehensively she tested her bloody lip with her finger. "I am but scratched. My family will be worried about me if I do not start for home now."

"Your family does not look to your whereabouts, Liberty Boudreaux. Wipe your apprehension from your mind. You have nothing to fear from me. I have watched you for years as you played along the bayou. I have seen the animals eat from your hand. I have seen the tears you cried when you thought no one was near. Today I saw you place yourself in danger to save my grandson from the slavers."

For the first time Liberty glanced down at the boy. His dark eyes were shining and his smile was sweet. "He does not seem to be injured," she said, dropping to her knees and looking him over. "He must have been more frightened than hurt."

"Thanks to you, Liberty Boudreaux. Now you will come home with me so I can repay your kindness."

Liberty stood, undecided, as Zippora turned and walked away. She wanted to go, yet she still feared the old woman. She thought how exciting it would be to tell her sister, Bandera, that she had gone to the house of the witch Zippora. The young boy tugged at her hand, making up her mind for her. She gathered her courage and allowed the boy to lead her down a worn pathway. Perhaps she would die from some awful curse, but if she lived, what a tale she would have to relay to Bandera.

Liberty had to rush to catch up with Zippora, who set a zestful pace for someone of her obviously advanced age. As they walked along, the young girl studied the old woman out of the corner of her eye. Zippora was tall and slender. Her face was like cinnamon, yet parched and leathery. Her strange catlike yellow eyes were filled with shrewdness. Her gnarled hands were evidence of years spent toiling for other people. Liberty wondered how the witch knew her name. Did she, indeed, have strange powers of perception?

Liberty looked into Zippora's eyes and found they were dancing with mirth. "You are wondering how I know so much about you, Liberty Boudreaux," she said with startling accuracy.

"Oui."

Crackling laughter issued from the old woman's lips. "It is said I am a witch and can see into people's mind. Do you believe this to be true?"

"I . . . *oui*—are you?"

"I will wait until I leave this world and let God judge what I am, Liberty."

"Do you believe in God?" Liberty asked in shocked surprise. "I had heard that you worshiped—"

"The devil?" Zippora broke in. "No, I am no disciple of the underworld, although it pleases some people to believe I am."

Liberty had been pondering Zippora's words, and she hadn't realized they had entered a dark part of the swamp until the trail narrowed and thorny bushes tore at her skirt. She stopped short for right in the middle of the path, just in front of them was a human skull perched atop a tall spike!

Liberty gasped from fear, and her heart pounded against her ribs. She wished she had never consented to come with the old woman. Her feet seemed rooted to the spot, and she wished she could take flight.

33

Seeing Liberty's fear, Zippora's laughter crackled. "This was not intended to frighten you, my welcome guest. It is intended to keep all intruders away."

"Did you . . . is that . . . ?"

Again amused laughter echoed around the swamp, and Zippora turned her strange yellow eyes on Liberty. "There is nothing here that will harm you. I have lived in these swamps for years, and find them safer than the streets of New Orleans."

The old woman turned away and walked down the path. The young boy tugged at her hand, and Liberty took a hesitant step forward, her eyes glued to the hideous bleached-white skull with gaping holes where eyes had once been. In that moment she called on all her courage to step around the spike and follow Zippora down the dark pathway. The path became a long narrow tunnel with very little light penetrating the gloom. Moss from the trees tangled in Liberty's hair and thorns tore at her clothing. It was dank and dark. Just ahead Liberty saw a ray of light, and she hurried toward it.

The cabin at the end of the path was nothing like Liberty had expected. Surrounded by an arc of light, it was a neat, trim structure made of cypress logs. Nearby, several goats grazed on the swamp grass. A stone walkway was lined with exotic flowers, and lace curtains were visible at the window.

Zippora stood in the doorway motioning Liberty inside. "Come along. I want to see to that cut on your lip."

Apprehensively the young girl moved into the cabin. Again she was surprised by what she saw. The room was light and airy. Above the open fireplace hung an iron pot, its bubbling contents sending a delicious aroma through the room. A table and chairs, which had been painted bright yellow, added to the cheerful setting. Bottles and jugs were neatly lined up on shelves.

Apprehensively, Liberty picked the young boy up. "I

think we should first make certain your grandson is unhurt."

Zippora looked her grandson over carefully and then smiled at him. "Reuben is not hurt," she said at last. "Go out in the yard and play, while I tend to our guest," she instructed her grandson.

The young boy's eyes were shining as he reached out and softly touched Liberty's cheek. She laughed and planted a kiss on his forehead just before he scampered out the door.

Zippora pointed to one of the kitchen chairs. "You will sit there while I tend your wound."

Without hesitation, Liberty obeyed. Zippora raised the young girl's face to the light and frowned. "This is not bad, and it will require only a little salve. It could have been much worse."

"Oui," Liberty agreed. "If you hadn't come along when you did, it could have been much worse for me."

Zippora mumbled to herself as she moved her bony finger over the labels of the bottles and tins. When she found what she was seeking, she nodded her head and returned to Liberty. Opening the tin, she liberally applied the rose-scented salve to the young girl's lips. Standing back, she nodded approvingly.

"Oui, that will do very nicely."

Liberty smiled. "Thank you for your care, but I really must be going now."

"Not yet. You will eat while I mend your gown. We cannot have you going about with your clothing half torn off." Zippora gave Liberty little time to refuse. Tossing a flowered robe into the girl's lap, she ordered Liberty to undress.

The girl obeyed slowly. "I shouldn't—"

"Tie the belt," Zippora ordered in a soft tone.

"I should be leav—"

Zippora silenced her with a glance. Pushing Liberty

down in a chair, she ladled some of the bubbling soup into a wooden bowl, which she placed on the table in front of Liberty. "I am a very good cook. You will like this."

"What is it?" Liberty questioned, unable to identify anything, except carrots, she saw in the milky substance.

"It is my own mixture. You will find it delicious."

Liberty took a deep breath and raised a spoonful to her lips. Her tongue peeped out and tasted the soup, and she smiled brightly. "This is delicious!"

"Did I not say it was?" Zippora asked. The old woman bent down and retrieved a sweet potato from among the red-hot ashes. Placing it on a plate, she broke it open, filled it with creamy yellow butter, and placed it beside Liberty's bowl. She then seated herself on a stool by the window, threaded a needle, took up Liberty's gown, and began to take neat little stitches.

"You are much too skinny. You should eat more," Zippora observed.

"I do eat, but I don't seem to gain weight," Liberty said, with her mouth full.

"It is not seemly for a young lady for your standing to talk with food in her mouth, Liberty Boudreaux," Zippora scolded mildly. "I am surprised your mother has not taught this to you."

"Oh, my mother does not bother with me. She says I am not pretty like Bandera. And I fear I am a constant trial to her, for I cannot seem to stay out of trouble. My father has very little money left, and the plantation is in a state of ruin. I fear Bandera will have to marry into money, while I may be forced to enter a convent." Now that Liberty had lost her fear of Zippora, the words flowed unchecked. Never had she had anyone to confide in, anyone who was interested in what she had to say.

Zippora stared at the young girl, searching for any sign of jealousy or resentfulness at her mother's neglect and cruelty, but saw none. Zippora knew that Liberty's mother, Ursula, had been married to a Spaniard who had died, leaving her desperate. Bandera had been the issue from that marriage. Ursula had then married Louis Boudreaux, and Liberty had been born to them.

"Do you not think you will one day be pretty, Liberty Boudreaux?"

Remembering the scolding she had just received, Liberty swallowed a mouthful of sweet potato before she answered. "No. Mother says the runt of the litter very rarely turns into a beautiful princess. I do not mind not being pretty, because I would detest having to go through all the rituals Bandera is forced to endure. She spends hours at her toilette each morning before she is allowed to come downstairs. She can never go abroad without a bonnet to protect her skin. At night she cannot go to bed without following a strict regime that my mother has drawn up for her. You cannot believe the torture she has to undergo each day. I believe it would be very tedious to be beautiful."

Zippora frowned. "So your mother believes you to be the runt of the litter? What does your father think?"

Liberty giggled. "My father is blinded by his love for me. He believes me to be a great beauty. He thinks I look like his sister whose name I bear."

Zippora looked into blue eyes with long sooty lashes. The sprinkle of freckles across the bridge of Liberty's nose gave her the look of a precocious child. There was a hint of something beyond beauty. Perhaps it was the laughter in those blue eyes . . . perhaps it was the proud tilt to the head. Whatever it was, the old woman knew this young girl would one day grow into a real beauty, admired by all who met her.

"I believe you are not a runt, but rather a bud that has not yet blossomed."

Liberty wiped butter from her chin with the back of

her hand. "Do you think so?" she asked, doubtful that Zippora's prediction would ever come to pass. She did not believe she would blossom into a beauty.

The old woman frowned. "You will never be a lady if you act with such disregard for manners. Never wipe your mouth with your hand. I am appalled that your education has been neglected. How old are you?"

Liberty hesitated for only a moment. "I — Today is my fifteenth birthday."

Now Zippora read hurt in those blue eyes. "It is your birthday, and your mother and father have forgotten."

"It isn't important. My mother is preparing for a dinner at our house tonight, and my father is in New Orleans."

"I see. Perhaps you can spend the day with me and Reuben. Together we will make it a special day for you."

"I must return home at once," Liberty said, coming to her feet. Slipping out of the borrowed robe, she pulled her gray gown over her head. "May I help you clean up?" she asked, stacking the dishes together.

"No, it is your birthday. I will give you a present, Liberty Boudreaux. It was given to me by someone special many years ago when I was young and beautiful. It has brought good luck to me; perhaps it will do the same for you as well."

Liberty watched the old woman take a bright red tin from the mantel and remove an object wrapped in blue paper. She held her breath as Zippora handed her a ring on which was set a huge pearl surrounded by several diamonds.

"It is beautiful," Liberty exclaimed. "But surely you do not mean for me to take it?"

"That is my intention."

"I could never accept this ring from you. It is much too valuable," Liberty said, holding the ring out to the old woman.

"Nonsense. It is mine to give, and I want you to accept

it as a token for saving my grandson from the slavers. You will take it to please me."

"I could not."

Zippora took the ring and pushed it onto Liberty's finger. "My daughter is long dead, and my grandson will never have any use for this ring. I will like knowing it is on your finger."

"But why me?"

"I told you before, I have been watching you for a long time and I like what I have seen."

On a sudden impulse, Liberty took the old woman's hand. "If it is your wish, I shall wear it for you. But should the time come when you want it back, you have only to say so."

"It is yours to keep. I will not want it back."

"Tell me who gave you the ring?" Liberty asked. The old woman had started to wash the dishes, so Liberty picked up a drying cloth and began to wipe them and stack them on the table. Zippora's eyes clouded over for a moment and then took on a soft glow, as if she were remembering something wonderful out of her past.

"It was long ago. The young gentleman who gave me the ring was named Beau Antoine. I grew up as a slave on his family's plantation in Haiti. He was handsome and dashing, and I fell in love with him." Zippora's eyes closed for a moment, as if she were remembering a particular incident from long ago.

"Did he love you also?" Liberty asked.

"*Oui.* You see I was very beautiful. I had been trained as a lady's maid and could speak French very well. It was my job to teach the niceties to Beau's two sisters."

"What happened?"

"Beau and I were so deeply in love that we became reckless. It wasn't long until his father found out about us and called me to him. He was a cold, hard man. I will not tell you what transpired that day, except to say I was beaten and sold to a slaver. My destination was not to be revealed lest Beau try to find me."

Liberty wiped the tears from her eyes. "How very sad."

The old woman's eyes clouded over once more. "Indeed it was sad. I could never cross into Beau's world, and he could never come into mine. Our love was doomed from the first. The black and white worlds can never merge. I found that out the hard way."

"What happened?"

"I was sent to New Orleans. To this day I can still feel the heartbreak of that time. I was so desperate for my love that I became ill. I wanted only to die."

Liberty's eyes blurred with tears. "Did you ever see Beau again?"

"*Oui*, but I wish I had not. For it cost him his life. Somehow my love found out where I had been sent, and he came to me. He bought my freedom and set me up in a house in New Orleans. Knowing that we could never find a priest to marry us, we entered a church late one night and exchanged our pledges to one another. I was as much Beau's wife as if we had been married by a holy man. But everyone thought I was his mistress, and this was acceptable to them. We were so happy when our daughter was born."

"That would have been Reuben's mother."

"*Oui*. Marie was our delight. She was light in color, like her father. Our little house was a sanctuary away from the world, and I was very happy. But I always feared Beau would one day be forced to leave me. I never dreamed it would be under such tragic circumstances."

Liberty held her breath as she became caught up in Zippora's tragic tale. "How did he leave you?"

Zippora leaned against the table and stared at the young girl as if not really seeing her. "Beau's father found us. He demanded that Beau return to Haiti at once, but Beau refused. It is my belief that his father hired a man

to kill me, but the man misfired and shot Beau instead."
The old woman's voice trembled. "As my love lay dying in
a pool of blood, he made me promise that I would flee
with our daughter. He knew his father was a vengeful
man and would try to have us killed. I changed my name
and hid out for many years. After the money Beau had
given me was gone, I had a difficult time feeding my
daughter."

"How did you live?"

"I made and sold baskets, as well as bottled herbs and
spices and flowers on the streets of New Orleans. After a
time I began to see that I could make money by reading
palms. The wealthy white ladies paid much to have me
look into the future for them. And they began to ask me
for love potions and all kinds of charms. I was astounded
at how fast my reputation grew. It was considered in
vogue to have one's future told by Madame Zippora."

Liberty didn't know at what moment her fear of the
old woman had disappeared. She was so moved by the
tragic story, that her heart went out to the young lovers.
"When did you leave New Orleans to live in the swamps,
Zippora?"

The old woman took the drying cloth from Liberty and
hung it on a peg. "That was thirteen years ago. My
beautiful Marie was brutally attacked by two white, so-
called gentlemen, who were on a drunken spree. When I
learned she was going to have a baby, I brought her here.
Reuben was born the night my daughter died. He is
simple-minded and cannot speak. None of my medicine
will cure him. But what my grandson lacks in intelligence,
he was gifted with in his heart. He is of a kind and loving
nature. He is my joy in life. In him I see much of Beau."

"Oh, Zippora, what a lonely life you have lived. Have
you no friends?"

"No . . . but I have had the added joy of watching you
grow up. You cannot know how your presence has often

41

brightened up my loneliness. Just watching you with the animals brought me pleasure. I dared not approach you, fearing you would be frightened and never return to the swamp, and I would never see you again."

Liberty brushed a tear from her cheek. "May I come to see you again?"

"Come whenever you want to, Liberty Boudreaux. You will always find a welcome for you in this house. Come to me and I will teach you the social graces that are lacking in your education." Zippora pressed a bright red tin into Liberty's hand. "This is another gift for you."

"What is it?"

"It is a special scent that I made for you several months ago. I thought I might leave it for you to find in the swamp, but decided against it. You must use it to wash your hair and put it in your bath. It is a scent that will be distinctly you. No one else will ever match it."

"How can I thank you for your kindness?"

"There is no need to thank me. We are friends, you and I, Liberty."

Liberty was having such a good time she was reluctant to leave. "I must go now. Thank you for rescuing me, and thank you for the lovely ring. I am glad you shared your beautiful story with me."

Zippora turned toward the door and nodded. "Go, Liberty. You must be home before dark."

Liberty was almost light-hearted as she skipped down the path on the way to the bayou where she had left her skiff. Deep inside she knew that, after meeting Zippora, her life would never be the same. She had found a friend in the most unexpected place. She could not wait to show Bandera the wondrous ring the old voodoo woman had given her.

Chapter Three

Briar Oaks Plantation

The afternoon was hot and steamy as Liberty dragged her boat up on the grassy slope and ran toward the stately, old plantation house. She was so accustomed to the house, that she did not notice the chipped and cracking paint on the barns and outbuildings, or the shutters and doors that needed repairing at the main house. As to the inside, many of the valuable paintings and rugs had been discreetly sold, but even though the furniture was in need of covering, there was still an elegance about the rooms, a hint of the bygone luxury that had been enjoyed by long-dead Boudreaux ancestors.

Liberty saw an all too familiar buggy pull out of the driveway, and she wrinkled her nose in distaste. She did not like Sebastian Montesquieu, who was becoming a frequent visitor at Briar Oaks. Though he was not to Liberty's taste, her mother seemed to have singled him out as a prospective husband for Liberty's sister, Bandera. Sebastian was the nephew of Gustave Montesquieu, and the only heir, to the vast Bend of the River Plantation. Yet something about Sebastian made Liberty's skin crawl. She did not know how Bandera could endure the thought of having him as her husband.

Breathing a sigh of relief, she stepped behind a pine

tree and watched Sebastian depart. At least she would not have to face him today. She hastily ran her fingers through her tangled curls, then tried to press the creases out of her muddy gown by running her hands down the skirt. She was glad that Zippora had mended the tear—it hardly showed at all. If only she could make it to her room without being discovered. Neither her mother nor Bandera would have been pleased if Sebastian had seen her in this bedraggled condition.

She rushed toward the house, deciding to use the back stairs. Automatically her eyes went to the bell tower as silver tones vibrated in the breeze. Liberty always loved the sound of the bell when it tolled the beginning of the work day or called the workers from the fields in the evening. She stopped momentarily to gauge the time by the white marble sundial. Here, surrounded by the beautiful grounds of the proud old manor, people did not often measure time by a clock, but rather by the rising and the setting of the sun, the starting and the ending of the workday. Here, the Boudreaux family had lived and died for four generations. Like her father, Liberty loved this land. It was her home—a part of her very life and soul. She was sorely grieved that it had fallen on hard times.

A grassy slope meandered down to the brown waters of the Mississippi. The river's wide avenue was often crowded with barges filled with indigo, and the newcomer, sugar cane. The ageless waters flowed past lazy bayous toward New Orleans, the heart and lifeblood of the Orleans Territory.

Huge oak trees and delicately-scented magnolias dominated the air she breathed as Liberty moved past a pine grove, glancing at the house where she had been born. The south side of the red brick mansion was covered with climbing ivy and wisteria, whereas a full-length veranda ran the length of the front of the house and around the north side. Now, as always in the heat of the day, the green shutters were closed because Liberty's mother claimed that the sun faded the already threadbare carpets.

Behind the house Liberty could see the whitewashed slave cabins, and beyond them, the rich meadowlands where cattle grazed. Pride flowed through her veins like a hearty tonic as she neared the house. She was so caught up in her warm feeling of tranquility that she forgot it had been her intention to use the back entrance to the house.

"Liberty, what you done to yourself, *ma chère!*" Oralee chided, her hands on her hips, her black face drawn up in a disapproving frown. "If your mother sees you looking like an urchin, she will skin you and me both."

Oralee was a tall *femme de couleur,* who spoke Haitian French. She was the sovereign voice at Briar Oaks, but though she ran the house with authority, she rarely chided Liberty, who was her favorite.

"Get up the stairs at once before your mother learns you are home." Oralee swung her bandanna-wrapped head toward the stairs. "Get! And do not come down until you are dressed to receive guests. M'sieu Montesquieu will be returning for dinner."

"Again? Does he never dine at his own home?"

Oralee raised her hand and pointed up the stairs. Seeing the determined light in her eyes, Liberty lost no time in bounding up those stairs. When she reached the wide landing, she tiptoed past her mother's room, and then dashed through her own bedroom door. Feeling safe, she leaned against the closed door, drawing in a deep sigh of relief.

Suddenly her eyes were drawn to the window, and her heart skipped a beat when she saw her mother staring at her. Ursula was impatiently tapping the toe of her shoe, and her mouth was drawn up in anger.

"Where have you been, Liberty? What in God's name have you done to yourself?"

Liberty swallowed a lump in her throat, knowing she had again displeased her mother. "I took the boat into the swamp, *Maman*. I would have been home sooner but—"

Ursula abruptly raised her hand. "Spare me the details of your mundane adventure. I swear, you will be the death of me yet, Liberty. One can only guess what our neighbors say about your unladylike conduct. You have ever been a trial to me. Why can you not be more like your sister?"

Liberty ducked her head in shame. "I am sorry, *Maman*. I try to be good, honestly I do. I always seem to do the wrong thing."

Ursula Boudreaux raised her dark brows in exasperation. Liberty looked so pathetic, with her woebegone expression and the damp gown clinging to her slender body, that her mother's heart softened. "Do not distress yourself. I do not have the time to go into this with you at the moment. Sebastian Montesquieu will be dining with us tonight, and I want you to make a passable impression on him. I will set your punishment at a later time."

Liberty was flooded with relief, for her mother would be so caught up in helping Bandera impress Sebastian that she would soon forget her displeasure. This was the way it always ended, her mother showing disapproval and then letting the matter drop until Liberty disgraced herself again.

Sometimes Liberty wished her mother would punish her, that at least would mean she was aware that Liberty was alive. She would have liked to have told her mother all that had happened today, but she feared her mother would never again allow her to go into the swamps.

She watched her mother advance toward her. Ursula Boudreaux owed her black hair and striking good looks to her Spanish blood. Her soft classic features set her apart from most other women. She had been married to an impoverished young Spaniard in her youth, but he had died of the flux shortly before Bandera was born, leaving his young wife destitute. When Bandera was six years old, Ursula had met and married Louis Boudreaux, and Liberty was the issue from their union.

"Get out of those wet clothes before you catch your death," her mother scolded, brushing Liberty aside and stepping out the door. "I'll send Oralee up with hot water for your bath," she called over her shoulder, before disappearing down the hallway.

Liberty wished she could tell someone about her exciting afternoon, about meeting Zippora. She glanced down at the ring that sparkled on her finger. She would tell Bandera about her adventure!

She bolted out of her room, and paused before her sister's bedroom. Hearing her mother's voice, she realized Ursula must have gone directly to Bandera's room. When Liberty heard her name spoken, she knew her mother and sister were discussing her. She closed her eyes tightly, not wanting to hear what was being said, and yet, she was unable to shut out their voices.

"I simply do not know what you are going to do about Liberty, *Maman*. She is becoming a constant embarrassment to us all. Why do you not send her away to a school for young ladies and see if they can smooth off the rough edges? Something has got to be done . . . and soon. She goes abroad heedless of her toilette. Even if she is a homely little mouse, she would be more presentable if she would take more time with her appearance."

Liberty backed away, but not before she heard her mother's reply. "You should not speak unkindly of your sister. Besides, Louis has forbidden me to punish her. He says she is a lively child and I am not to crush her spirit."

"Papa indulges her too much in this folly. He does not realize that Liberty is growing up. I wish he would treat me more like he does Liberty. She is his little darling. He

47

would keep her in baby silk and pamper her shamelessly, while he hardly knows I am alive."

"Do not say that. Your stepfather has been kind to you. Has he not been like a real father to you, Bandera?"

"I never receive imported silks, bonnets, and shoes like all my friends. Sometimes I am embarrassed to appear in public in my pathetic rags."

"Nonsense, you have lovely gowns. Louis is more than generous with you. Goodness knows he never denies you when you ask for something."

Liberty could hear her sister's voice rise in volume. "We are in dire straits. There is never enough money for me to do the things my friends do."

"There, there, *ma chère*. You must not cry or your eyes will be red. Your stepfather does the best he can. He cannot help it if the last five crops have failed. I have hopes that, in time, Briar Oaks will shine again."

"I do not have time to wait for that to happen — if it ever does. I am twenty-three. Most of my friends are already married, and have children. I have wasted years waiting for Sebastian to ask for my hand in marriage."

"It will be worth the wait. As his wife, you will be the envy of all your friends. Think of the power you will have as the mistress of Bend of the River Plantation."

"He had better offer soon. I do not intend to wait much longer."

"You were so sure he was getting close to asking you to marry him."

"*Oui,* but when? I suppose I should be grateful that I am pretty and do not look like Liberty. When she comes of age, she will have a difficult time getting someone of worth to offer for her. She will have nothing but a dilapidated plantation, and no beauty to lure a man."

Liberty caught the spitefulness in her sister's voice, but she did not hear her mother's reply. At the sound of footsteps approaching the door, Liberty moved quickly to the landing that led to the attic. Flattening herself against the wall, she waited until her mother passed before she allowed the tears to fall down her cheeks. She knew she was homely, but it hurt to hear it from her own mother and sister. And her heart was breaking for the trouble she caused her mother. Why could she not be a lady like Bandera? Why did she always have to displease her mother?

Liberty sat down on the steps and buried her head in her lap. When she could cry no more, she dried her eyes and stood up. Liberty was never one to bemoan that which she could not change. She knew that no good ever came from self-pity. She was ugly, and that was all there was to it. She would accept that fact and learn to live with it.

Liberty looked down at the pearl and diamond ring Zippora had given her. Then she stood up and went to her sister's room because she still wanted to share the day's adventure with someone. Perhaps Bandera would be impressed. Liberty rapped softly on the closed door, and waited until Bandera invited her in before turning the knob.

Bandera was seated before the *table de toilette,* brushing her dark hair until it sparkled. She was beautiful, draped in a soft yellow dressing gown that showed the swell of her smooth breasts and the creamy texture of her skin. Her ebony hair shimmered like a midnight sky as it fell down her back. Bandera was a classic beauty like their mother, and men flocked to her like bees to a honey pot. Liberty wondered, for the hundredth time, why Bandera had chosen Sebastian when she could have any man she wanted.

As Bandera coiled her hair on top of her head and secured it with an ivory comb, Liberty wished she had been blessed with lovely black hair instead of the straw-colored tresses that hung limply about her shoulders.

Why were her eyes a nondescript color instead of soft brown like her sister's?

Bandera gave her young sister a scathing glance as her eyes moved over her with disapproval. "Why must you always look like a *gamin*, Liberty? You never take pride in your appearance. Why could I not have had a well-mannered little sister with pleasing looks? You are such an embarrassment to me."

Liberty had heard all this before. It no longer hurt her when Bandera took her to task as it did when her mother criticized her. She merely shrugged her shoulders. "We cannot all be born beautiful like you, Bandera." Liberty smiled. "Besides you would not like it if I were beautiful. You have never liked to compete with other women."

Bandera arched an eyebrow, looking very like their mother. "I never have to compete with other women. But . . . you could be right, *ma chère*. Perhaps I would not like it if you were beautiful."

Even though Bandera had been born of Spanish parents, she chose to think of herself as French. She had never known her own father, and Louis Boudreaux had always treated her as his own flesh and blood. When she was twelve, he had even legally adopted her.

Liberty kicked off her muddy boots and curled up on the edge of Bandera's bed, tucking her feet beneath her. "I had a wonderful adventure today. Would you like to hear about it?"

Bandera applied rouge to her cheeks, then wiped most of it off so only a trace remained, before answering in a bored voice. "From the looks of you, I would say that you tromped through the swamps. What makes you think I would be interested?"

Liberty watched her sister's eyes as she spoke. "I met the swamp witch today, but she isn't really a witch, at least I do not believe she is." Liberty was bubbling with excitement. "I even went to her house."

Bandera swung around, skepticism written on her face. "You did not. Even you would not dare cross Zippora's threshold."

"I did. She invited me in, and I even ate at her table. She gave me this." Liberty extended her hand so Bandera could see the ring. "Is it not beautiful?"

Bandera sucked in her breath as she stared at the ring. "Where did you really get that?" she demanded, standing up and crossing the room. She stared at the magnificent pearl surrounded by diamonds that caught the sunlight and sent a rainbow of color dancing across the walls. "Do not tell me that old Zippora gave you this thing, because I do not believe it."

Liberty hesitated to tell her sister about the two slavers, fearing she would press their mother to stop the excursions into the swamps. "It's true, Bandera. Zippora gave it to me."

Bandera held out her hand and said in a demanding voice. "Let me see it."

Liberty readily removed the ring and dropped it into her sister's hand. Bandera turned it over and examined it closely. "This is worth a great deal of money. However you came by this, it is much too fine for you." Slipping it on her finger, Bandera held it up to the light, admiring the prisms of light that danced in the fiery depths of the diamonds.

A devious gleam came into Bandera's eyes. "If you don't give me this ring, I will tell *Maman* that you went into Zippora's cabin."

"No! It is a gift to me. Zippora said it would bring me good fortune."

Bandera turned a poisonous gaze on her sister. "It would appear the opposite has happened, little sister, because I am the possessor now. Run along and dress for dinner, while I finish my toilette. I am weary of your company."

"Give me the ring back!" Liberty demanded, coming to her feet and holding out her hand. "It's mine. You have no right to it."

Bandera grabbed a handful of hair and jerked until she brought tears to Liberty's eyes. When Liberty tried to free herself, Bandera yanked so hard that she sent her sister to her knees. "The ring is mine," Bandera said through clenched teeth. "Mine, do you hear?"

Liberty felt Bandera's hand tighten on her hair even more. Although the pain was excruciating, Liberty managed to land an elbow on Bandera's stomach. Bandera cried out in pain, and quickly loosened her grip on Liberty's hair.

At that moment their mother chose to enter the room. Misreading the whole situation, she saw her precious Bandera doubled over in pain and assumed that Liberty was the perpetrator. "What have you done to your sister?" she cried, rushing to Bandera's side. "There, there, *ma petite,* what has happened?"

Liberty saw Bandera press her knuckles into her eyes to make them tear—a trick Bandera had learned long ago, and it usually won her mother's sympathy. "Liberty is a beast, *Maman.* She struck me!" Tears glistened in Bandera's eyes as her mother gathered her close.

"You will be punished for this, miss," her mother said in a cold voice. "What have you got to say for yourself?"

Bandera raised her head and gave her young sister a malicious smile. "*Oui,* Liberty, what have you to say?"

Liberty knew she was beaten, and merely shrugged her shoulders in defeat.

"Go to your room at once, Liberty." Her mother spoke in bitterness. "You are getting out of hand. Your father will hear of this."

Liberty slowly crossed the room, her eyes locking with Bandera's, in which a self-satisfied gleam was reflected. She knew from long experience it would do no good to tell her side of the incident, her mother always took Bandera's word as truth.

As Liberty left the room, her mother's voice followed her. "You will come down to dinner tonight, but you will speak only when spoken to — is that clear? I will no longer tolerate your bad conduct. If your father does not punish you, I will deal with you myself."

As Liberty made her way back to her own bedroom she felt a coldness around her heart. Could her mother not see the games Bandera always played? Today Liberty had turned fifteen, but no one seemed to remember or care. In the past she had always made excuses for her mother and Bandera, but the truth of the situation had finally hit her full-force. Neither of them cared about her. She was nothing but a troublesome child to them. It was a heart-breaking lesson for Liberty. With bitter disappointment, she realized her only friends and allies were her father and Oralee. Of course, today she had found a new friend in Zippora.

Dressed in a hand-me-down yellow empire-waist gown that Bandera had discarded, Liberty descended the stairs. While the bright yellow gown had been lovely on her sister, she knew its color made her look pale and washed out. Instead of wearing her hair in soft Grecian curls like Bandera, Liberty's hair was shoulder length and pulled back in a yellow ribbon.

Her footsteps quickened as she neared the salon, for she dared not be late for dinner. She was already in enough trouble; she did not need to add more fuel to the flame. Liberty paused at the door, drawing in a deep breath and gathering her courage. On entering the room, she walked slowly toward her mother. Ursula Boudreaux offered her younger daughter her cheek and smiled stiffly. Liberty gave her a quick kiss, then moved past her sister, barely noticing her. Knowing it was expected of her, she made a quick curtsy in front of Sebastian Montesquieu.

"Good evening, *Monsieur*. I trust your uncle is in good health."

Sebastian smiled down at her. "The truth of the matter is he is not quite himself lately, *Mademoiselle*. He sends his regards and his regrets that he cannot be with us tonight. He always asks about you."

Liberty felt her mother's eyes on her, warning her not to make a mistake. "I find your uncle a very enlightened conversationalist, *Monsieur*."

Sebastian's eyes moved across Liberty's face, then lowered to her high-cut neckline. Something about him repulsed her. "You are one of the few people my uncle consents to talk to, *Mademoiselle*. For some reason he seems to find you fascinating."

Liberty had never liked Sebastian. He was what she termed a dandy. Even so, his lineage was impeccable, for his father was of the old French aristocracy. Sebastian's short-clipped black hair was disheveled, *à la Titus* as was the fashion. He wore sage green, tight-fitted trousers, and his elaborately tied neckcloth was complimented by an upright collar. He was clean-shaven, but wore side whiskers. For some reason his features did not seem to go together. His square-cut jaw seemed out of proportion with his aquiline nose. His blue eyes were dull, and he had the annoying habit of never looking into the eyes of the person he was addressing.

Bandera's laughter rang out as she slipped her arm through Sebastian's. "La, but our little mouse has pretty manners tonight, does she not, Sebastian?"

At last Liberty turned to her sister, knowing she could no longer ignore her. As usual, Bandera wore a lovely gown, smelled of some sweet, exotic scent, and looked beautiful. No one but Bandera could have worn the deep purple and carried it off so well. Beside her, Liberty indeed felt like a homely little mouse.

A deep French voice spoke up from the other side of

the room. "*Ma petite,* is not a mouse. She will show us all one day how the bud turns into the rose."

Liberty's father had just entered the room, and her eyes lit up when she saw his encouraging smile. Evidently he had just returned from New Orleans, because he wasn't dressed for dinner, and he still wore mud-splattered riding boots. Louis Boudreaux was a handsome man of forty-five. His sandy hair held no hint of gray and his blue eyes twinkled as he held a hand out to Liberty, who raced across the polished cypress floor, and threw herself into his comforting arms.

"I am so glad you came home tonight," she whispered against his ear, feeling like a condemned felon who has just been handed a reprieve.

"Did you think I would miss your fifteenth birthday?" he said, so only she could hear. "We will speak of it later," he added in a soft voice. "I see your mother is feeling neglected."

Taking Liberty by the arm, Louis strode to his wife. Reaching for Ursula's hand, he raised it to his lips. "You are lovely tonight, *ma chère,*" he said with warmth.

Ursula blushed with maidenly delight as her husband gave her a tender look. That she loved him was apparent to everyone in the room. Not to be left out of the family circle, Bandera elbowed her way forward to receive a kiss and a hug.

"Do you wish to change before we dine?" Ursula asked her husband. "We can hold dinner if you wish."

"No, no. Let us proceed with the meal. I assume there is a party tonight. I feared I wouldn't make it home in time for the festivities."

Ursula looked puzzled for a moment; then she smiled. "No, you have the dates wrong, Louis. Bandera's masquerade party is not until next Saturday. Did you remember to pick up Bandera's gowns from the dressmaker?"

A frown creased Louis's brow, and he caught the

sadness in Liberty's eyes. "*Oui* . . . the gowns were ready, but—"

"Oh, Papa," Bandera cried excitedly, forgetting to act *distingué* for Sebastian's benefit. "When can I see them? Do I have to wait until after we have dined?"

Louis turned his soft blue eyes on Liberty. "All in good time, Bandera. First, however, I have a gift for Liberty."

Bandera's lips drooped into a pout when Louis removed a black velvet-covered box from his pocket and held it out to his young daughter. "Happy fifteenth birthday, *ma petite*."

Silence followed his announcement. Ursula shook her head and reached out to Liberty, distressed that in all the excitement she had forgotten her daughter's birthday. "I . . . happy birthday, Liberty. It seems only yesterday you turned fourteen. Time passes so swiftly," she managed to choke out.

As Liberty felt her mother's cool lips brush her cheek, she noted the momentary sadness reflected in Ursula's dark eyes. Even Bandera had the good grace to look ashamed, but she said nothing.

Sebastian saved the awkward situation by stepping forward and extending his best wishes to Liberty. Your father is right, you are a bud almost ready to bloom." Sebastian's eyes saw past the ill-fitting gown to the girl's delicate bone structure. He did not mistake the future promise of beauty.

"Thank you," Liberty said, thinking this was the third time today she had been compared to a bud about to bloom. She could not stop the blush that tinted her cheeks. She was not accustomed to receiving compliments from gentlemen, even if this one was only from Sebastian.

Bandera, not liking the attention Liberty was receiving, laced her arm through Sebastian's, her lips curling viciously.

Liberty took the velvet box and opened it slowly,

savoring the moment. Joy lit her face as she picked up a golden bracelet with a tiny dangling heart. "Oh, Papa, this is lovely. This is the best birthday ever," she said through a mist of tears. Liberty's father hugged her to him, so she did not see the look that passed between her parents. Louis was not at all pleased that no one had remembered his daughter's birthday.

"Is it the best birthday you have ever had, my darling daughter?" he asked, watching his wife. "It seems to take so little to bring you joy." Ursula caught the sarcasm in her husband's voice, and she knew he was displeased with her.

But Bandera was watching Liberty slide the bracelet onto her arm. "A pretty bauble," she said under her breath, while thumping the dangling heart with her finger.

"It will do you no good to covet this, Bandera," Liberty told her. "Papa had it engraved with my name."

Bandera's eyes gleamed with jealousy. "What does it say?" she demanded to know.

"Here," Liberty said, removing the bracelet and handing it to her sister. "Read it for yourself."

Bandera's face reddened and her eyes gleamed spitefully. "To my daughter, Liberty, on her fifteenth birthday," she read aloud, then tossed the bracelet back to Liberty. "Who would want that old thing anyway."

"I do," Liberty said, once more slipping the gift onto her arm. Her eyes moved to her sister's finger where the ring Zippora had given her gleamed in the candlelight. Liberty wanted the ring back, but she decided it would be unwise to make an issue out of it. Better to let the whole matter drop, she decided.

No one saw the old woman's face pressed against the window as she watched the proceedings. No one could hear Zippora's softly muttered words. "What goes around, comes around. A hurt inflicted will come back tenfold."

As the small party gathered in the dining-room, candle-light glistened on the surface of the mahogany table, hiding the shabbiness of the room. Since it was her birthday, Liberty was accorded the honor of sitting to her father's right. She saw her mother watching her, and she knew Ursula was feeling guilty because she had forgotten her birthday. Liberty wished she could assure her mother that it was unimportant. She did not want regret to drive another wedge between the two of them.

Bandera was caught up in trying to impress Sebastian, and for the moment she was ignoring her family. As the desert was served, Louis leaned back in his chair to survey his family. For too long he had ignored the treatment Liberty had been receiving from her mother and stepsister. He intended to see that the child was never neglected again. His eyes were cold as they rested on his wife.

Feeling the tension in the air, Liberty tried to lighten the atmosphere. "What news from Paris, Papa?" she asked, since news from France was always welcome dinner conversation.

Louis smiled at his young daughter. "It is not easy to gain information from Paris these days, with the hostilities between the United States and France." He was thoughtful for a moment. "Let me see now . . . I did hear one interesting bit of news. It is said that Napoleon despairs at the flimsy gowns women are wearing, and he has had the fireplaces at Tuileries bricked up so that women will be forced to dress more warmly."

Liberty giggled behind her hand. "I doubt that even that will work. Women seem to be beyond good judgment when it comes to fashion, Papa."

"Little you would know about fashion," Bandera snarled. "You are certainly not an authority on how a woman should dress."

Louis leaned toward his wife and whispered in her ear. "Put an end to your daughter's insults, *Madame.* I will not tolerate her cruelty any longer." Ursula merely lowered her head, saying nothing, for fear Sebastian would realize something was amiss.

Bandera saw that she had displeased Louis, so she smiled prettily at him. "Of course, I could teach Liberty style if she were to show an interest in learning."

"Tell us more news from France, Papa," Liberty urged, trying to steer the conversation away from herself.

"I was told a funny story that came out of England," he said thoughtfully. "Again this has to do with women's fashions. It seems that a Russian army officer was visiting London. On a cold day he strolled down Bond Street and spied a fashionably dressed lady walking by. He was accustomed to judging a woman's circumstances by the warmth of her clothing, rather than the stylishness of mode. Seeing the woman's flimsy gown, he presumed she was a pauper, and out of sympathy, offered her money to buy a proper coat. The woman was a duke's daughter, and incensed to say the least."

Delighted laughter bubbled from Liberty's lips, and Sebastian joined in. By the time dinner was over they all moved to the salon, where a lighter mood ensued.

"I have a bit of unexpected news," Sebastian stated, as he took the glass of wine Louis offered him. Taking a sip, he then balanced the glass on his knee. "My uncle has just learned that my cousin is to return home."

Ursula's brow furrowed as she stared at her husband. She had heard talk that at one time Louis had been in love with Gabrielle Montesquieu. "Can you be speaking of Monsieur Montesquieu's daughter?" she inquired.

"Oui," Sebastian answered, studying the amber-colored liquid in his glass. "I have not seen her in years. Of course, she is some ten years older than I."

Louis seemed to tense. "I know very little about Gabrielle's life since she left Bend of the River. Is she still married, Sebastian?"

"No, her husband died several years ago. She has a son . . . I suppose he would be my second cousin. My uncle assumes she will bring his grandson with her."

Bandera's eyes narrowed in speculation. The Montesquieu fortune was so near her grasp. Could this grandson be a threat to Sebastian's future? She did not want to see her dreams shattered by some long-forgotten family member. "I never knew your uncle had a daughter or a grandson," she stated guardedly. "I always assumed you and your mother were Monsieur Montesquieu's only living relative."

"There is no reason you should have heard about Gabrielle and her son. When my cousin married the American, my uncle disowned her and never acknowledged the birth of her son. My mother and I are surprised he has done so now."

"Can this mean that your uncle has forgiven his daughter?" Bandera wanted to know.

Sebastian shrugged his padded shoulders. "Who can say? I can assure you, I am not looking forward to meeting my American cousin."

"We are all Americans in this room," Liberty reminded Sebastian.

He gave her a half-smile. "Some of us are more American than others."

"My father believes it is a good thing to be a part of America. He hopes Orleans Territory will one day become a state," Liberty declared.

Sebastian seemed not to hear. He stared into Bandera's eyes and said softly. "It seems I now have a rival for my uncle's affection."

"Gabrielle," Louis said softly. "So she is coming home after all these years. I wonder if she is much changed?"

Ursula felt jealousy tug at her heart. If this Gabrielle

was a widow, would she try to win Louis away from her? No, Louis would never love anyone but her. Still she felt a prickle of uneasiness. Louis had been displeased with her quite frequently of late. Did he think she had deliberately ignored their daughter's birthday? she wondered. Good lord, Liberty was her daughter, as she was his. Did he not know that she loved the child?

The night was still, and not a breath of wind stirred the trees outside the plantation house. Darkness covered the land as ominous clouds moved across the moon.

Bandera tossed and turned on her bed, moaning in her sleep. She dreamed that she was running through the swamp, trying to escape from something horrible. Cold sweat popped out on her brow, and she felt herself falling . . . falling . . . falling.

Finally, she landed with a plop, only to find to her dismay that she was in quicksand and sinking fast. Whimpering and whining, she tried to save herself, but each time she struggled, she sank deeper and deeper in the mire. Finally, she saw a shadowy creature standing on the slope, and she reached out her hand for help.

A scream issued from Bandera's lips when she recognized the old voodoo woman, Zippora. Fear encased her mind, and she was unable to move when the old woman grabbed her hand. But instead of saving her, Zippora brandished a knife and cut off Bandera's finger!

Sitting up in bed, Bandera made little whimpering sounds. The nightmare had been so real that it took her moments to realize she was safe. She felt her finger, and was relieved to find it still intact.

Bandera leaped from her bed, and raced down the hallway to Liberty's bedroom. She jerked the ring from her finger, trying to still the tremors of fear that shook her body. Liberty raised up and sleepily wondered why

Bandera was in her bedroom in the middle of the night.

"Take your old ring!" Bandera cried, pressing it into Liberty's hand. "I don't want it!"

Liberty slipped the ring on her finger and turned over, already reclaimed by the comforting arms of the sleep that comes only to the innocent. Bandera was not as fortunate as her sister, for it took a good hour before she was brave enough to, again, close her eyes in sleep.

The moon came out from behind the cloud, and a sudden gust of wind rustled the leaves of the magnolia tree that grew beside the riverbank. A dark figure slipped into a boat and paddled toward the swamps, her crackling laughter carried away by the heightening wind.

Chapter Four

Judah glanced over the iron balcony of his second-floor room at the Royale Inn. Nothing his mother had told him about New Orleans had prepared him for the picturesque sight that met his eyes. Across the street an unlatched grillwork doorway led to a courtyard where banana plants, palm trees, and exotic flowers enhanced a colorful garden. In the distance he could see the tall steeple of the magnificent old Saint Louis Cathedral, its inspiring presence looming, like a sentinel, over the city.

A tall black woman, her hair wrapped in a white turban, balanced a basket of oranges on her head, calling out her chant. "Oranges for *mam'zelle,* oranges for *m'sieu,* oranges to ward off the sickness."

Judah's eyes moved down the banquettes on which ladies and gentlemen of fashion strolled leisurely, stopping occasionally to peer in a shop window. This newly acquired territory did not seem to fit the view he had of the American territories. New Orleans would never be molded to resemble her sister cities of America. She was alive with old traditions that she would cling to jealously.

Judah had the oddest feeling that he was no stranger to this land. Perhaps it was because his mother had always talked of New Orleans with such love that he felt akin to this place. Yes, the feeling was strong—he felt as if he had come home. This was where he belonged.

Trying to shake other feelings he did not understand or welcome, he turned his head upward to let the golden sunlight warm his face. Even the air he breathed was heady, as were the many aromas that filled his nostrils. Vivid colors — yellows, pinks, and reds — blended as if they had been painted by a master painter.

Judah felt a hand close over his, and he glanced down at his mother. "Did you have a nice visit with your friend, Minette?"

"Yes, it was lovely. You impressed her very much when you came to tea yesterday. She says my son is very handsome, and she believes you will turn the heads of all the young ladies of New Orleans."

His mouth eased into a smile. "You aren't going to promote a romance between me and your friend, are you?"

Her eyes danced with amusement. "No. Minette is too old for you. Still, you might learn something from an older, more experienced woman."

Judah raised his brow in mock horror. "You are shameless, Mother."

Her laughter was light, almost girlish. "No, my son — I am French. I had almost forgotten that. You are half-French you know."

Judah's eyes followed his mother's as she glanced lovingly down Royal Street. "I can see why you love New Orleans, Mother. It is unique among cities."

"I am glad you discovered that. I cannot explain how happy I am to be home at last. According to my father's letter, we are to spend only three nights here. That being the case, someone will call for us and escort us to Bend of the River Plantation tomorrow. Just wait until you see the place. You cannot help but be impressed."

Judah noticed the flush of excitement on his mother's face. She was happier than he had seen her in a long time. He was glad he had consented to bring her for

64

returning brought her much joy. He only hoped her happiness did not fade when they reached their destination tomorrow.

Judah stared angrily at the mass of people on the docks. They were waiting to be transported upriver. He and his mother had been waiting in New Orleans for over a week with no word from his grandfather. Judah might have considered returning to Boston with his mother had it not been for the fact that the *Winged Victory* had already sailed.

In light of that, he had decided to take matters into his own hands. He had acquired space on a keelboat that would take them to Bend of the River. It angered him further that his mother would be forced to ride on public transportation, with livestock and farm implements.

Helping his mother on board, he steadied her while the boat pitched slightly. Gabrielle raised her lace handkerchief to her nose, then turned her face to the wind, hoping to escape the offensive odor of the goats, swine, and cattle packed aboard. Lumber was piled on both sides of the flatboat, and the crew of four seemed in no way concerned with the comfort of their passengers.

Judah stood with his legs widespread, a gleam of unleashed anger in the depths of his turquoise eyes. Soon he would face the man who had caused his mother so much grief. He ached to tell Montesquieu what he thought of him, and couldn't wait to warn his grandfather never to hurt his mother again. He glanced at Gabrielle, and saw the softness in her eyes as she watched New Orleans fade into the distance.

"Everything is so much larger than it was when I was a girl, Judah," Gabrielle observed wistfully, lapsing easily into her native French. "When I left, the languages spoken on the streets were Spanish and French. Now it seems English is more widely used."

"I believe you said Orleans Territory at one time belonged to Spain."

"Yes. That is why there is such a heavy Spanish influence in the architecture. The iron latticework you saw on the balconies can be attributed to the Spanish. Minette says that the Spanish and French population are not all pleased with the American takeover."

"I am an American," Judah reminded her.

His mother smiled sweetly and patted his hand. "So you are, and so am I. I would not have it any other way. But you will have to realize that the aristocracy, looks on "the American" with only slightly less horror than they look on leprosy. See the dwellings on the opposite side of the river? That is where the English-speaking people elected to live, since they were snubbed by the French. Minette says the Creoles feel that the Americans were forced down their throats."

"I can see where they might feel that way. I do not suppose they had a choice in the matter."

"Minette says the Americans found it much more to their liking to live outside the Vieux Carré. They just did not fit in."

His smile took the sting out of his words. "Can it be that my mother is becoming a snob?"

Judah looked into her eyes and read confusion there. "I do not think I am prejudiced, Judah. At least I hope not."

"Put your mind at rest. How can you be prejudiced when your only son is one of those 'horrible Americans'?" His eyes danced merrily. "Of course, you could always pass me off as someone else's son."

Gabrielle became silent, and Judah knew she was thinking about her father. "Why do you suppose he did not send someone to escort us to Bend of the River as he promised in his letter?"

66

Judah frowned. It was his belief that his grandfather was merely asserting his authority, letting them know he was still in command. This was just another insult his mother was forced to endure. He wanted to erase the hurt he saw in her eyes, so he changed the subject. "Tell me what it was like when you were a girl," he said, waving his hand toward the shore.

She was thoughtful for a moment, as if she knew what he was trying to do. "It was a glorious time that knew no equal. There were frivolous, joyous parties. The masquerade ball was the most anticipated of all. Each year it was held at a different plantation. We would use any excuse to have a party. The French Revolution was at its height, and many aristocrats found their way to our shores after escaping the flashing blade of 'Madame Guillotine.' It was a gallant age of chivalry, with a stiff code of honor, and many duels were fought over a young lady's favor. A man's honor was sacred, and he stood ready to defend it with his life. There was a saying, in New Orleans, that sums up that period perfectly. 'Rapiers for two, coffee for one.' That was the way of life when I was a girl."

"I remember you saying that the entertainment was lavish at Bend of the River," Judah declared, noticing the excited blush on his mother's cheeks.

"*Oui.* At my father's plantation, hospitality was offered to all of gentle breeding. Often as many as fifty guests would descend on us, and we would entertain them in a lavish style for a week. That was a time of much laughter and gaiety. Before my mother died, she made sure that no food was served twice during those visits."

"Were you not sorry to give it all up when you married my father?"

Gabrielle's eyes saddened once more. "No, I never regretted marrying your father—not ever. As I tried to explain to you many times, my father was a proud man—I knew he would think I married beneath my station—

and he was a hard man, Judah. If he has ever admitted to making a mistake, I have never heard him. Try to be patient with him, for he is now old. I suspect he wants to make amends."

Judah doubted it. There had been no evidence of such an intention since their arrival in New Orleans. His temper had not cooled, and he was still not looking forward to meeting his grandfather. "What of your father's brother? You rarely speak of him."

"André was twelve years younger than my father. He was a disappointment to his family in many ways. He was always dueling and drinking, never accepting responsibility. However, he married well according to my father's standards, so he was never in disgrace as I have been. When my uncle was killed in a duel, my father took Sebastian and his mother, Alicia, into his home. Minette told me that my father pinned all his hopes and dreams on Sebastian. She says that father has lately become disillusioned by him as well. I believe this is another reason why he has sent for you. He wants to see if you will live up to his expectations."

Judah clamped his lips tightly together. There would be no danger of his being accepted by his grandfather. Not after he stood eye to eye with the old tyrant and let him know how much he disliked him.

Both Judah and his mother lapsed into silence as they watched the keelboat move up the winding Mississippi River. The sounds of the street vendors hawking their wares faded in the distance as New Orleans was left behind and they moved slowly upstream. The earth-colored water flowed in an indecisive manner, past green farmlands and narrow forks half-covered with dense undergrowth amid the lazy bayous. Atop softly rolling hills, grand plantation houses stood as graceful reminders of a genteel lifestyle.

Against his will, Judah was drawn to the beauty and

graciousness of the hillside mansions that lined the waterway. The Mississippi valley, with its fertile valleys and rich farmlands, seemed to beckon to him. The beauty of the green meadows was timeless. The melodious sounds of the mimicking mockingbird trilled through the morning air.

"I am home," Gabrielle murmured. "Like the prodigal son I have returned."

Before Judah could reply, his mother's eyes sparkled with warmth. "Look, just around that next turn is Bend of the River Plantation!" Her voice rose with excitement as the flatboat maneuvered the curve.

When the boat passed a wide glade of trees choked with underbrush, it pulled within sight of the huge manor house. Nothing Judah had been told by his mother prepared him for the magnificent sight that met his eyes. The stately mansion was located on a distant cliff overlooking the Mississippi. Built in 1725, it was a testament to the finest French architecture. Unlike many of the other plantations that had been built along the Mississippi, the house was set half a mile from the river. Twenty acres of manicured lawns, pasture, and woodland surrounded the great house, and the roof of the red brick structure was graced by twelve chimneys. It was a three-story dwelling that boasted fifty-nine rooms.

Indeed, the mansion seemed to dwarf everything around it — even the tall stately magnolia trees that lined the drive leading to the front door. Iron latticework ran the length of the veranda as well as the second-story balcony.

As the keelboat pulled in at the wooden pier that jutted out into the water, the captain tossed a rope to a young boy, who jumped ashore to secure it to a post. There were several slaves standing on the dock. One, a tall man with stooped shoulders, white hair, and wide-set black eyes, seemed to be in charge, and ordered the others to unload the supplies. He watched closely when Judah and his mother disembarked, noting from their mode of dress that they were obviously of great import.

He looked at Judah for direction. "I was not told to expect visitors, *M'sieu*, or I would not have brought the mule-drawn wagon. Would you be so kind as to wait until I can send back to the house for the buggy?"

Judah noticed that the man spoke a broken kind of French that lent a certain charm and elegance to his speech. Before he could reply, however, Gabrielle stepped forward and startled the old man when she placed her hand on his arm. "Do you not know me, Biff?"

The man stepped back a pace, his dark eyes moving over her face. Suddenly there was recognition in his eyes, and a smile lit his face. *"Mon dieu!"* he cried, shaking his head, his eyes bright with genuine joy. "Can it be Ma-'dame Gabrielle? I thought these tired old eyes would never behold your pretty face again."

"I am home, Biff. At least for a while. Were you not told that I was coming?"

"No, but I am glad to see you all the same." The old man raised his voice and yelled down the dock. "Make quick and bring the buggy down, Ma'dame Gabrielle's come home!"

When the buggy pulled up at the front of the house, Biff jumped down to assist Gabrielle to the ground. His wrinkled face was creased in a smile as he piled the baggage on the front steps, knowing he could go no farther. There were strict codes to be observed. He was the foreman of the plantation, and outside the white overseer, Biff's word was law when it came to the field hands and the fishermen. But here at the big house, the house servants jealously guarded their domain; he was not allowed to intrude.

A tall slender black man with a regal bearing, dressed in red and white livery, opened the door and haughtily glanced down his nose at Biff. Seeing Gabrielle and Judah, he looked taken aback for a moment, but he quickly recovered. The snap of his fingers brought three other liveried servants. He ordered them to carry the baggage inside. Then he turned to Gabrielle and Judah.

"Whom shall I say is calling, *Ma'dame?*" the man asked with a crisp French accent.

Biff, still grinning, spoke up. "You may want to tell Cora to get her fancy cook pot going, cause there going to be a good time—"

The liveried servant cut Biff off. "Be so kind as to tend to your own affairs and leave others to tend to theirs. Move along." He shooed him away with the wave of a white glove.

"Just a moment," Gabrielle said, stopping Biff's hasty departure by the touch of her hand. "Who is this man, Biff? I do not recall ever seeing him."

Biff turned back, with a look of superiority, at the still unbending butler. "His name is Noal, *Ma'dame*. He is someone Ma'dame Alicia brought in from New Orleans. She say we need more— She say we needed him to make more nice the manners of the house servants."

"I told you to be gone," the butler said loftily. Turning to Judah, who had watched the whole proceeding with bored indifference, he asked. "Who shall I say is calling?"

Gabrielle pushed past the man and ascended the steps. "You may inform M'sieu Montesquieu that his daughter is home, and in the future you will never talk down to Biff in my presence, is that understood?"

Noal's face fell, and he stepped quickly to the door. "*Oui, Ma'dame,* it will be as you say. Come with me, and I will show you to your rooms so you can freshen up. When the master asks for you, I will come for you at once."

Judah followed the stiff-backed servant into the house. In the massive entrance hall, the white marble floor was immaculate, leading Judah to believe that not a single speck of dust marred its perfection. Golden Louis XIV armchairs faced each other, while urns and benches carved of Carrara marble stood on either side of the six steps that led to the landing. Off the landing were two sets of steps that went off in different directions, and Judah noted that several cherubs adorned the painted canvas ceiling. He had never imagined such wealth, but was cynically unimpressed. He did, however, now realize what his mother had sacrificed for loving of his father.

As he climbed the wide polished staircase, he paused to look at the floor-to-ceiling stained-glass window depicting the coronation of some distant French King. He drew in a deep breath, knowing he would soon meet the man behind this vast kingdom. Judah was well aware that when he stood before this tyrant who had made his mother's homecoming such a humbling experience, nothing would keep him from voicing his displeasure.

Judah buttoned his jade green jacket and adjusted the snowy-white cravat to his satisfaction. Gray pantaloons disappeared inside black knee boots. Impatiently, he paced the floor of the spacious bedroom, waiting for a summons from the great man himself. The long delay had not helped his temper. He did not care that he was being insulted, but he resented the treatment for his mother's sake. He was on the verge of demanding to be taken to his grandfather, when a knock came on his door.

Jerking the door open, he discovered his mother smiling up at him. "My father will see us now, Judah." She ran a nervous hand over the skirt of her pale green empire-waist gown. "How do I look? Do you think my

72

hair is right?"

Judah only half glanced at his mother's appearance. His anger was still too raw and too near the surface to do more than nod. "You are lovely as always," he said, taking her arm and steering her toward the staircase.

After they descended the stairs, Judah allowed his mother to lead the way. Their feet sank into rare thick rugs in the hallway as they passed by rooms where candles burned in crystal chandeliers, their flames reflected in glided French mirrors.

His mother knew where she was going as they walked down brightly lit hallways, past a host of servants who were cleaning and polishing floors and furniture. When at last Gabrielle stopped before a heavy mahogany door which was decorated with shining brasswork, she wrapped softly, then pushed the door open.

The room was almost dazzling in its magnificence. It was the largest room Judah had ever seen. The ceilings, painted in brilliant blues and whites, depicted the life of Jeanne d'Arc. An Aubusson carpet of white and gold graced the white marble floor. The floor-to-ceiling windows were draped with gold velvet and white lace, and a ten-foot-high white marble fireplace dominated the delicate French gilded chairs and sofas. Gilded mirrors lined one wall, making the room appear twice the size it actually was.

Judah felt his mother's trembling hand on his arm, and he placed his hand over it to give her courage. His eyes moved across the room to the man who was seated near the fireplace, haloed in the beam of light filtering through the open window. Judah met his grandfather's stare without flinching. His jaw clamped shut, stubbornly, as the man motioned for them to approach.

Judah was aware that the old man followed their progress, and when he drew near, he saw that his grandfather wore a blue satin coat and white knee britches, in the

73

outmoded style of a grand era. The old man's white hair, tied back with a black velvet ribbon, also represented the style of another era. Judah met faded turquoise eyes not unlike his own. He perceived heightened interest, curiosity, intelligence, and a mocking light in those shrewd old eyes.

Extending a trembling blue-veined hand to his daughter, while his eyes never left his grandson's face, Gustave Montesquieu spoke in French. "So, my daughter has returned home at last?"

"Oh, Papa," Gabrielle cried, clasping his hand in both hers. "I have missed you so desperately." Judah knew his mother waited for some sign of affection or welcome from the old man, who only studied her with cold indifference.

"Do not snivel, Gabrielle," Gustave scolded, removing his hand from her clasp. "You were overemotional even as a child. I see you have not changed, except to age somewhat."

Judah saw the pain in his mother's eyes, and he stepped forward, wrapping her in a protective embrace. "You have no right to insult my mother." Without thinking, he spoke in English. "I will not allow her to remain in this house for one moment longer than it takes to pack our belongings. You are a bastard, and I am glad to be able to say it to your face. It makes the journey worthwhile."

Gabrielle gasped, as two pairs of turquoise eyes locked in combat. She clutched her son's coatfront, waiting for her father's reaction to his insult. She knew that both her father and her son were stubborn and proud, and she wondered if either of them would relent. She was startled when she saw her father's face ease into what was almost a smile.

"If I am to be insulted, I prefer it be done in French. The English language is so vulgar and common. It has always grated on my ears. I assume your mother taught you her native tongue?"

Judah glanced at the old man through half-closed lashes. "My mother taught me several languages. If you would like, I can insult you in each one of them."

This time Gabrielle was dumbstruck by the laughter that issued from her father's throat. "I damned sure do not intend to stand here and listen to insults from a young pup who is barely old enough to shave. I happen to know how old you are, so we will assume it is your youth which makes you speak so rashly, and not bad manners."

"Were I beyond your age, I would still tell you what I think of your treatment of my mother. You have broken her heart every time you returned one of her letters unopened. You have caused her sleepless nights, and days of yearning for her girlhood home. She has suffered much because of you. I do not intend that you hurt her anymore."

The old man's eyes narrowed, and a spark ignited. "Gabrielle is my daughter. I will treat her as I believe she deserves."

"No, *Monsieur,* you will not," Judah declared, lapsing into French. "You have the earlier claim on her, but you forfeited your right to that claim. I am taking her away now!"

Gabrielle reached out her hand to her father. "Please, Papa, do not do this. I can stand it if you do not want me, but do not put Judah through this torment."

Gustave Montesquieu waved his daughter aside. "What makes you think I am the tormentor, *Madame?* Was it not your son who first started with the insults?"

Gabrielle glanced up at her tall son, her eyes shining with love and pride. With a determination that surprised her father, she spoke. "If you do not see that when you hurt me, you hurt Judah, then we have nothing more to say to one another, Papa."

The old man's shoulders sagged, and he seemed to

visibly age before their eyes. "Have done, Gabrielle. The time for insults is over. I sent for you; how can you doubt that I wanted you home?"

"If that is so, Papa, why were there no arrangements made for us in New Orleans. Why was the buggy not ready to receive us when we arrived at the docks of Bend of the River? If you meant to belittle me and my son, you have succeeded."

The old man's face whitened, and his hand trembled as he reached for his gold-handled cane. "What are you saying? I told Sebastian that I—"

"Did I hear my name spoken?" Sebastian ambled into the room, his hands crammed into his pockets. After his eyes moved briefly over Gabrielle, they came to rest on his cousin, Judah Slaughter. Sebastian had been listening outside the door, and this was not the puny American he had expected. No, this was a man who could sweep anyone who displeased him out of the way. And he had a closer blood tie to his Uncle Gustave—he was a real threat, and Sebastian knew it.

"Did I, or did I not, tell you to make arrangements for my daughter's arrival?" the elder man demanded, his head rearing up like a charging bull's.

"That you did, Uncle, and I did make arrangements. However, I see I was very remiss in my calculations on the time of their arrival. I made the arrangements for next week." He shrugged his shoulders. "Oh, well, you are here now, and that is all that counts, is it not?"

Judah eyed his cousin with distaste, his lips curling somewhat. He didn't care for the man's foppish manner. Sebastian strutted like a peacock in his vermilion coat and tight-fitting pink pantaloons. Judah realized it had been Sebastian Montesquieu who had caused his mother's humiliation, not his grandfather as he had formerly thought, but that revelation in no way excused his grandfather for years of neglect, nor did it cool Judah's anger.

Sebastian bowed slightly to Gabrielle Slaughter and gave her a weak smile. "Cousin Gabrielle, a long-overdue pleasure. Allow me to welcome you home." His words sounded sincere, but there was a half-hidden dullness in his watery blue eyes that bespoke something undefinable.

When Sebastian turned to face Judah, there was no hint of a smile. The two men's warring eyes locked. Sebastian's sparkled with belligerence and unleashed hatred, while Judah's were cool and lethal.

Seeing that his uncle was watching the meeting between him and his cousin, Sebastian smiled. "Cousin, this is indeed a happy day for Bend of the River. We are all eager to make your visit a happy one."

Judah glared over Sebastian's shoulder to lock eyes with his grandfather. This had not been the welcome his mother had hoped for. There were strange hidden undertones in this room.

"Sebastian, escort my daughter to her room. I want to talk to this young whelp alone." There was a hint of mirth in the shrewd old eyes. "I want to see if he can take insults as well as he can deliver them."

Sebastian looked as if he would like to protest, but his uncle silenced him with a nod. Gabrielle was not in the least bit happy about leaving her son in the clutches of her father. However, the old man reached out and touched his daughter's flushed cheek with a tenderness that startled her. "It will be all right, *ma chère*. Go to your room and wait."

Gabrielle gave her son a soft smile before turning to walk away, and when his mother and cousin had gone out the door, Judah turned back to his grandfather. "You and I have nothing to talk about, save the way you have treated my mother through the years. She is special in every way, and you have hurt her far too often."

Gustave merely smiled and pointed with his cane at the chair opposite him. "Be seated. I always resented having

77

to look up to a man. I like a man to be at eye level with me so I can see what he is thinking."

Judah nodded grimly and seated himself in the chair, his eyes locked once more with his grandfather's. He would like nothing better than to spirit his mother out of this house, but not before he told this old tyrant a few truths.

"I am taking my mother away from here tomorrow. I should have known you would only hurt her again."

"I will ask you once more to speak in French," the old man commanded. "As for your mother, must I remind you again that she is my daughter?"

"No," Judah bit out. "I have not forgotten. It is *you* who needs reminding."

Gustave's hand trembled as it tightened on the handle of his cane. "I would like to make amends now, Judah. I am an old man who has made many mistakes. When you reach my age, I doubt that you will be able to say otherwise. I regret every day I was without my daughter. I know what she has been through. I also know many things about you and your growing-up years."

"How can that be?" Judah asked scornfully.

"I have my ways. It might surprise you what I know about you. My spies have kept me well informed of your progress over the years. I . . ." Gustave paused. "I am proud of the man you have become. Captain of your own ship at your age."

Astonishment sealed Judah's lips, as his grandfather continued. "I know of the valiant struggle you made to fill your father's shoes. I also know about the sacrifices my daughter made to allow you to follow your dream, and of the loan she received so you could get the *Winged Victory* out of dry dock."

Judah remembered the money they had borrowed to make the *Winged Victory* seaworthy. At the time he had been surprised that the bank had loaned him such a large sum of money and had made the payments low so he would have no trouble repaying them. Now he looked at his grandfather suspiciously. "Are you the one who was behind the bank loan?"

The old man shifted his eyes away. "Why would I want to interfere in your life? Let us talk about your future, and not dwell on your past. I know you could use money now."

"You know nothing about me."

"I know that every penny you borrowed from the bank was paid back in full." Gustave chuckled. "I even know about Adriane Pierce, but I will wager your mother does not know about your mistress."

Judah was surprised at how closely his grandfather had followed his life. He lowered his lashes so the man would not read his astonishment. "I do not believe it is customary for a son to inform his mother of his mistresses."

"I have also learned that you are a young man with high values and a strong code of honor." The old man's eyes bore into Judah. "A man must put honor above everything else. It was so in my father's day; it must be so in your day. I cannot leave Bend of the River to a man who is unaware of the sacred trust and the responsibility he will be taking on. The man I choose to take over when I am gone must be above reproach."

Judah stood up slowly, forcing his grandfather to crane his neck to look into his eyes. "If you are hinting that I might be that man, you are mistaken. I want nothing from you." Judah sneered. "You can take your Bend of the River Plantation and be damned, old man. If you know about me, as you say you do, then you know I am not stupid and I will not play your little games. How dare you think you can bring me here and play me against your nephew, Sebastian."

The old man's eyes glowed with excitement. "Speak in French," he said again. "What makes you think I would

79

entrust my fortune and my home to a young whelp like you," he said, watching Judah with the same predatory instincts a hawk might watch a rattlesnake.

Judah deliberately spoke in English. "I suspect you would like to watch a battle brewing—some upheaval that would take your mind off the fact that you are an old man and will soon have to release your hold on everything that you greedily clutched for so long. You overlooked one aspect, *Grandfather*. You will have to have two willing prospects to play out your little game. When I leave, you will only have one."

"You need money. Are you not tempted by a fortune? Do you know what it is like to have the power to rule an empire? Power beyond your wildest imagination?"

Judah's lips curled in disgust. "In the name of all that is holy, do you think to lure me into your trap with the promise of wealth? I told you, I want nothing that belongs to you. It galls me that I am forced to remain under your roof this one night."

Instead of being insulted, the old man's eyes danced merrily. "What if I told you I would leave you everything I have, with no strings attached?"

"I would know it was a trick."

Gustave chuckled. "You would be right. I would have to lay down a few stipulations."

Judah's eyes seemed to spit blue fire. "Then I would tell you to take your offer and go straight to hell. I am sorry to say that you have lived up to my worst expectations. I had hoped, for my mother's sake, that you were sincere in your desire to see her."

Gustave's eyes took on a cunning glow. "So you will leave us tomorrow?"

"As soon as I can walk out that front door."

At that moment the old man grabbed his chest and began to gasp for breath. "My heart," he whispered through trembling lips. "This is . . . a . . . bad one."

Judah watched helplessly as his grandfather slumped back in the chair. Dropping to his knees, he felt guilty for having been so rough on the old man. After all, Gustave Montesquieu was quite frail. "Tell me what to do!" he urged. "Have you had these attacks before?"

"Moses will know what to do—get Moses!"

Judah dashed across the room, flung open the door leading to the hallway, and almost collided with a giant black man who appeared out of nowhere. "Find someone named Moses," Judah told him. "Your master is ill."

The big man looked Judah over from head to foot before he answered. "I am called Moses. I will tend to my master."

Judah watched Moses lumber into the room. As he stood by helplessly, the big man lifted his grandfather into his arms. "Shall I send someone for a doctor?" Judah asked, not knowing what to do.

"No, that will not be necessary. My master has had these attacks before. I know what to do. He will need much rest and no excitement, *M'sieu*. Any strain might mean the end for him."

Moses carried Gustave Montesquieu as if he weighed no more than a child, Judah's guilt deepened. He should never have argued with his grandfather. His mother would take it hard if anything happened to her father.

Judah did not hear the door at the far end of the room shut with a soft thud. He was aware that the butler, Noal, hurried down the hallway and up the stairs to relay what had occurred to Sebastian's mother, Alicia.

Judah crossed the room in heavy strides. He stepped into the hallway and ascended the stairs to tell his mother what had happened. His heart was heavy, for he knew she would never leave this house now that her father was ill. He had the feeling that he was in a situation over which he had no control. His feet had started down a path on which there was no returning.

Moses seated his master in the heavily cushioned chair by the bedroom window. The old man's eyes were lively with excitement, and there was no trace of illness on his smiling face. His body shook with laughter as he looked to the man who had faithfully served him for forty years. "What do you think, Moses? Was I convincing?"

"He was most concerned, *M'sieu*."

"What did you think of the boy?"

"It was as you said, he has a high sense of honor." The old black face broke into a wide grin. "I believe him to be not unlike yourself, *M'sieu*."

"Yes, by damn, he is like me. I am sick to death of my nephew, *Sebastian*, and his conniving mother. They both sit by like poisonous snakes, waiting to strike. They cannot wait until I pass from this world so they can get their hands on Bend of the River. But we will show them. We still have a few tricks up our sleeves, Moses."

The old man's eyes were clear and sparkled with a new awareness and joy. "He really is like me, isn't he now, Moses? You would not say it if it were not true, would you?"

"He is you when you were a young man, *M'sieu*."

"Did you hear him when he told me what I could do with Bend of the River?" Gustave's laughter filled the room. "He cannot be bought, Moses. I will have to earn his respect. Damn me if my daughter did not do well — what a grandson I have in Judah Slaughter!"

The room was stiflingly hot, and the air was heavy with the overpoweringly sweet scent of *eau de toilette*. The woman who reclined on the satin-draped bed held no hint of her former beauty. Her plump figure was evidence of over-indulgence in rich food, and her face was painted and rouged in an attempt to disguise the wrinkles that fanned out around her eyes and mouth. Her lusterless eyes looked as if they would bulge out of their sockets as her lips twisted in anger.

"That old man has gone too far this time!" Alicia Montesquieu pounded her fists into a pillow. I will not be put out by this . . . this upstart, Judah Slaughter. We have lived under your uncle's tyranny for years—indulging his every whim, bowing to his slightest wishes. He led us to believe that Bend of the River would one day belong to you. Now he plays with our emotions. I will not have it!"

Sebastian's eyes darkened slyly. "Judah Slaughter will never be master of Bend of the River—it is mine and mine alone."

"What shall we do?" his mother asked, plopping a chocolate bonbon into her mouth.

"We will wait and bide our time until it is the right moment to strike. Meanwhile, I believe it would be wise to try to get on the good side of Gabrielle and her son. We do not want my uncle to become suspicious."

Alicia's eyes twitched with delight. "You mean lull them into passiveness, make them and the old man think we are genuinely happy to see them?"

"Exactly."

She clapped her hands together like a child who has just been promised a treat. "We will outfox them all, will we not, Sebastian? They are no match for the two of us."

With their heads together like a couple of conspirators, Sebastian and his mother began to formulate their plans.

"I knew the moment I saw Judah Slaughter that he was everything my uncle expected me to be, though he never did give me a chance to live up to his expectations. I would have done anything to please him."

"I warned you that your gambling would get you into trouble. I tried to tell your father the same thing, but he

83

would not listen either. You should never have promised Ben Carson fifty acres of the bottom land to pay off a gambling debt. You should never have done that. Did you not know your uncle would find out. He has ears and eyes everywhere."

Sebastian's eyes became cold. "I will not lose Bend of the River!"

"Do not worry, my son. We will find a way to discredit Judah Slaughter in your uncle's eyes."

Chapter Five

Judah Slaughter glanced around the grand ballroom with bored indifference. It was his first experience with a masquerade ball. He remembered his mother telling him that this was the ball everyone looked forward to all year, and he noted that everyone was in a joyous mood, seeming to approach life with frivolous abandon. Sebastian wore brown velvet and had come dressed as a cavalier. Judah, looking handsome dressed all in black but for his white shirt, had refused to wear a costume.

This party was unlike any of the functions Judah had attended in Boston, and he could not think why he had allowed Sebastian to talk him into putting in an appearance. Perhaps it was because he wanted to get away from Bend of the River and the ominous cloud that seem to cling about it. Judah had not seen his grandfather since their first meeting, although his mother visited the old man each day. According to her, his grandfather was still too ill for them to think of leaving.

Judah glanced back at the people who danced by. One was dressed as a court jester, others as eighteenth-century royalty. Roman soldiers danced with peasant maids. As the music slowed, Judah took stock of the young ladies that danced by amid swishes of silk, trailing enticing fragrances. Stepping back into the shadows, he hoped to go unobserved while he watched the gaiety around him.

Above the din of music and murmuring voices, Judah heard his name mentioned. Turning, he saw two white-headed matrons discussing him. He decided one or both of them must be hard of hearing because they were talking loudly enough for their voices to carry. It was apparent they did not know he stood just behind them.

The older of the two, a woman with a prominent nose and an eager gleam in her eyes had said, "My dear, how can Gustave Montesquieu, who is from our finest family, have a grandson like the Slaughter youth? And further-more, from what nationality is the name Slaughter? It sounds positively primitive to me."

"Haven't you heard?" her companion asked with gleaming eyes, glad she could enlighten her friend. "Gustave's daughter married an American some years back!"

With a twist of his upper lip Judah noticed his nationality had just been pronounced in the same tone one would have used if announcing he had the pox.

"No! How can that be? An American!"

The woman lowered her voice. "Indeed, *oui*. I remember the disgrace as if it happened only yesterday. Gabrielle Montesquieu met the American the year Gustave sent her to visit relatives in France. I believe the man was a common seaman. Gabrielle and this Slaughter fell in love and were married right there in Paris, without so much as consulting her father."

"How dreadful. Was the marriage the reason why Gustave Montesquieu disowned his daughter?"

"Indeed it was. You know what a proud man he is. The disgrace must have been a bitter pill for him to swallow. I have heard that poor Gabrielle has been a widow for years, cut off from her family and friends, living in the wilds of America."

"In my opinion, she brought it all on herself. When one marries beneath oneself, one must suffer the conse-quences." This pronouncement was delivered smugly by the second woman.

"You are right of course. Dear Sebastian told me that Gustave issued the invitation for his daughter to come home. It is hard to believe Judah Slaughter and dear Sebastian are related. I hope Monsieur Montesquieu will not leave any part of his fortune to this Slaughter. Everything should, by rights, go to Sebastian—he has been so devoted."

"Surely Gustave Montesquieu will never consider leaving anything to this American. Everyone knows how steadfast and loyal Sebastian is. He is such a dear boy, while I doubt this American will ever be accepted."

"Make no mistake about it, if he is the one chosen to inherit the Montesquieu fortune, he will be accepted," the other lady wisely observed. "There will be a rush of mamas who seek to acquire him as a husband for their daughters."

Judah's finely molded lips eased into an amused smile as he listened to the two ladies discuss him in such unflattering terms. If only they knew how little he cared about his grandfather's fortune, they would be shocked.

Judah looked about the room, searching for Sebastian. His cousin had not made a very favorable first impression, but he now seemed eager to make Judah feel welcome. Judah did not trust his motives, however. All those he had met at Bend of the River seemed to be hiding their true feelings. None was as he appeared, and there were hidden meanings behind everything said. Judah decided not to let his guard down around any of them.

Tonight Sebastian had convinced him to attend this ball at a neighboring plantation. It seemed Sebastian was smitten with the elder daughter of the host, and had every intention of marrying her. Judah waited with little interest for his cousin's ladylove to enter. He doubted that anyone could be as beautiful as Sebastian claimed his goddess to be.

Judah felt movement behind him and turned in amazement to see a young urchin standing beside him. It took him a moment to realize the child was female. She was covered with mud from the tip of her head to the toes of her scuffed brown boots. Her skirt was tucked into her waistband, allowing her skinny knees to show, and her strange blue eyes were made more prominent because of her smudged face. Her pert little nose was wrinkled with mirth. As she smiled at Judah, her eyes danced merrily. Lifting her finger to her lips, she cautioned him to be silent.

"In case you don't know it, *Monsieur,* you have been crucified by the *crème de la crème,*" she whispered. That is Madame Dancy and that, Madame Pessac. Their joy in life is to gossip."

His laughter was soft. "So it would seem. It does not concern me overmuch what they think of me. But, if you are a servant, shouldn't you slip out quickly? I would not want to see you get into trouble."

She smothered a giggle. "Would that I were only a servant—then my penalty would be far less severe. You see before you, *Monsieur,* a daughter of the house. There is no way for me to reach the privacy of my room but across that dance floor. Someone locked the back door."

"Did you go swimming in the river?" he wanted to know.

"Not by choice. My boat capsized." She gave him a woeful smile. "I will be in disgrace after tonight."

His smile was warm. "You have my sympathy."

The music had stopped, and Judah's face showed amazement when the young girl squared her shoulders and strolled leisurely away, heading in the direction of the massive, polished cypress staircase. Everyone's attention seemed to be drawn to her, but she pretended not to notice. Liberty knew she would face her mother's anger later on that night, but the damage was done so she was determined to make the best of it.

Sharp gasps could be heard from the two matrons who had been discussing Judah in such unflattering terms. "Well I never," one of them declared in horror. "What will Liberty be thinking of next? She is a disgrace to her family. A total disgrace!"

"Oui," agreed her friend. "I fear they will never make a silk purse out of that sow's ear. How unlike her sister she is."

Judah watched the young girl dash up the stairs two at a time. He smiled as she turned back to him and then tossed a woebegone glance at the ceiling. Inspired by her courage, he straightened his snowy-white cravat, stepped out of the shadows, and bowed before the two *grandes dames.* "If either of you ladies has a marriageable daughter, I may consider her" — he paused for effect — "but only if my grandfather leaves me his holdings. Otherwise, I would not dare aspire so high for a wife."

Hearing a giggle, Judah's attention was drawn to the stairs in time for him to see the girl called Liberty burst into laughter. With a wink in her direction, he walked out the double doors into the garden, leaving the two matrons gaping.

As he gazed up at the crescent moon, he wondered how the young girl had come to be named Liberty. Poor little homely creature, her name was the most promising thing about her. He laughed at the memory of the humor he had seen in her dancing blue eyes. She might never grow into a beauty, but she was certainly an adorable little minx.

The music had started again. Violins sweetly filled the air with a haunting melody. Judah glanced back at the house. He was certain that he did not fit in with his mother's people. He was an American, and proud of it! His father's family, the Slaughters, had come from a distinguished, old family. He would never apologize to anyone for who he was.

Suddenly the balcony doors were pushed open, and he recognized his cousin's voice. "I thought you would never come down. Are you happy now that you made the grand entrance?"

Judah assumed the woman beside his cousin was the *femme fatale* Sebastian had described. He allowed his eyes to rove to her, and he was disappointed that she wore a mask. There was no mistaking her costume; it was meant to represent Queen Elizabeth of England. Her gown was all red, but for the white ruff at her throat, and her hair was covered with a red wig. When she laughingly removed the mask and the red wig and tossed them aside, ebony locks spilled down her back. Her face was like an angel's, and her voice was musical when she spoke.

"When I have an expensive new gown, I like to show it off," Bandera stated. Opening her fan, she tapped Sebastian on the shoulder. "You cannot deny that I fooled everyone here tonight. At least they pretended not to know me."

"No disguise can hide your beauty, Bandera." Sebastian stared down at her. "I am the envy of every man here because you are with me," he said with feeling. Pulling her into his arms, he tried to kiss her, but she ducked her head and laughed at his attempt.

"Surely you do not expect the Queen of England to be of easy virtue, Sebastian."

Judah was so caught up in the woman's spell that he did not realize he was not alone until he heard Liberty speak. "That's my sister, Bandera. Men always think she's beautiful. I just think she's tiresome." Liberty bit into a carrot and continued talking with her mouth full. "All she ever thinks about is clothes and her gentlemen friends. She never has fun because she is too busy trying to look beautiful."

Judah noticed that the young girl's face had been scrubbed clean and her light-colored hair was now tied back with a ribbon. The shapeless smock she wore was also clean. "And what do you do for fun, Mademoiselle Liberty?"

She tossed aside her uneaten carrot. "Mostly I like to be in the swamps, but I also like to ride horses and to help out in the stable. But I have to sneak off to do that. I like horses more than most people I know."

Judah smiled. "So do I, Liberty. So do I. Why are you not dressed in costume?"

"I am too young to attend the ball this year. My mother says I have to wait two more years before I can participate in the masquerade ball."

His eyes went back to the balcony where that lovely vision, Bandera, had been joined by three other gentlemen. Her laughter was enchanting—everything about her was enchanting.

"*Monsieur,* what does it feel like to be an American?" Liberty wanted to know.

Through lowered lashes, he looked down at her. "Comfortable. I suspect you will find out before long. It is my guess that Orleans Territory will soon become a state."

"Do you think so?"

"I do."

"Is it true that you are Sebastian's cousin?"

"Guilty."

"I suppose that will make us relatives of a sort. It seems almost a certainty that Bandera will marry Sebastian. He is considered a prize catch, you know"—Liberty smiled impishly—" unless, of course, you walk off with the Montesquieu holdings as Madame Tulorose suggested. Should that happen, Bandera will probably try for you."

Judah glanced back to Bandera and watched her disappear inside the ballroom. "You aren't being very kind to your sister. You make her sound as if she were only after

91

Sebastian for his prospects."

"Not at all. I believe it is a game most women play. My mother says when one is pretty, one needs nothing else. As you have seen, Bandera is beautiful."

He smiled. "How would you classify yourself?"

"I am reasonably intelligent."

The self-appraisal was spoken earnestly. Liberty leaned close to Judah. "Bandera says ladies are not supposed to be intelligent. She says men don't want them to be. Can that be true?"

Judah laughed at the little charmer. "I have very little doubt that you will grow up and outsmart all the competition."

Liberty seated herself on a marble bench and spread her smock out about her. "Is that just a polite way of saying you do not think me pretty?"

His laughter rang out. "You are about the most precocious little girl it has ever been my pleasure to meet."

"I am not a little girl," she insisted. "Just last week I turned—"

"No, don't tell me—allow me to guess. You have just celebrated your twelfth birthday. You see, I am somewhat of an authority on a young lady's age."

"I am not twelve," Liberty said indignantly. "I am much older than that."

"I see." He tried not to smile. "How much older?"

She gave him a supercilious glance. "I . . . am fifteen."

"Ah," he said, making a gracious bow before her. "Mademoiselle Liberty, you will forgive my ignorance. How can I have been so mistaken? I see now that you are much older than I first suspected. Is there some way I can make amends for my miscalculation?" The smile that played around his lips was quickly hidden as he bent to kiss her fingers.

When he glanced up, Liberty saw his turquoise blue eyes twinkle with humor. As she stared into his handsome face, she felt a quickening in her heart — a strange feeling she had never before experienced, one which left her shaken.

For the first time, she noticed that Judah Slaughter was taller than the average man. He had not come in costume, and her eyes were drawn to the breadth of his shoulders and to how snugly they fit into his black velvet jacket. Her eyes moved down his long muscular pantaloon-clad legs, to his shiny black boots. He was all male, and she had the feeling there was unleased strength and power behind this man. Before now, Liberty had never dwelled on the differences between a man and a woman. But this man had made her all too aware that he was out of the ordinary. He would stand out anywhere because there was something different about him. It was more than the fact that he spoke French with an American accent; it went past the humor that now curved his lips.

"How may I make amends?" he asked once more, while clicking his heels and giving her an exaggerated bow.

The mischievous smile that hit Liberty's face, made her eyes sparkle. "You could dance with me, Monsieur. I know the quadrille quite well."

He presented his arm, and she placed her hand on it. "As, my lady wishes," he said, the mirth still dancing in his eyes.

While the music filtered through the air and thousands of stars twinkled in the ebony sky, Judah danced Liberty around the garden. While he seemed to find the whole incident humorous, Liberty was having an entirely different reaction. She could feel the corded muscles, the whipcord sinews, as her hand rested on his arm. His gaze was fixed on her face, and suddenly Liberty was finding it hard to breathe. When his hard thigh accidentally brushed against her during a quick whirl, she felt her body come awake with a painful jolt.

Staring through thick lashes, Judah caught her eye.

"You are indeed a fine dancer, Mademoiselle. Rarely have I danced with a partner to equal you." As a lock of her hair brushed against his cheek, Judah became aware of a lingering scent. It was not one of the exotic or powerful scents that most women preferred, but a sweet, soft, haunting scent. One that he was sure he would remember for the rest of his life. And she was soft in his arms—as if she belonged there. With restraint, Judah kept reminding himself of her young age.

Liberty tried to speak, but her voice caught in her throat. She was aware of her limitations when it came to holding this man's attention. She realized how young she must appear, dressed in her childish smock. She wished with all her young heart that she had paid more attention to her toilette on this night. She could at least have worn her violet-colored silk gown with the green embroidery around the skirt. She remembered with horror what his first impression of her must have been. He had seen her at her worst in that mud-covered state.

"I like a lady who doesn't talk," he said, sweeping her around a hedge to circle the small fountain.

"I speak three languages," she blurted out, wondering what had ever possessed her to make such a mundane statement. He would not be interested in her trivial accomplishments. Why had she not said something clever to impress him? Bandera would have known just how to keep his attention.

"Do you?"

She lowered her head. "It is unimportant."

Without breaking his stride, he placed a finger under her chin and raised her face to his. "I believe any accomplishment is important. Which languages to you speak?"

"I . . . the obvious, French . . . Spanish and English."

He smiled indulgently, as though sensing her discomfort. *Merveilleuse, brava,* and hurrah!"

Liberty lifted her lashes, meeting his gaze. A shiver ran

94

through her body, and she spoke quickly, hoping he had not noticed. "My mother says a woman should never point out her accomplishments to a gentleman. She says if she acts with the proper decorum, her attributes will be apparent.

Judah threw back his head and laughed deeply. This little charmer would all too soon have the gentlemen aware of her accomplishments. Even though she was a mere child, he found her fascinating. "What else does your mother say, little Liberty?"

"Her mother says children should be seen and not heard." A musical voice spoke up just behind Judah. Liberty felt her heart thud as she saw her sister standing under the moon's glow, looking like a beautiful princess. "Her mother says that she should not pester the adults."

Judah turned, not at all pleased with the way this woman had embarrassed and humiliated Liberty. He was about to voice his displeasure when his eyes fell on Bandera, and all else was pushed from his mind. Her dark hair seemed to shimmer in the moonlight, as did her bright red gown, and her creamy skin was like alabaster. His heart hammered in his temples as she smiled at him.

"Has my sister been annoying you?"

"To the contrary; I find her enchanting."

Liberty knew she might have been on the moon for all Bandera and Judah cared. Liberty saw the way her sister's eyes assessed their guest, and she knew Bandera was on the trail of another conquest. She quickly glanced up at Judah, hoping he could see through her sister's practiced ploys. But like a man caught in a dream, Judah released Liberty's hand and gravitated toward Bandera.

"Liberty, where are your manners?" Bandera scolded. "You have not yet introduced me to your friend."

Liberty bit back her disappointment. Now was not the time to act like a spoiled child. "This is Sebastian's cousin, Judah Slaughter. Monsieur Slaughter, meet my

sister, Bandera."

"Ah, yes, the sister." Clicking his heels together, Judah bowed from the waist, not in mockery as he had earlier with Liberty, but with politeness and gallantry. "I believe I am in the presence of Good Queen Bess."

Bandera's eyes sparkled with renewed fascination as she stared at the handsome stranger. She could feel her pulse racing as his eyes moved over her face with evident attentiveness. "So," she breathed, "you are Sebastian's cousin."

"I am."

She circled slowly around him, her eyes taking in the cut of his coat, the breath of his shoulders. Magnetism seemed to ooze from every pore of his body. Bandera's movements were graceful, practiced to draw a man's eyes, and she definitely had drawn Judah's attention. When at last she stopped in front of him, knowing he was attracted to her, she smiled. "You do not look like a Montesquieu."

"I am not. I am a Slaughter."

Bandera licked her lips, making them moist and soft, then tapped her black satin fan against her open palm. Both gestures caught Judah's attention. "Sebastian is worried lest you came to steal away his inheritance. Need he be?" Her voice was low and musical. He did not see the urgency in her eyes as she waited for an answer to her question.

"Sebastian need have no fear of me. I will not be staying long enough to take anything away from him."

Bandera's thick lashes fluttered, and she met Judah's brilliant turquoise gaze. "Has Sebastian nothing that would interest you?"

His eyes swept across her face to light on her parted lips. "Perhaps, but it has nothing to do with money."

Low laughter trilled from Bandera's throat. "You will have this country girl's heart all atwitter, Monsieur

Slaughter." His smile took her breath away.

"Indeed, that might well be my intention."

Her eyes coyly dropped, and she held out a delicate hand. "You danced with my sister, Monsieur. Will you not also dance with me?"

"Indeed Mademoiselle, it would be my pleasure."

Bandera gave her sister a tight smile as she placed her hand on Judah's arm. With a feeling of helplessness, Liberty watched the two of them walk toward the house. She had just met this man who set her heart on fire, and Bandera was stealing him away. How could she ever hope to compete with her beautiful sister? Why did Judah not see that Bandera was playing a game with him? She had hoped he would be different from all the other gentlemen that trailed after Bandera—but apparently he was not.

By now Judah and Bandera had reached the polished dance floor, and he swung her into the stream of dancers. He could not drag his eyes away from her face. Her beauty was flawless, her body enticing, her smile flirtations.

"I wonder if I could steal you away from my cousin?" he murmured, as if in a trance.

"That depends," she said with a slow smile.

"On what?"

"Whether I want to be stolen away."

Bandera felt her skin tingle. She had never experienced such strong emotions with a man before. This man was different from all others; he was the forbidden fruit, the outsider. Her mother had trained her well, but she had never told her what to do if a man set her heart to throbbing like the hooves of a runway horse. Bandera thought of Sebastian. He had never stirred any emotion within her, only boredom and complacency. But he was the favorite, and destined to inherit the Montesquieu fortune. Money and power were the most important things in Bandera's life. Emotions would not buy lovely

gowns, and love would not provide her with a home like Bend of the River.

"Why have you come among us?" she asked, raising her eyes to meet his turquoise gaze. If there was the slightest chance that this man would inherit instead of Sebastian, Bandera would gladly throw in her lot with him.

"Actually, I came only as an escort for my mother."

"Will you not stay?"

"I think not."

"What if your grandfather were to leave Bend of the River to you? Would you stay then?"

"No. If he were to saddle me with his holdings I would leave them to the nearest charitable organization." His voice was bitter. "I want nothing from my grandfather."

Bandera felt her heart sink. For one brief moment she had entertained the thought of being the wife of this handsome rogue. In comparison, how tiresome it would be to marry Sebastian. She shrugged her shoulders, resigning herself to the fact that being Sebastian's wife would be her lot in life.

Smiling up at Judah, she moved just the slightest fraction so her breasts brushed against his chest. She saw the fire leap into his eyes, and her heart raced. She was not married yet. There was no reason she couldn't enjoy this man's company for a time.

Liberty stared up at the ballroom, unmindful of the music and laughter. The glow from the numerous chandeliers shone like a beacon out the windows and into the garden. To her it was all so ridiculous. The dancers in their colorful costumes were like children playing at being grown-up.

As she walked down the path leading toward the river, her mind was troubled. What had happened to her tonight? Was it possible she was becoming a woman?

Liberty leaned against a tall magnolia tree, and was overcome with melancholy. Tonight, Judah Slaughter had

stirred her young body to life. She was experiencing her first womanly feelings. She now knew why girls acted so silly when a gentleman was near. She had been unable to breathe when Judah Slaughter had held her in his arms. And she now knew why Bandera spent hours at her toilette, so she would look her best. This was what it felt like to be touched by a man.

Liberty raised her face to the sky, and watched a shooting star streaking across the heavens. She closed her eyes, and wished with all her young heart: "Please, please make me pretty so Judah Slaughter will look at me the way he looked at Bandera tonight!"

Chapter Six

Liberty stood on the bank of the Mississippi River, watching the sun make its first appearance of the day. The air was fragrant with the scent of the nearby pine forest, and the fertile valley seemed to stretch on for as far as the eye could see. It was often her habit to ride out before sunrise so she could be alone and drink in the beauty of Briar Oaks.

Her horse, Goliath, trailed his reins as he grazed on the sweet grass that grew beneath a cypress tree. Dressed in a pair of britches she had found in the attic, her hair carelessly pushed beneath a black cap, Liberty made her way down to the river. Casting her line into the slow-moving current, she then secured it between two large rocks which came together in a vee.

Liberty had been troubled since the night of the masquerade ball when she had met Judah Slaughter. Now, lost in thought, she wondered if she were becoming a woman, with a woman's needs and desires? Why did she get so little pleasure out of the things that had once brought her so much joy? This was the first time she had been fishing in weeks. She had been back to the swamp only once to see Zippora, and lately she found herself staring into the mirror, wondering why she had been born so homely.

She flopped over onto her stomach, and trailed her

hand in the water, watching it ripple away from the shore. If this was what it was like becoming a woman, then Liberty could very well do without growing up; it was much too painful.

Liberty pensively watched a dragonfly skimming across the river, dipping its wings in the water. She was feeling lost and unsure of what direction her life was taking. She wondered if every girl felt this way when she started to grow up. Had Bandera?

"Hey there, young lad. Have you caught anything yet?"

Liberty froze at the sound of Judah Slaughter's voice. No! she thought in a panic, do not let it be him. Why must he always find her in the worst possible situation, and looking her most wretched? For the moment he seemed to believe her to be a boy. How horrified he would be when he discovered who she really was. Perhaps there was a chance that he would not discover her identity. She prayed his view of her had not been very clear the night of the ball and he would not recognize her now. Perhaps if she did not engage him in conversation, he would just ride away.

Slightly turning her head, Liberty watched Judah dismount and secure his horse to a tree. In frustration she pulled the cap lower over her forehead, and ducked her chin. "If you have come here to fish, you will be disappointed, *Monsieur*. The fish are not biting this morning," she said, trying to persuade him to leave.

Against her will, her eyes moved over him as he drew near. He stood with his muscled legs apart, staring absent-mindedly across the river. "I would think this is a fisherman's paradise. Rarely have I seen such an abundance of wildlife." His eyes dropped to her face. "Do you mind if I join you?"

She shrugged her shoulders, pretending indifference, while warring emotions battled inside her. She wanted to be near him, but feared he would discover she was not the

boy he believed her to be.

"I thought I was the only one who was an early riser around here. I am glad to see I was wrong," he said, seating himself beside her.

Liberty drew up her legs and rested her head on her knees. What she would give to be wearing one of Bandera's lovely frocks at the moment. She wished she could think of something witty and charming to say. She wished she could crawl off somewhere and hide so she would not have to watch the horror in his eyes when he discovered she was not a boy at all.

"I see the river is running smoothly today," he observed, trying to draw her into conversation.

"That is true," she mumbled. "It often does."

"You don't talk much, do you, lad?"

"No."

"Do you often fish here?"

"Oui."

"Do you live around here?"

"Not around . . . here."

Judah looked about him. "So, you live on Bend of the River Plantation. Is your father perhaps the overseer?"

"You are not on Bend of the River Plantation, *Monsieur*. You are on Briar Oaks. The dividing line is that row of pine trees to the right."

He arched a dark brow at her. "I seem to be trespassing."

"It is of little matter. Neighbors are always welcome at Briar Oaks."

There was a moment of silence before Judah spoke again. "Is the river always so muddy?"

"I suppose it is, but you will find that we French love our river."

"Even when she runs over her banks and floods the land?"

"Then we love her as a mother would love a wayward

child."

"Eloquently put."

"You will forgive me if I have to leave now, *Monsieur,*" Liberty said, rising unsteadily to her feet. "If you like, you can keep the fishing pole." Picking up the cane pole, she thrust it into his hands, wanting to make a hasty retreat.

As she moved back a pace, Judah's eyes followed the slender line of her body, which was well defined by the boyish clothing. He saw the gentle swell of breasts thrust against the stiff linen shirt . . . and he caught the sweet aroma that he now associated with young Liberty.

A smile suddenly tugged at his lips. He took a closer look at the freckles sprinkled over the pert upturned nose. As his eyes locked with shining blue eyes that held a hint of apprehension, he turned away.

"I will stay only if you stay with me, *Mademoiselle* Liberty."

"You . . . you know it is me?"

Gripping the fishing pole, he cast the line into the water before securing it between the rocks. "I didn't at first. You had me thoroughly fooled." Sitting down on the riverbank, he nodded to his right, indicating that she should join him.

Liberty removed her cap, and her hair tumbled across her shoulders and down her back. Reluctantly, she dropped down beside him, knowing her cheeks had turned a bright scarlet color. Turning her face toward the river, she hoped to quell her thundering heart. Why did she always have the feeling she was drowning whenever Judah Slaughter was near?

Judah stretched out his long form beside her as his eyes followed the bobbing cork that moved restlessly with the waves. "You are an amazing young woman, Liberty. I know of no other lady who would go out alone to fish."

She swung around to face him, and her hair made a silken swirl about her head. "What you meant to say is

you don't think I am a lady at all? You believe, like so many of your sex, that a woman should spend her time sewing and making senseless chatter. Well, I am not like that. Sewing bores me, and I care not for asinine chatter. I find it all so artificial." She stopped, horrified that she had said too much. She had wanted to impress Judah Slaughter; she had ended up shocking and amusing him.

In that moment, her blue eyes blazed and the pulse throbbed in her arched neck. Judah drew in his breath as he saw the promise of beauty yet undeveloped. While this young girl had none of the graces that her sister possessed she had something more, something that he could not define. A refreshing honesty . . . a zest for life . . . a sense of humor that allowed her to view herself and others with amusement. He was fascinated by her, and it bothered him a great deal because of her young years.

"I, myself, have never been overly fond of idle chatter. However, I do like stimulating conversation. Mundane, everyday platitudes bore me."

Liberty began to relax. Unfolding her legs, she raised her face to the sun, feeling the warming rays caress her skin. "I detest hypocrisy of any kind, *Monsieur*. I find the the games men and women play to attract each other tiresome and, perhaps, even a little humorous."

"In what way?" He was enchanted with this little minx. She was like no one he had ever known.

"Well," she began thoughtfully, "my sister has been schooled in what to talk about, what subjects not to broach with a gentleman. She has been taught how to use a fan to her advantage, how to walk, how to sit, even how to catch a man's eye from across the room. It is an old game, yet one would think all the men dull-witted because they fall for it every time. You should see how—"

Suddenly Liberty saw the smile on Judah's face, and she covered her mouth in horror. She was mortified by what she had been telling him. *"Monsieur,* I beg you to

disregard everything I have said today. A man should never be told about the preparation a woman makes to trap . . . I mean . . ." She was getting herself in deeper and deeper, while the smile on his face widened. ". . . My mother would be very displeased with me if she knew I had spoken so boldly," Liberty said, ducking her head, and feeling like a complete fool.

Leaning back against the soft grass, Judah folded his hands behind his head and stared into her blue eyes. "I find your refreshing approach to the act of the male-female ritual fascinating."

"I am sure it is not at all proper to tell a gentleman secrets that only a woman should know."

"I can see you standing back observing the rest of us with quiet indulgence. How tiresome it must be for you."

"Oh, I pray, *Monsieur,* you will not think me conde-scending. I beg that you forget what I have said to you today. My mother always accuses me of speaking before I have taken time to think. It is a habit I cannot seem to break, *Monsieur*—though I have often tried."

His delighted laughter filled the air. "I would like to press you not to change your ways, Liberty. Stay us charming and honest as you are. Allow the other ladies to play their little games. I have the feeling you are laughing at us all."

"Oh, no, *Monsieur,* I would never laugh at you." Reaching out to her scuffed brown boots, she traced the sole with her finger. "I . . . find you different from your cousin, Sebastian."

"In what way?"

"I . . . you . . . when I saw you that first night, you seemed to be detached from the others. I could see the scorn on your face as you watched the make-believe world that was created for grandes dames who want an advanta-geous marriage for their sons, and mothers with marriageable daughters who want to make a grand

106

match."

"Are you not interested in making a favorable marriage?"

"No. I may have to enter a convent."

His dark brow arched. "In heaven's name why?"

"I have given this much thought. It is not unusual that the less favorable daughters in a family sometimes are forced to join an order to save face."

Judah's eyes narrowed against the glare of the sun as he watched her face. He detected hurt in the depth of her eyes, and he wondered what her life had been like, lived in the shadow of her beautiful sister. No wonder she had turned tomboy. Apparently someone was always pointing out her shortcomings and comparing her to Bandera.

"Is there not some young gentleman who interests you?"

Liberty met his eyes. "Only one. If it is possible, I suppose I shall one day marry him."

A smile parted his lips. "So, there will be no taking of the veil for you, Liberty. Does the fortunate boy know about your plans?"

"He is not a boy, but a man. He does not yet know how I feel about him. I hope that one day I can tell him — one day when I am grown up."

"The man is most fortunate," Judah whispered under his breath. His eyes moved up her trouser-clad legs, past the slight swell of her breasts, to her pixyish face. "Most fortunate. I doubt he will ever be bored with you at his side."

Liberty blushed and ducked her head at his words of praise. She felt her heart beating a wild tempo. What would Judah do if she were to tell him that he was that man? In that moment, she wanted more than anything to be beautiful. If she were to work very hard and adhere to her mother's demands, could she turn into a lady Judah would admire?

Turning to face him, Liberty saw that he was now lying on his back, staring at the sky. Her young eyes moved across his powerful legs, clad in gray pantloons which were stretched taut across bulging muscles. His black English riding boots came to his knees, and shone with a high gloss. The ruffles at the cuff of his white linen shirt rested against strong, sun-tanned hands. The blood ran hot in her veins, as she thought of those hands touching her in the most intimate way.

Judah had removed his gray, cutaway jacket and casually tossed it aside. Her eyes were drawn to the hollow at the base of his throat; the golden hair on his chest was just visible above the top button on his shirt. His chin was strong; his face handsome beyond belief. Golden skinned and golden haired; surely there was no other man like Judah Slaughter. Liberty could almost feel the strength of him radiate through the crisp morning air, and she was almost giddy from the effect. There was about him a sense of vitality and strength that no one could ignore. He was so alive, so male. She had no doubt that he had always been spoiled by the fair sex. Most probably he could have any woman he wanted.

Liberty remembered how Bandera had reacted to him, and she felt dread in her heart. Suppose Bandera decided she wanted Judah Slaughter? Bandera had certainly been attracted to him, and to Liberty's knowledge, no man could resist her sister's charm.

Judah turned to face Liberty, and she was caught in a tide of confusion when his turquoise eyes held her gaze. It was as if this were the moment in time that she had been created for. Judah Slaughter was the only man she would ever love. Would a man like him, who must have scores of lady friends, laugh at the love she felt for him?

There was complete silence as his eyes narrowed. It was a strange moment, and he felt the young girl pulling at him. Judah reached out his hand toward her, but drew it

back before it made contact. What in the hell was wrong with him? he wondered. Liberty was a child, and he was having very grown-up thoughts about her. "How did you ever come by a name like Liberty?" he asked in a soft voice.

Liberty turned away so she could find her voice. "It was the name of my father's only sister. She died in a yellow fever epidemic."

"I see, a family name."

"*Oui*, my mother was not in favor of the name, but my father, who usually gives in to her, held out stubbornly in this."

"I think it is a lovely and unusual name."

Liberty reached for the saddlebags she had tossed on the ground earlier, and withdrew two apples. Pitching one to Judah, she shined hers on the leg of her trousers. "My father says it is a name to live up to. He says it demands integrity, honor, and honesty. I told him I would endeavor not to shame his sister's name."

Judah bit into the apple, all the while watching her face ease into her devilish little smile. "Sometimes it is very difficult to live up to my father's expectations, *Monsieur.*"

His smile was warm as he reached out to catch a golden wisp of hair and tuck it behind her ear. "I believe you are already in possession of the traits your father expects of you, little Liberty. I am very proud that I have come to know you."

Her eyes brightened, and she caught her breath as his finger trailed across her chin. "Are you ready, Judah?" They had both unconsciously slipped into a first-name basis.

"Indeed I am."

Suddenly she wanted to know everything about him — his likes and dislikes, his favorite pastime, his plans for the future. "What did you do before you came to your grandfather's house?"

He chuckled. "You see before you a sea captain, Liberty. I hope you are properly impressed."

Her eyes rounded in surprise. "A sea captain! I never suspected, but *oui,* it fits." Now she could better understand why his skin was so beautifully tanned. "How did you come to be a captain?"

"I suppose it's in my blood. My father was a sea captain."

"But you are so young. One always thinks of a sea captain as an elderly, more mature gentleman."

He laughed again. "If you are wondering if I am qualified to captain a ship, the answer is yes."

"What is the name of your ship?"

"The *Winged Victory.*"

"I like that. What kind of ship is she?"

"She is a frigate. Do you know anything about ships?"

"No, but I would very much like to. Where is she now? Did you sail her here?"

He took another bite of apple and chewed it before answering. "My first mate, Philippe Cease, took the *Winged Victory* to the Spanish Territory. On his return I will leave for Boston."

Suddenly her heart felt heavy, and she shook her head. "Does that mean you will be leaving as soon as he arrives?"

"Perhaps." He traced the stem of the apple with a long finger, then pulled it out and tossed it away. "That will depend on my mother. But I need to get back to sea, Liberty. That is the way I make my living."

"Your grandfather is a very wealthy man."

"I agree."

"You could—"

"Let me explain something to you, my new little friend. What my grandfather has, or does not have, does not affect me in any case. I make my own way."

She caught the bite to his words, and felt an even

110

deeper admiration for Judah. "I know your grandfather quite well. It is strange that he never told me about you. He is really very nice, once you realize he talks gruffly to cover a kind heart."

Judah looked at her doubtfully. "Perhaps you have seen this side of him. I doubt I ever shall." He shifted his weight. "It is much too nice a day to talk about my grandfather."

Liberty could read the anger in the depths of Judah's eyes, and she realized it was time to change the subject. "I have never sailed on a big ship. The only times I have been on a boat are on occasional trips down the Mississippi to New Orleans, or of course when peddling my skiff down the bayous—but that doesn't qualify."

"Do you go into the swamps alone?" His voice was filled with wonder.

"Of course. My father says I know the swamps better than anyone. Besides, I have a friend that I visit there."

"Who would live in the swamps besides alligators?"

Liberty smiled slightly. "A woman named Zippora. Some people believe her to be a witch, but she's not. She lives in a cabin where she weaves her spells and mixes her potions." Her eyes danced merrily. "Are you impressed?"

"Indeed. I have heard it said that voodoo is still secretly practiced among many of the slaves."

"As I said, Zippora is not really a witch, and she claims she does not practice voodoo. But she has strange powers. She is my best friend. I find her company preferable to that of most people I know."

"Let me see if I have this right. "You prefer the company of horses and witches, to that of people of your own kind—is that correct?"

"*Oui,* I do."

After a long moment of silence, Liberty asked. "What do you think of Sebastian?"

"He is everything I expected him to be."

"Which is no answer at all."

He arched an eyebrow. "You catch on quickly. I like a woman with a fast mind."

Liberty took a bite of her apple while studying him closely. "You don't think much of us do you?"

His smile was genuine. "I like you."

"You like Bandera, too, don't you?"

"Tell me about her," he said with sudden attentiveness. "What is she really like?"

"No need for me to tell you she is lovely; you already know that. Bandera is everything a young lady of quality should be. She will one day adorn some gentleman's home and make him the perfect wife." She could have added that Bandera was cold and calculating, but she did not. In spite of her sister's shortcomings, Liberty loved her. And it was not in Liberty's nature to be unkind.

"I find it strange that your sister has dark hair and yours is so fair," Judah observed aloud.

"In truth, Bandera is only my half sister. My mother was married and widowed before she met my father."

"That would explain the difference in coloring."

"*Oui*. Bandera is Spanish, while I am only half-Spanish.

At that moment, the fishing pole began to wiggle, and Judah and Liberty both made a dive for it. Laughing and tugging at the line, she handed the pole to him. With a strong jerk, he pulled the fish in, and it landed with a plop on the riverbank.

Liberty picked up the two-pound catfish, steadied it with one hand, then deftly removed the hook from its mouth. "Have you had breakfast yet?"

"No, as a matter of fact I haven't."

"How would you like to have a freshly cooked catfish?"

"I would like nothing better. How will you arrange it?"

"Come with me," she said, shouldering her fishing pole. "You are in for a real feast." Liberty made her way

down the sun-baked brick path, which was moss covered and almost hidden from view. Judah gathered up the reins of his horse and followed, while Liberty's horse grazed beside the river. Rounding a bend, Judah stopped short when he saw the huge barn that fallen into disrepair.

Judah followed Liberty inside, and tied his horse to a broken stall post. He watched her gather wood and place it inside a white brick oven. Then Liberty reached into her pocket, withdrew a flint, and ignited a fire.

"Do you come here often?" Judah asked, his eyes following the pigeons that were nesting in the loft.

"*Oui.* Usually my father and I come here to clean and cook our catch. We laugh and he speaks to me of the past, when Briar Oaks was the grandest plantation around." Her eyes softened with sadness. "I am sure it has not escaped your notice that my home has fallen on hard times."

He watched her expertly clean the fish and place it on a red-hot stone to bake. The delicious aroma quickly filled the air. "I know how you must feel, although I never knew my father. After he died, my mother and I knew hard times."

Liberty plopped herself down on a wooden barrel and gave him a sympathetic smile. "I am sorry. It must be sad to lose one's father."

He smiled. "How did we get on such a serious subject? Tell me, though," he said with interest, "how is it that a plantation like Briar Oaks can fall on hard times?"

"My father says that the indigo crop is on its way out, and he should have realized it long before now. He wants to concentrate on cotton and perhaps even tobacco. He believes sugarcane is the way of the future. He hopes one day to restore Briar Oaks to its former beauty."

Judah was impressed and amused that one so young would be so wise. He refrained from commenting on her intelligence, knowing her well enough by now to realize

113

that she would think he was being condescending. "I would not have thought tobacco would do well this far west, but cotton, perhaps."

"You will find this land very fertile. One has but to drop a seed in the soil and, most probably, it will take root."

Nature chose that moment to press her authority. A sudden flash of lightning split the air while thunder rolled across the river. Rain fell in torrents, and Liberty and Judah were forced to take shelter under the protected side of the barn, where the cypress shingles were still intact.

A feeling of comradeship joined them together as they ate the delicious-tasting baked catfish and stood beneath the shelter of the barn, watching the rain swell the muddy river.

Liberty looked up at Judah and smiled. "I love it when it rains. It washes the earth clean, and the smell of damp earth is so invigorating. I love to sleep with the rain pounding on the roof and thunder echoing down the valley."

"I have heard my mother tell stories of the Mississippi River on a rampage. I am sure that is an aspect of the rain that you don't enjoy."

"*Oui,* when it floods, it is not pleasant. But as I told you, we love our River; when one loves, one must take the bitter with the sweet."

Judah couldn't keep from laughing. Her little face was drawn up with such concern, and she appeared much older at that moment. With a sudden impulse, he reached out and hugged her to him. "Well, little one, you are my first friend in New Orleans. Perhaps you and your sister will be my only friends."

She closed her eyes and leaned her head on his broad shoulder, listening to the steady beat of his heart. She did not want to be just his friend. Oh, no, she wanted to be so much more. To her, his arms encased her in a dream

114

world; she could almost imagine what it would feel like to be kissed by him.

Liberty raised her face, and met the soft look in his eyes. With a daring that came from her newfound love, she raised up on tiptoes and pressed her lips against his.

For the briefest moment, Judah's hands came up to cup her head, and he deepened the kiss. Liberty felt her breathing stop as his lips pressed more tightly against hers. Then suddenly, he jerked his head up and roughly pushed her aside.

Judah drew in several steadying breaths, before he spoke in a shaky voice. "Don't ever do that again, Liberty." Anger flashed in his eyes. "Do you know what can happen to you if you go around kissing strange men? If I were of a mind to, I could have easily taken advantage of your innocence."

Embarrassed by his stinging words, she backed away from him, then turned and dashed out of the barn, to race down the brick walk toward her horse. In the distance she could hear him calling out to her, but she didn't turn around. Gathering up a handful of Goliath's mane, she bounded onto his back and galloped toward the house.

Tears and raindrops washed down her face. She loved Judah Slaughter, and he thought she was just a troublesome child. Why had she acted so boldly with him? They were having such a wonderful time before she had spoiled it.

Liberty rode Goliath up to the docks. Bounding to the ground, she jumped into her skiff, knowing her horse would find his way back to the stable.

The heavy rain did not deter her from her course—she needed to see Zippora. Her only friend would explain what was happening to her mind and body since she had met Judah Slaughter. Perhaps Zippora had a potion that would wipe him from her heart. No, she wanted to keep

the image of him in her heart forever.

Zippora held Liberty in her arms and spoke soothingly to her as she cried out her heartache. When it was over, she handed the girl an ivory comb and stood her before a mirror.

"From this day forward, you will not go about the countryside looking like a drowned river rat. You will learn to dress and move with pride. You are no longer a child. If you have the heart of a woman, you must act like a woman."

Through the mirror, Liberty stared into Zippora's strange yellow eyes. "Do you think I will ever be pretty?"

"How can I say? I am not a fortuneteller. You will never look other than you do today, unless you take pride in who you are. It is time you stopped running from life and faced some truths, Liberty Boudreaux. Most of us only have one chance at happiness, and it does not usually land in our laps. Anything worthwhile must be earned, or it has no value. Regardless of what you believe, your appearance does matter."

Liberty was finding that Zippora often spoke in riddles, and she did not always understand her meaning. "I suppose on several occasions I have been an embarrassment to my family. My mother is justified in her criticism."

"I am glad you see this for yourself."

Liberty smiled. "I will do as you say. Will you teach me how to become a lady?"

"This I will do."

Liberty hugged Zippora before turning away. "I am going to be pretty, just you wait and see. Judah will one day look at me and think I am beautiful."

Zippora watched as the young girl ran down the path to her boat. *"Oui,* little one," she said aloud, "you will one

day be a beauty, but it will be more of a curse to you than a blessing. I will watch over you if I can."

It was almost sundown by the time Liberty reached home. The clouds had cleared, and a sky of dark purple dominated the western horizon. Her heart was lighter as she picked a wild rose and slipped it behind her ear. The talk with Zippora had given her a new direction in life. If it were possible, she would win Judah Slaughter. She hoped he would not sail away before she could put her new plan into effect. There was not much money for new clothing. Perhaps she could take some of Bandera's old gowns, those that would be flattering to her skin and hair coloring, and have them restyled for herself.

Liberty's head was so filled with plans that she had no warning there were guests in the house until it was too late. Before entering, she wiped her muddy boots on the mat. As she made her way toward the stairs, she hummed a happy little tune. Her mind was not on her appearance, and for that moment she had forgotten that she wore damp trousers.

Oralee was coming down the stairs when she encountered Liberty. The maid's eyes roved over Liberty's wet garments and she shook her head.

"*Mon dieu,* will you never learn to be a lady? You know your mother will not like you to come dragging in looking like a barnyard cat. Your sister has guests. M'sieu Sebastian is here with another gentleman. You must get upstairs quickly before you are discovered."

Hearing voices and laughter coming from the salon, Liberty hastened to the stairs. If Judah was with Sebastian, she certainly did not want him to see her until she had changed into a gown. Every time they met, she looked less than favorable. She wanted tonight to be different.

In her haste, Liberty caught her foot on the edge of the

117

tattered rug, and she lost her balance. She clutched at the bannister as she felt her body tumble backward. Rolling down three steps, she landed with a thud against the ornate pedestal. Liberty felt pain shoot through her side as she helplessly watched the bust of Louis XVI teeter on the edge of the pedestal.

"No!" she cried, reaching out her hand to her father's most valued treasure. The statue had been presented to her father by the king himself, when, as a young man, Louis Boudreaux had visited France on his grand tour. The pain in her side did not matter. It was not important that her mother and sister came rushing out of the salon to see what the commotion was. She did not care that Sebastian Montesquieu was staring at her with disbelief written on his face. The only thing that was important was to save her father's treasure.

Lunging forward, she watched in horror as the bust tipped over the edge and fell crashing to the floor. For what seemed like an eternity, a hush fell over the house. Liberty crawled over to the broken treasure, tenderly touching the shattered fragments. She raised tear-bright eyes to her mother, whose face was rigid with anger; then she spoke, a sob in her voice.

"I am sorry, *Maman*. I did not intend—"

"That's right, Liberty, you never intend to cause trouble, but you always do. Go to your room at once. I will attend to you later."

Liberty felt utter humilation when she saw the slight smile on Sebastian's face. He made her aware that her tangled hair had spilled across her face, that her clothing was rumpled and muddy. Liberty's heart skipped a beat when she saw Judah Slaughter looking down at her with sympathy in his eyes. Now her humilation was complete. The worst that could happen had happened.

Without ceremony Judah reached out his hand, and she placed hers in his warm clasp. With a short tug, he helped

her to her feet. "This, too, shall pass," he whispered near her ear, as if he knew what she was feeling.

Shame kept Liberty from meeting Judah's eyes, as she murmured a hasty, thank you. Worse than her embarrassment was the fact that she had destroyed her father's treasure. Without a backward glance, she hurried up the stairs, wishing she were dead. After today, how would she ever face Judah? On entering her room, Liberty threw herself down on the bed and stared, dry-eyed, out the window.

This evening her reckless ways had brought shame on her mother and a loss to her father. She made a silent vow that this was the last day she would act without considering the consequences. Zippora was right, it was time she behaved like a woman.

Hours passed and the house became quiet. Oralee had brought Liberty a tray of food, but it sat on the small table, uneaten. Liberty paced the floor, knowing the hardest thing she would ever have to do in her whole life would be to face her father and explain to him that she had broken his bust of Louis XVI. She knew he must be home by now. As difficult as it was, she would have to tell him how sorry she was.

Squaring her shoulders and setting her chin, she slowly descended the stairs. Even though the rest of the house slept, she knew her father would still be working on his ledgers. Rapping on the door, she entered at his invitation.

Louis, seeing his daughter's stricken face, motioned her closer. She stood stiffly at the edge of his big mahogany desk, trying to gather the courage to tell him of her sin.

"Come here, Liberty. Nothing can be so dreadful as to make you this sad."

She took his hand. "This is worse than dreadful, Papa. I have done the unforgivable." Tears trailed down her cheeks, and she tried to turn away; but her father would

not allow it. "What is your infraction, *ma chère?*" he asked kindly.

"I . . . broke your bust of Louis XVI!" she cried out. "It was an accident, but none the less unforgivable."

He raised her face and wiped her tears away with his thumb. "That old thing. It is just as well that it is broken. We are about to become a new nation. It is time to throw off the monarchy and embrace a president."

Liberty searched his face, knowing he treasured the bust more than anything he possessed, outside Briar Oaks itself. "I know you loved that statue, Papa. You are just saying that to make me feel better."

He placed his cheek next to hers. "Things are not important, Liberty—people are important. As far as I am concerned, that old bust isn't worth one of your precious tears."

Liberty threw her arms around her father. He was the kindest man she had ever known. He had demonstrated how much he loved her tonight by not making her feel guilty. Fresh tears wet her eyes, and she mumbled against his shoulder.

"I hope if I ever have children of my own, I will remember the example you set for me tonight, Papa."

"What example is that, my dearest daughter?"

She smiled through her tears. "That people are more important than things. I do not believe I shall ever spank a child of mine, no matter what he or she may break."

Her father was silent for a long time. When he spoke, it was in a trembling voice. "I cannot tell you what it means for you to say that to me, Liberty. You are my only child, and I love you more than anything else in the world. My father was a cruel, unloving man. I swore that I would be a better father to my children than he was to me. I hope I have at least succeeded in that. It seems that I have failed in everything else."

"Oh, no, Papa, you are not a failure. No one ever had

a kinder, more loving father than you. I count myself very fortunate."

Louis took his daughter by the shoulders and led her to the window. "Look out there, *ma chère*. Briar Oaks will one day belong to you." He smiled down at her sadly. "If I can manage to save it for you, this will pass to you as a trust for your children. My hope is, that along with the land, I can pass love through you to future generations. This is the legacy I will leave you. That bust of a French king was not worth one handful of Briar Oak's bottom land, Liberty—always remember that."

Father and daughter stood together, silently surveying the land they both loved. "I will probably never marry, Papa. You will never have grandchildren, except through Bandera."

He laughed softly. "You will marry, *ma chère.* Soon your beauty will bloom, and you will have your choice of young gentlemen to select from. Choose well, and do not allow blind pride to rob you of love."

Liberty glanced up at her father, but his thoughts seemed far away. She got the impression he was remembering some lady out of his past, and she did not think it was her mother.

Glancing down at her upturned face, he smiled. "I understand you have met Judah Slaughter."

"*Oui*, Papa."

"What do you think of him?"

"I . . . he is wonderful."

His eyes twinkled beneath arched brows. "Is he?"

"I think so."

"I knew his mother many years ago. I thought she was wonderful." Louis Boudreaux placed a soft kiss on his daughter's cheek and walked her to the door. "Go to bed, Liberty, and allow nothing to trouble your dreams. Weave dreams of love and happiness."

She paused with her hand on the door. "Papa, about

the bust—"

"It is all but forgotten."

She turned away and slowly walked up the stairs. When she reached her room, she undressed and climbed into bed. Tonight her father had taught her a valuable lesson about love. Liberty swore that she would never disappoint anyone in her family again—especially not her father, hopefully not her mother.

Chapter Seven

Liberty moved along the garden path which sloped toward the Mississippi River. From her vantage point she could see the opulent farm lands, the soil in hues of gray, black, and red. The rich land was suited to a multitude of different crops, but it was a constant fight to keep the ever-moving undergrowth from reclaiming it.

Liberty had kept the promise she made to herself. Each day she tried to improve her manners and her appearance. But no matter how she tried, she decided she could never turn herself into a beauty. No matter how much she brushed her hair, the damp climate made the unruly curls spiral around her face and down her back, and she could do nothing about the straw color of her hair. When she looked into the mirror, she saw the face of a child staring back at her. She had tried applying color from Bandera's rouge pot, but that merely made her look like a little girl playing at being a grownup. If her mother and sister noticed a change in Liberty's appearance, neither of them commented on it. Liberty would like to have talked to her mother abut the unsettling feelings she was experiencing. But her mother neither solicitated Liberty's confidence, nor gave any indication she was interested in her troubles. Indeed, Ursula took no notice that Liberty had problems; only Zippora held out a helping hand to the lonely, confused girl who was on the brink of womanhood.

Deeply breathing in the magnolia-scented air, Liberty moved toward the house, hoping to have breakfast with her father. When she entered the small family dining room, she was surprised to find not only her father, but her mother and sister as well. After a hasty good morning, Liberty slipped into her chair.

She gasped in surprise when she saw the white rose beside her plate. Catching her father's eye, she watched a smile spread over his face. "Thank you, Papa," she said, raising the delicate blossom to her nose.

Bandera slammed her fork against her plate, venting her displeasure, until her mother's hand closed over hers, stilling any angry outburst she might have made. Louis looked down the table, studying each face carefully. He still felt guilty because he had waited so long to do anything about Liberty's plight. Today he would take the first steps to help her find her way.

"I am leaving at the end of the week," he said, dipping his spoon into thick cream and fishing out a plump blueberry.

"Must you go?" Liberty asked, already feeling alone and isolated due to his impending absence.

"Yes, I fear I must. I am going to Natchez for three weeks. I have to see about a loan, and I want to learn more about growing sugar cane."

"I am going with your father," Ursula announced to the surprise of both girls. "While we are away, Oralee will see to your needs."

"What about the ball at Bend of the River next week?" Bandera wanted to know. "Who will make certain I am properly clothed?"

Louis stared at Bandera for a moment. "You must assume that your mother knows where her priorities lie. When we return, many things around here are going to change."

"That's right," his wife agreed. "Your father and I have

been talking, and we have decided that we are going to become a closer family. Each of us must put forth more effort."

Louis turned to his youngest daughter and gave her his brightest smile. How alone and vulnerable she looked at the moment. "I have a surprise that I believe you will like, Liberty," he said, hoping to make her smile.

Before she could answer, Bandera spoke up. "You always have a surprise for Liberty. You never seem to know I am alive, Papa."

Louis gave Bandera a hard glance. "I believe we are all aware that you are alive, Bandera. I have given you a home as well as my name. I have loved you like a daughter, and in so doing, I sometimes neglected Liberty. It is my intention to right any mistakes I may have made in the past. Besides, you would be bored this afternoon. I am taking Liberty to meet an old friend of mine at Bend of the River."

Liberty did not notice the jealousy that gleamed in her mother's eyes. "You haven't asked me to go along with you, Louis."

"No, not this time, Ursula. This is just for Liberty."

"You are taking her to meet Gabrielle Slaughter," Ursula said, a pout on her lips. "Don't try to deny it. I know you are."

"I do not deny it. I believe Liberty and Gabrielle are very much of a kind, and will take an instant liking to one another." His eyes narrowed. "I believe knowing Gabrielle will be good for Liberty."

Liberty stared from her mother to her father. There had been very little love between them for years. She could not remember the two of them ever going away together. Her heart ached as her mother lowered her head in defeat. Liberty did not know what the trouble was. She realized that her parents were making this trip together to try to recapture some of the love they had lost. Her father

must have insisted on it.

Liberty sat beside her father, watching the scenery fly by. It was a lovely clear day, and she was excited about going to Bend of the River to meet Judah's mother. However, she couldn't help but hope that Judah would not be there. Liberty had not seen Judah since the day she had made a fool of herself, and she was still too embarrassed to face him. She knew that Bandera was frequently in Judah's company. It was obvious that her sister had begun playing Judah against Sebastian; that way, no mater who inherited Bend of the River, Bandera would have the heir in the palm of her hand.

Several times a week, Liberty had visited Zippora, and the old woman had instructed her on how a properly brought-up young lady would act. Always in the back of Liberty's mind was the vision of Judah Slaughter. Someday he would look at her and think she was pretty — he had to.

The one thing that bothered Liberty was the fear that Judah would leave Bend of the River and sail back to Boston. She knew that he had not already departed because Bandera kept him dangling. Even if Liberty could not have him, she hoped he would not fall in love with her sister. He deserved so much better than Bandera.

Gabrielle Slaughter was in deep thought as she walked in the garden. How wonderful it was to be home. She had not realized how much she had missed Bend of the River until she had returned. The only thing that marred her happiness was knowing that her son was restless, eager to leave. Since that first day, her father had ignored Judah. Each day she feared a summons would come from her father, and the two stubborn men, so much alike, would

lock horns, and Judah would be driven away forever.

Gabrielle was often left in the company of Sebastian's mother, Alicia. She did not care much for her aunt, because the woman was always so sullen and complaining. Apparently Alicia was lazy and spent her days lying abed or lounging in the morning room, eating chocolates. Gabrielle had very little patience with anyone who constantly bemoaned their lot in life as Alicia did. Gabrielle had always been the eternal optimist, and she expected no less from others. But Sebastian was always pleasant, and Gabrielle found him charming, even though Judah did not like him overmuch and was suspicious of his motives.

Stopping beneath a flowering dogwood tree, Gabrielle was overcome with a feeling of nostalgia. So much of her life had been spent here at Bend of the River. She remembered a scene that had been played out beneath this very tree—a scene that had broken her heart when she'd been a young girl.

Her mind was spinning backward to the year of her eighteenth birthday. Bittersweet memories now wrapped her in dreams of days gone by. How well she remembered the feeling of devastation when the young man she loved stood in the spot where she was now standing and told her he was going away. She still had the image of him in her mind, of his pain-filled blue eyes, begging her to understand why he had to leave.

"Why, Louis?" she had begged to know that day. "Why are you turning your back on me? I thought you loved me?"

"Try to understand, Gabrielle. I cannot marry you until I have the money. I will not have people saying I married you for your fortune. Briar Oaks has fallen on hard times, and my father has borrowed heavily against it."

"Louis, do not do this to us. Everyone knows we have loved each other since childhood. No one will believe that you are marrying me for any reason except love. My

127

father approves of the match, why cannot you?"

"If I loved you less, I would take you for my wife, and the world be damned. But my pride will not allow me to live on your father's money."

"We will not take money from my father, if you do not want to. I will live anywhere with you. We can get a small place in New Orleans."

"My father has ordered me to leave Briar Oaks, Gabrielle. There is no way I can support you at this time, and I cannot ask you to wait for me. I will not ask you to give up everything you are accustomed to and live in poverty with me."

Gabrielle knew that Louis's father had married a woman twenty years younger than he. Louis had told her how his stepmother, Anna, had tried to entice him into her bedroom when his father was away. She had been horrified by the woman's wanton behavior. Gabrielle knew that Anna was at the bottom of Louis's troubles. Anna had spent money lavishly, and now Briar Oaks was in financial trouble.

"Anna caused the rift between you and your father, didn't she, Louis?"

"Yes. She has told my father that . . . that I made advances toward her, which we both know is not true. I could not tell him the real truth about her. He would never believe his beloved Anna is nothing but a . . . that is the one who . . . I have to go away, do you not see that? I could never hurt my father by telling him the truth."

Gabrielle had grabbed Louis's shirt front, trying to hold on to him. "You do not mind hurting me, Louis. You are tearing my heart out."

His eyes had misted with tears. "My dearest and only love, no one will ever care for you as deeply as I. But I have nothing to offer you. I will not drag you down with me."

She had clasped his hand tightly, knowing he was slipping away from her. "I ask no more than to be your wife."

"No matter what happens, Gabrielle, you will always be my only true love—will you remember that?"

Gabrielle could feel the pain of that day as if it had been yesterday. She had called after Louis as he turned and walked out of her life, but he did not heed her call. Shortly thereafter, she had left on a tour of France and had met Judah's father. She had loved him deeply, but a woman never quite gets over her first love. The past was as dead as Louis's father and Anna. But Gabrielle had heard that Louis was still paying off debts incurred by his stepmother. She wondered if he ever thought of her. He was married, and she hoped he had found happiness.

Wiping the tears from her eyes, she heard footsteps and spun around. Blinded by the sun, she stared at the man walking toward her. Her heart pounded like a young girl's as he reached her side. Softly, his eyes caressed her face, and she reached out to clasp his hand.

"I see tears in your eyes, Gabrielle. The last time I saw you, you were standing here, and there were tears in your eyes then also."

"Yes, I remember, Louis," she answered, feeling his hand tighten about hers.

"Time has been kind to you, and has only enhanced your beauty, Gabby."

She smiled. "You always knew how to make me feel good about myself, Louis."

"I have not yet met your son, Gabrielle."

"He is a fine young man."

He smiled and tucked her hand into the crook of his arm, leading her in the direction of the river. "My daughter finds him charming."

She returned his smile. "Which daughter? I hear you have two."

"My wife, Ursula, had a daughter by her first marriage, whom I adopted; but I was speaking of my own little Liberty."

"You named her after your sister. I am so glad. Tell me about her?"

So easily did they fall into conversation, it was as if the years fell away and they had never been parted. After Louis described his daughter to Gabrielle, he allowed his eyes to roam at will over her face. "I wish Liberty had someone with your patience and kindness to guide her. I fear she is left much to her own devices, and knows nothing about a gentle upbringing."

"Your wife?"

"She has been a good wife, but I fear she neglects Liberty in favor of Bandera."

"When can I meet your Liberty?"

"She came with me this morning, and is waiting in the salon. Will you see her now? I was hoping she could spend the day with you. I wanted more than anything for her to get to know you."

Gabrielle nodded, knowing they were both thinking Liberty could have been their daughter. Overcome with tender feelings, she pulled away. Louis caught her hand and raised it to his lips. Naked love was reflected in his soft blue eyes, but Gabrielle knew he would not speak of his feelings; for he was an honorable man. It was enough for her to know he still held her in high regard.

Liberty loosened the lace collar at her throat and kicked her shoes off, since they were new and pinching her toes. She was very familiar with this room. Before Monsieur Montesquieu became ill, she had often visited him in the afternoon. She was one of the few people Gustave had tolerated. He had confided in her many times that Alicia and Sebastian were both fools. She had

agreed with him on that and many other subjects. There had been a time when she had read to Monsieur Montesquieu twice a week. But when his illness kept him confined to his bedroom, her visits had become less frequent. Liberty had missed the grizzly old man, who was not nearly as gruff as he would have everyone believe.

Liberty heard footsteps on the garden steps, and turned to see her father and a woman she knew would be Judah's mother enter the room.

"Gabrielle," Louis said with pride. "This is my Liberty. Liberty, this is an old and very dear friend."

Liberty realized, when the woman looked down at her feet, that her shoes were across the room, under the chair where she had kicked them. There was nothing to do but admit her mistake and hope that Judah's mother would not think her a complete fool.

The lovely vision smiled and took her hand. "I am Louis's friend, but not as old as he claims. I am so delighted to meet you, my dear. You are so lovely. You remind me of another Liberty, who was my dearest childhood friend."

"I . . . my shoes . . . they are new, *Madame,* and . . ."

Gabrielle laughed softly. "I, too, detest new shoes. We shall ask your father to leave us alone so we can visit, then I may also take off my shoes." Liberty knew this lovely lady would never be caught without her shoes, and was merely trying to put her at ease.

Louis chuckled as he bowed to Gabrielle and winked at his daughter. "I leave you in good hands. I will call for you this afternoon at four."

Liberty could not remember a day when she had been more entertained. She and Gabrielle Slaughter walked in the garden, while the older woman told her many things about her father when he was younger. She spoke of her life in Boston, and her pride in her son, Judah.

"Are you coming to the ball here at Bend of the River

131

on Saturday, Liberty?" Gabrielle wanted to know.

"No, I . . . am too young."

"Nonsense. I will speak to your father and promise to look after you. I am sure he can be persuaded to let you attend."

Liberty beamed with happiness, and the day passed so quickly that she was sorry when her father came to take her home.

In the coach, Liberty chatted endlessly about Gabrielle, declaring that she would one day be a great lady, just like Judah's mother. She did not notice the soft faraway look that came into her father's eyes, or the grateful sigh that escaped his lips. Louis was relieved that Gabrielle had instilled in Liberty a sense of pride — a desire to become a lady. Yes, he thought, Gabrielle had given Liberty what her own mother had neglected to give.

Judah had just ridden into the stable, when he received the summons from his grandfather. Tired and irritated, he was not in the best of moods when he climbed the stairs to Gustave Montesquieu's room. It was time he told his grandfather that he was leaving. This life of leisure was not for him. Soon the *Winged Victory* would be returning, and he planned to sail for Boston.

When Judah neared his grandfather's chamber, the door swung open, and a smiling Moses greeted him. "It is good that your grandfather is feeling strong today so you can see him. He has been very ill. Have a care, it would not be good to upset him."

Judah caught the warning in the big man's voice. Looking around the chamber, he saw it was empty. Moses nodded toward the wide terrace. "You will find your grandfather out there taking the air."

There was a cloudless blue sky as Judah stepped onto the terrace. His grandfather was reclining on a chair, and

even though the day was hot, there was a wool coverlet tucked about his legs.

"I understand you have been seeing some of the countryside, Judah. I also understand you have been seeing something of the Boudreaux daughters. I'm sure that does not please Sebastian overmuch."

"How about a greeting such as, 'Hello, Judah, how are you feeling?" the young man mocked. "I'm just fine, Grandfather, and how are you?"

The old man smiled. "I can see how you are; I don't have to ask. Now what about the Boudreaux sisters?"

"I have met them both."

"I am told that you are often in the company of Bandera Boudreaux."

Judah seated himself on the iron grillwork and folded his arms across his chest, not knowing if it was humor or disapproval that gleamed in his grandfather's eyes. "If your spies told you that, they must also have told you that I cannot wait to leave this place."

"I heard that from you the first day you arrived. I was hoping I could convince you to stay."

"Not likely."

"What would it take to induce you to remain with us?"

"Nothing you have would entice me to stay here."

The old man stared out over the green hills. "Perhaps there are certain young ladies who could persuade you otherwise. I speak of one of the Boudreaux sisters."

Apparently nothing happened in this valley that his grandfather did not know about. He must have learned that Judah was infatuated with Bandera. What Judah did not know was the point his grandfather was trying to make. He was sure he would be enlightened when it suited the old man. "You are well informed. Do you have a watchdog following me?"

The old man ignored the biting remark. "I gave you more credit than Sebastian. I see I was mistaken. Like

him, you cannot see past a pretty face. If you were wise, you would wish a fond farewell to the elder Boudreaux daughter, and wait for the younger one to grow up."

Judah studied his grandfather for a moment. "Unfortunately, that will not be my choice to make. I leave the older daughter to Sebastian, and the younger to Providence. My future does not lie here."

"Where does it lie?"

"You know about the *Winged Victory.*"

"Hah, that ship is no more than a rust bucket. You do not have the money to make her into a seaworthy vessel. You have to hug the shore in case she goes under. That is why you will never make a decent living at sea." Gustave's turquoise eyes gleamed with an excited light. "What would you say if I told you I had my will changed, leaving Bend of the River to you?"

Judah flicked an imaginary speck from the sleeve of his powder-blue coat. "I would tell you to go to hell."

Instead of being angry, the old man laughed delightedly. "By, God, you are the one who could hold this place together. Like it or not, you are my grandson, and I like the fact that you can spit in my face and turn your back on my fortune. However, I would caution you not to be foolhardy. Have you considered your mother."

"I can take care of my mother. She will come away with me."

"Will she? Have you noticed how content she has become?" The old man waved a gnarled hand in the air. "Gabrielle would leave if you asked it of her, but are you such a selfish bastard that you are willing to take her away from all this? What kind of life did she have in Boston? Most of her friends are here."

"You are the last one who can preach to me about my mother."

"Would you throw away a fortune?"

Judah's eyes narrowed. "I do not know what game you

are playing, but Sebastian is your heir. I will not allow you to use me as a pawn in your little game."

The old man's eyes darkened. "I do not play games—not when it comes to Bend of the River Plantation. If you had grown up here, you would know without being told that land is the only thing that endures. This is your heritage, whether you like it or not. You have my blood running in your veins, and you cannot turn your back on this land. Sebastian is a fool. He would marry Bandera, and between the two of them they would squander the inheritance within a few years. Within five years, he would have lost Bend of the River, and I cannot allow that to happen."

"Why should that matter to you? Should that happen, you will be dead and past caring."

"Have you no pity for an old man, Judah? Is there no mercy in your heart?"

"Was there any pity in your heart when you turned your back on my mother?"

"Perhaps not, but I am trying to make amends for it now."

"You are not trying to make amends. You are a selfish old man, who merely wants his own way. You know the only way you can keep me here is by using my mother. You are not sorry for the way you treated her."

"I find I have missed my daughter, and I am glad she is home."

"But you are not sorry for the way you treated her."

The old man smiled. "We understand each other perfectly. I will leave Bend of the River to you, with only one stipulation. You are to forget about Bandera and marry Liberty Boudreaux."

Judah's jaw clamped tightly together and his turquoise eyes burned like flames. "Not you, or anyone, can tell me who I will marry. I told you that I do not want your damned plantation. Perhaps you will believe me when I

sail away without a backward glance."

At that point the old man started coughing, and Moses rushed forward. "You had better go now; your grandfather is tiring. It would not be wise to upset him with more talk of your leaving."

His look of concern was genuine as Judah glanced at his grandfather's closed eyes. I shouldn't have come. Will he be all right?"

"Leave him to me," Moses said. "Go on about your business. I been taking care of *M'sieu* for many years."

When Judah was out of earshot, the old man opened his eyes a crack. "Did you hear, Moses?"

"I did. Your grandson does not like your offer."

"He will come around in time. Right now he would rather tell me to go to hell, than take what I offer him. I have little doubt that good sense will soon prevail."

"He is a man much like you. I know of several times you told someone to go to hell, and meant it."

"Yes, he is very like me. That is why he must not leave. Bend of the River needs him."

"He has the ship," Moses reminded Gustave.

"I happen to know he has very little money to pay the crew and keep that ship afloat. He will take my offer, if for no other reason than to have money to repair his damned ship."

Alicia edged her way out of the shadows and rushed across the hallway to her bedroom to avoid meeting Judah on his way out. Her worst fears had been realized; she had heard enough to know her son was no longer to be the future master of Bend of the River.

How dare that old man hand everything she and Sebastian had worked for over to Judah Slaughter and his mother. Something had to be done quickly. This was a desperate situation, and it called for desperate action. She

would tell Sebastian what she had overheard; he would know what to do.

"They will never put me out," she muttered to herself, as she rushed to the stables where she knew she would find Sebastian.

Judah's boots clicked against the cypress boards as he crossed the ornamental bridge that spanned the wide pond. He was remembering the conversation he'd had with his grandfather earlier, and paying little heed to where his footsteps were taking him.

Finding himself on a wooded hill with a wide vista of the surrounding countryside, he drew in his breath at the magnificent sight that met his eyes. There was no mistake, Bend of the River Plantation was queen of this valley. There were fruit orchards in full bloom, and vegetable and flower gardens that were larger than most farms in Boston. Beyond the orderly barns and stables, was the blacksmith shop and a smokehouse, and beyond that, whitewashed slave quarters. The pastures were so green it was almost painful to the eye. On them, cattle, horses, and sheep grazed in peaceful contentment. As always, dominating the landscape, was the mighty Mississippi, meandering its way through the countryside with complicated twists and turns.

Judah felt a stirring in his heart. Some small part of him recognized this as his heritage. Some part of him wanted to reach out and take what had been offered. No, he thought, Bend of the River did not belong to him. This was Sebastian's domain. Even if he did not like his cousin, he recognized the man's right to inherit this land.

Judah heard someone approach from the pine woods just below, and he turned to see Bandera climbing the hill toward him. Her midnight-colored hair swirled about her face; her pink gown clung to her like a second skin.

Through the thin material, with the sun behind her, Judah could see the outline of her body.

Unconsciously, he took a step toward her, holding out his hand to help her up the last few steps of the hill. She was panting slightly, and his eyes were drawn to the rise and fall of her rounded breasts.

"I was told, by your mother, that I would find you here," she said breathlessly.

"I was walking and found myself on this hill." He made a wide gesture with his hand. "This is magnificent, don't you think?"

Bandera gravitated toward him, her arm brushing against his. *"Oui,* there can be no place on earth like Bend of the River." She stared at him for a moment before she spoke. "I have heard that your grandfather is considering making you his heir over Sebastian."

"From whom did you hear that?"

"Sebastian."

Judah was aware of her closeness, and his pulse quickened as he stared into her lovely face. "Sebastian must be made aware that I turned down my grandfather's offer."

She placed her hand on his, and raised her face, a gesture that was staged to call attention to her long, white neck. "Why? Surely you cannot turn your back on all this. Why do you not accept it?"

"Have you heard my grandfather's conditions?"

She shook her head. "What conditions?"

"In order to acquire the plantation, I must marry your sister, Liberty."

Bandera's face drained of color, and she shook her head in disbelief. Ever since Bandera could remember, she had coveted the position of mistress to this vast domain. When Sebastian had confessed his fear that his uncle might change his will in favor of Judah, she had been secretly pleased. She wanted to be the bride of this man who fired her blood, but only if Bend of the River was

included in the bargain. Now it appeared Gustave Montesquieu had other plans. Hatred and envy burned in her heart. Liberty would never be mistress of Bend of the River—never! And she would never have Judah; Bandera would see to that.

"Do you want to marry my sister?" She held her breath, waiting for his answer.

"Liberty is a child. I cannot see myself as her husband. When I marry, it will not be to a child." Judah was still angry at his grandfather, and it showed in his hard tone.

There was a pout on Bandera's lips, and tears gathered in her eyes. "Your grandfather has never liked me, and I never knew why."

Without thinking, Judah took her hand in his, wanting to comfort her. Her tears were like a knife in his heart. "If my grandfather thinks ill of you, that is an excellent representation of your fine character as far as I'm concerned."

She smiled slightly. "Are you saying you like me just a little?"

"I believe I am falling in love with you," he confessed, the admission coming as a surprise to him. "I shouldn't have said that," he added, dropping her hand and stepping back a pace. "Forgive my boldness." Bandera was such a lady, that Judah feared he had shocked her with his forwardness.

But she took the step that brought her up against him, and her heart was pounding as she looked into his unusual eyes. For the moment she had forgotten her ambition to rule Bend of the River Plantation. All she could think about was this exciting man who had just admitted his love for her.

She raised her face, and invited his kiss. Judah felt his body tremble as her soft hands slid around his neck. As his lips touched hers, he was momentarily startled when she thrust her tongue into his mouth. Aching to possess

her, he pulled her body tightly against his.

Time and space were forgotten as Bandera boldly nipped at his lips with her sharp teeth. It did not occur to him to wonder how she had become so wise in the ways of pleasing a man. He was experiencing love for the first time. To him, Bandera was a pure and sweet angel.

Bandera took his hand, pulling him toward the pine-scented woods. When they reached the cover of the trees, away from prying eyes, she melted against him again.

Raw passion tore at Judah as her hands moved across his chest. Somehow, he could not quite remember how, he found himself lying on the soft green grass, with her body pressed against his.

Passionate gasps ripped from Bandera's lips as Judah pressed her against his body, and she could feel the tight bulge that announced his desire for her.

Bandera felt her blood running hot in her veins. But her lust for power was still greater than her desire. She would do what she must to gain the Montesquieu fortune. For now, she had to use her charms to keep Judah near. She had to keep both men interested in her. That way, no matter which one Gustave Montesquieu decided to make his heir, she would have him in the palm of her hand.

Judah's lips devoured Bandera's and she trembled with excitement. Suddenly she was losing control. This man's body beckoned to her, and she ached for him to thrust his manhood into her. Real tears gathered in her eyes as she arched away from him. If she gave in to him now, all would be lost. Judah must not discover that she was not the coy young maiden she pretended to be. He must not learn that she had given herself to Sebastian many times. Her instinct told her it would be dangerous to play games with Judah as she did with Sebastian.

"No!" she cried, turning away and straightening her gown. "No." She scampered to her feet and turned her face away. Raw passion burned in her heart, but she could

not allow it to make her forget her real goal.

Judah, mistaking her refusal for maidenly coyness, felt guilty and remorseful, thinking his overwrought desire frightened someone with her sensitive nature. Pulling his shirt together, he rose to his feet. "There is no excuse for my behavior, Bandera, but I beg you to forgive me. I can only say I was so taken by you that I lost my head."

"I am so ashamed," she said, hiding her face. 'You must believe the worst of me."

"It is I who took advantage of your innocence." Judah walked around her and reached for her hand. "You have my word as a gentleman that this will never happen again. Will you trust me?"

With real tears running down her cheeks, Bandera walked up the hillside, while he stayed in step with her. "I will always trust you, Judah. I . . . believe I am beginning to feel . . . affection for you."

His heart took wing, and it was all he could do to keep from shouting his joy to the heavens. "Can I hope that it will turn into love?"

She lowered her lashes, knowing his charm was still pulling at her. "I believe it may be so. But I need time to think. I know there is no future for us if you take your grandfather's offer."

"Come away with me. We will sail the world and visit faraway places with names you have never heard."

For a fraction of a second she was tempted, but as always, her greed took charge. "I cannot live so frivolous a life. I would rather be your wife at Bend of the River."

Judah thought of his grandfather's outrageous offer. How dare he use little Liberty in his devious plans. "Alas, that can never be, Bandera. My grandfather made his terms clear. If I am to inherit Bend of the River, I must marry Liberty. I would not take his offer on any terms."

Bandera's dark eyes were now half-closed, almost slits. Liberty had always had everything. She was the true

daughter at Briar Oaks. She was the one who always brought out tenderness in their father. Liberty was not going to have Bend of the River, nor would she have Judah—Bandera would see to that. "Your grandfather chose my sister because he believes her to be of superior breeding. My real father was not of the aristocracy."

Judah felt bitterness in his heart. "Yes, I know what importance my grandfather places on proper breeding. He did not think my father was good enough for his daughter either."

By now Judah and Bandera had reached the hill, and Judah gazed out over the land. "What has me perplexed is why my grandfather now prefers me over Sebastian."

"That is not so hard to guess. Sebastian is headstrong and has a passion for gambling. I am told he is not very good at it, and loses large sums of money. Once, while in New Orleans, Sebastian lost heavily. To pay his debt, he agreed to deed over certain property that would be taken over when he inherited Bend of the River. He offered two hundred acres of prime bottom land. When your grandfather discovered what had happened, he was in a rage for days. He threatened to throw Sebastian out of the house and cut him out of his will. That is when he sent for you. I believe in time Monsieur Montesquieu would have forgiven Sebastian's indiscretion."

"I see. If I had never come, then Sebastian would have been back in Grandfather's good graces."

"Perhaps. But I know your grandfather did not want Sebastian to marry my sister."

"How can you know that?"

She smiled, hoping to make Judah jealous. "He thinks Sebastian and I were made for one another. According to Sebastian, he believes we deserve one another."

"What do you think?" Judah asked in a deep voice, as possessiveness burned in his heart. He could not stand the thought of Sebastian touching Bandera. "I have never

hesitated to take any woman I wanted. But with you it is different. I hope you know that I respect you, and would never do anything to shame you."

"Do you hesitate because you think I belong to Sebastian?"

His eyes burned into hers. "Yes. After all he is my cousin. I cannot take from a man when I am living under the same roof with him." Judah took her hand and raised it to his lips. "Be warned, however. The moment I leave, I am no longer honor bound to keep my distance from you."

His deep voice made Bandera tremble with excitement. As he brushed his lips across her fingers, she felt her legs go limp. Never, had she desired a man as much as she desired Judah Slaughter.

"Are you sure that you will never change your mind and decide to marry my sister?"

"Yes, I am sure. Liberty is young and vulnerable—too young to be a player in my grandfather's game. I would never drag her into this conflict."

"Yet you would drag me in," Bandera said with feeling. "Is she so much better than I?"

Judah watched Bandera's lips part, and he had to control the urge to take her in his arms and crush her mouth with a burning kiss. "Will you marry my cousin?"

"I—We have planned to marry one day."

Judah smiled as he released her hand. "I will not take Sebastian's inheritance, but I had better leave before I take his woman."

She threw herself into his arms. "I do not want you to go away. Promise you will not leave until we have talked again."

"I will not leave until we have come to some kind of understanding," he promised.

She brushed her lips against his cheek and turned to walk away. Judah watched her until she disappeared into

the pine woods. He wondered what kind of people was he dealing with here? His grandfather was a man who would do anything to get his way. Sebastian he did not trust at all, and beautiful Bandera was the most baffling of them all. Judah thought of little Liberty and smiled. She was like a breath of fresh air. He wondered what she would think if she knew his grandfather had offered her to him in sacrificial matrimony. He could almost envision the humor that would gleam in her eyes if she were to learn about the plans that had been made for her future.

His life was becoming a tangle. He had come here for his mother's sake, never dreaming that he would become involved in a love triangle. If he wanted Bandera, why didn't he just take her, and say to hell with Sebastian! He was caught in a crosscurrent and would be pulled under if he did not watch his step.

Chapter Eight

The scents of wisteria, jasmine, and magnolia blended to enrich the evening breeze and welcome the guests to Bend of the River Plantation. The sound of music and laughter filled the air, and the brightly lit chandeliers displayed hundreds of candles.

From miles around, the *haut monde* came in response to the coveted invitation issued by Gustave Montesquieu. Inside the mansion, ladies in brightly colored silk skirts swished across the polished floor of the *grand salon*, while gentlemen in pantaloons and elaborate neckpieces bowed gracefully to some passing beauty. The delicious aroma of food gave promise of a feast later in the evening; the gala would last into the night, and in the morning, breakfast would be served. The doors were thrown wide, as the stiff-backed butler, Noal, admitted only those who handed him the coveted gilt-edged invitation.

Judah had adhered to his mother's wishes, so he reluctantly stood in the receiving line with the rest of the family. His grandfather seemed to have made a miraculous recovery, and was jovially greeting the guests. Rigidly Judah waited beside him, trying to hide his boredom. To

Judah's right was his mother, looking lovely in a green silk gown. Beside Gabrielle, with a dour face and her lips compressed, stood Alicia. Her eyes were red rimmed, and she had almost shredded the white lace handkerchief she clasped tightly in her hands. Sebastian stood at the end of the line, polite as always, his eyes watchful and cunning.

When there was a lull in the steady stream of newcomers, Gustave, leaning heavily on his gold-tipped cane, eyed Judah. "I was proud to present you as my grandson, Judah. What do you think of my friends and neighbors? Do you think you would like living around them?"

Judah's eyes narrowed in on the old man's face, and he answered without hesitation, "For the most part, I find them snobbish and haughty, as well as careless in their need to find pleasure. No, I would not like to live within a hundred miles of any of your friends."

Gustave chuckled. "When your Americans first came to this land, we found them intolerant and provincial. They did not seem to know how to have fun. It is easy to see why the two do not mix. I fear we have come together for mutual benefit and a mutual desire to make money. Your Americans are shrewder than we are when it comes to money matters. Many of my friends cannot match wits with them. I see my friends becoming poorer, while the Americans become wealthy. I fear they will win in the end and destroy our way of life forever."

"If your friends have your attitude, you will probably never acquire statehood."

The old man smiled indulgently at his grandson. "You will pardon me if I do not look forward to that prospect with great enthusiasm. We were governing ourselves long before you were acquiring your independence."

Judah drew in a deep breath. "That is the attitude I was talking about."

Gustave smiled and clapped his grandson on the back. "Perhaps you will be the one to change things for the

better. Take what I offer you, and you can Americanize Bend of the River until your heart is content."

At that moment, Judah caught Sebastian's eye and saw the hatred burning there. Looking into his grandfather's eyes, he spoke so everyone in the receiving line could hear. "Bend of the River be damned. I would sooner see it put to the torch than accept any part of it." He was tired of playing games and wanted everyone to know what his feelings were concerning his grandfather's plantation.

Gustave laughed heartily, while turning to the next guest, which happened to be Liberty Boudreaux. "Did you hear how the young pup just insulted his frail old grandfather?" His eyes were dancing merrily as they met the young girl's.

"I have every confidence that you bring most of the insults upon yourself," Liberty observed laughingly.

Gustave lifted Liberty's hand to his lips. "Well said. Most probably you are right. I am finding that you young people have very little respect for the older generation."

Again Liberty laughed. "I have every respect for you, *Monsieur*."

Liberty stepped forward as Judah bowed to her. Her serious little face was drawn up in a frown; her lovely eyes searched his face to see if he was glad to see her.

"Hello, little friend," Judah said, forgetting to be formal. "I have not seen you these two weeks past. Have you gone fishing lately?"

"No, I no longer fish. I am growing up."

His laughter was warm. "I hope you do not grow up too quickly. I like you just the way you are."

"Do you really?" she asked breathlessly.

He glanced at the green gown that somehow did not look right on her. It did not take a man who was well versed on ladies fashions to guess it had been Bandera's and had been altered to fit Liberty. She looked like an adorable child who was trying on her mother's gown, one

that was too sophisticated for her.

"Indeed, I speak the truth. I like your impertinence, I admire your honesty, and most of all, I adore your pert little nose." Judah glanced up at that moment and caught his grandfather's satisfied smile and his blood flamed with rage. He knew his grandfather was reminding him of their bargain concerning Liberty. Judah bit back the angry remark that begged to be spoken.

"I was so pleased when your mother invited me," Liberty said innocently, unaware that she was a source of contention between grandfather and grandson.

"You have always been welcome in this house *ma chère*," Gustave declared. "If I were a younger man, I would seek you as my bride. It takes a stupid man not to see your qualities." He was looking at Liberty, but his words were for Judah.

Liberty felt light-hearted and happy. She was attending her first ball, and Judah was glad to see her. She moved on down the line and was greeted warmly by Gabrielle.

Judah might have voiced his anger to his grandfather had his eyes not fallen on the vision of loveliness that came through the door. He had not seen Bandera since their encounter on the hill, but she had never been far from his thoughts. She seemed to shimmer in a lovely cream-colored gown embroidered with golden threads. When she approached and pressed her hand into Judah's, he realized she had placed a note in his palm, and he quickly pushed it into his pocket, to read later.

"Good evening, Monsieur Slaughter. One hopes you are enjoying our nice spring weather." Her voice was polite and stiff, but he did not miss the warm glow in her eyes. His grandfather and Sebastian did not miss the melting glance either.

"Spring comes earlier here than it does in Boston, Mademoiselle Boudreaux." Judah's voice was equally stiff, but Bandera shivered with delight as his eyes rested

on her lips. Seeing Sebastian at the end of the line, she smiled prettily and moved away, trailing a tantalizing scent of wild honeysuckle.

Judah was watching Bandera, so he noticed the strange look that passed between her and Sebastian, but he had no time to speculate on it, as another guest claimed his attention. He could hardly wait to be alone so he could read Bandera's note. He wondered what she would have to say that she could not tell him in person. As Judah watched Bandera walk away on Sebastian's arm, he became more certain he would soon have Bandera for his very own. It never occurred to him that there was a woman he could not have just for the taking.

When the last of the guests had arrived, Judah slipped into his grandfather's study and removed Bandera's note from his pocket. By the dim candlelight he read:

It is most imperative that I see you.
Meet me in the barn at eleven.

Judah was puzzled as he crammed the note back into his pocket. Why would Bandera want to meet him in secret? Whatever the reason, he knew he would be there at the appointed time.

As the evening progressed, Liberty noticed that Bandera and Sebastian danced every dance together, and since Judah's grandfather had shown his approval of his grandson by placing him at his side in the receiving line, Judah had become very popular with the young ladies. He was surrounded by a number of them who were flirting outrageously with him. Many saw him as the new heir to the Montesquieu fortune. Judah was unimpressed with his sudden popularity, however, and while he was polite, he did not ask any of the ladies to dance with him. His

eyes seemed to be on Bandera as she danced around the room with Sebastian.

Liberty spent most of the evening sitting beside Gabrielle Slaughter, watching happy couples dance by. As she looked at all the lovely gowns the ladies were wearing, it made her more aware of her own shabby appearance. The happiness she had known earlier in the day disappeared. Not one gentleman had thus far asked her to dance. She wished she had not attended the ball.

Gabrielle seemed to sense how the young girl felt, and she patted Liberty's hand. "You have no notion how lovely you look. Not even that gown can disguise the fact. It is only respect for your young age that keeps the gentlemen from asking you to dance."

Liberty gave her a weak smile. "You are kind to say so, *Madame,* but I—" A shadow fell across Liberty's face. Glancing up, she saw Judah holding his arm out to her.

"Would you honor me with this dance, Mademoiselle Liberty?"

All eyes were suddenly trained on Liberty. She was now the envy of every young lady who had coveted a dance with the handsome Captain Slaughter. There was much whispering behind fans, and wondering why the young girl had been singled out by Judah.

Liberty shook her head. "I do not think—"

"But I insist Liberty," Judah pressed. "I want to dance with the loveliest young lady in the room."

Reluctantly Liberty gave him her hand. As he whirled her onto the floor, she glanced up at him, and Judah was surprised to see anger flashing in her eyes. A smile parted his lips. "Am I in trouble?"

"I do not want a gentleman to tell me an untruth, Judah. I do not like false flattery. You know that."

"Are you referring to the fact that I said you were the loveliest young lady here tonight?"

"*Oui.* We both know you do not believe that."

His eyes brushed across her face. "Do I not? I wish you could see yourself through my eyes, little Liberty. You are the most charming, the most honest, the most — "

"If you say intelligent, I will scream. Please do not take inventory of my good points." A smile touched her lips. "That might take all night."

"You little devil," he said, swinging her wide. "You do not know how tempted I am to take my grandfather's offer tonight."

They had to move apart. When they came back together, Liberty said, "I do not understand. What offer?"

"I pray God you do not ever find out," he murmured.

"It seems I am the envy of all the ladies and their ambitious mamas. You have become the rage."

His face was grim. "So it would seem. You and I know how fickle fame can be. If they knew how I felt about my grandfather's holding, they would turn a cold shoulder to me."

Liberty giggled. "You underestimate your own charms, Captain Slaughter." She batted her eyes and tapped him with her fan, mimicking some of the flirtatious ladies.

Judah threw back his head and laughed. "You little minx. You will always put me in my place, will you not?"

"Where is your place?"

His mouth eased into a lazy smile. "Right now . . . right here with you."

Suddenly Liberty became aware of the heat of his hand through her white gloves. In a fluid motion he swung her around, and her shoulder pressed against his chest. Liberty stumbled and was steadied by his hand at the small of her back. The violins were playing as she looked into Judah's eyes, and she wanted to melt against him, to have him hold her very, very close.

Judah smiled down at the little face that had become so dear to him. He was about to make some joking remark when he looked into her eyes, and for a moment it was as

151

if he were being drawn into swirling, bottomless pools of blue. The soft scent of her filled his senses, and he felt as if the floor moved under his feet.

Damn, he thought, tearing his eyes away from hers. What in the hell is happening to me? Liberty is a child—she trusts me like a brother. Why do I keep having these disturbing thoughts about her?

Liberty watched Judah's dark lashes come down to cover his blue eyes. She could feel something physical between the two of them, and she wondered if Judah could feel it also. Realizing there had been a long silence she tried to think of something clever to say—anything to cover up her confusion.

"Judah, you really should choose one of the ladies as a partner after me."

He was silent a moment as his eyes rested on her golden hair. "What if I don't want to dance with anyone but you, little one?"

Her heart was hammering in her throat, and she had to look away from the warm glow in his eyes. "I—"

The dance ended abruptly, saving Liberty from having to answer. Judah escorted her back to his mother and then disappeared through the door that led to the dining room. Gabrielle smiled and patted Liberty's hand. "You and my son dance divinely together. It was as if each knew what move the other would make."

Liberty was too disturbed by her strange feelings to answer. She just wished the evening would be over and she could go home.

Sebastian pulled Bandera behind the wisteria bush and clasped her tightly in his arms. He bent his head and swirled his tongue around her lips, then plunged it into her mouth. Bandera felt bile rise in her throat, but she knew it would not be wise to show her distaste for

152

Sebastian's crude lovemaking. She closed her eyes, allowing him access to her creamy neck, and his wet lips moved down her throat to the valley between her breasts.

"I want you now," he breathed against her skin. By now Bandera realized Sebastian was her only hope of being mistress of Bend of the River. Judah had made it very plain that he wanted no part of his grandfather's fortune. She would have to do whatever Sebastian wanted. "It would not be good if we were found in this compromising situation, Sebastian. You said that every move we made tonight had to be well planned. It would not do for someone to come upon us now."

"You are right," he said, stepping back on the path and looking around to make sure no one was about. "Did you give Judah the note?"

"*Oui,* I told you twice that I did. Are you sure this is the best way to discredit your cousin? If we are not careful, it could backfire on you, Sebastian."

"Not on me — on us." His eyes were cold as he stared toward the ballroom. "I have thought this out carefully. There is no other way, and we are running out of time. My uncle has asked his attorney to come to Bend of the River next week. I know he is going to change his will in favor of Judah, if he hasn't already."

Bandera shook her head. "We cannot allow that to happen, Sebastian."

"We can stop it if we are very clever. Will you do exactly what I tell you?"

"*Oui,* I will! But it will be so humiliating for me."

"No, *ma chère,* Judah is the one who will look bad. You will have the sympathy of all our friends. It is getting close to eleven; you had better start for the barn. I will just go back inside so everyone can see me."

Bandera shivered, thinking about what she must do, but she would endure it. She must. Sebastian was clever. She would never have thought of so bold a plan. She only

hoped she could carry her part off. She had to! Bend of the River was within her grasp. All she had to do was follow Sebastian's directions.

Gustave was tiring, so Gabrielle excused herself to go upstairs with him, and Liberty went out onto the gallery. Weary of the gaiety, she was searching for a quiet place to be alone. A painful lump formed in her throat. She was hopelessly in love with Judah, and he still thought of her as a child—his little one. She had come to the heartbreaking conclusion that no matter what she did, Judah would never think of her as a woman. She has seen him watching Bandera, had realized he cared about her sister.

Liberty heard someone come out onto the gallery, and she flattened herself against the iron rail, hoping to go undetected. Her heart skipped a beat when she saw it was Judah. He was the last person in the world she wanted to see.

"I know you are there, Liberty. I saw your shadow as I came out. Why do you hide from your old friend?"

She stepped into the light, embarrassed at having been caught hiding like a child. "We are not old friends," she said evenly. "To tell the truth, we hardly know each other."

Judah whistled through his teeth. "I would say something has you in a spin. Care to tell me what it is?"

"I just do not like men," Liberty announced breezily. "I find them very tedious." She made a wide sweep with her hand. "I am bored with all this."

His laughter was amused. "When one is so worldly as yourself, other, less astute people tend to bore one."

She drew in her breath and straightened her shoulders. "I am wise enough to know when I am being made sport of. I do not care for your humor, Monsieur Slaughter. I never have."

He reached out and cupped her chin, studying her face in the soft moonlight. "I would never make sport of you, Liberty. Of all the people I have met since coming to Bend of the River, you are the most memorable."

"You talk as if you are going away, Judah."

He smiled. "Are we back on a first-name basis?"

"Are you going away?"

"Soon. The *Winged Victory* will be docked at New Orleans. I will be leaving then."

Pain cut through Liberty's heart like a knife. How could she live if she never saw Judah again? Tears she could not stop flowed from her eyes. She turned away not wanting him to see her cry.

Judah gripped her shoulders and turned her to face him. With his thumb, he wiped a tear away. "Little one, are those tears for me?"

"Will you not stay?" she sobbed, burying her face against his chest. Judah gathered her close, feeling anguish at her tears. He was besieged by a flood of emotions he dared not put a name to, and there was a sudden emptiness in his heart at the thought of never seeing Liberty again. He would like to be around to watch her grow into a woman.

"I cannot stay, Liberty. My life is not here."

She shrugged his hands off and turned away. If her heart was going to break, she certainly was not going to allow Judah Slaughter to watch. Running back inside the house, Liberty made her escape. Hearing Judah call out to her, she ducked into the empty library and sank down in a window seat, where she lost herself to total misery. She wished Bandera would tire of the ball, so they could go home.

Judah glanced at the clock on the mantel and saw that it was five minutes until the appointed time he was to meet Bandera. Pushing Liberty to the back of his mind, he left the house and walked in the direction of the barn.

Perhaps Bandera had decided she loved him and was willing to go away with him after all.

When Judah entered the barn, it was pitch-dark inside. He called out. "Bandera, are you here?"

"I am at the end of the stalls," she called softly.

Judah thought the whole situation was odd, but he made his way slowly toward the back of the barn.

Sebastian was hidden in the loft. As he heard Judah approaching beneath him, he removed the small flintlock revolver from his breast pocket and fired.

Judah saw a flash of light, felt something hit him in the chest; then he knew agonizing pain. For a moment he was too stunned to react. His hand went up to his shirt front and he felt something warm and sticky oozing from his chest. It was blood — his own blood. He had been shot!

With a gasp, he crumped to his knees as pain drained him of his strength.

In the pinnacle of light that came from the loft, Judah watched a shadowy figure materialize from the darkness. His face showed his confusion when Sebastian bent over him, gun in hand.

"I don't understand, Sebastian," Judah gasped out. His head was swimming, and blood now covered his whole shirt front. ". . . Why, Sebastian?"

Sebastian's face was drawn up in anger. "Don't you know? Haven't you guessed?"

Judah tried to stand, but there was no strength in his limbs and he fell back to his knees. "Yes, it must be because of Bandera. You . . . found out . . . that I was to meet her here, and you are jealous." Sweat had popped out on Judah's face and he felt as if the barn were spinning. He watched helplessly as Sebastian hastily reloaded the gun and pointed it at his head.

Sebastian's laughter was threaded with hatred. "I have nothing to be jealous of. You can come out now, Bandera. I believe Providence has smiled on us tonight, *ma*

156

chère. Judah fell for the oldest trick known to man. He allowed a woman to lure him into a trap."

Judah watched in disbelief as Bandera stepped out of the shadows. He was dazed and his thinking was unclear. "Bandera, help me," he said, reaching out to her.

For a fraction of a second there was pity in her eyes, until she remembered that Judah Slaughter stood between her and all that she desired. Lifting her skirt, she stepped over him, and stood beside Sebastian.

The harsh taste of disillusionment filled Judah's mouth like bitter wine. Bandera read the contempt in his eyes, and raised her chin to hide the shame she felt.

"What are we going to do now, Sebastian?" Bandera asked, in a calm voice that surprised her.

Sebastian glanced at his cousin while he took aim with his pistol. "I'll tell you what we are going to do, *ma chère*. I heard you scream and ran to investigate. I found my cousin dragging you into the barn, and before I could prevent it, he had practically ripped your gown off. Alas, I had to shoot him to get him away from you. It took two shots."

"No!" Bandera cried, looking at Judah. "We cannot get away with this. I will not be a party to his death. You said we would only dishonor him."

"Perhaps you are right. We do not want him dead, at least not yet, Bandera," Sebastian said in a silky voice. "If you back my story, we will have Bend of the River in the palm of our hands."

"I do not—"

"You must back me up in everything that I say. Is that clear, Bandera?"

"I— no."

By now they could hear voices in the distance. Several people from the house had heard the shot and were coming to investigate. "Hurry and make up your mind, Bandera. There isn't much time. If you want to be

157

mistress of Bend of the River, I suggest you do exactly what I say."

Bandera glanced back at Judah, who was lying in a pool of blood. He was having trouble focusing his eyes, and he was so pale. It appeared that he was already half-dead. *"Oui,* I will do what you say."

Sebastian startled Bandera when he grabbed the neck of her gown, and with a swift jerk, ripped it to the waist. She tried to cover her nakedness as Sebastian turned his attention back to Judah. "You see how it is, cousin. You tried to rape Bandera, and I had to stop you the only way I could."

Judah slowly turned his head and stared at Bandera. He was too heartsick to care what they did. When he saw her lower her lashes to keep from meeting his eyes, he realized what a fool he had been. Bandera had only used him. He should have seen through her, but he had been too blinded by her beauty. Apparently she would lie, cheat, and even kill to get her hands on Bend of the River.

"I am sorry, Judah," Bandera whispered. "You see how it is."

"I do now," he said, trying once more to rise, but falling back in pain. He was grasping for breath and his voice was no more than a whisper. "I was once . . . told if you lie with pigs . . . you pick up the smell. I would say . . . you have lain with Sebastian many times before, because I smell the . . . stench."

Sebastian's eyes contracted as fury overcame his reason. He delivered a powerful kick to Judah's head, then kicked the wounded man again and again. Blood ran into Judah's eyes, while pain and agony pinned him to the ground.

"You bastard," Judah said between clenched teeth. He cursed the weakness that kept him from rising, but he knew he had been a fool, and deserved anything that

happened to him.

With a strength that surprised Sebastian, Judah managed to pull himself up to his knees by using the stall door. Blood was oozing from the gash on his temple, and his head was swimming drunkenly.

"Don't bother getting up any farther," Sebastian said through gritted teeth. "You can die on your knees."

Bandera grabbed Sebastian's arm. "Do not kill him. What good would he be to us dead?"

Sebastian nodded as his reasoning powers returned. "She is right. As much as I would like to see you dead, I believe I would rather see you disgraced in my uncle's eyes. I will like watching his newly acquired grandson fall from grace right before his eyes."

Slowly Judah rose to his feet. "I'll see you in hell first." Leaping forward, he grabbed for Sebastian, just as the gun exploded. Pain tore at his arm but he managed to take a step before he fell to the ground. This time he did not try to rise, because he was unconscious.

Suddenly they were surrounded by people who had come from the house. The men were trying to hold the ladies back so they could not see the ghastly sight.

Liberty refused to be restrained. She elbowed her way through. She was confused when she saw that Bandera's gown was torn. "Give me your coat," she said to one of the men. When he obediently handed it to her, Liberty placed it around her sister's shoulders.

"In God's name what happened to you, Bandera?"

Before anyone could speak, a moaning came from the shadows. Liberty spun around and saw a man lying on the ground. His face was all bloody and he was not moving. Everyone was talking at once and there was mass confusion.

"What happened here?" Liberty demanded.

"Judah Slaughter," Bandera murmured, pointing at the body on the ground. "He may be dead!"

159

"No, no!" Liberty cried, dropping to her knees beside Judah.

Bandera played her part convincingly. She was trying to pull her torn gown together, and while tears made a path down her face, she sobbed in a broken voice. "Sebastian has saved me. Judah Slaughter went crazy. He dragged me in here and . . . he . . . he would have . . . It was awful!"

Several men tried to pull Liberty away from Judah, but she pushed their hands away. In a haze of confusion and fear, she felt his warm breath against her hand and knew he still lived. She quickly examined his head and saw that the wound was bleeding profusely. Fear for his life caused her hand to tremble when she pulled his shirt aside and saw the bullet hole in his chest.

Liberty paid no attention to the commotion that went on around her. "Judah, dearest, Judah," she whispered as she tried to wipe the blood from his face with her handkerchief. "Why have they done this to you?"

Liberty fought Sebastian when he gripped her shoulders and pulled her up beside him. "Let me go!" she cried, struggling with him. "I will not leave Judah. You cannot make me."

"Get a grip on yourself, Liberty. Think of your sister and what she had been through," Sebastian demanded. "I will tend to Judah."

Sebastian pulled her away from Judah, but she spun away from him.

"I am not going to leave Judah," Liberty declared stubbornly.

Bandera saw that Liberty was intent on making trouble, so she clutched her arm. "Help me up to the house, Liberty. Judah tried to . . . he attacked me. I feel faint."

"No! I will not leave until Judah's wounds have been tended." The girl looked around at the people who were supposed to be her friends and neighbors. "What is the

matter with everyone. Can you not see Judah needs help? He is bleeding. Someone carry him to the house. Get a doctor." She saw doubt and uncertainty on the faces around her, and knew she would get no help from them. "What is the matter with everyone? Don't you know Bandera is not being truthful."

Liberty softly touched Judah's face. Her heart was breaking; she wanted so badly to help him. "He will die if someone does not help him," she pleaded.

"Perhaps it would be a mercy for him if he did die," Sebastian declared. "It would be cruel to patch him up for the hangman. How my cousin must hate me to brutally attack my fiancée."

"You lie!" Liberty cried. "Judah would never have done what you accuse him of."

Bandera knew she had to do something quickly or her sister would spoil everything. She grabbed Liberty, dug her fingernails into her arm, and dragged her to her feet. "Make my sister come with me, Sebastian. She is becoming hysterical, and making a spectacle of herself."

Before Liberty could protest, Sebastian gathered her in his arms, and carried her away. Liberty kicked and squirmed, but Sebastian merely tightened his grip. Bandera clung to Sebastian's arm. She couldn't get away quickly enough to suit her. The onlookers moved aside to clear a path for them, shock and disbelief on their faces.

Every instinct Liberty had cried out for her to stay with Judah. "I do not know why you and Bandera have lied, Sebastian. Judah would never have done such a thing," she cried, trying to make sense out of what had happened. "He—"

Bandera clamped her hand over Liberty's mouth, while Sebastian held her arms. "Be quiet, you little fool." The more Liberty struggled, the more Bandera tightened her grip and cut off her breathing.

Finally Liberty stopped struggling, knowing it was get-

161

ting her nowhere. If only her father were here—he would believe her—he would help Judah. She wondered why Judah's mother and grandfather didn't come forward to help him. Then she remembered that they were upstairs and probably didn't know what had happened. If she could only get free, she could make her way upstairs and tell them.

Sebastian must have read Liberty's thoughts, because he tightened his grip on her. "Don't even think about warning my uncle, Liberty. You would not even make it as far as the house."

By now they had reached the buggy of one of the guests and Sebastian placed her inside. "Mademoiselle Liberty is overwrought," he explained to the driver who was standing nearby. "I am sure your master will not mind if you drive her and her sister home. Wait here while I get something to calm her down."

Liberty lunged at the door, but Bandera caught her and dragged her back. "Where do you think you are going, little sister?" she asked between clenched teeth.

"I am going to tell Judah's mother and grandfather about the lie you and Sebastian are spreading. I do not know why you are doing this, but his grandfather will believe me."

"What makes you think he is innocent?" Bandera asked pointedly. "Anyone with eyes could see that Judah Slaughter has been panting after me for weeks."

"He would never attack you."

"And I say he did," Bandera snarled, baring her teeth. She grabbed a handful of Liberty's hair and jerked with all her might. "Take warning, little sister. If you keep your mouth shut, Judah may get out of this. If you do not, Sebastian will see him dead!"

Again Liberty tried to free herself, but Bandera was too strong for her. She fell back against the cushioned seat, overcome with pain. "Surely you do not think I will stand

by while you lodge false charges against Judah," she managed to say. "I will tell everyone what you and Sebastian are trying to do."

Bandera's nails dug into Liberty's shoulders. "You do, and you never see Judah alive again. Do nothing, and in a few days, this will all blow over and you can have your precious American if he wants you." Bandera's features were distorted, and her eyes gleamed maliciously.

"Judah is not my American," Liberty said, jerking free of her sister's grip. "It is you he loves. How can you repay his love with betrayal? How can you prefer Sebastian to Judah?"

Bandera smiled, reminding Liberty of a predatory cat ready to strike. "I would do anything—betray anyone—to be mistress of Bend of the River. Sebastian is my only hope of fulfilling that goal."

"But Judah—"

Soft laughter rolled off Bandera's lips. "I do not know why you are so loyal to Judah. He doesn't give a fig for you. No man will ever want you. Look at yourself. You remind me of a homely little mouse."

Bandera's cruel words pierced Liberty's heart. Even though the night was warm, she shivered with cold, and was hardly aware that Sebastian appeared beside her. Obediently she took a drink from the flask he held to her lips, without question swallowing a fiery liquid that burned a trail down her throat. Almost immediately her head became fuzzy and she had to grasp her sister to keep from falling. It had not occurred to her that Sebastian had put something into the brandy flask to make her sleep.

"Relax, little sister," Bandera said in a silky-smooth voice. "I will take you home. Tomorrow will be soon enough for you to grieve about your lost love."

As if in a dream, Liberty heard Bandera talking to Sebastian. "What have you given her? I will not allow you

to harm my sister."

"I merely gave her a dose of my mother's laudanum. It should keep her from making trouble until morning." He leaned closer and caught Bandera's chin in a hard grip. "You had better see that she does not spoil our plans. We are both in this together. If I go under, I take you with me."

Sebastian thrust the flask into Bandera's hand. "When you think she is regaining consciousness, give her another drink of this."

"What will you say to Judah's mother and grandfather? They are not fools, you know."

"Leave it to me. Can you handle your sister?"

"*Oui.* I want it understood that I do not want any harm to come to Liberty; after all, she is my sister."

"As you wish," Sebastian said, glancing down at Liberty and seeing that she had fallen into a drugged sleep. Taking Bandera's hand, he raised it to his lips. "I believe we have won, Bandera. You and Bend of the River will soon be mine. My uncle will turn his back on my cousin, because he cannot tolerate disgrace."

"What will happen to Judah?"

"Without seeming to, I must persuade our friends that he should be locked in the shed until the authorities can get here. Of course, if my plan holds, Judah will have escaped before anyone can question him." Sinister laughter issued from his lips. "Actually, it would not surprise me in the least if my dear cousin were to take his own life when he learns of his disgrace.

"Do you mean—"

Sebastian patted his breast pocket, where he had placed the pistol. *"Oui,* that is exactly what I mean. All you have to worry about is keeping your sister's mouth shut."

"You can depend on me for that. I will keep her away from everyone."

Stepping back, Sebastian motioned for the driver to

move on. Raising his hand in a salute, he smiled at Bandera.

As Bandera leaned back against the padded seat, her mind was in a whirl. Everything had happened too quickly and she could not put all the details together. Bandera glanced at her sister and noticed she was in a deep sleep. Softly touching Liberty's face, she felt warm breath on her hand. She had to keep Liberty from defending Judah. Someone might believe her. It is strange, she thought. If anyone had asked me before tonight whether I cared if my sister lived or died, I would have thought no, but surprisingly I was ready to fight Sebastian if he tried to harm Liberty.

But Sebastian had been very clever. If the plan worked, she would soon be installed at Bend of the River as his wife. An involuntary shudder shook her. She could not stand it when Sebastian touched her, and his lovemaking left her feeling unfulfilled.

Bandera thought of Judah Slaughter and she remembered how she had trembled at his touch. There had been moments when he had almost made her forget her goal in life. How beautiful it could have been if only . . . if only . . .

Judah moaned as he regained consciousness. Pain pinned him to the hard ground and he could not see anything because it was pitch-black. He tried to rise, but he gasped and fell back. A strange weakness held him in its grasp. Where was he? What had happened?

After struggling, he managed to get to his knees. He reached out his hand, and it came in contact with a splintery wall. Dear, lord, what was happening to him? Where was he?

A feeling of nausea rose up inside him. Gasping for breath, he fell backward. He felt something sticky run-

165

ning down his face, and knew it was blood. What was the unbearable pain in his chest? he wondered. Feeling light-headed, he rolled over on his side, trying to find relief. Soon unconsciousness took him to a soft dark world where there was no pain and no memory of betrayal.

Chapter Nine

Gustave Montesquieu stood at the window watching the last of the guests depart while he waited for Sebastian. Moses had told him everything that had happened, and Gustave was angry. He cursed the sickness that kept him prisoner in the house. How could an evening that had started with such promise, end in such tragedy? He stared out the window vacantly, unaware that rain fell to the earth in heavy drops and pelted against the glass window-panes. He wanted some answers, and he wanted them immediately!

Since Judah had come to Bend of the River, Gustave had found a new joy in life. It had sharpened his wits to bandy words with his grandson. Where was Judah? Why had he not come forward to face his accusers? His jaw tightened. He wanted Sebastian and Bandera to stand before him and repeat those ludicrous accusations.

He was an old man, who felt all of his eighty-three years tonight. No one could make him believe that Judah had committed the atrocity of which he had been ac-cused, especially not Sebastian.

When Gustave heard the swish of silk and the hurried footsteps, he turned to see his daughter rushing toward him. Her face was pale and he could tell she had been crying.

"Papa," she cried, running forward and dropping to her

knees before him. "It isn't true, it isn't true. Judah could never have committed the monstrous deed he has been accused of. Someone is not telling the truth."

"Have done with your whimpering, *Madame*. The seed of your body has caused enough grief for one night. He does not need your tears."

She reached out her hand to him pleadingly. "Allow me to see my son. No one will tell me where he is being kept. If you have ever loved me, Papa, have mercy. You know in your heart that no son of mine would ever attack an innocent girl."

Gustave laid a trembling hand on his daughter's head. "Bandera is no innocent. I have my suspicious as to who is behind tonight's business, but nothing was ever gained by hasty action. Have no fear, I will get to the bottom of this, *ma petite*. I wait only for them to dig themselves into a hole, so I can push the dirt in after them."

Gabrielle gazed up into her father's face. "You believe Judah innocent, Papa, I know you do. I can see it in your eyes."

"If he is innocent, he will suffer no more than this one night under lock and key. Tomorrow I intend to take a hand in this matter."

Grateful tears ran down Gabrielle's cheeks. "I have heard that Judah was hurt, Papa. May I see him and tend his wounds?"

"No. I have sent for a doctor to look after him. I have heard that your son suffers from no more than a scratch." The lie did not come easily to Gustave's lips. Moses had told him that Judah had been shot, but he did not know how serious the wound was and he did not see any reason to worry Gabrielle at this time. He had already ordered Sebastian to have his grandson brought to the house at once.

"Take comfort in the fact that tomorrow your son will be reinstated to his rightful place. Now off to bed with

you, before you wear my nerves thin."

Gabrielle smiled half-heartedly. "I shan't sleep, knowing Judah is locked away."

"If you trust me, Gabrielle, do as I say. You have my promise that I shall get to the bottom of this. Go and rest. I will send you word as soon as I hear anything." Gustave turned his eyes back to the window, and watched rain make runnels down the glass panes. "Leave me in peace so I might untangle this web of truths and untruths."

"You promise you will let me know, no matter how late it is?"

"You have my word." The old man was so deep in thought, that he did not hear his daughter depart. His senses became alert only when, moments later, he heard the sound of Sebastian's familiar footsteps.

"I was told you wanted to see me, Uncle. Forgive me for not coming at once, but I had pressing business."

Gustave glanced up through bushy eyebrows and sneered. *"Oui,* the business of betraying someone of your own blood could be referred to as pressing business."

Sebastian seated himself on the window seat and stared at his uncle, knowing he must proceed carefully. "If you do not believe me, at least believe Bandera. I can assure you that if I had not come along when I did, Judah would have raped her."

"I would sooner believe the deed of you. It was always your style to sneak around corners and practice mischief. When you were a boy, you would torture the plantation horses and dogs, and later my slaves bore the mark of your cruel deeds. At that time I realized you were slightly mad. I did not know how mad until tonight."

"Those were a young boy's pranks. I—"

"So your mother tried to convince me at the time. I know about you, Sebastian. You are unscrupulous and ambitious. You always wanted Bend of the River, and you

169

know Judah stands in your way. You chose to remove him as a threat."

"No, I would never—"

Gustave broke in. "Let me finish. You and Bandera cooked this up, but you forgot one very important thing. You forgot I am not so easily duped."

"My God, Uncle Gustave, Bandera would not lie about something like this. Do you think she wanted all our friends to know about her shame? This will be a cruel blow to her reputation. She was so overwrought, that I had to send her home."

Gustave whirled around and snarled. "I will not believe his guilt until I hear it from his own lips. Where is Judah? Why have you not brought him to the house? Moses gave you my order."

"Our neighbors became so incensed when they saw what had happened, they would have done Judah bodily harm if I had not insisted on locking him in the tack room. I can assure you it was done for his protection."

"What devilish plan is afoot here? I order you to bring Judah to this house immediately. I thought many things about you, Sebastian, but I never thought you would betray one of your own kind. It seems I was wrong."

To Sebastian, it appeared that his uncle had aged right before his eyes. His frail hands shook as they rested against the arms of the leather chair.

"How badly is my grandson hurt?" The old man asked, his voice so low, Sebastian had to lean forward to hear him.

"He had been wounded. I am sure you have already heard I had to shoot him to get him away from Bandera. He was like a mad man."

"Damn you, Sebastian, you will pay for this," Gustave roared. "How dare you take it upon yourself to harm my grandson? I will have you horsewhipped."

Sebastian's eyes blazed. "I had hoped you would believe

170

me. After all, you have known me all my life. What do you know about Judah Slaughter?"

"I know Judah is as honorable, as you are dishonorable. You covet what I have, while he wants no part of it. You are a disgrace to me and to the Montesquieu name."

"You never had anything good to say about my son!" Alicia Montesquieu screamed, stepping from her hiding place behind the draperies at the end of the room. "I have stayed with you when your own daughter turned her back on you. My son has always carried out your orders as if he were one of the slaves. We have lived on your crumbs and abided by your wishes. Now you want to replace my son with an outsider, Judah Slaughter! I will not be shoved aside by this upstart and his mother!"

Gustave shook his cane at Alicia. "You can take whatever you believe is owed to you, *Madame,* and leave this house tonight. I will tolerate your presence here no longer. I should have put you and your son out long ago."

There was madness in Alicia's eyes as she flung herself on the frail old man. She licked the foam from her lips as she pinned him back in the chair. "I will see you dead!" she screamed, trying to take the cane away from him. "I hate you and your precious daughter and grandson," she muttered, finally gaining possession of the cane and striking Gustave with the heavy gold tip.

Sebastian rushed forward and grabbed his mother, using all of his strength to restrain her. There was horror on his face as he saw the blood that flowed from his uncle's forehead. He shoved his mother against the wall, and slapped her twice across the face in an effort to calm her.

"He is badly injured!" Sebastian cried, going down on his knees and lifting his uncle's limp hand to his cheek. Gustave's eyes were closed, and he appeared to be dead or unconscious. "All I ever wanted was your approval, Uncle Gustave," Sebastian said in a strangely tender voice. "You never saw me as I wanted you to. I wanted Bend of the

River, but I did not want you dead to get it."

Sebastian buried his face in his hands and sobbed like a baby while Alicia dropped down beside him. "I just saw his eyelids flicker, Sebastian. We had better finish him off, before he calls for help."

Sebastian shoved his mother away as his thoughts became more rational. "You are not to touch him, do you hear me? Where is Moses?"

Alicia's eyes cleared. "Gustave sent him after the doctor."

"Good," he said. Tenderly picking up his uncle's body, he started for the stairs, while Alicia merely stood by, wringing her hands and moaning. Sebastian spoke to her sharply. "Run ahead of me and make sure none of the servants are about."

Alicia dashed across the floor, knowing she had gone too far on this. If the old man lived, he would force her to leave, or perhaps he would have her arrested. She hoped he would die because that would solve all their problems. Sebastian might be angry at her for now, but in time he would realize that she had done the right thing.

Sebastian carried his light burden up the stairs and into the master suite. He gently laid Gustave on the bed. Then he picked up a cloth and attempted to wipe the blood from his uncle's face. He knew he could never allow his uncle to regain consciousness.

For just a moment he bowed his head in sorrow. Then he pulled the mosquito net down around the bed, and picked up the lamp from the round table.

"I send you to hell, Uncle Gustave, and Bend of the River along with you."

"No, no, what are you doing?" his mother cried when she realized he was going to burn the house down. "Are you mad! You will ruin everything!"

Sebastian pushed Alicia toward the door before he threw the lamp against the wall, and watched as hungry

flames ignited the mosquito netting.

"You have done it, Sebastian," Alicia cried. "Now we shall have nothing."

Sebastian shivered, thinking how horrible it would be to be burned alive. There was no longer any anger in him, only sadness, and cold, calculating reason. "Come and help me push the bookshelf against Gabrielle's door. She must not be allowed to escape the fire either."

Unable to sleep, Gabrielle heard the sound of the heavy piece of furniture being shoved against her door. As she sat up in bed, she smelled smoke! Without bothering to pull on her robe, she ran to the door and pushed against it, but it would not budge. Pounding on it, she cried out in fear as the smell of smoke crept into her room.

"Papa!" she cried, knowing his room was just next door. "Papa, help me!"

Sebastian led his mother toward the stairs, trying to calm her. "Do not tell anyone I have been here, *Maman*. It must look as if I was not here when the fire started. I have to make everyone believe that Judah started the fire."

Alicia stared in disbelief at the flames that were devouring the second floor. "You have ruined it all!" she cried. "The house will be destroyed!"

"Do not be addle-brained, *Maman*. A house can be rebuilt. Do as I say, and we will still come out of this."

Sebastian slipped out the back door and headed toward the barn, while his mother, on his instructions, ran out the front, screaming: "Fire, fire!"

It appeared that the whole second floor was in flames. Somewhere in the recess of the house screams could be heard. Slaves came running from their quarters and immediately began a bucket brigade.

No one saw Sebastian make his way toward the barn, because he took advantage of the confusion that was brought on by the fire. He grabbed an axe from the wall and smashed the rusted lock on the tack room. With an

ominous creak, the door swung open, and Sebastian cautiously stepped inside. The flames from the fire gave off enough light to allow him to find his way to Judah. With considerable effort, he hoisted the body of his unconscious cousin upon his shoulder. Staggering to a horse, he then slung Judah across the animal and led the beast out the side door.

When Sebastian reached the river, he pulled Judah from the horse. His cousin was a big man, and it took all of Sebastian's strength to lift him so he could carry him to a flat-bottomed boat.

With sinister laughter, Sebastian pushed the boat away from shore. He watched it become caught in the swift current. "Sorry, cousin, but it has to look as though someone helped you escape and you set fire to the house. Your misfortune lay in the fact that your grandfather liked you too well. You will die without ever knowing your mother's and grandfather's lives also ended tonight."

Turning back to the house, Sebastian saw to his astonishment that, with the help of the rain, the fire had almost been extinguished. He rushed forward, pretending he had just arrived on the scene. Taking charge, he stood at the head of the bucket brigade, issuing orders and making a great show of trying to enter the house to rescue his uncle and Gabrielle.

At daybreak the exhausted firefighters stared at the half-burned manor house with disbelief. Neighbors had begun to arrive. They offered their sympathy to Sebastian, who had lost his uncle and his cousin Gabrielle in the fire. Sebastian was, of course, inconsolable until Bandera arrived to comfort him.

The blackened windows, crumbling stairs, and the telltale odor left by the fire marred the magnificence of the old dwelling. A crumpled ivory fan was a grim reminder

that just the night before, there had been gaiety and laughter in this house.

Sebastian had managed to convince his neighbors that his cousin had escaped and had probably set the fire. Tempers flared, and an angry mob gathered, demanding revenge on the man who had done this awful deed. Gustave Montesquieu had been an important man, and a cry rose up to find his murderer, Judah Slaughter, and punish him. The men were fast becoming uncontrollable, a mob bent on a lynching. Hunting dogs were leashed to saddles, guns were loaded. All present swore to Sebastian that they would bring Judah Slaughter back, dead or alive!

In truth, Sebastian did not have to pretend bereavement; his grief was genuine for he had loved his uncle almost possessively. Yet he felt no guilt for Gustave Montesquieu death. After all, he reasoned it had not been his fault that his mother had lost control last night. He had no qualms about allowing his cousin to take the blame for his mother's crime—in fact nothing would please him more than to have Judah discredited before the whole world. He did feel a prickle of remorse because Gabrielle had died. He had nothing against her. She had just happened to be in the way and had had to be eliminated. Cold and calculating was the gleam in Sebastian's eyes as he accepted his neighbors' sympathy.

Already his mind was racing ahead to the year of mourning that would have to be observed before he could marry Bandera. He would use that time to rebuild Bend of the River.

Sebastian heard the rain hiss on the smoldering embers; he was glad the fire had been contained in the left side of the house. The damage wasn't as bad as he had feared.

He glanced at the Mississippi, and he wondered where his cousin's boat had drifted. It was possible that it had drifted into one of the numerous bayous, or perhaps it

had capsized on the river. He hoped the latter was the case. In any case, Judah would have died from his wounds by now. Sebastian could not have him around proclaiming his innocence and seeking revenge. Not that anyone would believe Judah anyway. Everyone's sympathy was with Sebastian. If the mob found Judah, they were likely to shoot first and ask questions later.

It was the early morning hour just before daylight. Rain pelted Judah in the face, but still he did not regain consciousness. He was not aware that the boat bumped up against the riverbank, disturbing a huge green alligator that reared its ugly head and then slithered into the water.

Zippora, on her early morning walk, was gathering roots and berries, while her grandson chased a brightly colored butterfly. When she saw the boat, she cautiously moved closer and saw the unconscious man whose head and chest were covered with blood. Bending over him she touched his forehead to see if he was alive, and he cried out. "So much pain, so much pain."

She called to her grandson, Reuben, and bade him help her remove the man from the boat. The rain continued to fall as they made their way slowly toward a nearby shelter. Often the old woman and the young boy paused in their task to rest, for the unconscious man was very heavy. From the looks of him, Zippora thought he would be dead before morning.

The room was small and had the musty smell of rotting vegetation. When Judah opened his eyes and stared through a rotted roof at a cloudy gray sky, he realized he was lying on the dirt floor of a tumble-down house. There was an air of dilapidation about the place. The windows were shuttered, and it was difficult to see with

the light of a candle casting grotesque shadows against the crumbling walls.

An old woman stepped out of the shadows. Around her head she wore a white *tignon*. Her gray gown was spotlessly clean, belying her filthy surroundings. Through half-closed eyes, she regarded him narrowly, her masklike face unreadable. When she spoke it was with a heavy French accent, but her voice had a strangely soothing effect on Judah's jumbled mind.

"You have been injured, but are in good hands. My grandson and I will attempt to take you to my cabin so I can tend your wounds. Can you assist us in getting you into the boat?"

Judah's mouth felt like he had swallowed cotton. "Where am I?"

"You are in an old abandoned farmhouse. We had to bring you here until the rain stopped."

"Who are you?"

The old woman shook her head. "It is of no matter. You are in friendly hands. Come," she said, assisting him to his feet. "You have got to remain conscious long enough to help me get you away from here."

Zippora saw the pain in Judah's eyes as he took a staggering step forward. He was in a bad way. Not only was there danger from his wounds; he had caught a chill from being so long in the rain. Each step Judah took brought on a jarring pain. He was too ill to think past the next step . . . and the next. Finally they reached a boat, and Judah fell forward, to be lost in the a world of darkness.

It was much later when Judah awoke to find the same woman at his side. His eyes vaguely followed her as she bent over the fireplace and lit a fire. Shadows played across her cinnamon-colored face, and there was dignity,

almost hauteur, in those strange yellow eyes that held his glance.

"Am I dead and in hell?" he mumbled.

Her hand touched his fevered brow, and the last words he heard were a strange prediction. "You may wish many times that you were only in hell, Judah Slaughter."

Judah did not know that he now lay upon the snowy-white bedcovers of Zippora's own bed. As the old woman cleansed his arm and removed the bullet which was still embedded close to his heart, Judah did not even regain consciousness. Zippora's sagacious eyes saw beneath the surface and into the cloudy future. She knew who this man was, having seen him from a distance several times. Judah Slaughter was important to Liberty, but he had much trouble coming to him. Zippora applied salve to the gash on his forehead, then bound it in a white cloth.

She felt his forehead and discovered that his fever was now dangerously high. The next few hours would be critical. They would determine if this man would live or die. And something else would, too. She could feel this young man's unrest. She was experiencing his outrage at being betrayed. He was going to need more than she could give him if he was going to make it through the hours ahead. He needed someone to take his hand and pull him out of his torment.

Zippora stood up, took her scarf, and wrapped it about her head. "Stay by his side, Reuben," she told her grandson. "I am going to bring Liberty to sit with this man whom she loves."

The young boy nodded and plopped down on the floor beside the bed so he could watch over the strange white man.

When Zippora stepped outside the cabin, the wind was so strong it almost whipped the door out of her hand. This is good, she thought. She could sneak onto Briar Oaks Plantation without being detected.

erty stood at the open window, allowing the wind to her face. Having realized she was being drugged by sister, she had pretended to take the liquid that had een spooned into her mouth earlier, but when her sister had departed, she had slid out of bed and staggered to the window. There she had spit out the bitter-tasting potion, and had tried to clear her mind.

Her thoughts were in a turmoil; she kept trying to remember what was nagging at the back of her brain. Digging her fingers into the soft, gold velvet curtains at the window, she remembered that Judah was in trouble. He had been accused of a crime he had not committed. Dear, God, he had been hurt!

Liberty knew she had to do something to help him. Her legs were shaky as she weaved her way across the room. She found her old gray gown and slipped into it, then pushed her feet into her boots. Grabbing her black cloak, she pulled it over her shoulders. It would be impossible to leave through her bedroom door, so she went to the window.

Many times in the past years Liberty had used the magnolia tree as a means of escape from her room. She stepped out on the ledge and eased herself onto a branch. The ground looked a long way off as she climbed down to a lower limb. She took a deep breath, wishing her head would stop swimming.

Moments passed as Liberty clung to the tree for support. Still shaken by the effects of the drug that had been administered to her, she felt her grip slipping and knew she was about to fall. She reached out her hand to grasp another branch, then sighed in relief when she secured it. A whimper escaped her lips as she fought down the churning nausea that assaulted her.

Cautiously, she glanced around, making sure no one was about before she dropped to the ground. She leaned against the trunk of the tree for support, wondering if her

trembling legs would hold her weight.

A hand fell on Liberty's shoulder, and she whi[r]
around, fearing she had been discovered. Relief wash[ed]
over her when she saw Zippora standing there. The blac[k]
woman raised a finger to her lips and motioned Liberty to
follow her. "Come, I will take you to Judah Slaughter."

Without question, Liberty followed Zippora. They
clung to the shadows as they made their way down to the
river. Once they were in Zippora's boat, and away from
the house, the old woman spoke.

"The white man is very ill. I have come for you,
knowing you can do more for him than the medicine I
have given him."

Liberty grasped Zippora's hand. "Is he . . . going to
die?"

"It is not well with him."

"How did you find him?"

"That is not important."

"He didn't do what Bandera accused him of, Zippora.
Judah Slaughter is innocent."

"I do not know about such things. But I will tell you
this, I saw that there had been a fire at Bend of the River.
I felt death in the air."

Liberty leaned back against the splintered boat while
her eyes searched the eastern skies for some sign of the
fire. By the time they rounded the bend, she saw people
milling about the site of the fire and she shivered. It
seemed the second floor had received the heaviest damage. The first floor had somehow survived.

Liberty's eyes sought Zippora's. "Do you know if anyone was hurt?"

"This I do not know, but I will find out after I take you
to the white man. The fire happened two nights ago."

Liberty looked astonished. "How is it possible that my
sister kept me drugged for two days?"

Zippora applied the oars to the water, and the boat

quickly skimmed over the surface. "We will talk of that later. Right now I want to get you to my cabin as quickly as possible."

The journey downriver seemed endless. By now Liberty's head had cleared, and she was most anxious to see Judah. She did not know what had happened in the days she had been drugged, but as soon as she could, she intended to go to Judah's grandfather and tell him that his grandson was innocent. Liberty didn't care if Bandera faced ruin and disgrace for her part in the deception; she only knew that Judah had to be cleared.

Judah was dreaming of Bandera. He could feel her soft hand on his forehead, cooling his fevered brow. Her smile melted his heart as she took his hand and held it to her cheek. He could feel that her face was wet with tears. Was she crying for him? Surely he had only dreamed she had betrayed him. Bandera was too angelic—too honest—to lie. "Bandera," he muttered. "Bandera."

Liberty held Judah's hand to her lips. Even after being betrayed by her sister, he still called out to Bandera. If it would make him feel better, she would pretend to be Bandera.

She stared at his pale face, then she softly kissed his lips. "Sleep," she whispered. "Sleep, so you can heal, Judah. I will stay beside you until you wake."

Judah's hand tightened on hers, and his chest rose and fell with a relieved sigh.

Throughout the night his fever raged, and he called out to Bandera many times, but it was always Liberty who soothed his nightmares, and Liberty who spoke to him, imitating her sister's voice.

Chapter Ten

Judah was gripped in the thralls of a nightmare world. When he opened his eyes, he found dark, unfamiliar surroundings. His head was throbbing painfully, and he felt as if the bed beneath him was spinning. He clung to the headboard until his knuckles whitened, while trying to bring his eyes into focus. He squeezed his eyes together tightly, hoping the room would right itself and the sick feeling in his stomach would go away. How did I get here? he wondered, and where am I?

Slowly, fragments of his memory fell into place, and his mind began to clear. It was as if he had stepped out of a thick fog into the light. He remembered the treachery that had brought him to his present circumstances—whatever those circumstances were. He now suffered all the cutting pain of betrayal. It did not matter to Judah that Sebastian had tricked him, but it tore at his heart that the beautiful Bandera had helped Sebastian.

"No, not Bandera," he moaned, hoping his memory was at fault. Surely he had misunderstood what had happened in the barn. Bandera was too sweet to cause another person harm. "No, she would not betray me," he said aloud.

"It is better not to talk." A soft voice came to him from out of the darkened room. "Close your eyes and try to sleep." He felt a cool hand on his brow, and it immedi-

ately soothed him. He thought he could hear little Liberty's voice, feel her cool hand touch his cheek.

"Say you will stay with me. Swear it." He tried to focus his eyes so he could see in the dark, but all he could make out was a shadowy outline.

Liberty felt tears drop from her lashes onto her cheeks and roll down them. In his fevered mind, he must have again mistaken her for Bandera. What harm would it do to bring him comfort by pretending to be her sister? The room was dark, and he couldn't see her face. All she had to do was imitate Bandera's voice.

"I did not betray you, Judah. If I had, would I be here now?"

His hand tightened on hers. "Say you love me," he demanded. "Say it!"

A sob was building up in Liberty's throat, and she could hardly speak. "I love you with all my heart," she choked out.

In the darkness, she could feel him groping for her face. His fingers outlined her mouth as he brought her head down to his. "Kiss me, sweet love. Let me once again feel your soft lips against mine."

Liberty did not know what was expected of her, but she didn't see any harm in pretending to be Bandera if she just gave him one kiss. No one would ever know. His hot mouth settled on her trembling lips, causing Liberty's breath to catch in her throat and her whole body to be filled with an emotion she could not put a name to. She quickly drew away, fearing what these new feelings might evoke.

Judah's voice broke through the stillness as his searching hands found and clamped on her arm. "No, do not leave me in my nightmare world. If you have any regard for me, stay for a while."

"I . . . shouldn't."

"I need you. Lie beside me."

s plea was Liberty's undoing. She would do anything Judah if he needed her. What did it matter that he ought she was someone else? She eased her weight onto the bed, fearing she might cause him pain. When he pulled her against his fever-hot body, she tried to hold herself rigid. She had never been this close to a man before. Since Judah's chest was bare, Liberty feared he might not be wearing clothing beneath the patchwork quilt.

His hand moved softly from her shoulder to her breasts. Liberty's first instinct was to push him away, but she didn't. She decided that if she lay very still he would realize he was being far too bold and stop.

At first Judah did not move the hand that rested against her tender young breast, and he was seemingly content to gently cup it in his palm. When his thumb slowly circled the taut nipple, however, Liberty felt waves of excitement awaken in every nerve-end of her body. Through the thin material of her linen gown, his finger circled around and around, softly, sensuously.

Liberty caught his hand and moved it away. "You must not, Judah. This isn't right."

"If I do no more than touch you, can there be harm in that?"

"You know there is."

"I need something to hold onto." He moistened his dry lips and Liberty saw that his eyes were glazed with fever.

What if Judah where to die! she thought frantically.

"Help me get through the pain," he pleaded, striking a cord of pity in Liberty's heart.

She suddenly felt older than her fifteen years. The man she loved was in agony, and only she could help him. "Hush, hush, my darling. You are very ill. If you will but rest, everything will look brighter in the morning." She tried to soothe him, much as a mother would soothe a troubled child.

"Stay with me," he begged, clasping her closely burying his face against her soft breasts. Dear lord, was burning up with fever. She could feel the heat of body even through her gown. Liberty wished that Zippor would return because she would know how to help Judah.

Tears wet her cheeks, and sobs built up from deep inside. The pain she felt was so intense that it ripped at her heart. "I will not leave you," she promised. "I will help you get through this night, my love."

Taking Judah's face between her hands Liberty raised it up to her own. Softly, almost shyly she pressed her lips against his.

A low sound tore from his throat, as he tasted the saltiness of her lips. "You do care," he breathed. "You do love me." In Judah's mind Bandera's face faded and Liberty's materialized. "I tried not to love you. You are too young and I would only hurt you. But I cannot help myself. I could sooner die than forget you."

"*Oui*, I do love you, Judah."

"Let me make love to you," he groaned, reaching for the fastenings on her gown. "If I be damned for it, I will die a happy man."

For a moment, Liberty had forgotten Judah believed her to be her sister. The pain of being reminded did not discourage her from bringing him comfort. Let him think she was Bandera if it would bring him peace.

Liberty stiffened as his burning lips settled on hers. She gasped at the tender feelings he put into the kiss. Surely it was the kiss of a man in love—a man who worshiped the woman whose lips he devoured. She parted her lips and his tongue slid into her mouth, tasting the sweetness.

Everything was so new to Liberty. She battled with her ignorance of not knowing what was happening to her. Her young body reacted wildly to his every touch. As his tongue moved in and out of her mouth, building up a tempo, heat was building in her veins, and finally her

was trembling with thrill after thrill. Driven by a need she could not control she touched her tongue his.

Instantly Judah pulled her so tightly against him that she could scarcely breath, and his hammering heart beat a quick tempo against her breasts. His need had reached a fevered pitch. He craved the soft body that was driving him slowly out of his mind. The soft gentle fragrance he always associated with Liberty was weaving through his brain.

"I love you," he whispered. "You belong to me."

Liberty was so carried away by the new feelings she was experiencing that she was only vaguely aware that Judah had slipped her gown off her shoulders. When his hands untied the laces on her chemise, she could only moan a weak protest that was quickly smothered beneath a searing kiss.

His lips played with the tips of her silken lashes. Then, slowly, and with mind-destroying patience, his mouth moved across her lips, down her arched neck, to find bliss in her firm satiny breasts. His tongue circled, tasted, then circled again with featherlike softness.

No longer did Judah feel the pain of his wounds. He was driven by stronger feelings — by a need to possess this female creature who was driving him out of his mind. He had never felt so alive.

He realized that she was inexperienced, but he would be tender and loving with her. He would not complete the act, but would save her virginity for their wedding night. She was fever in his brain, fire in his blood. He would make this a night she would remember. Afterward, they would be married and he would take her away from this hell.

When she raised her trembling fingers to touch the rough outline of his face, he kissed them one by one. Again his mind was becoming fuzzy, and he realized that

fever was clouding his reasoning. Tomorrow wou
time enough to worry about the future; tonight he w
be in paradise.

Liberty bit her lips as Judah's tongue moved across o
breast, leaving a moist trail, to tease and torment the
other. She groaned with pleasure and arched her body,
wanting to be closer to the heat of his mouth. Clasping
his arm, she felt muscles bulge against her fingers. She
vaguely remembered her mother telling Bandera it was a
woman's duty to please her husband. How could it be a
duty to please a man when there was so much pleasure.

As Judah's hand moved over Liberty's hips, the breath
seemed trapped in her lungs--she couldn't breathe. She
wanted to be a part of him and for him to be a part of
her. Perhaps by using her body, she could burn Bandera
out of his mind forever.

With that thought in mind, she decided to forget about
maidenly shyness. Tonight would give Judah everything
she had to give.

"I must stop now," he groaned. "I should never have
allowed it to go this far, but I want you with every beat of
my heart."

Liberty could feel him moving away from her. She
couldn't let him go. She would lose him if he stopped
now. She had to give him something to remember her
by—something she could hold on to after he went away.
Boldly, her hand moved across his broad chest to circle
his stomach. In her innocence, she wanted to please him.
When she heard his breath come out in a hiss, she knew
she had succeeded.

"No," he groaned. "You don't know what you are
doing."

"I do not want to you to stop," she whispered, feeling
the muscles in his stomach go taut beneath her fingers.

"I must. I do not want you to suffer the consequences
of this night."

will pay any price to make you happy," she declared
y.

Liberty discovered that Judah wore nothing beneath the
anket when her hand brushed against his swollen,
hrobbing, hardness. She quickly drew back, but he
grabbed her hand, clasping it in a firm grip. "You must
not touch me," he whispered, trying to control his desire.
"You must not . . . you . . . shouldn't . . ."

Liberty extracted her hand and placed it against his
stomach, unable to venture further down. When Judah
gasped, she gloried in the power she had over him. No
one had ever told her that a woman could control a man
with the touch of her hand. In the next moment Liberty
realized her mistake. She was no longer in control. She
had pushed him too far.

Judah gathered her to him, pressing her into the soft
mattress. "I cannot help myself. I cannot stop, now."
Liberty didn't know if it was a plea or an apology, but it
did not matter. All that mattered was the hot hand that
was moving across her abdomen, spreading her legs
apart—the finger that circled her moist opening, teasing,
then slowly, softly moving into the entrance.

At first Liberty tried to pull away. She hadn't meant
things to go this far, had she? His hot breath touched her
cheek as his hand moved nearer to paradise. "No," she
moaned, feeling as if she would die if he stopped.

A sob escaped Liberty's throat as she moved her body
against his hand. He teased her with gentle massaging
motions. Suddenly Liberty could stand it no more. She
begged him to go deeper, to put out the fire, to soothe the
ache he had built up inside her.

"Easy," he whispered hotly in her ear. "I do not want to
cause you undue pain." Softly, his finger moved forward,
finding the barrier of her maidenhead. Momentarily, he
paused. Even in his fevered condition, he realized she had
never been with a man. "I have no right to—"

189

"You have a perfect right," she whispered in his e
will never allow anyone to touch me but you."

"My dearest, sweet love," he groaned. "I will die hap
if I can have one moment of paradise with you."

Liberty wanted to protest when he withdrew his hand,
and when he positioned himself between her legs, she was
puzzled as to what would happen next. She thought she
would faint from pleasure as his swollen member entered
her body slowly at first, until it broke through the barrier
of skin, then deeper, until an all-consuming passion
shook her to the very core.

Judah pulled her close to him, kissing her lips, murmuring an apology for any pain he might have caused her.
Liberty clung to him as his rhythmic movements set up a
tempo that echoed in her brain. The tempo became
wilder, and wilder, as he penetrated her further.

Liberty's pleasure grew with each forward thrust he
made. Whimpering, she tried to draw him deeper into her,
wanting and needing to make him part of her. She wanted
to give so much of herself that he would never forget this
night. Her skin was dewy with perspiration as she welcomed his forward thrusts, and her pleasure was building
to a fevered pitch. Joy sang in her heart. All at once, she
drew in her breath, as a shock wave shivered through her,
alerting Judah that he was about to introduce her to a
new and far more pleasurable tide of feelings.

Need and want fired her. Magic, beauty, everlasting joy
burst forth from their bodies. Judah had never known
such pleasure. This was the woman who had been created
to receive his lovemaking. This was his perfect love—the
other half of himself that made him a whole man. Never
had he felt this oneness with a woman, never had he felt
so vulnerable. A shuddering release rocked both their
bodies, and Judah clasped her to him tightly while he
sprinkled burning kisses over her face. His mind was
playing tricks on him again, because he almost called out

Liberty's name.

"From this day forward, I will love no other woman. You have given me joy beyond belief. I worship you—I adore you," he murmured.

Liberty's heart took wing as he ran a soothing hand over her tangled hair, brushing it from her face and then kissing her swollen lips.

"I am a woman," she whispered. "Your woman."

His hand gently cupped her face. "Yes, you belong to me alone. No other man will ever touch you as I have."

Liberty felt her heart shatter into thousands of fragments. Judah didn't love her, she had almost forgotten that he thought she was Bandera! He had taken her body, believing her to be Bandera.

Tears ran down her cheeks, as she eased herself off the bed. She had no one to blame but herself. She had left herself open to this hurt. It was she alone who was to blame.

"Stay with me," he pleaded, reaching out to her. "I never want you to leave me." He could see no more than a vague outline, but he could tell she was slipping into her gown.

"I must go. It would not go well if they came searching for me and found you."

Already Judah was becoming drowsy. In his fevered state, he had been drained. "Will you come again?"

"I do not know. You must sleep now."

Judah's eyes fluttered shut, and Liberty bent to pull the bedcovers over him. Placing a kiss on his cheek, she discovered that he was still feverish.

With a heavy heart, she left the cabin and headed for the boat. Her life had changed dramatically in the last two days. Liberty doubted she would ever be the silly naive girl who had believed she could make Judah love her.

Liberty was now caught up in the middle of a whirl-

wind, with no way out. Her feet were set upon a path from which there was no return. She would always love Judah. Tonight she had given herself to him, while he thought he was taking Bandera. Everything was in a turmoil, and she had a feeling that in the days ahead, Judah would need her more than ever. She hoped he would soon be well enough so she would no longer have to pretend to be her sister.

Zippora waited until Liberty was out of sight before entering the cabin. She had come too late to prevent the inevitable from happening. She saw that the flame in the fireplace had gone out, and she bent to relight it. Then she moved to the bed and felt her patient's brow, discovering that he was still feverish.

A scrap of brightly colored material caught her eye, and she reached to the floor to pick it up. It was Liberty's pink satin ribbon. Zippora shook her head sadly. She had seen the tears in the young girl's eyes when she had run off into the night. Liberty was hurting, and there was nothing she could do about it, because she knew what had taken place in this room. *Oui*, she had come home too late to keep it from happening.

Zippora's shrewd old eyes took in the condition of the bed, and a sadness touched her. In his sleep, Judah reached out his hand. "Little one," he murmured. "You smell so sweet. Your lips are like honey. After tonight, you are a part of my body, Bandera."

"Be silent," Zippora snapped. "I do not want to hear this from you. You can't even decide which sister you want. You do not deserve Liberty." She was quiet for a moment. "But you do not deserve the black spider that is in her sister either. I should have seen this coming, but I did not. You have taken Liberty and used her for your needs. It is my fault."

e you," Judah muttered in his delirium.

ora seated herself beside the bed, and stared into
ckering fire. "I must fix this. It wasn't supposed to
en like this. I do not want Liberty to be hurt."

Bandera," Judah rambled on in his sleep, until Zip-
ora clamped a hand on his arm.

"You are most fortunate that you did not bed that
hellion, *M'sieu*, but you do not know it yet. Soon enough
you will remember that it was your precious Bandera who
betrayed you." She chuckled. "Already you do not want
to admit that you love Liberty. Your mind will not let you
accept that you love one so young. You call for Bandera,
but you desire Liberty."

Zippora knew Judah couldn't hear or understand her.
Her eyes glowed yellow in the firelight, and a smile parted
her lips. Reaching into the leather bag she wore at her
waist, she removed a powder and sprinkled it over Judah's
face.

"You will remember this night you lay with Liberty. No
matter where you go, you will remember everything that
happened here tonight. No. woman will satisfy you. No
woman will ease the hunger and need that will burn
within your body like a slow fire. You will know no
easing of that need until you again lie with your one true
love."

With a crackling laugh, she rose and padded across the
floor. "That should give you many sleepless nights,
M'sieu. I'll teach you to hurt the little one."

But as she turned back to Judah, Zippora's face softened with pity for the man who had been so ill used.
"You will travel a long way before you finally find that
which you seek. May God in his mercy give you a helping
hand, for I will be unable to smooth your pathway."

Liberty climbed up the magnolia tree and slipped in

through her bedroom window just as the sun w
over the Mississippi like a giant ball of fire. She r
her wrinkled gown and quickly slipped into her
gown. She hastily ran a brush through her tangled
and glanced in the mirror. Whose was the face that sta
back at her? With the soft flush on her cheeks she w
almost pretty. Her lips were still swollen from Judah's
kisses, and she touched them, remembering those burning
kisses.

Inhaling deeply, Liberty crossed the room and stepped
out into the hallway. The time for playing games was over.
It was time she did something to help Judah. She entered
Bandera's bedroom without knocking. She had to find
out what had caused the fire.

Liberty found Bandera's room empty and went downstairs, walking across the threadbare rug in the hallway
and into the dining room. She let her breath out slowly
when she found Bandera alone at the table.

"Liberty, are you feeling better? I know you have been
ill. I would have looked in on you, but I didn't want to
disturb your sleep."

"Spare me your concern, Bandera. I know you tried to
keep me drugged." Liberty seated herself across the table
from her sister so she could watch her eyes. "And I know
why you drugged me. You wanted to keep me from
talking."

Bandera smiled. "No one will believe that. Are you not
even the least bit curious as to what has happened in the
two days you have been . . . ill."

"Suppose you tell me."

"So much sadness. Poor Sebastian is beside himself
with grief."

Liberty felt as if something was dreadfully wrong and
Bandera was merely playing with her. "What sadness? Do
you mean the house at Bend of the River burning, or the
fact that Judah Slaughter—?"

"Do not speak his name in this house. He is the devil come to earth in human form. I hope they catch him and hang him or throw him into quicksand and let the alligators wrestle for his remains."

Liberty grabbed Bandera's hand. "You do not have to pretend with me, sister dear. I know you and Sebastian lied about Judah, and I intend to prove it."

Bandera looked into her sister's eyes for the first time. "You couldn't know what that man has done. You were too ill." She dabbed at her eyes. "Prepare yourself for a shock. That madman—that American—set fire to the house at Bend of the River. It is believed that his grandfather and his mother were killed in the blaze!"

Liberty came quickly to her feet. "Dear God, no! How can that be?" Grief tugged at her heart. "Surely there is some mistake. Judah doesn't even know about it."

Bandera's eyes narrowed suspiciously. "How would you know? You have been in your room. Has he come to your bedroom?"

Liberty realized her mistake. In her grief, she had almost given herself away. "Of course not. You should know—I am sure you have had me watched."

Bandera studied her face with a long and hard look. "You are always against me, Liberty. It is my hope that you will stand by me in my hour of need. *Maman* isn't here, and I need your support. I have sent word asking *Maman* and Papa to come home at once. Let us hope they will be more understanding than you are."

Liberty hardly heard her sister's words. She was thinking about Judah and the grief he would feel when he learned about the fire at Bend of the River, and the death of his gentle mother and his grandfather. The web of treachery was closing in on Judah, and he was too ill to defend himself.

She knew that Sebastian was behind all the trouble. Couldn't everyone see that Sebastian had made it look as though Judah were guilty, when all along it was he who was the guilty one. Liberty wondered how deeply her sister was involved in the plot. Would she go so far as to sanction the burning of Bend of the River to get what she wanted?

"You said it was believed that Judah's mother and grandfather were killed. Is there any doubt that they are dead, Bandera?"

"They have not yet found their bodies, but it is doubtful that they could have survived. Most of the second floor was gutted. If they were alive, they would have come forward by now."

Liberty ran quickly from the room and into the garden. She leaned her head against a magnolia tree and closed her eyes against the tears that spilled down her cheeks. She prayed with all her heart that the lovely Gabrielle, who had been so kind to her, had somehow escaped the fire, and she found it hard to believe that Monsieur Gustave could be killed by anything so insignificant as a fire. He had been too alive—too vital.

"Oh, Judah," she cried out. "How ill you have been treated since coming to Bend of the River. I cannot bear the pain you will feel when you learn about your mother and grandfather!"

Chapter Eleven

Judah leaned his head against the cypress headboard and glanced about the small bedroom. The floor was polished, and the yellow and gray rug added color to the otherwise drab appearance of the room. Now that his wound was healing and the weakness that had sapped his strength was passing, he had begun to question many things. Had he only dreamed that Bandera had come to him? Had he taken her to him, or had it all been just hallucination brought on by his high fever?

One thing was certain, he had to get out of this bed and make his way back to Bend of the River Plantation. He wanted to confront Sebastian. His cousin had much to answer for. Judah realized Sebastian had tried to discredit him in the hope of turning his grandfather away from him. If only Sebastian had known that he did not want any part of Bend of the River, Sebastian could have saved himself a lot of trouble.

Judah heard movement outside the bedroom door, and he guessed it would be the old black woman who had been administering to his needs. Who in the hell was she? he wondered. And what was he doing in her cabin? So many things were foggy in his mind. Somewhere in the back of his head, he seemed to remember Liberty's voice, soothing and encouraging. But how could that be?

In irritation, he unwound the white bandage that had

been wrapped around his head, and tossed it aside. Slowly, he began to ease himself toward the edge of the bed. He had to get going, for he had no way of knowing how long he had been ill. Surely the *Winged Victory* had anchored at New Orleans by now. Judah wanted only to collect his mother and get out of this place where mystery and intrigue seemed a part of everyday life.

But before his feet touched the floor, his head started to swim and he fell back against the pillows. He swore under his breath, realizing he was still too weak to get up. For a long moment he stared at the ceiling, trying to stop the room from spinning. Suddenly, the door was pushed open, and he watched the old black woman enter, carrying a tray of food.

Zippora stood over her patient, noting how pale he looked. *"M'sieu,* it is not wise to try to get up until you have had something to eat," she cautioned.

Despite his dizziness, Judah managed to rise to a sitting position. "Who are you?" he asked, looking at the woman suspiciously. "If you are working with Sebastian, I warn you, it will take more than you to keep me confined to this bed."

Crackling laughter rolled off Zippora's lips. *"Mon dieu,"* she said, with a shake of her head. "I have no more love for your cousin than you do, *M'sieu.* You are not a prisoner here. You are free to leave as soon as your health permits."

"How did I get here?" He was still not convinced of her good faith.

Humor lines fanned out around her eyes. "I found you in the swamps, where an alligator was showing a great deal of interest in you. I should have left you there, but I took pity on you." Zippora balanced the tray in one hand while she reached into her pocket and withdrew a bullet and dropped it into Judah's hand. "I kept this for you as a souvenir after I took it out of your chest. You had been

198

shot in the arm as well, but the bullet passed through without harm."

Judah stared at the offending object. "It seems I owe you an apology. You probably saved my life."

"Most probably I did, but I had help," Zippora admitted, placing the tray across Judah's lap. "Eat as much as you can so your strength will return."

"Liberty was here, wasn't she?" he asked, eying the thin broth and crusty bread with distaste.

Zippora's eyes veiled. "Yes, she was here, *M'sieu*."

"How about her sister? Was Bandera here?"

Zippora's eyes snapped. "That one would not be welcome in my house."

"I must have dreamed—" He broke off, knowing he could not tell the old woman about the strange dream that had haunted him. He dipped the spoon into the broth and raised it to his lips. The taste was not at all unpleasant.

"After you have eaten, we must talk, Judah Slaughter. There are some bad things that have happened, and it falls to me to tell you about them."

"I know that Sebastian has told lies about me, but that does not bother me overmuch. Bandera will tell the truth, if she hasn't already."

Zippora seated herself in a cane-bottomed chair and fixed her dark gaze on the handsome young man. "Bandera has done no such thing. You are in far more trouble than you realize." Zippora lowered her eyes. "And . . . there is much sadness that I must tell you of."

Judah shoved the tray aside and stared at the old woman. "Has something happened to my grandfather?"

Zippora met his eyes. "Yes. There was a fire at Bend of the River. Most of the second floor was destroyed. Your mother and grandfather are missing."

Judah felt his heart stop beating. "What do you mean they are missing?"

Zippora could see the agony in Judah's eyes. "Their bodies have not been found. It is believed they perished in the fire."

Trying not to believe what he was hearing, Judah shook his head. "If they were dead there would be . . . bodies."

"I do not know of such things. I can only tell you what is being said."

Judah moved off the mattress and grabbed the bedpost for support. "I have to see for myself. My mother could not be . . . dead. If she were, I would know it."

Zippora grabbed his arm as his knees buckled under him. She helped him back to bed and removed the tray, tucking the covers about him. "You are not going anywhere until you have fully recovered, *M'sieu*. You haven't the strength to take me on—how could you face the trouble that awaits you at Bend of the River?"

Judah's thoughts were of his sweet, gentle mother. No, God would not take her away from him. There had to be another explanation—there had to be! "I have to get up. I must find my mother," he said in desperation. But when he tried to rise again, he fell back in a flash of blinding pain.

Zippora placed her hand on his brow. "Rest and recover, Judah Slaughter. There are worse things that you do not know."

He stared, dry-eyed, at the old woman. "What could be worse?"

"You are accused, not only of attacking Bandera Boudreaux, but of setting fire to the house at Bend of the River. You are a hunted man. It is believed that you are responsible for the death of your mother and grandfather. The charge against you . . . is now murder!"

Confusion furrowed his brow. "I do not understand. How can anyone believe that I would—"

Zippora held his gaze. "That is not so hard to understand. You are a stranger, while Sebastian is well thought of around here. People will believe anything he tells them, especially since Bandera will back him up."

Judah stared at the old woman in disbelief. "Bandera would never . . . no, I will not believe that of her."

"Believe what you will, but know this, *M'sieu,* if you are found, you will be shot on sight. Sebastian has the countryside howling for your blood. They are combing the whole area, searching for you. It is said that your ship has docked in New Orleans, and your crew is not allowed to come ashore. I am told there are three men guarding the ship at all times."

Judah's head was pounding and his heart felt as if it had just been delivered a death blow. Anger and frustration waged a war within him. He didn't know where to go or where to turn. He was in a hostile land with no friends. His only companion was this old black woman who he suspected, couldn't care less about what happened to him.

Zippora's eyes took on a strange yellow glow as she smiled slightly. When she spoke, it was as if she had read his mind. "You have friends, *M'sieu.* Liberty has believed in you all along. She will not desert you, nor for her sake will I."

"Why should you care what happens to me?"

"I do not, *M'sieu.* I care about Liberty, and she cares about you."

Judah looked into the woman's eyes. "It seems I owe you much, and I do not even know your name."

"You can call me, Zippora. And you owe me nothing. As I told you, what I do, is done out of love for Liberty."

"Yes, Liberty. Where is she?"

"For the last few days she has been forced to stay away, fearing she is being watched. She did not want to lead anyone to you. I have made plans to get you safely away as soon as you are stronger."

"Why should I sneak away? I am innocent, and I can

201

prove it."

"A dead man can prove nothing, *M'sieu.*"

"I will not leave until I have proof that my mother is ... dead. I will clear my name, and I have to see Bandera."

"When you are strong enough, you can do what you like. Right now, you couldn't find your way to the door, much less out of these swamps."

"I have never been good at playing waiting games," he said weakly.

"Sometimes it is wiser to leave a fight and return at a later time. You cannot help yourself if you are dead."

Judah closed his eyes, feeling as if the whole world had just fallen on him. It was too painful to think about his mother. In his mind he could see the face of his grandfather, and he realized he had cared deeply for Gustave Montesquieu. He felt sick inside. His mind and his body were in need of mending. He was so weak, it was an effort to even raise his hand. Yet inside he raged. How could he allow Sebastian to make him cower in a corner. The man would pay for what he had done!

Judah cursed the weakness that kept him from going to Bend of the River, facing his cousin, and demanding he tell the truth. He reached back into the far recesses of his mind, trying to make some sense out of the situation. He was exhausted and weak. He was feeling drained emotionally, and he sought forgetfulness in sleep.

Zippora tiptoed out of the room and softly closed the door behind her. She had not told Judah Slaughter that he had been abed for over two weeks. The young man had grief to deal with; later he would deal with his other problems. Her only concern now lay in keeping him out of the clutches of his cousin and of the men who were searching for him.

She smiled slightly. Justice sometimes ground out slowly, and revenge was a bitter pill to swallow. Sometimes both were all the sweeter after a long wait. Zippora knew it would be a very long time before Judah Slaughter tasted the triumph of justice and revenge . . . if ever.

Bandera waited in the sun-bright garden for Sebastian to arrive. Tension hung in the air, and she jumped as a fleeting shadow crossed her face. Seeing it was no more than a bird, she tried to relax.

Nothing was going as it should. Sebastian still hadn't explained to her why there had been a fire at Bend of the River, and there was a hue and cry for Judah's arrest. Surely no one would believe that he had set fire to Bend of the River and had killed his own mother. Anger encased her mind. If Sebastian was responsible for the fire, she would not easily forgive him. She couldn't bear to think of the valuable treasures that had been ruined in it—treasures that would one day have belonged to her.

She heard footsteps behind her, and she spun around, expecting to see Sebastian but instead discovering it was only Liberty. "Well, little sister, have you taken to skulking in shadows and sneaking up on people?"

"No, Bandera. I leave sneaking around to you and Sebastian. The two of you do it better than anyone I know."

Bandera instinctively slapped at her sister, missing her by inches when Liberty ducked out of the way.

"I wouldn't try that again, Bandera. I have no intention of allowing you to push me around any longer."

Bandera grabbed her arm and shook her. "I would guard my tongue if I were you, Liberty. If you do not, you could find yourself in more trouble than you can handle."

Liberty wrenched her arm free. "I am no longer frightened of you, Bandera. I have learned how to fight for what I believe in—you have taught me that."

Bandera's eyes narrowed. Yes, she could see that a change had come over Liberty. She couldn't put her finger on what it was. Liberty was . . . pretty—no more than that, she was almost beautiful. When had that happened? Most certainly there was nothing of the untamed young girl about her now.

"How quaint. What will we have to talk about now that you are all grown-up, little sister? How about old Zippora's love potions . . . huh? Did you convince that old witch to give you an herb or a root that would make you pretty?"

"No, Zippora does not offer me her cures and potions. And as for what you and I can talk about, we could start with truth. We both know that you lied about Judah. One word from you, and the authorities would change their mind about his guilt."

"What makes you think I would lift a finger to help your Judah Slaughter."

"I can think of one very good reason, Bandera. Judah loves you."

Bandera raised one shoulder in a shrug of indifference. "Many men love me. They are of no concern to me, and neither is Judah Slaughter."

"You are not seeing very clearly Bandera. If Judah's grandfather is dead, who do you think will inherit Bend of the River? Think . . . it may not be Sebastian. What if Monsieur Montesquieu left everything to Judah?"

Bandera stared at her sister. "You know even if Judah were to inherit I could never be the mistress of Bend of the River. His grandfather would have had that stipulation added to the will."

"What stipulation?"

Bandera watched Liberty's face carefully. Was it possible that Liberty did not know that Gustave Montesquieu wanted her for Judah's wife? "You don't know, do you?"

"Know what?"

204

"Never mind," Bandera said, thinking it was better not to tell Liberty that Gustave had favored her as mistress of Bend of the River.

"Perhaps Monsieur Montesquieu cut Sebastian out of his will," Liberty said, planting seeds of doubt in her sister's mind. She was finding out that Bandera was not very intelligent, and could be easily led by others.

Bandera was quiet for a moment while she digested all that her sister had said. Then she spoke without thinking. "Judah would never forgive me for what I did to him in the barn."

Liberty heard the confession, but she realized Bandera didn't know what she had just said. "I believe Judah would forgive you anything, Bandera. Just suppose, for a moment, that Monsieur Montesquieu had left everything to Judah, would you not be casting your lot with the wrong man by joining forces with Sebastian?"

"I need time to think," Bandera said, rubbing her temples. "I am confused."

"Yes," Liberty said sarcastically. "You think, Bandera. That is always what you do best." Liberty no longer felt like a little girl basking in the sunshine of her sister's beauty. After what Bandera and Sebastian had done to Judah, she felt only contempt for them both.

"Let me see if I have this right," Bandera said with a soft laugh. "You have come to me offering the supreme sacrifice. You love Judah, but you will give him to me . . . I wonder why."

"It is very simple. He loves you, and he isn't mine to give."

"Love is an emotion I have no wish to feel. *Maman* says money and power are the only lasting things. Desire is often mistaken for love. I will admit that in the past I had a strong desire to be with Judah. I am not ashamed to admit it. He is a most handsome man."

"Crudely put, Bandera," Liberty said, as her lips curled

with contempt. "I will make a deal with you. If you help clear Judah's name, I will say nothing about the lies you and Sebastian have told about him. You can have Judah and Bend of the River, and everyone but Sebastian will be happy. In my estimation, Sebastian does not deserve to be happy."

Bandera's eyes sparkled with just a hint of admiration. "I can see you have given this a great deal of thought, Liberty."

Sebastian had come up behind them undetected. With a slight smile on his face he spoke. "How bloodthirsty your little sister has become, Bandera. Would she throw me to the wolves because my cousin sprinkles star dust in her eyes?"

Bandera lowered her eyes, wondering how much of the conversation Sebastian had overheard. She willingly allowed him to pull her to his side in a show of possessiveness. "You never told me your sister could be so vicious."

Bandera slipped her arm through Sebastian's. "Did you hear what she said?"

"Most of it, but I do not believe we have anything to fear. I came by to tell you that tomorrow we will be holding a memorial service for my uncle and Gabrielle."

Bandera shivered. "I suppose it is necessary."

"Yes, it is," Sebastian replied. He reached out to catch Liberty's hand and pull her to him. His eyes roamed over her face, and he wondered why he had never noticed that her eyes were an exceptional color of blue. "You have changed somehow. There is something new about you that I cannot define, Liberty."

"It is the disgust you see in my eyes," she spat out, pulling away from that odious man. "I am disgusted by you and my sister."

Sebastian laughed. "It would seem, my love, that your sister does not hold us in high esteem. Can it be that, in defending my cousin, she has turned away from us?"

"She threatened to make trouble," Bandera warned.

Sebastian's eyes grew cold. "That would not be advisable, and anyway, no one will believe her. I have spread the word that your sister is — how can I put this delicately? — enamored of Judah. Everyone feels sorry for her for being taken in by such a monster." He shrugged, "You see how it is, Liberty."

"I see what you want people to believe, Sebastian, and one day Judah will see you dead for this. I believe it was you who set fire to the house at Bend of the River, the fire that took the life of Judah's mother and grandfather."

Sebastian swaggered over to Liberty and stared down at her, his upper lip curling. "I challenge you to prove it."

"Judah will prove it."

"I don't think so. Personally I have my doubts that he is even alive. Knowing my cousin, I would expect him to be making trouble if he were able."

Liberty was glaring at Sebastian, and for the first time, she noticed how strangely he was staring at her. His eyes ran almost caressingly over her face. He was looking at her the way he always looked at Bandera. Revulsion made her step back. "Judah will come back, Sebastian, and when he does, you and Bandera will have to face his wrath."

Sebastian turned to Bandera. "Can it be that your sister has grown into a woman? Has it escaped your notice that she defends my cousin very eloquently. It raises the question in my mind of whether Judah has been taking liberties with our little Liberty." His lurid laughter filled the air, but there was no laughter in his eyes.

Liberty could no longer stand to be near her sister or Sebastian. Turning quickly away, she rushed toward the house. Did her guilt show in her face? she wondered. Could Sebastian tell Judah had made love to her?

Bandera pulled away from Sebastian, suddenly aware that he was intrigued by her sister. "You show far too

207

much interest in Liberty, Sebastian. One would think you were in love with her instead of me."

He swung around and smiled slightly. "There is something new about Liberty, a promise of excitement in her eyes. I believe she is beginning to grow up."

"She is just a child," Bandera snapped, her eyes narrowing as she glanced toward Liberty, who was disappearing around a hedge.

"Child or no, Bandera, I can tell you that if she talks she could make a lot of trouble for us."

Bandera's eyes gleamed. "You said no one would believe her."

"When her father comes home, he may believe her, and that could be a mistake, because Louis Boudreaux is greatly respected in these parts."

"Do you really believe Judah is dead?"

"Yes, I believe so. His boat was found drifting upside down in one of the bayous."

Bandera shook her head regretfully. Judah Slaughter had been an unusual man. He had swept into her life like a tidal wave, and she realized that she could easily have fallen in love with him. "Sebastian, did you have anything to do with the fire at Bend of the River?" she asked, putting Judah out of her mind.

He pulled her into his arms. "Of course not. Are you beginning to believe your sister's wild ravings? Come with me," he said, leading her to the far side of the garden out of sight of the house. "I have need of you."

Judah slipped through the gate that was hanging on rusted hinges. Driven by a need to see Bandera, he had come into her garden, hoping to find her alone. On hearing voices, he had pulled back into the shadows. Instinctive hatred burned within his heart when he heard Sebastian's laughter.

"We have won, Bandera. There are no more obstacles in our way. Bend of the River will soon be mine."

"I wish we did not have to observe a year of mourning before we can be married, Sebastian. I want to be your wife as soon as possible."

Judah's eyes burned with disgust as he watched his cousin run his hands familiarly over Bandera's breasts. "I may devise a plan by which we can speed things up a bit, my love. Since it is believed you were attacked by Judah, my friends will think I am being magnanimous by marrying you to save you from possible disgrace."

There was a pout on Bandera's lips. "I do not like my friends believing I was almost violated. I wish there had been another way to—"

Sebastian unfastened the top hook of her gown and fumbled with one of her breasts. "What a little hypocrite you are. You do not mind being a party to ruining a man's reputation, but you do not want the slightest smudge on yours." Running his fingers across her nipples, he stared into her face. "What would your friends think if they knew I first took you when you were fifteen, h'm?"

Bandera laughed breathlessly, pretending to be moved by his searching hands. "You were very persuasive that first time, Sebastian. You swept me off my feet."

Sebastian took her chin and forced her face up to his. "I have no illusions about you, Bandera. The first time you gave yourself to me, it was with the promise of a diamond ring that had once belonged to my grandmother. Your price has gone up considerably. You now demand to be mistress of Bend of the River."

Her laughter was warm as she pressed her body against his. "Neither of us has any illusions about the other. We are not guided by love and devotion."

"No, my sweet. That is why we make such a good pair; we are both guided by money and power."

Judah felt sick inside. The woman he had made love to

in Zippora's cabin had been pure and innocent, and Bandera was not. Had he dreamed the whole incident? In his fevered imagination had he dreamed he had made love to someone unforgettably sweet? The woman he had thought to be an angel had turned out to be a devil. If he had anything to say about it, she would never be mistress of Bend of the River! Stepping out of the shadows, Judah spoke.

"What a pretty picture." Sarcasm laced his voice. "True love shines through."

Sebastian's eyes narrowed, and he jerked his head around to face Judah while the color drained out of his face. "I thought you were—"

"Dead," Judah furnished. "No, I am sorry to spoil your plans, but I am very much alive." Judah's eyes moved to Bandera. "I would say the two of you deserve one another, Bandera. But you see, Sebastian will not live long enough to become your husband."

Fear made Sebastian's hand tremble when he reached inside his breast pocket for his pistol. As his fingers touched the weapon, he felt his confidence return. He aimed the gun at Judah's heart, and laughter filled the air. "I would say you are the one who will not live long, Judah. I'll say this for you, you are a persistent bastard, not as easy to kill as I thought."

Judah took a step forward, but halted when Sebastian cocked the hammer.

"Careful, cousin. I would be praised for killing a fugitive if I were to shoot you now."

"I should have known you were up to something from the beginning, Sebastian. I underestimated you, and that's a mistake I will not make again."

"That's because you will be dead, Judah."

"Not yet, Sebastian—not today," Liberty said, propelling herself against Sebastian and knocking the gun from his hand. The weapon fell to the ground, discharging the one bullet in the chamber.

"Run, Judah, flee!" Liberty pleaded, kicking the gun out of Sebastian's reach. "Do you not see that you will die if you stay. The place is surrounded by men who know you are here. Your only chance to escape is by way of the river—hurry!"

Sebastian, not so brave now that he had no weapon, hung back, eying his cousin warily. Judah's eyes swept Bandera's face for a brief moment. "I have looked at the face of an angel and seen a devil," he whispered.

Bandera took a step toward Judah, something akin to shame and sorrow reflected in her eyes. "Judah, forgive me," she pleaded.

Judah didn't even look at Bandera. He glanced back at his cousin. "I will be back. Perhaps not today or even tomorrow, but I will return. I would advise you to look over your shoulder and lock your doors at night."

"Judah!" Liberty cried as the heavy footfalls of advancing men could be heard on the garden path. "Please leave now!"

Casting a quick glance at Liberty, Judah smiled slightly. "For your help I thank you, little Liberty. If I never see you again, I will long remember your sweetness."

"Judah!" she cried, as he whirled around and melted into the shadows. Her heart was shattered, and she had the feeling she wouldn't see him for a very long time.

As the men approached, Sebastian pointed out the way the fugitive had taken. Liberty glanced at her sister and saw the tear that rolled down Bandera's cheek. "I hope you are proud of yourself," she declared. "I wouldn't like to be in your shoes when Judah returns. A desperate man is very dangerous. Judah is more than desperate . . . and he will be back!"

Liberty stood on the riverbank, scanning the horizon.

Storm clouds clung to the sky, and her heart was heavy with sadness. Zippora had told her how easily the crew of the *Winged Victory* had tricked the men watching the ship. Judah was now safely aboard and he had sailed with the morning tide. Tears stung Liberty's eyes as she said a silent prayer for his safety. Someday Judah would come back, and she would be waiting for him . . .

The early morning sun was hidden behind dense black storm clouds. In the strange yellow light, the Mississippi River appeared to be a gun-metal gray color. Frothy white caps rushed to the shore, as if trying to escape the impending storm. In the distance, a flash of lightning split through the heavens, followed by a rumble of thunder.

Despite the oncoming storm, the *Winged Victory* slipped her anchor and headed for the open sea. The men who had been guarding her, at Sebastian's orders, had been easily dealt with by the crew of the *Winged Victory*. They were now gagged and bound, and locked in a warehouse on the waterfront.

Judah watched with cold eyes as New Orleans faded into the distance. "Thank you for saving me my friend. I could never have escaped without your help."

"Don't thank me, Captain. It was your friend, Zippora, who showed us the way. She was remarkable. It was her idea to lure the guards into the warehouse with a promise to tell their fortunes. Where did you find her anyway?"

Judah shivered, knowing he would have died had it not been for Zippora. "I didn't find her, she found me. I owe her a debt I can never repay."

"You are still not well, Captain. I promised Zippora I would make you stay in your bed for a few days."

Judah was too weak to protest as Philippe led him to his cabin. He eased himself down onto his bed and spoke

212

in a calm voice, trying to cover the rage that governed his thinking. "I feel like I am running away, Philippe. I swear to you the day will come when I will return, and when I do, blood will be spilled at Bend of the River Plantation!"

"When you return, Captain, I will be beside you. All the crew thought well of your mother, and they will help you in any way they can."

Judah lay back on the bed and closed his eyes. His head was pounding, and he still felt weak and shaken.

"What course do I set, Captain?" Philippe asked, trying to draw Judah's mind away from his troubles.

Raising up on his elbow, Judah managed a smile. "Set a course of the Caribbean, Philippe. It is time the *Winged Victory* earned her keep. How do you think the crew will take to a little privateering? The Governor of Martinique was a friend of my father's. I feel sure he will issue me a letter of marque, so we can operate in the Caribbean without being called pirates."

A big grin spread over Philippe's face. "I believe I speak for every one of the crew when I say, they will like it just fine, Captain."

Liberty shaded her eyes against the bright glare of the sun as she watched the approaching boat. For over a week she had kept a close eye on the Mississippi, hoping her father would return. If anyone could help Judah, it would be her father. He would believe her when she told him Judah was innocent. Then she recognized Mr. Forester, her father's attorney. When she waved to him, he only acknowledged her by the merest nod of his head. Mr. Forester had always been glad to see her. Why was he acting so distant? she wondered. And why were the two long boxes beside him. They looked like . . . like . . . coffins!

Fear and dread tugged at her heart. "Please, no," she moaned softly, seeing the sadness in Mr. Forester's eyes.

"Not my father—not my mother!"

With a quick word to the pilot of the boat, the attorney stepped ashore. He walked over to Liberty, and with sympathy in his eyes, reached for her hand. "I am sorry to be the bearer of grievous news, my dear. Your father and mother met with an accident."

Liberty stared in disbelief at the men whom were unloading the coffins onto the pier. She became acutely aware that the sun was still shining and birds were singing in the nearby oak tree. Why was life going on as usual when the ones she loved were dead? Her mother and father could no longer feel the warmth of the sun or hear the sweet bird songs.

"How?" she managed to choke out. She stared directly into the attorney's face.

"I am told the boat on which they sailed hit a sudden squall and capsized. Many of the bodies were not recovered."

Tears gathered in Liberty's eyes. "There must be some mistake. My father was a strong swimmer. He would have been able to save himself and my mother."

The old lawyer rubbed her cold hands, wanting to bring her comfort. Not only had he been Louis Boudreaux's attorney, but his friend and confidant as well. Louis had left Briar Oaks to Liberty, and had made Forester her guardian. He would do the best he could for her, but there would be dark days ahead. She was too young and inexperienced to hold on to a plantation the size of Briar Oaks, not with the staggering debts that were increasing every day. Out of his friendship for Louis, Forester was determined to help Liberty in any way he could, but he knew she would not keep the plantation for very long.

Liberty slowly walked over to the coffins. By now she was blinded by tears. Her hand trembled as she touched the roughened wood. *"Oh, Papa, Maman"*— she sobbed—"I cannot bear a world without you."

Through her tears Liberty, saw that the boat's crew had moved back a respectable distance so they would not intrude on her grief, and she did feel the need to be alone to express her sorrow. "Monsieur Forester, will you see that my father and mother are taken to the house?"

"Of course, but—"

Before he could finish, Liberty turned away and scampered into her small boat. He watched her paddle toward the swamp, knowing this was her way of dealing with her parents' untimely deaths. With a heavy heart, he turned his attention to the heartbreaking task at hand. He still had to inform Bandera that her mother and stepfather were dead.

The rain was falling heavily against the black umbrella Liberty held over her head. She stood silently beside the graves of her mother and father, unable to believe they were gone. She snapped the umbrella shut, allowing the rain to saturate her clothing, to plaster the thin muslin to her slim body. She shivered with cold, and her tears mixed with the rain. Suddenly she raised her face to the heavens, crying out her anguish.

"Papa, I miss you so desperately. Briar Oaks is in trouble. I try to think what you would do if you were here. I know how much you love this land, Papa, and I will try to make you proud of me. With my last breath, I will fight to save it, but I do not know how!"

Part Two

A Woman's Conquest

Chapter Twelve

October, 1814

There was a feeling of unrest as rumblings of the war between America and England were drawing ever nearer to Louisiana. General Andrew Jackson had invaded Spanish Florida, and captured Pensacola from the English. It was reputed that a fleet of British soldiers had set sail from Jamaica, their destination unknown. Some feared they were heading for Louisiana. Amid the rumors and speculations, not all the French Creole populace were steadfast in their loyalty. While they had no liking for the English, they were not inclined to offer the Americans their wholehearted support.

In any case, neither the cold wind that howled down the valley, nor fear of impending war kept the elite of Louisiana from arriving at Briar Oaks Plantation to attend the wedding of Sebastian Montesquieu and Bandera Boudreaux.

Madame Darcy and Madame Pessac, the two matrons who attended all the parties and weddings, and spent their time gossiping about the guests, had their heads together. "I must say," Madame Darcy stated, "all and all it was a lovely wedding. Everyone knew that Sebastian and Bandera were meant for each other. It's a pity that the death of Bandera's parents caused such a delay, not to mention the odd happenings with Gustave and his daughter Gabrielle."

"What happened there?" Madame Pessac inquired, her eyes gleaming with curiosity.

"Well, it is all very strange. You know about the fire at Bend of the River about three years back?"

"*Oui*, does not everyone know about that?"

"At the time we all believed that Gustave and Gabrielle had perished in the fire, but it seems that Gustave's major-domo, Moses, arrived at the burning house in time to rescue them both by way of the second-floor balcony. For some strange reason, they took a boat to New Orleans and did not tell anyone they were unharmed. A very curious business. I can tell you Sebastian was beside himself with grief. He thought they were dead, while all along they were in New Orleans."

"It has not escaped anyone's notice that Gustave and Gabrielle did not attend the wedding. I think it is a shame to treat Sebastian in such a shabby manner."

"*Oui*, Sebastian is such a dear boy. I wonder why he and his mother left Bend of the River after the fire? I had thought he would inherit the plantation."

"So did we all, and so he should. There was much speculation as to why Gustave Montesquieu no longer allowed Sebastian and his mother to live under his roof. Of course the Montesquieus are proud and secretive and they keep their troubles to themselves. One can only guess that the trouble came from Gustave's grandson, that American."

"*Oui*, what a nasty business. Some say he is dead, and rightly so, I should think."

"I cannot say for sure. Gustave and his daughter never entertain, and no one is invited to Bend of the River, except Liberty Boudreaux. Both Gustave and Gabrielle have become very reclusive."

"It is my understanding that even though Liberty inherited Briar Oaks, the married couple will be residing here. At one time Liberty was a strange wild child. Now she is more subdued. The poor child has much to weigh on her shoulders. She labors like a slave, trying to keep Briar Oaks from being taken over by the money lenders. I admire her spirit."

"She is such a pretty little thing. My grandson has lost his heart to her, but she brushes him aside as she does all the others. They are calling her a heart-breaker—an incomparable."

"So true," the friend agreed, "so true. At one time I thought Bandera was the beauty in the family. But now Liberty outshines her."

Sebastian took a sip of wine, savoring the bouquet. The wine cellar at Briar Oaks still had fine wines. He bowed to the two matrons as he walked by them, and when he caught the end of their conversation, his lips curved into a smile. As he gazed across the room, the sound of Bandera's musical laughter met his ears. Today a part of his ambitions had been fulfilled; Bandera was his wife. It was but a matter of time before he would have everything he wanted. Sebastian was determined to settle down and act the model citizen so his uncle would soon realize that he was a worthy heir for Bend of the River. The old man must now know that Judah would never come back.

Sebastian's eyes momentarily clouded. It angered him that Gustave had refused to attend his wedding, and he was further annoyed by the fact that he and Bandera would have to reside at Briar Oaks for the time being. That was more aggravating because Louis Boudreaux had left everything to Liberty; Bandera had inherited no part of the Plantation.

He gazed across the room to the golden vision of loveliness that stood apart from the crowd of dancers as if she were not of the earth, but some mystical princess, lost in an enchanted world. Sebastian realized with a jolt that the two matrons had been right: Liberty had matured into a delicate beauty who far surpassed Bandera in looks.

There was such a radiance about her that Sebastian drew in an excited breath. Liberty was as unattainable to him as the moon. She had been cold and distant since Judah Slaughter had disappeared, and he knew that she detested him. For some reason it bothered him. Nevertheless, for Bandera's sake, Liberty had agreed that Sebastian and his mother could live at Briar Oaks until they found a place of their own.

Liberty felt Sebastian's intense gaze upon her, and she turned, her eyes locking with his. He nodded and smiled, raising his glass in a silent tribute, but she ignored the overture and turned back to the window. Her mind was on another man. As always, she wondered where Judah could be. Was he safe? What was he doing? Did he ever think of her? Each night Liberty prayed for Judah's safety. One thing she knew: if he were alive, he would one day return to Bend of the River Plantation to settle an old score.

"Pipe dreaming, little sister?" Bandera asked. "Why do you not join with the others in celebrating my wedding?"

Without looking up, Liberty answered in a soft voice. "I see nothing to celebrate. You are married to a trickster and a thief. However, the two of you are well suited to one another." Liberty made a wide sweep with her hand. "You and your new husband may enjoy my hospitality while you can. When Judah returns, there is nowhere the two of you can hide to be safe from him."

Bandera grabbed Liberty's arm and dug her nails into its soft flesh. "Hush. You will not talk like that. I am warning you, Liberty, have done with your accusations, or I will . . . I will . . ."

Liberty pushed her sister's hand away and stared back

at her, not in the least intimidated. "Or you will what, Bandera? I am no longer afraid of your threats."

Bandera's eyes dropped before Liberty's. No, Liberty was no longer so easy to control now that she was the mistress of Briar Oaks. Many changes had occurred in her sister. She had ceased to be a homely little river rat who spent her time in the swamps, and she had turned into a lovely swan with polished and graceful manners. Bandera knew that even her beauty paled when compared to Liberty's. Now, when they attended a party or ball, it was Liberty who was surrounded by all the gentlemen, and Bandera who waited to be asked to dance.

Jealousy flamed in Bandera's heart. "You would do well to guard your tongue or Sebastian will have it lopped off."

"I do not fear Sebastian, any more than I fear the water moccasin who slithers through the water. Neither is a threat if one watches one's back."

Soft laughter met Liberty's ears, and Sebastian's hand came down heavily on her shoulder. "If I am the snake, should you not fear me, little sister? I might wrap myself around you and squeeze tightly." As he spoke, Sebastian's hand moved caressingly over Liberty's shoulder. "I could easily crush you," he whispered into her ear.

Liberty swept away from him, and his hand dropped to his side. "Save your threats for someone who is afraid of them. I merely loathe you, Sebastian. It is because I do not want to see my sister live in the streets that I invited you to share my roof. Just remember at all times that you are a guest in my home, and do not abuse the privilege."

Anger clouded Sebastian's eyes. "Do you want everyone to hear you air our family problems?"

Liberty saw that no one was close enough to hear her words. "I do not care that the world knows I do not like you, Sebastian."

Anger fired his eyes, and he grabbed Liberty's hand.

Before she could react, he pulled her toward the stream of dancers, forcing her to dance with him and leaving Bandera glaring after them both.

"Have a care, Liberty," Sebastian warned. "We would not want our neighbors to think you do not love me and your sister."

She raised her chin and returned his bold stare. His grip was tight, and she knew he wouldn't let her go without a struggle. "I keep my mouth shut only because I know my mother would have wanted me to look after my sister. I can do nothing about your deception, but be warned, Sebastian, one day Judah will return, and you and my sister will be forced to face his fury."

A smile tugged at his lips. "You are breathtaking when you are angry, do you know that?"

She tried to pull away, but he would not relinquish his hold on her. "Save your compliments for your wife. You will find she needs an enormous amount of flattering to make it through every day."

Sebastian's breath came out in a hiss, and he felt his body come alive. "You little firebrand. Don't you know that I desire you? I have watched you bloom into a beauty. You are wild and unpredictable and every man here wants you. Have I not had to stand by while others lusted after you?"

"Let me go," Liberty said in a disgusted voice, feeling sick to her stomach. "I detest you!"

"You should be nice to me, little sister. I happen to know that before your father died he borrowed heavily against Briar Oaks Plantation, and you face the possibility of losing everything. Perhaps I can help you."

"You cannot even help yourself, Sebastian. You will be living here on my charity. Because of my sister, you and your mother will have a place to stay. I know that both of you have been living with friends in New Orleans, and that your welcome was growing very thin. Everyone believes that your uncle is being unreasonable in throwing you out of his home—I happen to know you deserve far worse."

Again he smiled. "Do you know your eyes sparkle like blue fire when you are angry?"

"How dare you insult me so. If my father were here he would—"

His eyes darkened. "Your father is dead," he said flatly.

"I wonder what our neighbors would say if I were to slap you right now?" Her eyes held a hint of warning.

His brow furrowed. "Try it and see."

Suddenly, unable to stand his touch any longer, Liberty wrenched her hand from his grasp and spun away. Unmindful of the curious stares that followed her, or the anger on her sister's face, she rushed across the floor and outside. Standing on the terrace, Liberty breathed in large gulps of cold, cleansing air.

Tears washed down her face as she gazed up at the moon. Somewhere that same moon shone down on Judah. Was he with a woman at this moment? "Please come back soon," she sobbed. "I have waited so long for your return. I have grown up, and became a proper lady, hoping you will be pleased when you see me."

A dark, ominous cloud moved over the moon, and Liberty shivered. Tonight her heart was troubled. Sebastian had been right. If she didn't do something soon, she would lose Briar Oaks. She had received several marriage proposals from wealthy young gentlemen who would help her save Briar Oaks, but she had turned them all down. Her heart and body belonged to a man who had probably forgotten her very existence.

Hearing a rustle of silk, Liberty turned to find her sister at her side. "Once again you have drawn attention to yourself, Liberty. I will not have this kind of behavior from you, especially on my wedding day."

Liberty suddenly felt pity for her sister. The death of

their mother had been hard on her, because Bandera no longer had a close confidante. "I am truly sorry, Bandera. I just do not feel well tonight."

"Come back inside, and at least pretend that you are happy for me. Lord knows what kind of impression you made when you bolted out the way you did."

"You are right, Bandera," Liberty said, drying her eyes on a lace handkerchief. "It was unforgivable of me."

"From your behavior tonight, one would think that you had designs on Sebastian yourself. Have you not enough men paying court to you that you would covet my husband? I believe you only pretend to despise Sebastian to cover up your true feelings. Why else would you allow him to move in with us?"

Liberty sighed heavily, knowing it would do no good to tell her sister she had only agreed to have Sebastian and his mother at Briar Oaks for her sake. "Believe me, Bandera, Sebastian is safe from me. I would not take him if he were the last man on earth."

For a moment, Bandera looked as if she might cry, but then she straightened her shoulders. "You may not like Sebastian, but he is my key to wealth and power. Do you think I would have married him had I not known he would one day be master of Bend of the River?"

Liberty watched Bandera whirl away and storm into the house. She could not see how Sebastian had convinced her sister that he would one day be master of Bend of the River. Monsieur Montesquieu has forbid Sebastian to ever step foot onto his land. Liberty dreaded the thought of having Sebastian in her house. Sometimes the obligations she felt for her sister weighed very heavily on her.

When Liberty reentered the room, she saw that Sebastian and Bandera were dancing. She could tell that her sister was angry, and she knew Sebastian would not have an untroubled wedding night. Poor Bandera—she did not want Sebastian, but she wanted his undivided attention.

Liberty doubted that her sister would have his attention or his faithfulness for many days. She almost found it in her heart to feel sorry for Bandera . . . almost, but not quite.

The square-rigging of the *Winged Victory* filled the sky as she smoothly rode the choppy waves with a grace and dignity that proclaimed her to be a lady of the sea. No longer did sea water have to be pumped from below her leaky decks to keep her afloat in a storm, and no longer did her sails bear the signs of numerous patchings. She was clean and sleek. Having been modified to her captain's exact specifications, she was reputed to be the fastest vessel in the Atlantic. She was now a privateer. Her captain was famous for his quick strikes and his ability to disappear without a trace. The men that sailed on the *Winged Victory* had made their fortunes by capturing English and Spanish ships, nevertheless, it was said that their favorite targets were the Barbary pirates!

The *Winged Victory's* sun-bleached canvas was unfurled and playing with the stiff breeze. Majestically, her bow caught a wave, and lurched upward, seeming to reach for a piece of the heavens.

Her captain stood on deck his eyes trained on the distant pyramid of sail on the eastern horizon. His attention shifted for the moment, to his left, and he saw a second ship appear on the horizon.

The brisk north wind ruffled Captain Judah Slaughter's golden hair, but not his poise. There was a coldness in the captain's turquoise eyes, and maturity and confidence etched on his handsome face. No longer was he the confused and bitter young man who had fled New Orleans. His wits were sharpened, and he captained the *Winged Victory* and her crew with a firm hand and an easy confidence. The adoration of numerous females had added a certain arrogance to his stance, even though they had all left him feeling unsatisfied and unfilled. Many things had changed about Judah, but the passage of time had not lessened his need for revenge on his cousin and Bandera.

Philippe Cease stood at Judah's right, a telescope aiding him to gauge the distance to the two oncoming ships. "They are British, Captain. It looks as if one of them is flying the Blue Ensign, so there must be an admiral on board."

Judah reached for the telescope and gazed at the approaching vessel. "There's a third ship," he said, adjusting the lens to his eyes. "It's an American Naval vessel. I make her out to be a twelve-gunner."

"She's in trouble, Captain! They're closing on her fast, and will soon catch her. She's outnumbered and outgunned!" Philippe observed.

Judah had not set foot on American soil since that night he had fled to New Orleans. He knew returning would mean immediate arrest. However, he was very aware that his country was fighting a war with the British. Although he had thus far not been drawn into the conflict, he had felt particular satisfaction, each time he had taken an English ship as prize. Now, seeing the small American vessel in danger from the enemy, he was outraged. Closing the telescope with a snap, he narrowed his eyes.

"Suppose we even the odds, Philippe? How do you feel about helping a sister ship in trouble?"

A smile spread over the Frenchman's face. "I'd like that fine, Captain."

"I have but to win the approval of the crew and convince them to take on a fight that will net them more trouble than booty."

"They like a good scrap, Captain. I believe they could be easily persuaded," Philippe responded. "Put it to

228

them, Captain, and see if they are willing to go along."

"Assemble the men on deck, and I'll do that." Judah's eyes brightened. "Meanwhile, heave to, Philippe, and allow the ships to gain on us. We do not want to outrun the fight before it begins."

By the time every crew member had gathered to hear what the captain had to say, the three ships were less than half an hour away. The smaller American ship was trying without success to escape her powerful enemies. Soon the three vessels would play out their life-and-death struggle within distance of the *Winged Victory*. Every eye was trained on the captain to see what his plans were concerning the impending battle.

Judah was a dashing figure as he stood on the quarterdeck, one booted foot resting on the railing. He wore black leather britches and a white ruffled shirt. A knife and a pistol were pushed into the folds of the red sash wound about his waist, and a rapier dangled from a black leather strap.

Judah's eyes moved over his thirty-man crew, all of whom he had come to know very well over the years they had sailed together. The *Winged Victory* was renowned for her battles with the Barbary pirates, as well as her attacks on French and English merchantmen. Each man present had made his fortune under the command of Captain Judah Slaughter—each man trusted and admired him—but Judah did not yet know how far their loyalty went. Many of his crew were fugitives from American justice; some were of foreign birth and had no interest in the war with England.

"Men," Judah began, fingering the hilt of his rapier. "As you are all aware, there is a battle about to take place just off our starboard. Like you, I know this battle is none of our affair." Judah paused for effect. "Why should we care that the small American ship hasn't a chance against two larger British ships? It is no concern of ours that the British are at war with the United States. It does not effect us that the British have been firing on American ships and impressing their crews into her service. No, I say we turn tail and run. We have more important things to do. In a week or less, we will be in Martinique where we can celebrate our last three victories and count our booty."

Judah saw a troubled look appear on many of the men's faces as their eyes moved to the American ship that was losing in the sea chase. Her enemies were bearing down on her.

Crossing his arms, Judah took the few steps that brought him down to the lower deck. Climbing up on the hatch so he would be above the crew, thus focusing them to look up at him, he played the men as an actor would play his audience. "Let the American Navy look after their own. We certainly have no reason to fight her battles."

To Judah's surprise it was a Spanish sailor, known only as Rojo, who spoke up first. "It does not seem fair to let the two bigger ships attack the smaller one, Captain. We have never before run from a fight." A murmur of agreement arose from many of the others. "We take pride in serving aboard the *Winged Victory*, and we do not want word to get around Martinique that we are cowards.

"Perhaps you have a point," Judah speculated. "We have never run from a fight . . . neither have we interfered in one that didn't directly concern us. What do you think we should do, men?" He acted as if the decision rested with his crew.

"Begging your pardon, Captain," a man called Gordon said, respectfully removing his cap and tucking it under his arm. "It kind of gets my ears to burning, knowing them English are about to fire on my own countrymen. It don't hardly seem right to turn our backs when we could help. Hell, sir, there could be some men from my home state of Virginia on board. I vote that we teach the English dogs a lesson they won't soon forget!"

"Aye, sir," the others agreed in chorus.

"Let's give them what for!" Gordon rallied the men. "Let's blow them clear out of the water!"

Judah took a deep breath and laughed heartily. "All right, men, you've won your point. If it's a fight you want, then it's a fight you'll get."

A chorus of voices rose in deafening approval. In one lithe stride, Judah moved up the quarter-deck and began to issue orders. "Hoist sail, Philippe. Gunners, make your cannons ready to fire. Look lively men—prepare to do battle."

Philippe caught Judah's eye, and he almost laughed aloud at how easily Judah had maneuvered the crew to do his bidding. Judah knows a lot about human nature, he thought. "Man your stations," Philippe yelled across deck. "Like the captain says, prepare to do battle."

In the distance, several volleys were fired, and the American Naval vessel sustained two direct hits. Her bow splintered, and one of her masts toppled onto the deck.

It did not take long for the *Winged Victory* to be drawn into battle. One of the crew, Philippe suspected it was Gordon, raised an American flag above the mast. That drew almost immediate fire from one of the English frigates, but the shot was clean and wide, sailing harmlesly across the bow of the *Winged Victory*.

By now the American Naval craft had spotted her only salvation, and was swinging wide so the *Winged Victory* could stand between her and harm. Judah saw that the larger of the two British ships, a fifty-two gun ship-of-war, named *Freemont*, had turned and was heading straight for him. Judah knew he was outgunned and he had to get closer so it would be harder for the enemy to deliver a heavy broadside. A quick glance told him the small American craft had turned to take on the other

British ship. Damaged as she was, he knew she couldn't last long.

With the wind at his back, Judah brought the *Winged Victory* so near the *Freemont* that Philippe shouted across the deck.

"Do you want us in their laps, Captain?"

"Aye," came the smiling reply, "that I do."

The *Winged Victory* caught a wave, and her hull reached toward the heavens. As Judah brought her about, she raked the stern of the *Freemont* with a broadside. Now it was impossible for the English ship to fire her cannons, not so the *Winged Victory*. Simultaneously, her guns flashed fire. She couldn't miss her target at this close range. Each shot resulted in an explosion on board the English vessel, and in no time at all the enemy ship was crippled and taking on water.

No longer seeing the *Freemont* as a threat, Judah turned his attention to the other English ship, the *Royal George*. The American Naval ship was in trouble, and since it was apparent that she was sinking fast, Judah wanted to finish off the *Royal George* quickly so he might rescue the American crew.

As the English ship bore down on the *Winged Victory*, Judah ordered the sails filled so it would look like he was trying to escape. "Make ready for a sharp turn, men," Judah bellowed. "Pass the word on for everyone to grab hold of something and wait for an impact!"

With the enemy in close pursuit, Judah quickly turned into the wind and caught his opponent by surprise. The two warring ships came together with a grinding crash that was felt from bow to stern. As Judah had hoped, the enemy had been taken by surprise, and many of her crew had been sent flying across deck, whereas most of Judah's men had braced themselves and were now armed and ready for a fight.

"Toss grapples!" Judah commanded, as he swung himself over the side and onto the deck of the *Royal George*. A mighty roar rose up from the crew of the *Winged Victory* and they followed their daring captain into battle.

The captain of the British ship, seeing the mass of men surging onto his deck, ordered his gunners to fire on the *Winged Victory*, but he had missed his chance. The fight was now limited to hand-to-hand combat, with the privateers clearly having the advantage of surprise.

Amid the confusion, Judah had no trouble finding the English admiral on the forward deck. "I have no wish to see more bloodshed," he declared, brandishing his rapier. "Do you give quarter, sir?"

"Not on your life," the Englishmen returned, bravely lunging forward to meet Judah with his own blade.

With a slight smile, Judah defended himself against the thrust. The two men crossed swords again and again, taking little notice of the chaos around them. There was fighting on the upper and lower decks, on the platforms and riggings. The planking was slick with blood spilled by both sides. Judah thrust and parried, agilely side-stepping his opponent's thrusts, and it was soon obvious to the British commander that he was outmatched by the American captain.

The admiral of the *Royal George*, seeing the tide of battle was going against him, and knowing he had already lost one ship, threw down his sword and, to be heard above the noise, yelled loudly, "Quarter, sir, we beg quarter!"

Judah order an immediate halt to the hostilities, then turned to see how the crippled American ship was faring. She was riding low in the water and slowly beginning to list to her right side. Judah knew that in another hour she would be at the bottom of the sea. The *Freemont*, although not as severely damaged as the American vessel, was likely to suffer the same fate.

"Make haste, men," he cried. "Place the prisoners

below. Philippe, put men at the helm and rescue the American sailors, then rescue the men from the *Freemont*." Judah grabbed a rope and swung back on board his ship. "And, Philippe," he called out. "When you see him, offer my respects to the captain of the American ship and invite him to dine in my cabin with me and the English admiral."

The Americans were grateful for their rescue, and joyful shouts arose from the English ship as impressed American sailors again tasted sweet freedom.

Captain Étienne Banard took a sip of claret from a crystal wineglass while he studied the man who had saved him and his crew from disaster earlier in the day. "The dinner was excellent, Captain Slaughter. I feel fortunate to be alive and able to indulge in such a feast. Can you imagine how I felt today when I had all but lost hope? Then I saw your ship with the American flag flying above her mast. It was like a miracle!" He raised his glass to Judah. "Again, I thank you for coming to my aid. I owe this day, my life, and that of my crew to you, sir."

Judah studied his guest with a practiced eye. Judging from his slight accent, he guessed the man was of French descent and about his own age. In spite of the mishap today, the American captain was meticulously dressed in the white and blue dress uniform of the American Navy.

"Please," Judah dismissed Étienne's gratitude. "It was nothing. To speak of it further will only cause me embarrassment."

"It is I who suffer the embarrassment, gentlemen," the Englishman, Admiral Sills, stated. "I thank you for your kind hospitality, but may I ask what you have in store for me and my men?"

Judah nodded. "I will tell you of my plans tomorrow. Rest assured that none of you will come to harm." Judah stood up. "I have given you my own cabin, and I hope you will pass a restful night there. My first mate, Philippe, will show you to your quarters."

"May I see my men so I can be satisfied as to their well-being?" Admiral Sills asked.

"Yes. Philippe will take you below so you can see that we Americans do not misuse our captives."

The admiral looked at Judah, respect evident in his pale blue eyes. "I have fallen into the hands of a kind enemy, sir." Bowing stiffly, he turned to be led out of the room by Philippe.

"What are your plans for the English admiral and his men?" Étienne Banard inquired.

"I am not sure at this time. You will help me decide later."

"Again, I am grateful for your intervention today. I will always know that I owe my life to you," Étienne declared passionately, his French nature coming to the fore. "If ever you are in need of a favor, you have only to ask and I will immediately oblige."

A smile smoothed Judah's brow. "You can start by calling me Judah."

"And you will call me Étienne. I will be your friend for life."

"To good friends," Judah said, tipping his glass to Étienne.

"Will you drink a toast with me, Judah?"

"I will. What shall we drink to?"

"To the United States of America, and to President Madison. May we have a quick victory over our enemies."

Judah raised his glass, a sober look in his eyes. "To the land of my birth, may she ever be free!"

Ballard, the ship's cook, cleared away the dishes and the remains of the meal, while Judah poured Étienne a glass of brandy. The Frenchman waited until Ballard had left the cabin before he asked, "What do you plan to do

235

with the English ship, Judah?" He smiled. "I am just curious."

Judah took a sip of brandy before answering. "I will tell you later. Right now I want you to look at something and give me your opinion on it." Reaching behind him to a shelf on the wall, Judah picked up a parchment and unrolled it. "As you can see, it has been burned around the edges. Apparently someone tried to destroy it."

Spreading the parchment out on the table, Judah motioned for Étienne to examine it. "My first mate found this in Admiral Sills's cabin. It appears to be a dispatch from London. See what you make of it."

Étienne eyed the document carefully, before whistling through his teeth. Quickly glancing at Judah, he shook his head, "It is hard to make out the exact meaning since it is so charred, but apparently it is from someone named Lord North. He seems to be very important."

"Yes, that is what I thought."

Étienne held the paper closer to the candle so he could read the words. "I believe it has to do with—Good, God! This talks about an attack on New Orleans! I am from New Orleans. Those bastards are going to try to take Louisiana!"

"That is what it looks like to me," Judah agreed, nodding slightly.

Étienne glanced up, excitement burning in his eyes. "It is imperative that this dispatch reach the proper hands. It could turn the tide of war in our favor."

"Yes, I agree."

"General Andrew Jackson would be the best person to receive this."

"I agree," Judah said, shaking his head. "The trouble is, where do we find him?"

"If you will trust me, I will take you to General Jackson."

Judah stood and propped his booted foot on the chair.

"We hear rumors about Andrew Jackson. Some say he is headed for Louisiana. It pains me to tell you this, but I would not exactly be welcome in Louisiana. I am a wanted man there."

Étienne's eyes clouded with disbelief. "What have you done that this should be?"

"To use an old, worn-out phrase, I was accused falsely." Laughter took the edge off his words. "You may not believe this, but I fell into a trap that was set by a woman."

"I believe that you are innocent," Étienne said earnestly. "Do you want to tell me about it?"

Judah found himself telling Étienne about his trouble, taking care not to mention any names. After he finished, there was silence in the cabin until Étienne stared into Judah's eyes.

"I will put myself at your disposal and help free you of the false charges," Étienne stated with feeling. "I will tell the authorities what you have done today, and they will have to let you go free."

A smile twitched at the corners of Judah's lips. "I am afraid that will not happen, my friend. You see, I have powerful enemies."

"My father is also a power to reckon with. He is a judge in New Orleans. I know he will be grateful to you for saving my life, and will help clear your name."

"I would never ask a friend to put his good name on the line for me, Étienne. I will deal with my enemies in my own way. Nevertheless, I thank you for the offer of help."

"But if you are innocent . . . ?

"I cannot prove my innocence." Judah's eyes lit up and he clapped Étienne on the back. "Do not distress yourself on my account. I will take care of the matter in my own good time. Until then, I am a prisoner of the past."

Étienne saw the dangerous glow that suddenly lit Judah's eyes, but the naked hatred he saw in them was quickly masked by indifference. He wondered at the power of the hate that had driven this man to privateering?

"When will you go back to New Orleans, and try to clear your name, Judah?"

"Soon, I think."

"My family will be giving the annual masquerade ball two months from now? Would that not be a good time for you to return? Everyone who is of any importance in Louisiana will attend. You would never be discovered if you wore a disguise."

Judah was thoughtful for a moment. At last he spoke in a soft voice. "Are you issuing me an invitation?"

"Indeed I am."

"Perhaps it is time I revisited my past. If I come, will you send an invitation to Briar Oaks Plantation?"

"But of course." Étienne smiled. "Since I am from New Orleans, I know Bandera Boudreaux very well. Would she be the one you want to receive the invitation?"

"Yes."

"I have not been home in over three years," Étienne said, "but I still remember how lovely Bandera was."

Judah was in no mood to discuss Bandera. "Come," he said, walking across the room. "Let us see about getting you a ship. If I know my men, and I believe I do, they will be begging you to take the *Royal George* off our hands. It is my estimation that they have all imbibed a dose of patriotism today and are itching to get into this war. When you take over the ship, you can also take the prisoners off my hands."

Étienne's eyes lit up. "The United States Navy could use men like you and your crew. We need all the good men we can muster. Why do you not enlist your services in our cause?"

"Understand me, Étienne, I love my country as much

238

as any man. My father died in her service. But I am not yet ready to expose myself to my enemies. If I help the United States, it will be in my own way . . . and in my own time." Suddenly Judah's turquoise eyes twinkled. "Perhaps the way is through you, and the time is nearer than we think."

Judah was restless as he tossed and turned on the small cot that had been placed in Phillipe's quarters to accommodate him. He was dreaming, and in his dream, a soft hand touched his brow. He reached for the hand and raised it to his lips. Then love washed over him, and he trembled as he heard a woman's voice.

"I will not leave you, Judah. I will stay as long as you need me."

"I love you," he cried out, as he crushed her to him. "I have been in torment since I left you."

"I must go now, Judah. I cannot stay with you any longer."

"But you promised," he said, trying to keep her with him.

"I must go," she said, disappearing.

Judah felt empty inside. He yearned for her return. "I love you, Liberty. I will always love you," he called out, as the sweet scent that she had always used came to him.

Startled by her departure, Judah was jarred awake. As he sat up and glanced around the darkened room, he swore aloud. "Damn! What is the matter with me?" The dreams were becoming more and more frequent. And why did he always call out to Liberty when she was just a child? Why was he never able to find another woman to satisfy his deep yearnings?

As always, guilt settled on him for desiring the sweet, innocent Liberty. She was like a fever in his brain. It was strange and disturbing that, when asleep, he dreamed of

239

Liberty, yet upon waking, he thought only of Bandera. Judah knew he would not sleep the rest of the night, so he quickly dressed and went up on deck. He found Philippe at the helm, and sent him below to his cabin.

Then he stared out over the calm ocean at the big, bright moon that turned the waves a shimmering silver. He was helplessly caught up in an unreal world, hopelessly in love with a dream that had two faces—one, that of a woman who had betrayed him, and the other, that of the sweet child, Liberty.

As Judah looked up at the moon, he could see a shadowy likeness of Bandera's face. "Why?" he said aloud. "Why did you betray me?"

Suddenly Bandera's face faded into a childlike image—Liberty. In the silver splendor of moontide, Judah felt his heart skip a beat. "Liberty, why do you haunt me? You are nothing but a child. Why will you not let me be?"

Chapter Thirteen

Bandera had refused to come downstairs, so Alicia huddled before the fire, trying to ward off the chill she felt in her bones. At times like this, she missed the splendor of Bend of the River, where an army of servants had been available to fulfill her slightest whim. Here at Briar Oaks there were only two house servants, and they were always doing menial tasks instead of tending to her comfort. There was no end to her troubles. Alicia hadn't had a new gown in over a year, and though she had never gone hungry, there was never a feast like those she had enjoyed at Bend of the River. This was a house oppressed by poverty, she thought miserably.

Then, as if she didn't have enough problems, war was practically on their doorstep, and it seemed that her son and Bandera did not have an ideal marriage.

Last evening, because Bandera had been told that there was no money for a new costume for the masquerade ball, she had stormed out of the dining room. No one, not even the servants, had been safe from her verbal onslaught.

Alicia's hand trembled when she handed a steaming cup of tea to Sebastian. "I fear your wife is still having her little tantrum this morning," she said quietly. "We will just have to humor her until she forgets about her disappointment. We cannot afford to offend anyone here, for if we do, Liberty might order us to leave."

Liberty was seated across the room, polishing a pair of silver candlesticks, and Sebastian had been staring at her.

He knew she would be sending the silver ornaments into New Orleans to see if they could be sold. Many of the Boudreaux treasures had gone on the auction block in New Orleans.

Liberty was dressed in pink, and she was so lovely that Sebastian realized he was staring at her. He glanced back at his mother. Remembering Bandera's bad behavior, he slammed his cup down, spilling the hot liquid on the rosewood table. "You humor your daughter-in-law, *Maman*. I am weary of her stalking off to her room every time she does not get her own way." Sebastian raised his voice so Liberty could hear. "Bandera has been spoiled excessively, and is intolerable to live with."

Liberty turned to Sebastian, her eyes spitting fire. "You would do well to remember that Bandera is your responsibility now. Look to yourself for the solution to her tantrums."

Alicia gasped at Liberty's angry statement, but Sebastian only smiled, his eyes raking Liberty's soft curves. "I seem unequal to the task of quelling Bandera's ill humor. Perhaps you could deal with your sister better than I."

Liberty felt a prickle of pity for Sebastian. He had discovered that marriage to Bandera was not all he had dreamed it would be. He must have thought that his uncle would finally give in and allow him and Bandera to move to Bend of the River, but that had not happened. They must be content to live at Briar Oaks until such time as Monsieur Montesquieu relented, though Liberty doubted he ever would. She almost wished Judah's grandfather would ask Sebastian back. She was weary of trying to keep peace between Bandera and Sebastian, and she was equally weary of listening to Alicia's constant complaining.

"I will see if Bandera can be reasoned with," Liberty said, pouring a cup of tea and wrapping a sugar cake in a thick white napkin. She could feel Sebastian's eyes on her as she moved out of the sitting room and into the hallway. She ascended the stairs, knowing he was still staring at her, and when she reached her sister's and Sebastian's bedroom, she rapped softly before pushing the door open.

Even though it was a bleak, damp December day, there was no fire in the fireplace, and there was a chill in the room. Bandera was huddled beneath the covers, shivering.

"It is about time someone came in answer to my summons. I could freeze to death around here and no one would care."

Liberty placed the tea and cake within Bandera's reach, then went to the wood bin. She gathered an armload of logs and placed them on the grate. "If I know you, you have probably frightened poor Oralee away. You could get out of bed and light a fire yourself, Bandera."

Bandera dabbed at her eyes. "How would you feel if you were unable to have a new gown for the masquerade ball."

"The gown I am wearing is one of the your castoffs. I am going as Queen Elizabeth, in your old costume. In case you haven't heard, Bandera, there is a war going on. It would be in the poorest taste to have a new gown at this time."

Bandera took a sip of the tea. "I do not want to hear about that silly old war. And if I have to wear an old gown, I will not attend the masquerade ball. I would be mortified to be seen in a castoff, if I were you."

Liberty fluffed up her sister's pillow and then tucked the covers about her shoulders. "I feel no shame in wearing an old gown, Bandera. You can stay home if you like, but you will be missing all the fun."

"Who is taking you to the ball, Liberty?"

"I will be going with Madame de Boise and her daughter. As a matter-of-fact, I will be staying the night with them, and will not be home until late tomorrow afternoon."

"When I was your age, I wouldn't dream of going to a ball without a gentleman escort. I would have been too humiliated."

"Apparently it takes far more to humiliate me, Bandera. If you get out of bed, I feel sure your husband will be only too happy to escort you to the ball."

Bandera shook her head. "There is no joy in life anymore," she whined. "I find that I do not like being married in the least. I had envisioned it quite differently than it actually is."

"What you envisioned was sitting at the head of the table at Bend of the River. That may never happen."

"It will happen when the old man dies. Sebastian will have his rightful place someday."

"Beware, Bandera, you are beginning to sound like Sebastian's mother."

A pout tugged at Bandera's lower lip. "If you are going to insult me, you can just leave."

Liberty shrugged her shoulders. "Have your way, Bandera. You will be missed at the ball tonight."

"No one understands me since *Maman* died. I have no friends," Bandera cried, dabbing at her eyes.

"At one time I would have given much to be your friend, Bandera . . . but no more. I will always look after you, because our mother would have expected it. That is all you can expect from me, however," Liberty said, as she went to the door and wrenched it open.

"You have become cold-hearted, Liberty. You still blame me for what happened to Judah Slaughter. I have paid for that mistake."

"No, you have not yet paid, Bandera, but you will." Liberty left and closed the door behind her. She heard the teacup shatter against the bedroom wall, and she shook her head. Would Bandera never grow up?

The music was loud and the laughter light-hearted. For the moment everyone seemed to have forgotten that the British were just outside New Orleans. Gaily clad ladies with silk masks moved among velvet-bedecked gentlemen, coyly searching for excitement.

Judah stood beside Étienne Banard, his eyes moving over the crowd, searching for the one person who had haunted his dreams for so long. "Are you sure they will come?" he asked his friend.

"The invitations were sent out. It is doubtful they would ignore this ball. Invitations are coveted by all, but only the elite are invited."

During the three weeks it had taken the *Winged Victory* to reach New Orleans, Étienne and Judah had become good friends. Étienne now knew the complete story of what had happened to Judah since he had left Boston. He knew that Judah was the grandson of Monsieur Gustave Montesquieu, and he had heard, from one of the ladies attending the ball, that Judah's grandfather and mother were still alive. He hesitated to tell his friend that until he was positive it was a fact.

Étienne had also not informed Judah that Bandera had married Sebastian Montesquieu. He realized he would have to tell him now, before Bandera arrived and Judah heard it from the lady herself. Perhaps when Judah knew the truth about Bandera, he would be able to put her out of his mind.

"Judah, I am loath to tell you a bit of news I discovered but this afternoon," Étienne declared.

Judah had been watching the dancers. He glanced back at his friend, dread in his heart. "What is it?" he asked insistently.

"Bandera is married to your cousin, Sebastian. I do not want to speak loosely of a lady's conduct, but I was told

245

by a friend that she is not what one would consider a faithful wife. It is said that she is not selective in her lovers."

To Étienne's surprise, Judah only laughed. "Is that all? I couldn't be more delighted. My cousin will grieve more over losing a wife to me, than he would over a prospective bride."

With relief in his heart, Étienne surveyed Judah, who was dressed in black leather, from his wide shoulders to the toes of his thigh-high boots. A black velvet cape was carelessly thrown over Judah's shoulders, and he wore a black patch over one eye. His black plumed hat was pulled low over his forehead. Étienne smiled, thinking his friend looked very like the dashing privateer he was.

"Do not worry, they will come," Étienne stated, as he adjusted the ruffles on the sleeve of his Louis XIV costume. Then he lowered his voice. "By the way, I have spoken to General Andrew Jackson about your situation. He would like to see you at your earliest convenience. He was more than pleased that you helped us against the British. He found the dispatch very useful. You might like to know that Admiral Sills and his crew are being detained here in New Orleans. I suspect they will be exchanged for some of the our captured officers."

Judah smiled down at his friend. "I'm pleased about the prisoner exchange, but I would be a fool to expose myself to discovery. I am afraid I will have to forgo the pleasure of meeting your Andrew Jackson."

Étienne lowered his voice even more. "I was told to tell you that if you go you will be under Jackson's protection. He has a proposition to offer you."

"If I should decided to see him, where can he be found?"

"I will take you to him. But for now, my friend, let us enjoy the evening. I believe I will do the ladies a favor and circulate among them. I saw a rather interesting prospect dressed as Cleopatra."

Judah moved around the edge of the room, his eyes searching the crowd. Bandera had not yet come. There was no disguise she could wear that could fool him. Halfway around the room, he happened to glance toward the door, and his breath caught in his throat as he watched a woman enter. She was dressed as Queen Elizabeth of England. She had come!

Judah walked toward her like a man possessed. His eyes burned with distrust. The years had eased neither his anger, nor the desire that burned in his body day and night. His sleeping hours had been spent in restless pursuit of an elusive dream. Like a ghost, she had haunted him, making him doubt his sanity.

Judah pulled his hat lower over his forehead, so he wouldn't be recognized, and he broke through the circle of men that already surrounded Bandera. Elbowing an admirer aside, he bowed before her. "I have come to serve the queen," he said, softly in French. "Dare I hope that you will honor me with a dance?"

Liberty felt her heart take wing! She had waited so long for Judah's return; now she could not believe he was actually standing before her. For the moment she was speechless. He held out his hand to her, and like a woman floating on air, she allowed him to lead her to the dance floor, then whirl her around and around in the lively steps of the quadrille.

"Have you missed me?" he breathed next to her ear, as the sweet scent of her dulled his mind.

"Oui," she replied. She could feel the heat of his hand through her red leather gloves. Her body was a trembling mass, and she thought she would faint had he not been holding her up.

"You lie, but then that is expected. Do you know who I am then?"

"Oui, I know who you are."

"You knew I would come back?"

"I never doubted it."

Judah stared at her soft lips. The rest of her face was concealed by a red silken mask, and her red wig was in place; but he remembered so well her midnight-black hair. He felt strangely alive, and his blood flowed hotly in his veins. The meeting had happened just the way we had planned. Now all he had to do was lure Bandera back to his room at the inn and make love to her. Revenge would be so sweet. Judah would see that Sebastian learned he had bedded his wife.

When the last chord of music died away, Judah led her across the floor and into a deserted study. Wordlessly he stared at her. He wanted to savor the moment to make her squirm. If she was frightened, however, she was not showing it.

"How did you know me? Have I not changed?" Liberty asked in a husky voice. She was so happy that Judah had recognized her.

He peeled back her red glove and planted a burning kiss on the inside of the wrist. "The dress, Bandera. You were wearing it the first night I saw you. Have you forgotten?"

Liberty felt her heart plummet. He had once again mistaken her for her sister. She resisted the urge to remove her mask. "Of course," she replied, deciding to play along with him for a time. "How foolish of me to have overlooked that."

He reached out and softly touched her lips. "What else have you forgotten, Bandera?"

"I have not forgotten you."

His voice came out in a hiss as he pulled her into his arms. "You still think to dangle me on a string? It could be dangerous to flirt with me. I am not like your husband or those milksops you call 'gentlemen.' "

Liberty knew she was playing with fire by pretending to

248

A <u>FREE</u> ZEBRA
HISTORICAL
ROMANCE
WORTH

$3.95

be Bandera, but she couldn't seem to help herself. "I am not trying to dangle you, Judah."

"Prove it."

She could feel the heat of his body as he pressed her more tightly to him. "How can I prove it?"

"Come away with me for this one night."

"I . . . that would not . . . be possible."

He shoved her away. "Are you afraid of me after all?"

"No, I have never been afraid of you."

He held out his hand to her. "Then come with me."

She hesitated for only a moment before reaching out and placing her hand in his. "Where shall we go?"

Judah was unsure. Her quick decision had thrown him off balance. He had expected an argument. "We will go to my room at the inn."

"All right."

His laughter was almost sinister. "Somehow I thought you might, Bandera. I did think, however, that it would take longer for you to make up your mind. Have you no doubts as to whether I will bring you back?"

"It does not matter?"

He drew in a deep breath. No, he couldn't allow her to pull him back into her web. He would be the one in control tonight. He had an old score to settle, and she would be the instrument of his revenge. His heart was pounding as he led her toward a side door.

"Wait. My cape," she reminded him.

He unhooded his own cape and fastened it about her neck. "It may be a little long, but you can hold it up." He smiled, as if waiting for her to find another excuse not to leave with him. "This is your last chance to change your mind," he warned.

"I will not change my mind," she assured him.

"I did not see Sebastian. Will he not think it strange that you have disappeared?"

"Sebastian did not attend the ball tonight. I was supposed to stay with a friend, but she and her mother feared the war was coming to New Orleans so they left for the country."

"How convenient for us," he said in a sarcastic voice. The moon was shining brightly as they stepped out into the garden. Judah led her to a waiting coach and gave the driver directions to the inn where he was residing.

Sitting back in the carriage, he pulled Liberty into his arms. She gasped when his lips came down hungrily on hers, stealing her breath and sapping her strength. His hand burned through her gown as it slipped up to softly caress her throbbing breasts. Suddenly breaking off the kiss, he stared at her. "Damn you, Bandera." His voice was thick with passion. "I thought I had forgotten what your lips felt like; it seems I was wrong. But be warned—I will not allow you to make me a slave to your body this time."

Liberty felt tears form in her eyes. Again she was playing a role that had been meant for her sister. She doubted Judah had given her a thought in the days, months, and years he had been away. There was pain in her heart as she tried to pull away. "I do not know what you mean, Judah." She was ready to end this farce, strip off her mask, and admit who she was. "You have never been my slave."

"Like hell," he said, even then needing to touch her. His hand, like a vise, clamped around her arm, and he brought her close to him. "You do not even know the hell you put me through, do you? I would have done anything to please you. After you helped Sebastian betray me, I thought I hated you. I dreamed that you gave yourself to me at Zippora's cabin. I have to know if it was a dream or madness?"

Liberty bit back a sob. "We are both mad, Judah. I am not what you think. I am—"

"Let me finish. "I thought about you, or I think it was

250

you," he said doubtfully. "For many lonely nights I was a prisoner of my dreams. That night in Zippora's cabin, you pulled me so tightly into your web that I can never escape. I cannot stop dreaming about that night. You are a fever in my brain, and I have lived for the day I could face you again. But I never thought you would be in command of the situation."

"Judah, I do not—"

"I was going to use you tonight, do you know that?"

"I began to suspect that was your intention."

"And still you came?"

"Oui."

This was not Bandera the betrayer . . . this was the sweet lover that had haunted his dreams. How could he hurt her? "Perhaps this was not such a good idea. Say the word, and I will immediately take you back to the ball."

"I want to be with you, Judah. But I think you should know—"

"I know you are married to Sebastian. Do you think that matters to me?"

"Judah, will you listen to me. Sebastian is not—"

He pulled her forward, his lips depriving her of speech. Liberty knew she was letting herself in for more heartbreak, but she wanted to be with Judah—just for tonight. If she told him the truth, he would surely take her back to the ball. When they reached the privacy of his room, she would tell him that she was not Bandera.

"There was a time when you had me where you wanted me," he said against her lips. "You know I have to destroy Sebastian, don't you?"

"Oui, I know."

He laughed softly. "You haven't changed. What a coldhearted wench you are. I'd bet you would even help me place the noose about his neck, wouldn't you?"

"I have no liking for Sebastian."

By now the coach had pulled up to the inn, and Judah

helped her alight. Liberty was glad she wore a mask, because of the knowing glances cast their way by the men and women in the public room. Nonetheless, she allowed Judah to lead her up the rickety stairs.

"Does it not bother you, what they are thinking?" Judah asked.

"It bothers me," she answered, staring straight ahead.

"One would think you were new at this sort of entertainment. I happen to know better." Again his voice was cold and accusing.

Liberty bore the insult in silence, and when they reached the top of the stairs, he whisked her into one of the rooms.

Liberty glanced around her, realizing they were quite alone. One candle burned low in a pewter sconce, casting shadows about the small room. Wine and two crystal glasses sat on the low mahogany table. Upon seeing them, Liberty knew that Judah had expected Bandera to come with him. She watched him remove the eye patch and his plumed hat and toss them aside.

"How easily you walked into my little trap, Bandera. Did you believe the lies I told you so I could lure you here?"

"*Oui,* I believed you. You don't think I'm in the habit of going to a gentleman's rooms, do you?"

He stepped closer, glaring at her, trying to see her face behind the red silk mask. "Your habits are reprehensible, even to me, Bandera. I know you find married life with my cousin less than fulfilling, and it is reported to me that you are not discriminating when you are looking for a lover. Rumor has it that you would as soon bed a common fisherman as one of your French blue bloods."

Liberty was glad that she was wearing her mask for it hid the blush that stained her cheeks. She knew about her sister's indiscretions, but she didn't like to hear about them from Judah. She decided it was time she ended this farce. Reaching up to remove her mask, she was startled when Judah stepped forward and trapped her hand in a viselike grip.

"No, leave it on. I don't want to look into your lying eyes while I make love to you. It is better if you wear the mask of deceit — it fits you very well. Later, I will remove the mask so I can look upon the face of betrayal."

"Judah, I —"

"Do not speak my name," he said, reaching up to unlace the bodice of her gown. He had already had numerous glasses of wine and his mind was muddled. Still, he sensed that something wasn't right. He kept seeing soft blue eyes filled with trust and compassion. Little Liberty was again weaving herself into his conscsciousness. He tried to push her aside. He wanted to hate the whole Boudreaux family. After all, Liberty had the same blood in her veins as her beautiful sister who played with men's hearts as if they were toys.

Liberty had dreamed of Judah's return. She had imagined that he would know her immediately and would realize he loved her. That fantasy had been shattered by cruel reality. Even if Judah knew her true identity, he was so obsessed with her sister that he would turn from her in disgust. But she had never, in her wildest imaginings, dreamed that he would look at her with such loathing.

"Now you will pay for your faithlessness and betrayal, Bandera," Judah hissed between clenched teeth. "How long I have dreamed of having you in my power, you scheming bitch!"

Liberty backed away from him, while fear pounded in her brain. "Judah, I am not Bandera. You know me . . . I am —"

His laughter was deep and sinister, causing the hair on the back of her neck to stand on end. "I told you that you took me for a fool once, Bandera; do not expect me to play the fool twice."

Liberty stepped back, coming up against the bed. "Judah, listen to me—please do not do this. You will only regret it later."

He drew closer. "I do not think so, Bandera. I will be taking my pleasure and striking out at Sebastian at the same time." He pushed her gown off her shoulders. "Do you think Sebastian will be in anguish when he finds out I have had his wife?"

Liberty knew she could stop Judah by just removing her mask. Why did she hesitate? His eyes were filled with burning passion. He might deny it, but he wanted her. She had seen his hand tremble when he touched her. Liberty stood like a statue while he pushed her gown past her waist. She saw the raw need in his eyes as he hastily untied ribbons, and did away with stays and undergarments.

Tears rolled down Liberty's cheeks. She now stood before him, naked and utterly defenseless. The only things between her and complete humiliation were a red silk mask and an equally red wig. Glancing into his eyes, her eyes begged for pity, but of course he could not see them. He reached for a wineglass and filled it with sparkling liquid.

"Here," he said, advancing toward her and holding out the glass. "Fortify yourself for what lies ahead, because I intend to use all the strength you have."

For the first time Judah allowed himself to look at her and his breath caught in his throat. She was even lovelier than he had thought. Her firm young breasts, with their dusky tips, were just made for a man's hand to caress. Her skin was like white velvet, her waist tiny, her hips rounded. A deep ache started in his groin as his eyes traveled across her flat stomach to the mat of golden hair nestled between her legs.

In the back of his mind a warning bell sounded. Something was not right here. Was it that she was not acting the part of a wanton? She was almost shy with him. Pouring himself a glass of wine, he raised it to her. "To a night of . . . desire, if not . . . love."

Judah was jolted when he saw a tear escape from beneath her mask. But he set his glass aside, determined not to weaken. He had Bandera just where he wanted her. "I know what your problem is," he stated in a shaky voice. "I have too many clothes on. He quickly removed his shirt and tossed it aside. Unfastening his britches, he smiled when she turned her head away. "You play your part to the hilt, Bandera. Go ahead, play the coy maiden if it pleases you."

"Judah, do not do this, I implore you." Her hand went out to him, but he ignored it and bent to remove his boots.

"I will not force myself on you, if that is what you fear, Bandera. No, I will not have to resort to that."

"Judah—" Liberty's eyes moved to his body, and she was stunned by his masculine beauty. Blond hair curled around the nape of his neck, and it sprung forth from his sun-bronzed chest. His waist was narrow, his hips and legs were well muscled. Hungrily, her eyes devoured his body. She was grateful that he could not see her eyes.

"No more talk," he said, bending to blow out the candle.

For a moment, until Liberty's eyes became accustomed to the darkness, she could see nothing. Then a hand came out of the darkness, and she was pulled against a hard, muscular body.

"Now, isn't this better," he breathed against her cheek. "Let me rid you of your wig and mask, Bandera. I want you to be completely undressed."

Liberty felt that a knife was plunged into her heart every time he called her Bandera. Would he use her body again, pretending she was her sister? His hot lips brushed against her mouth, and she stiffened. With gentle pres-

255

sure, he probed her lips apart, and his tongue darted inside. Wild sensations beat like drums in her ears. Then his hands circled her waist, and he brought her body to mesh with his.

His breathing was heavy, and he muttered in her ear. "You were made for a man's pleasure. I have never seen a body as desirable as yours. Please give yourself to me. Let me enter paradise just once more."

Liberty sensed that his whole attitude had changed again. He was so filled with love and hate for her sister that he didn't know which part to play. He was no longer the arrogant suitor. He was pleading with her. Was this another of his tricks? If it was, it was working. She pressed her hips more tightly against him, and a gasp escaped her as his swollen spear throbbed against her.

Judah kissed her slowly, pleasurably igniting a fire within the two of them that could only be extinguished by the joining of their bodies.

"I like the way your body answers mine," he whispered, picking her up in his arms and placing her on the bed. Even though it was dark in the room, he could imagine her golden hair spread across the pillow . . . No! he thought, his mind in a turmoil. Not golden hair—Bandera's hair is black. Why did his mind always play tricks on him?

The bed sagged as he joined her. He was hesitant, until she touched his face. Judah closed his eyes, reveling in the softness of her hand. Like a man who had found an island after being lost at sea, he gravitated toward her warmth. Rolling her beneath him, he knew he had completely lost control of the situation. He hungered for her like he had never hungered after a woman before. He cursed himself for drinking the wine, thinking he should have known he would need a clear head.

Suddenly Liberty panicked. Judah would take all she had to give, while thinking she was another woman. He would leave her with nothing, not even her self-respect. With a strangled cry, she tried to move from under him.

"Easy, little one," he said, in a gentle voice. "I would never hurt you."

Liberty stopped her thrashing. Did Judah realize he had called her little one—the name only he and Zippora had used for her. Liberty would have cried out, but he smothered her cry with his mouth. Lost . . . she was lost. Every time he touched her, she melted more into the mattress. Each time his lips took hers, she moaned passionately. His mouth moved down the satiny smoothness of her throat, until he found the valley between her breasts. He planted tiny kisses on each dusky tip, making her body tremble with want and need.

The curly hair on his chest tickled and tantalized her breasts when he clasped her to him. Hot flesh fused to hot flesh. Judah felt a pounding in his head, and he realized it was the beating of his heart. Her nearness was driving him to the brink of madness. He was wild to bury himself deeply inside her once more.

Judah was not gentle as he drove his aching, throbbing shaft into the softness of her body and shuddered with glorious pulsating feelings. This was what he had ached for. This was what his body craved.

The hot invasion into her inner core came unexpectedly, and Liberty bit her lips to keep from crying out. At first Judah did not move, but was content to merely hold her in place. The only sounds were a boat whistle from the Mississippi and the heavy breathing of the two people in the room.

Liberty could feel him imbedded inside her; it was as if she had taken him into herself and he had become a part of her body. Her fingers tightened against his arm as he moved ever so slightly, bringing a moan from him.

"This time it is no dream. It is so right, between us, little one." His shuddering breath teased her ear. "You are

257

right for me. I want no one but you."

Liberty felt delight rush through her body. *Oui,* she thought in a haze of pleasure, it *was* so right between them. Judah was not even aware of it, but he had called out to her, not Bandera.

"I have dreamed of you so often," he whispered, his forward thrusts still slow and easy. "In fact there was not a night I didn't dream of you."

His words penetrated her consciousness. "Why?" she needed to know.

"Damned if I know. I believe, that night in old Zippora's cabin, you put a spell on me. Since then I have wanted no one but you."

"I do not understand," she said, stilling his motion by placing her hand on his hip.

A burning ache seared his body, and he wanted to plunge even deeper into her. "I do not understand myself. How could you betray me at one moment, and give me such pleasure in the next? I have given up trying to reason it out."

Liberty was too confused to try to untangle the web of lies that bound her and Judah together. The only thing that mattered at the moment, was that he wanted her. Her hand slid up his back, and she moved her hips just a fraction. He laughed in her ear, and thrust forward until deeply buried in her body. They made love with wild abandonment, conscious only of each other.

Liberty heard Judah call out in a passionate voice. "Little one, little one, you take my breath away." She wasn't at all sure he knew whose body he plundered. Surely he had never called anyone but her by that name.

Amid burning, passionate lovemaking, Liberty and Judah found the paradise that they had once created for themselves, in a small cabin in the swamps. Again and again, he took her body throughout the night—neither wanted to sleep—until at last they lay exhausted in each other's arms.

"I will never forget this night," he said, pulling her head to rest against his chest. She could hear the thundering of his heart, and she curled up contentedly. "Do you love me?" she asked drowsily.

"Love?" he smiled against her cheek. "I do not know what that word means, but I desire you, and that is a far longer-lasting emotion than love."

All emotion had been drained out of him, and he yawned. "So sleepy," he murmured. "I have been tormented for so long . . . now I can sleep."

Liberty felt his grip loosen on her hand, and she knew he had fallen asleep. After waiting a few moments, she carefully eased off the bed. As she dressed, she feared Judah would awaken. She quickly replaced her mask and put on the wig; then she picked up Judah's cape and pulled it about her shoulders. Silently she crossed to the door.

Once out of Judah's room, she breathed a sigh of relief. When she reached the public room, she took money out of her drawstring bag and pressed it into the landlord's hand, asking him to find her a conveyance to take her to the waterfront.

Liberty thought the passenger boat would never arrive at Briar Oaks. It was almost sunup when she stepped ashore. As soon as the passenger boat was out of sight, she climbed into her own small boat and paddled toward the swamps.

In the half-darkness, hopelessness weighed heavily on Liberty's small shoulders. She had to see Zippora. Perhaps her friend would help her understand why she had given herself to Judah again tonight.

Chapter Fourteen

Judah awoke with the lingering scent of some haunting fragrance filling his senses and invoking bittersweet memories. Reaching out his hand in search of the soft warm body that had brought him so much delight, he found he was in bed alone. A quick glance about the room told him that she had gone.

Throwing the covers aside, Judah felt a great sense of loss. Had last night been just another dream? His eyes caught sight of something in the fold of the covers, and he picked up the red ribbon that had been torn from her gown. No, last night had not been a dream. Today Judah's body felt revived, and his spirits soared. Somewhere in the back of his mind he experienced a certain distaste in knowing that someone like Bandera should be the one woman who made him feel so alive, yet he now realized he could never use her to hurt Sebastian. He would have to find another way to get at his cousin.

Judah tried to push the preceding night to the back of his mind because he had important matters to attend to. He would ask Étienne to take him to the headquarters of Andrew Jackson in the afternoon. His country was at war, and he had decided to aid her defense. His vendetta with Sebastian would have to wait. There was a great possibility that he might be recognized and arrested, but that was a chance he would have to take.

Étienne instructed the driver of the carriage to take them to 106 Royal Street. It was a crisp, cold morning, and Judah could feel the tension in the air. This was not the New Orleans he remembered. Absent was the sound of children's laughter, and no servants plodded the streets, shopping for their masters' tables. Even the birds seemed silent. Judah fastened the brass button on his green velvet cutaway, as he smiled at his friend.

"What news of the war, Étienne?"

Étienne, looking every bit the dashing young naval officer, glanced speculatively toward the east. "The situation looks very grave, Judah. General Jackson received word today that the British fleet are in a position that suggests they will soon be landing."

"How near are they?"

"Within nine miles of striking distance."

The buggy came to a halt, so the two men stepped down. Étienne hastily shook Judah's hand and then climbed back into the buggy. "I will not be coming in with you. General Jackson has asked to see you alone."

After Étienne disappeared, Judah turned to the door, where a sentry stood at attention. The man obviously had been told to expect Judah, because he opened the door and stepped aside, allowing him admittance to the house.

The only occupant of the room Judah entered was one of Jackson's Tennessee Regulars. He was dressed in rough buckskin, his hat pulled down over his eyes, and the man appeared to be asleep, but Judah had the feeling that he was alert to everything that was going on around him and would come to full attention if the situation called for it.

Suddenly the door opened, and a man entered who could be none other than Andrew Jackson himself. His rough-hewn face was accented by a thick crop of white hair. His legs were long and gangly, his body lean and wiry. Bushy eyebrows sagged over his blue eyes in which there was a troubled look. For a moment he silently studied Judah with an intense stare. Then a slight smile curved his generous mouth. "I once met your father. I was trying to see if you resemble him . . . and you do."

"So my mother used to tell me, sir. I never knew my father."

Jackson waved Judah into a chair and then seated himself behind the desk. "Yes, that is a tragedy. I understand your father was set upon by the Barbary pirates, and still managed to save his ship before he died."

"Yes, sir."

"That is a matter I wish to talk to you about at a later date. For now, I am told you might be willing to help your country in her hour of need."

"I would gladly do anything I can, sir. But I believe you are already aware that I am considered a fugitive from justice here in New Orleans."

"Étienne filled me in on your problem." Jackson laced his long fingers together, his eyes looking deep into Judah's. "Étienne believes in your innocence, and I trust his judgment, so I am willing to offer you a deal. Are you interested?"

Judah could see the dark circles under Jackson's eyes, and he knew this man now had the weight of the war on his shoulders. "Will your proposition also include my men, sir?"

"Yes, that's understood. Do you want to hear my proposal?"

"I would be very interested, sir."

"I will make you the same offer I made to Jean Lafitte. If you and your men will help me defend this city, I will see that you get a full pardon for any past misdeeds."

Judah was thoughtful for a moment. "That is a very tempting offer, sir. Are you sure I should be pardoned?"

263

"Yes, I believe so. I will never be convinced that the son of Daniel Slaughter could have committed a very serious infraction."

Judah looked into humorous blue eyes. "I fear I committed the serious infraction of being a fool. I allowed a woman to become too important to me. I should have been on guard, but her beauty blinded me."

Jackson chuckled. "Ah, yes the fair sex. I notice you do not proclaim your innocence."

"Would you believe me if I told you I had been falsely accused?"

Again Jackson looked into his eyes. "Yes, I believe I would. But as I told you, Étienne believes you innocent, and that is good enough for me."

Judah noticed that the man who had been dozing in the corner stood up and quietly ambled out of the room. Jackson nodded in the man's direction. "Since arriving in this city, I have been amazed at the men who have volunteered to fight. I have French blue bloods, Spanish noblemen, free blacks, and even Indians. I am proud to have them all, but give me two hundred Tennesseans like that one, and I'll whip the tail off the British."

"Sir, I stand ready to help you in any way I can. I put my ship, my men, and my life at your disposal. You have only to tell me what to do."

The commander smiled. "I'll take your men and your ship, but I want you to keep your life. Report to Étienne, and he will tell you what to do."

Judah was tall, but when he stood up, he came eye to eye with Andrew Jackson. For a moment Jackson's face whitened and he clutched at his heart.

"Sir, are you ill? Can I help," Judah asked with concern.

Jackson waved him aside. "It is nothing. Few people know this, but I have three bullets in me that could not be removed. Sometimes they cause me pain. For the most part I try to ignore them. Sometimes I cannot."

Judah helped Jackson into a chair and poured him a glass of water from the pitcher on the desk. "Why cannot the bullets be removed, sir?"

Jackson took a sip of water, and some of the color returned to his cheeks. "One of them is too near my heart. But you did not come here today to talk about my health. I have been forced to place New Orleans under martial law. That gives me the authority to free you of all charges lodged against you. Of course, you will want to clear your name later on. I assume you can do that?"

"Yes, sir, I believe so."

"Fine." He reached for paper and quill and began to write. When he had finished, he pushed the document at Judah. "Your paper to freedom! No one will question this. For the time being you will consider yourself an unofficial officer in the United States Navy, Captain Slaughter."

"Thank you, sir. I am proud to serve you."

"Good, good. But you do not serve me, son. Like your father before you, you serve your country." Already the general's attention was turning to the maps that were laid out on his desk. Judah realized that he was in the presence of a great man, and he had very little doubt that this man could easily defeat America's enemies.

Liberty stood on the banks of the river, caught up in the beauty of the night. The moon cast a silvery path across the Mississippi, disguising its usual mud color. Beneath the clear sky, the temperature had dropped, and there was a bone-chilling iciness in the air. She was just returning from the slave quarters, where she had tended a child with the croup, and she could not resist the beauty of her river. She had been trying to keep busy so she wouldn't think too much about the night she had spent with Judah Slaughter. She wasn't very proud of the fact that Judah had so easily lured her into his bed.

She sighed, wondering where Judah was at that moment. She had told no one but Zippora that Judah had returned, and she wondered what Sebastian and Bandera would do if they learned he was back.

Liberty gazed toward the house. Lights streamed out of the drawing-room windows, and she knew the family would be gathered about the huge fireplace, waiting for dinner to be served. She was not in the mood to listen to Sebastian's mother complain about being forced to live on the charity of others, nor to Bandera bemoaning the fact that there was no money for a new gown, while Sebastian sipped brandy and made suggestive innuendoes and inane remarks. Liberty decided that if she went to the back of the house, she could slip upstairs and not have to face any of them tonight.

She shouldered her heavy medicine bag, but her footsteps lagged. She was weary because everything was falling on her shoulders, and she had no help from Sebastian. His favorite remark was that a gentleman did not dirty his hands with menial labor.

Since it was winter, the fields lay waiting for spring planting. Still, there was plenty of work to keep her busy. There were hogs to be slaughtered, meat to be cured, food to be preserved and dried. She was nurse, confessor, and peacemaker for everyone on Briar Oaks. She had to see that all were properly clothed and had plenty to eat. There had been a time when her mother had filled the role of mistress at Briar Oaks. Now that, too, fell to Liberty.

When Liberty entered the bright, cheery kitchen, Oralee met her with a stern look on her face. "Have I not warned you not to stay out in the damp night air, *ma petite?* You will become ill, and then where would the rest of us be?"

Liberty smiled at Oralee, her only friend in an otherwise hostile environment. She knew this servant was the only one who really cared about what happened to her. Handing Oralee her medicine bag, Liberty removed her damp cape and hung it on a peg.

"It looks like Matty's daughter has a bad case of the croup, Oralee. After I put her head over steaming water and gave her honey and vinegar, she seemed to calm down."

"I have a tub of hot water waiting for you in your bedroom . . . or it was hot, probably cold by now," Oralee stated, taking Liberty by the shoulders and pointing her toward the back stairs. "You have time for a quick bath before dinner is served."

Obediently Liberty climbed the stairs, wishing she did not have to come back down to dine with the family.

Liberty was preoccupied at dinner and hardly noticed the usual bickering that took place around the table, until Bandera spoke directly to her.

"Liberty did you hear me?"

"I . . . no, my mind was wandering, Bandera. What did you say?"

"I was telling you how demeaning it was today when the Dulongs called at tea time and I had only that old china tea set. You are stripping this house to the bone, selling off all that is valuable. Our neighbors are very aware that we are paupers. I will never be able to hold my head up if you do not stop selling off everything."

"I am not so worried about you holding your head up as I am about feeding you, Bandera. You would be hard pressed to hold your head up if you were starving. I am forced to sell everything but the bare necessities so that will not be the case."

"I think it is a disgrace," Alicia expressed her view, and

in a rare moment agreed with her daughter-in-law. "I have never before been forced to redo one of my old gowns so I could have something suitable to wear. Poor Sebastian's shirts are frayed, and he hasn't had a new coat in months."

Liberty wished herself anywhere but where she was. She doubted that the three of them understood how desperate their situation had become. If she didn't have money for this year's crops, they would all have to find another place to live, because the moneylenders would own Briar Oaks. "I have nothing to spare on clothing. All the money we have must be used for seed and a new plow."

"Not all," Alicia said, smiling. "last week I found where you keep the household money in your desk, and I gave it to Sebastian. He had more need of it than the rest of us. A gentleman should never be without money."

Bandera quickly glanced at her husband. "It isn't fair that you had money while I am forced to wear these old rags, Sebastian. It wasn't your money."

Liberty felt her calm slipping. "How much of the money did you take, Alicia?"

"Well . . . all of it, but there wasn't that much."

Liberty was angry, knowing that was all the money she had to buy the seed and tools necessary for the spring crops. She stood up slowly, holding her hand out to Sebastian. "Give me the money."

He smiled and leaned back in his chair, poking his hands in his pockets. "I no longer have it."

"Where is it?"

"I made a bad wager and lost it all," he said flippantly.

Liberty sank down onto her chair, feeling desperate and alone. "You don't realize what you have done, Sebastian. That was all the money I had."

He shrugged his shoulders. "I have every confidence you will find some other treasure to sell."

"It isn't fair, Liberty," Bandera stated angrily. "Sebastian had no right to the money. Why didn't you give it to me?"

Liberty stood up and left the room. She had to get away before she said something she would regret. She could feel Briar Oaks slipping away from her. There seemed no way to hold on to it now.

She left the house and quickly made her way toward the river. What was she going to do? That money had been her last hope of saving her father's home. She made her way to the pier and walked out on the wooden planks to the very end. Her mind was troubled as she spoke aloud. "I am sorry, Papa. I have done everything I can to save Briar Oaks, but I fear it was not enough."

Liberty was startled by the sound of footsteps on the wooden pier. She turned around, expecting to see Sebastian, but her heart skipped a beat. Even though it was dark, she recognized Judah's long stride. No one walked the way he did, as if he were on the rolling deck of a ship. She felt cornered, and wondered if he had learned of her deception and had come to confront her. There was nowhere to run because he blocked her only escape. All she could do was wait for him to approach.

Judah had just ridden up to the house when he saw a woman running toward the river. From the distance, he thought it was Bandera, and he blessed his good fortune in finding her alone. He had come here tonight ready to face Sebastian but had been secretly hoping to see Bandera alone.

As he neared, her face was in shadow, but he smelled the familiar sweet scent that he had begun to associate with her since that night in Zippora's cabin. "I was surprised to find you living at Briar Oaks, Bandera. I thought you and Sebastian would be well settled in Bend of the River by now."

"You have me confused with someone else," Liberty

answered, knowing she would never again pretend to be her sister. "I am not Bandera."

Judah reached out and tilted her face up to the moonlight. When his eyes moved over the beautiful, unfamiliar features, he dropped his hand and stepped back. "I am sorry. Please forgive me, *Mademoiselle*. It was my mistake. Forgive the intrusion—I will leave now." Yet he was reluctant to go, because there was something familiar about this startlingly beautiful woman. His eyes fastened on her features, and he shook his head in confusion.

"Do I know you?" Even in the half-darkness, he could tell she was the loveliest creature he had ever seen.

"You once did, Monsieur Slaughter. I do not believe you know me at all now."

"Are you someone I met at a party or a ball?"

Liberty felt pain in her heart. He had forgotten all about her, while there had not been a day that she did not think of him. *"Oui.* I first met you at a ball."

"I see," he said in a puzzled voice. "You must be one of Bandera's friends. I am sorry, but I do not recall your name."

Liberty turned her back to him and stared out on the river. It hurt to know that Judah looked at her with the eyes of a stranger. Were the gods angry with her that they tormented her so? "I am no one of importance, *Monsieur.* You do not know me very well."

At that moment Oralee's voice could be heard, calling from the path that led to the house. "Liberty, I know you are out here. I have brought your cloak. I have told you and told you that this night air will be the death of you."

"Good night, *Monsieur,"* Liberty said as she turned to step around Judah. "I am just coming in, Oralee. I won't be needing the cloak."

By now Oralee was at the pier and could see that a gentleman was with Liberty. "Do you want me to wait for you, *ma, petite?"* she asked.

Judah stared at Liberty in disbelief. No, this woman could not be his little one. Liberty was just a child. What cruel game was this?

As Liberty moved toward Oralee, Judah rushed after her, too bemused to speak. When Liberty took the cape and pulled it around her shoulders, she spoke to him. "You see, we did first meet at a ball if you will remember, *Monsieur.*"

Oralee walked away, shaking her head and mumbling about how some people didn't have sense enough to come in out of the cold.

"Liberty," Judah said, finally finding his voice, "you were not supposed to grow up." He searched for the freckle-faced little girl in this lovely vision. "This isn't fair," he said, too stunned to comprehend the nagging feeling that haunted him.

"Many things are not fair, Judah. You should know that by now."

"I . . . how are you?" he stammered like a schoolboy.

"I have been better, but no matter. Should you be here? Are you not afraid the authorities will find you?"

"I have been cleared of all charges," he said, still in a quandary. "Are you cold?" he asked, as she shivered. He stepped closer to Liberty, but stopped short of touching her.

"No, I am not cold. What do you mean, Judah? Are you no longer a hunted man?"

"Thanks to Andrew Jackson, who believed in my innocence, I am no longer a fugitive."

"I do not understand."

"It is not important. I want to hear all about you. What have you been doing? Are your mother and father well? How is Zippora?"

"Zippora is well." She took a deep swallow. "My mother and father are . . . no longer living. I received word of their deaths the day you left New Orleans."

He reached out and rested a hand on her shoulder. "Poor little one. I am grieved by your sorrow. It seems we have both lost our families."

She drew back and his hand fell away. "What do you mean we have both lost our families? I know your father is dead, but surely you know . . . you must have been told that . . . have you not heard about your mother and grandfather?"

"Yes, and there is not a day that goes by that I do not curse Sebastian for their deaths."

Liberty frantically reached for Judah. "No, you do not understand, Judah. Your mother and grandfather are not dead! They have been frantic for some word of you; they feared *you* were dead."

"What are you saying?" he asked brokenly, trying to deal with his rampaging emotions. He dared not hope that he had heard her correctly.

"Judah, your mother and grandfather are alive. Do you hear me? They are alive!"

He glanced up at the moon, trying to deal with all that had hit him in the last few moments. "You would not say it if it weren't true, would you, Liberty?"

"I can assure you I would not, Judah. You must go to them at once so they will know that you are unharmed. Your mother has been beside herself because they received no word . . . but of course you wouldn't have written them if you thought they were dead."

"I don't understand any of this. I thought they were burned in the fire."

"Moses saved them and took them into New Orleans. Your grandfather needed a doctor, and he thought that would be the best thing to do. It wasn't until weeks later that your grandfather let anyone know that he and your mother survived the fire."

Judah felt joy rush through him. "I can hardly credit what you have told me, Liberty. I believe God has given

272

me another chance at life. It is like a miracle."

Liberty felt tears in her eyes as Judah's happiness touched her heart. "I believe in miracles, Judah. In fact, I hope God has a few miracles in store for me."

"What do you mean?"

"Nothing. You do not have time to stand here talking with me. Go to your mother."

Judah reached for her hand. "So I shall, little one. But I will be back tomorrow. I have some unfinished business here. I am beginning to suspect that . . . but never mind. We will talk tomorrow."

Liberty wondered what Sebastian's reaction would be when he heard that Judah had returned. She didn't know why Judah was now allowed to walk around a free man, but she felt happiness for him. "*Oui*, I know you have unfinished business here. I always knew you would come back. I just did not know when."

He took her hand and briefly held it to his lips before releasing it. "Until tomorrow, little one."

"Until tomorrow," she said, as she watched him turn away to be swallowed up by the darkness.

Liberty brushed the tears away, knowing she would always love Judah but also knowing that most of Judah's unfinished business concerned Bandera. If he loved her sister in the same burning way Liberty loved him, then she pitied him. Bandera would never live up to the picture of her he had created in his mind. Judah knew Bandera had betrayed him, and still he wanted her.

Liberty now felt the chill of the night and hurried toward the house. The tally books needed her attention. She had no time for self-pity. Her heart felt bruised and bleeding, but she was a survivor.

Judah mounted his horse and rode in the direction of Bend of the River. His mind was in a whirl. Too many things had happened at once. His mother was alive! Judah had grieved for her, *death*, and now he would be able to see her!

What strange little quirks a man's life took, he thought. His eyes had been opened in many ways in the past few moments. He had been unable to see Liberty very clearly tonight, but his heart had known her. He remembered the scent she wore and closed his eyes. He had been such a fool in thinking the woman he wanted was Bandera. A part of him had known all along what his heart was trying to tell him. Bandera had never come to him in Zippora's cabin—it had been Liberty! That was why visions of Liberty always pushed Bandera to the back of his mind. Tomorrow he would come back to Briar Oaks and confirm what he already knew. Why had it taken so long to realize that Liberty was, and always had been, his heart's desire?

Gabrielle and her father were sitting before the big fireplace in quiet companionship. Gustave was covered with a woolen shawl, and would often nod off. Gabrielle was working on a tapestry to replace the one that had been destroyed by the fire.

The house no longer bore the scars left by the fire. Gustave had put his daughter in charge of restoring it to its former glory.

Not a day had gone by that Gabrielle did not wait for some word from her son, but it was as if the earth had swallowed him up without leaving a trace.

Gustave had used his influence in trying to locate Judah. He had engaged a man to go to Boston, but there had been no word of Judah there either. In desperation, Gabrielle had even put her pride aside and had written to Judah's mistress, Adriane Pierce. The response from Adriane had said only that she shared Gabrielle's concern for Judah's disappearance.

Gabrielle glanced at her father and saw he was dozing.

She smiled, thinking how he had come to depend on her. She had never understood him until now. It had come as a shock to her when she had learned that her father had always had a man in Boston looking after her and Judah. It was her father who had arranged for the bank loan so Judah would have the money to get the *Winged Victory* out of dry dock. Gustave had followed his grandson's life and had been proud of the man Judah had become.

Sebastian was still a source of irritation for Gustave. Both Gabrielle and her father realized the treachery that had been practiced the night Judah had disappeared. It was through Liberty that they had learned the whole story about what had happened that night. Gustave lived for the day his grandson would return, and together they would clear his good name.

Gabrielle pricked her finger with the needle and dropped the tapestry in her lap. She glanced up at the mantel clock and watched the minutes tick away. This house, and everyone in it, was waiting for Judah to return. She and her father never entertained or received guests. The only person they ever saw was Liberty, and she was always welcome, though she was not often able to get away from the demands of Briar Oaks.

Gabrielle had just closed her eyes, thinking she should summon Moses and have him take her father up to bed, when she heard someone rapping at the front door. She stirred, wondering who would be calling at this hour, and knowing, whoever it was, the caller would be turned away on her father's instructions. Again she closed her eyes and tried not to think about how lonely she was. She almost wished the caller would be allowed to come in and visit.

No sound alerted Gabrielle that someone was in the room with them. A feeling did. She opened her eyes and thought she must be hallucinating. "Dear God," she cried, holding out her trembling hand. "Judah, is that you?"

He bent down and gathered his mother in his arms,

275

thanking God that she was alive. "Yes, Mother, it is very definitely me."

"My son, my son,' she cried, burying her face against his shoulder. "You are alive! You have come back to us."

"Huh . . . huh? What's going on, Gabrielle?" her father questioned, trying to gather his thoughts. His eyes focused on his grandson, and he reached forward, his eyes sparkling with happiness. "The lord, be praised," he whispered. "Our boy has come home at last, Gabrielle."

Judah took his grandfather's hand in a strong grasp. "I am even glad to see you, Grandfather. Having thought you dead, I am delighted to see you are still in command."

"I can hold my own with you, if that is what you are worried about, you young pup," the old man said, a genuine smile smoothing the wrinkles about his mouth.

Judah laughed down at his mother. "I don't doubt it, sir. You could hold your own with the devil himself." There was a new respect in Judah's tone as he spoke to his grandfather.

The old man's eyes sparkled with new life and he called out to Moses. "Bring the brandy so we can celebrate. The prodigal son has returned, and I want to kill the fatted calf."

Liberty sat at her father's desk, trying to keep warm. The room was so cold, she gathered up the ledgers and moved to the big red leather chair in front of the fireplace. She could somehow feel her father's presence, and she wished he was there to advise her.

I really have my life in an tangle, Papa, she thought, looking up at the portrait of him she had moved from the library into the study. "I don't see how I can save Briar Oaks, and there are so many people depending on me. Judah is home, and there will be trouble from that direction. I don't know how this will all end with him and Sebastian, Papa. And there is a war on our doorstep. Life is so uncertain. I do so wish you were here. You would know what to do."

The door opened a crack, and Sebastian stuck his head in. "Can I talk to you for a moment, Liberty?"

Liberty was still angry with Sebastian for taking the only money they had and squandering it frivolously. She drew in a breath and then spoke. "It is getting late, but I have a few moments before I go upstairs."

He ambled in, his hands in his pockets, and stood next to the fire. "I have been meaning to speak to you for some time on an important matter. I suppose now is as good a time as any."

As always, Sebastian was looking at her in a most disturbing manner, his eyes often straying down her neck to her breasts. She closed the ledger with a snap, and motioned for him to sit across from her, because she didn't like to have to look up at him. "As I said, I have a few moments."

He cleared his throat, but remained standing. "I think you know by now that one puny little girl cannot save Briar Oaks. You must have realized that it is just a matter of months before it goes on the auction block."

Her ire was tapped. "I know no such thing, Sebastian. If you are worried about losing a place to lay your head, you needn't be concerned. I will keep this roof over you as long as I am able."

He smiled indulgently. "I have a proposal that I believe will help us all. I know a gentleman who is willing to buy Briar Oaks at a reasonable price. We could take the money from the sale and live comfortably in New Orleans for years to come."

Liberty hadn't known it was possible to detest Sebastian more than she already did, but it was. "What do you mean, *we,* Sebastian?"

"We are a family. Naturally, we will all want to stay together."

Liberty stood up and clutched the ledger, trying to hold on to her temper. "I do not consider you my family, Sebastian. I think of you and your mother as guests in my home, and you have about overstayed your welcome." Anger sparked in her eyes. "Let me say this so there will be no mistake in the future: I will sell no part of Briar Oaks. If the plantation goes down, then I go down with it. I am fighting in every way I know to keep from losing this plantation. Don't ever ask me to sell it again."

Sebastian hardly heard the words Liberty was speaking. He was mesmerized by the spark in her eyes and the rise and fall of her breasts. For years he had wanted her, but she was always cold and remote, like an ice princess. As he watched the firelight play on her golden hair, his restraint broke, and he grabbed her to him.

Liberty was so startled that she dropped the ledger and was frozen into immobility for a moment. "I want you," he said, trying to press her body against his, and running his wet mouth across her face.

Liberty shuddered in disgust, then came to life with a vengeance. She pushed against him and pounded him on his chest. When he laughed down at her, she twisted away and managed to get free. Reaching for the fireplace poker, she held it out in front of her. "If you ever come near me again, I will kill you! I don't like you, Sebastian—I never have. Mark my words, if you ever touch me again, I will throw you out of my house."

His eyes narrowed. "What makes you think you are so high and mighty? You dwell in your tower thinking you are so much better than the rest of us."

"I'm better than you," she proclaimed, taking a step toward the door.

"I know who you want, Liberty, but you will never have Judah Slaughter. He will never come back."

Liberty raised her head and smiled. "You take comfort in that thought, Sebastian, and lull yourself into passiveness. If I were you, I would look over my shoulder. He may be nearer than you think."

Sebastian moved closer and stared at her. "You are the one who is woolgathering, Liberty. Judah is intelligent enough to know he will be arrested the moment he comes back here."

"What are the charges against Judah, Sebastian? Surely you don't think the charge that he was trying to press his attentions on Bandera will stand up. You, and everyone else, knows that no one has to press anything on my sister."

Sebastian took a step toward Liberty. "You bitch. You think yourself a saint, while the rest of us are just mud beneath your feet." Several steps brought Sebastian even with Liberty. "I will be glad to see you fall on your face."

Liberty saw something in Sebastian's eyes that she had never seen before, and it frightened her. He was dangerous and would stop at nothing to get what he wanted. Relief washed over Liberty when the door opened and Bandera entered.

"What's going on here?" A smile curled her lips. "A midnight *tête à tête?*"

Sebastian turned burning eyes on his wife. "For your information, your sister just accused you of being a harlot."

Bandera smiled in amusement. "And you were going to defend my honor, Sebastian? How wonderfully gallant of you." She looked at Liberty. "My sister always had an eye for the truth, but then I have never tried to hide anything from her or you, Sebastian. Do we understand one another?"

"I don't know what you mean," Sebastian said, turning his anger on his wife.

"Don't you? I am aware that you covet my sister, but

279

you can never have her, and you can't stand that, can you, Sebastian?"

"Go to hell, Bandera."

"I have been in hell since the day I married you. You are nothing, Sebastian. You promised me the world, and now you live off my sister's charity. I could have married anyone I wanted—I must have been touched in the head to have chosen you."

Silently Liberty slipped out of the room. Sebastian and Bandera had forgotten about her, and she knew they would rage at each other for hours. As she made her way up the stairs, her footsteps lightened. She could imagine the happiness Judah was feeling at being reunited with his family. She also wondered what her sister and Sebastian would do when Judah came to Briar Oaks the following day.

Chapter Fifteen

The sun came up, spreading its light like a warm blanket over the valley. Liberty had been busy since sunup, supervising the storing of meat in the smokehouse. As the last of the ham hocks was hung from the ceiling, she stepped outside and breathed in the crisp, clean air.

Automatically, she turned toward Bend of the River Plantation. Judah had told her he would see her on this day and she knew he would come. What would he do when he faced Sebastian? she wondered. Judah had every right to demand satisfaction, yet his love for Bandera might keep him from harming Sebastian. Liberty had never been able to understand what a man like Judah could see in Bandera. Didn't he know that she would never care for anyone but herself?

Liberty's eyes moved toward the swamps, and she became aware of the ominous silence. Something strange was definitely in the air. There were rumors that the British were moving ever closer. Soon they would all be caught up in a war. She turned to Delton, the slave who had been her father's right hand, and on whom she had come to depend so heavily.

"Delton, put a padlock on the smokehouse and have the stock driven into the pens. Should the enemy come, we don't want to feed them."

"I have already had the cattle and horses brought in, *Mam'zelle*. I'll have someone put a lock on the smokehouse at once."

Liberty pulled her shawl about her, and smiled. "I don't know what I would do without you, Delton. Thank you for all your help."

The black man grinned at her praise. "I will always serve Briar Oaks, *Mam'zelle*. This was my father's home, as it is mine and my sons."

"I know that, Delton, and I have been meaning to speak to you about something. I don't have to tell you that we have fallen on hard times. I just want you to know, that no matter how difficult times become, you will never be sold to anyone else. You are a part of this land. Should I be forced to sell, I will give you and your family your freedom."

Delton's dark eyes misted, and it took him a moment to reply. *"Mam'zelle,* we are all going to work hard so we can keep our home."

Liberty turned away, reluctant to tell Delton that there was no hope of saving Briar Oaks since Sebastian had squandered the money she had been saving for seeds. Liberty had considered asking Monsieur Montesquieu for a loan, but her pride wouldn't let her. No, her father would not approve of her taking advantage of friends and neighbors. In her estimation, she might be able to keep Briar Oaks for four or five more months, a year at the most.

Nightfall found Liberty and Bandera alone in the sitting room. Sebastian had announced at noon that he was going into New Orleans, and Alicia had taken to her bed with one of her headaches.

Liberty was going over and over the ledger, hoping she had made a mistake in the addition, while Bandera moved restlessly around the room, examining every detail, as if seeing it for the first time. At last Bandera seated herself on the sofa and leaned her head back.

"I could die of boredom. Men are the fortunate ones. Look at Sebastian, he just takes off any time he wants to, and no one ever faults him for it. If I were to do the same, people would say terrible things about me."

Liberty put her bookwork aside. "I have never known you to care overmuch what people said about you, with the exception of never wanting to be accused of being poor."

"That's right. If you are wealthy, people will forgive you anything. I don't really care all that much about respect—I just want people to envy what I have. Unlike me, Sebastian seems to want respect, too."

"I would respect your husband more if he were to do an honest day's work, or at least join the men who are trying to defend our country."

"My, my, you have become quite a little American since you met Judah Slaughter, haven't you, Liberty?"

"I am an American because Papa convinced me that eventual statehood would be in our best interest. Surely Sebastian can see this. He must want to defend his homeland against the British."

"Ha, not Sebastian. He doesn't believe in the war, and to put it simply, he is a pleasure seeker. I am bored to tears with him. I cannot stand for him even to touch me."

Liberty watched her sister pop a chocolate in her mouth, a habit she had picked up from Alicia. She noticed for the first time that her sister was becoming plump. "You married Sebastian; you should have known what he was like."

"*Oui*, we all make mistakes. Sebastian was my biggest mistake."

Liberty glanced at the wall clock. It was late and Judah still hadn't yet come. Perhaps he won't come tonight, she told herself, almost with relief. Liberty had not looked forward to the prospect of watching Judah and Bandera together.

As Liberty rose to her feet, thinking she would go to bed and hopefully lose herself in sleep, she heard a horse whinny at the front of the house. Her heart skipped a beat when a loud rap came at the front door and she heard Judah speak to Oralee.

"I wonder who could be calling so late?" Bandera said, smoothing her hair and pinching her cheeks to give them color.

Liberty stood as though turned to stone when Oralee showed Judah into the room, but she was aware of her sister's gasp of fear. Bandera jumped to her feet, as her face whitened. For a long moment Judah stared at Bandera, not once taking his eyes off her.

Even from across the room, his turquoise eyes glittered. The force of him, the power and the strength, were almost overwhelming. Liberty noticed how his green jacket was stretched tightly across his broad shoulders. His buff-colored riding trousers smoothly fit his long, lean legs, and his black boots held a lightly glossed shine.

Liberty felt shaken, knowing that in the next few moments her deceit might well be exposed, but Judah leaned casually against the door and smiled at Bandera — a smile that did not reach his eyes.

"Good evening, ladies. I trust you are both in good health?"

"I . . . we . . . Sebastian isn't at home," Bandera blurted out, moving closer to her sister.

"I know," Judah answered, staring at the woman whom he had worshiped for so long. Bandera was still beautiful, but not as beautiful as he'd remembered. The pink gown she wore was too young for her, and it fit too snugly across her breasts. Her eyes, though frightened at the moment, were lusterless. She smiled at him coquettishly,

284

knowing such behavior had once attracted him.

Now his eyes were cold. "I know your husband is in New Orleans, Bandera. Oralee told me."

Bandera clutched Liberty's hand, and found it to be ice cold. "I . . . why have you come, Judah?" she asked in a shaky voice.

"Do not distress yourself, *Madame*. I want nothing more than to talk to you and your sister." At last his eyes moved to Liberty, who had not yet spoken. "I do have a purpose in mind which I would like to discuss with you."

For some reason Judah had been almost afraid to look at Liberty. A simple gown of slate blue outlined her slender form, and glorious golden hair formed a wreath around her lovely face and fell down her shoulders to her waist. Gone were the braids and the freckles. Gone was the uncertainty in her wonderful eyes. There was no evidence of the young girl she had been. He now saw only the most beautiful woman he had ever laid eyes on. No woman had a right to be so perfect. Her skin was creamy in the candlelight, and Liberty stood inches above her sister, her height giving her an aura of unconscious elegance.

A tide of feelings rushed through Judah like a raging flood. In the moment that their eyes locked, he knew without a doubt that Liberty was his love. He prayed that hers had been the hand that had soothed him when he had been wounded. It had to have been her body that had taken him to the heights of paradise. It must have been her, and not Bandera, whom he had taken to his room at the inn on Saturday night.

Judah stared at Liberty so long and hard that she began to squirm beneath his close scrutiny. "Hello, Judah," she said to break the tension. "Won't you please be seated? Would you like a cup of tea, or perhaps something stronger?"

"Not at the moment. Could we talk?"

"Of course," Liberty replied, motioning him toward a chair. He moved across the room with animal-like grace, while Bandera watched him with frightened eyes. When Liberty sat down, Bandera moved as close to her as she could without sitting in her lap.

"I am glad you have returned, Judah. I trust you found your mother and grandfather in good health?" Liberty felt a chill around her heart. She wondered if Judah wished she would leave the room so he could be alone with Bandera.

He smiled slightly. "I found them well and they praised you highly, Liberty. It seems you have looked in on them and have taken care of them while I have been away. My mother has taken you to her heart."

"Your mother is most gracious, Judah."

Who is this woman who is so cold and distant? Judah wondered in desperation. Now and then he caught a glimpse of his little one—a certain gesture, a look that would come in her eyes, or the proud tilt of her chin. Judah was feeling so much raw emotion that his hands trembled, and he crammed them into his pockets so Liberty wouldn't notice.

Bandera began to relax when she noticed that Judah directed no malice in her direction. Actually he hardly noticed her. In vexation, she asked the question that was uppermost on her mind. "Should you not have a care for your safety, Judah?"

He swung his gaze to Bandera. "Did your sister not tell you that I am no longer wanted by the authorities?"

"No." Bandera gave Liberty a hard glance. "She didn't. But that is not surprising. Liberty has always been closed-mouthed about everything." There was accusation in Bandera's biting tone.

"For several reasons I came here tonight," Judah said, glancing from one sister to the other. He hoped his suspicions were correct and it had been Liberty in Zippora's cabin. He would soon know which sister had been with him Saturday night. He hardly breathed as his eyes locked with Bandera's. "I have come for my cloak," he said softly.

Bandera looked bemused for a moment. "Can you be talking to me?"

"Yes, if you are the one who has my cloak."

Liberty wanted to bolt into the night, to flee anywhere to escape what was coming. Soon Judah would know that it was she and not Bandera who had given him her body. She couldn't bear the thought of his looking at her with loathing.

Bandera shook her head. "I don't know what you're asking me. Did you leave a cloak with me before you went away? No, you didn't—I would have remembered that."

Judah felt the flood pumping through his body. So far so good, he thought. "It is a black velvet cape, Bandera. I wore it to the masquerade ball Saturday."

"I did not go to the masquerade ball. You have mistaken me for someone else. What would I want with your cape?" Bandera looked at him questioningly.

Judah felt his heart lighten. He dared not look at Liberty, not until he asked a few more questions which Bandera seemed unwittingly able to answer. "Have you been to Zippora's cabin lately, Bandera?" He tried to act casual, though he felt anything but.

"Are you mad, *Monsieur?*" Bandera was beginning to wonder if Judah had lost his mind. "I have never been to Zippora's cabin. That old woman hates me, and I am terrified of her. She dotes on my sister, however."

Judah remembered Zippora telling him that she disliked Bandera but would do anything for Liberty. Why had he never considered Zippora's meaning before? Judah's eyes moved to Liberty, and he saw a tear roll down her cheek. He wanted to take her in his arms and assure her that

287

everything was going to be all right. His heart was overflowing with tender feelings, his lips ached to confess his love. He took a deep breath and stood up. "Liberty, is there any hope that you might have my cloak?"

Liberty tried to look away from him, but he held her gaze. She had the feeling that she had just been stripped naked. How cleverly Judah had found out what he needed to know. Shame weighed heavily on her shoulders as she slowly rose to her feet. Unable to look into his eyes, she murmured hurriedly. "I have your cloak in my room. I'll just go and get it for you now."

Judah's eyes followed Liberty as she moved with controlled grace across the room. "Tell me about her?" he asked, without looking at Bandera.

"Tell you about who? Liberty?"

"Yes."

"What do you want to know?

"Does she have many suitors? Is she committed to someone?"

"I suppose there are several gentlemen who admire her kind of prettiness. There are some I can think of who would like to have Liberty committed to them. Why do you want to know?"

"My mother says Liberty is having a hard time holding Briar Oaks together. She says Liberty is too proud to ask for help."

"Well, we don't like to talk about it, but times have been better. What about me, Judah?" Bandera allowed her eyes to move over his tall frame. If anything, he was even more handsome than when he had left. There was an arrogance about him, a light of indifference in his turquoise eyes. "Did your mother tell you how hard my life has been since your grandfather threw Sebastian out of his house."

His lips thinned. "No, she didn't mention it to me. Surely you do not expect my sympathy? I have a very

288

long memory, Bandera."

"Oh, that. Sebastian and I were just playing a game. Everyone took it far too seriously."

"Have done, Bandera. I didn't come here tonight to talk about you or Sebastian. I want you to leave when Liberty comes back. I have something I want to say to her."

"Surely you don't expect me to leave her alone in your company?" Bandera's eyes grew round with speculation. "How did she come by your cloak anyway—and why would you think I had it?"

"Forget about the cloak. You need have no worry about leaving your sister with me, Bandera. I can assure you my intentions are very honorable. I intend to ask her to marry me."

Bandera jumped to her feet. "If you think I am going to stand by and watch my sister become mistress of Bend of the River you are much mistaken, Judah. I will not have it, do you hear me? I will not have it!"

Judah looked at her lazily. "I don't see that you have any choice, Bandera. If Liberty will have me, I will most certainly make her my wife. As far as her becoming mistress of Bend of the River, that is another matter. Bend of the River belongs to my grandfather to dispose of as he chooses."

"Is this your way of getting back at me, Judah?"

A smile curved his lips. "I had thought of a hundred ways to make you suffer for what you did to me, but I find the hell you have made for yourself by marrying my cousin is far worse than anything I could have planned for you."

"She won't have you." Bandera's voice was rising in volume. "Perhaps you have heard that Liberty is called the 'ice princess.' No man can get close to her."

Judah merely stared at Bandera. It had been no ice princess that had thrilled him with the mere touch of her hand.

Bandera got up the courage to move over and sit beside Judah. "My sister isn't warm-blooded like me. I remember a time when you liked me a great deal."

He reached out and caught her face between his hands. "Yes, I once thought I saw something in you that was rare and lovely. I found I was mistaken."

Bandera stared into his eyes, wishing she had been the woman he had imagined her to be. If she had married Judah, she would not have been bored. "I know why you are doing this," she whispered. "I remember that your grandfather once told you that you could only inherit Bend of the River if you married Liberty. You want Bend of the River, and that's the only way you can get it!"

Judah smiled down at her. "If it will make you feel happy to believe that, I will not try to change your mind."

Liberty stood in the doorway with Judah's back velvet cloak draped over her arm. She felt an ache in her heart at seeing Bandera in Judah's arms. She resisted the urge to turn away and seek the comfort of her room.

Her legs were stiff as she forced one foot in front of the other. "Here is your cloak, Judah," she said, advancing into the room.

Judah released Bandera and came to his feet. "I would like a private word with you, Liberty." His eyes went back to Bandera. "I am sure your sister will leave us alone."

Liberty shoved the cloak at Judah. She had no wish to be left alone with him. She knew he would question her about the night of the masquerade ball. Her shame was great enough without having to admit it to him.

"The hour is late, and I am going to bed," she said, turning on her heel, but he was too quick for her. He rushed forward and caught her by the arm.

"No, Liberty, you will stay, and your sister will go to bed."

"Judah"—her eyes were begging him for mercy—"I

290

know what you want to ask, and I don't want to talk about it."

His eyes looked deeply into hers. "Do you know what I want to say, little one? I doubt that you do." Judah looked over Liberty's shoulder and watched Bandera silently leave the room, her face a mask of fury.

Taking Liberty's hands in his, he led her to the warmth of the fire. "Your hands are cold. We do not want you to become ill."

Liberty sat on the edge of the sofa, wishing she could flee. Judah was too near, and she couldn't think straight. Why was he looking at her so strangely?

Gently, he reached out and touched her hair. "You have grown up behind my back, Liberty. When I left, you were so young—I come back, and you are a lovely woman."

Her face flushed red, and her tongue flicked out to moisten her lips, catching his attention. "Don't," he said, tracing a pattern across her cheek. "Don't ever be embarrassed with me, Liberty. I want to be your best friend."

She looked at him, puzzled. "I have always considered that you were my friend."

"What would you say if I told you that I wanted to be more than your friend?"

She held her head up proudly. "I would say you had discovered what happened between us, and you have decided to make me your mistress."

He leaned his head back against the sofa and laughed delightedly. "There is still a trace of Liberty the minx in you after all. I half feared you had lost some of your most endearing qualities."

"Did you really think I would become your mistress, Judah?"

He could hardly contain his laughter. "No, not my mistress."

She looked past him to the clock on the wall. "I feared you would be angry with me . . . when you learned . . ."

"I should beat you. Do you know what a fool I felt when I discovered last night that you were the one—"

Liberty placed her hands over her ears. "Do we have to discuss this? I do not feel up to your recriminations."

He took her hand and held it in his warm clasp. "All right, no recriminations, but at some time in the future we will talk more about this. I have many unanswered suspicions about the two nights in question."

She peeped at him through her long lashes. "Are we through talking?"

Again he laughed. "No. I have something very important to ask you, and I don't want you to say anything until I have finished."

"All right. . . ."

Judah felt his heart skip a beat, knowing how important her answer would be to his future happiness. He was as deeply in love as some untried schoolboy. He wanted to take her in his arms and voice his feelings, but when he gazed into her troubled blue eyes, he stood up, knowing he needed to put some distance between them.

"Liberty, I want you to be my wife."

For one joyous moment she thought Judah had asked her to marry him! "What did you say?" she asked, fearing to learn she had misunderstood him.

He took her hand and pulled her up to stand beside him. "I have just asked you to do me the very great honor of becoming my wife."

She gasped as excitement robbed her of breath; then she waited tensely for him to tell her that he loved her. But no—he loved Bandera. Slowly the joy seeped out of her and reason prevailed. Judah, being the gentleman he was, wanted to offer her his name because he felt she had been dishonored.

Stubborn pride allowed her to raise her chin and meet his eyes. "I thank you for the offer. It is one of the nicest I have received, but I must decline."

Judah released her hand. "Do you care for someone else? I seem to remember you once telling me that you cared about someone. Is that why you won't marry me?"

"No. I just do not want to be your wife." She closed her eyes for a second, hoping she could get through this without crying. "Will you go now, Judah?"

"No, not until I have some answers. Why will you not marry me?"

Liberty held on to her composure, hoping he wouldn't discover how much she loved him. "You have not given me a good reason why I should become your wife."

Judah drew in the breath he had been releasing. "Don't you know that after Saturday night you may already be with child—my child?"

A tear escaped from Liberty's eyes to roll down her face. "I . . . do not hold you responsible. I knew what I was doing."

"I *am* responsible, Liberty, and I do not want a child of mine growing up without a father."

"How do you know I do not . . . that there have not been other men?"

He laughed at the adorable expression on her face. "Let us just say that I have vague memories of a night in Zippora's cabin when I was the first to be with you."

Her face burned, but she met his eyes. "What about when you left. Perhaps I was . . . free with my favors."

"Oh, little one. Your innocence shines forth in your eyes. I know you so well, probably better than you know yourself."

"Judah, I do not want to get married. Don't you see, I have obligations and people who depend on me. I could never ask a man to take on my problems. Besides, we don't . . . love one another."

He reached into his breast pocket, withdrew a handkerchief, and wiped her tears away. "Liberty, I want to be your husband, and by God, I will be!"

"I need to think," she said, turning away. "Everything is happening too quickly."

"There is no time to think. There is a war at your back door. I don't have time to pay court to you and to try to win you. If you will agree to marry me, I want you to come to Bend of the River with me tonight. A priest is waiting there to join the two of us in marriage."

Her heart was beating in her throat. More than anything she wanted to be Judah's wife. "I cannot," she said aloud.

"Liberty, what can I say to make you change your mind?"

She raised her head proudly. He had given her all the wrong reasons as to why she should become his wife. "I will not change my mind, Judah."

Judah could see her slipping away from him. "I suppose you have had many offers besides mine."

"I have had a few."

His eyes racked her face. "I was told that you are called 'the ice princess.' "

She smiled ever so slightly. "I have heard that."

"Liberty, if you will marry me, I will allow you to remain the ice maiden if you desire it."

"Why are you doing this, Judah?"

He thought about telling her that he loved her and wanted her as his wife. He ached to tell her how she had fulfilled him and how, even now, he wanted to take her in his arms and carry her up to the bedroom. But something stopped him from exposing his true feelings. "I know about the trouble you are having keeping Briar Oaks from the moneylenders. In all modesty, I admit that I have more money than I know what to do with. As your husband, I could help you save Briar Oaks."

She moved away from him and absently picked up his cloak, draping it about her shoulders for warmth. "I do not believe that is your true reason, Judah."

"What do you believe my motives are?" he asked, thinking how adorable she looked with his black cloak dragging the floor.

"I believe you are doing this to get back at Bandera and Sebastian for hurting you."

"Do you think I would go that far to revenge myself on your sister?"

"I . . . it doesn't make sense, does it?"

"No, not really."

"Then give me a reason, Judah."

He dropped down on the sofa and patted the cushion beside him. "Come sit with me, and I will tell you some of my reasons."

Reluctantly, she complied. Sitting stiffly on the edge of the sofa, she waited for him to continue. "Liberty, in truth, I find you to be exactly the kind of wife I would like to have. You are young and lovely. You are intelligent, and you won't bore me on those long winter nights when we are forced to endure each other's company." In a move that took her by surprise, he pulled her to him and softly brushed her mouth with his. "And you already know the most obvious reason, Liberty."

Her face burned, and she turned away from him. But he would not be put off. Forcing her to look at him, he continued. "Liberty, I am going to join Andrew Jackson's forces tomorrow." He hated playing on her sympathy, but he saw no other way. "I may not come out of this alive, so—"

"Judah," she cried out, placing her hand over his mouth. "Do not say that. Never say that!"

"It's true, Liberty. If I don't come back, I would like to know that my mother and grandfather are taken care of. They both love you, Liberty." He looked at her through lowered lashes. "You would take care of them for me, wouldn't you?"

"Of course, but you don't have to marry me for that. I

will always care what happens to them."

"Yes, but as my wife, you would be safe also."

"But, Judah."

"No more arguments, Liberty. Suppose you run upstairs and get your own cloak. I have brought a horse for you to ride. If you hurry, we can be at Bend of the River within the hour."

"I did not say I would—"

He stood up and pushed her toward the door. "Hurry, I do not have much time before I must join Andrew Jackson."

He watched different emotions play across her face. First indecision, then fear and uncertainty. "I shouldn't, Judah. You haven't given me one good reason to—"

He pushed her toward the door. "I will be waiting for you out front—don't disappoint me."

Hesitantly, she moved across the room. Her heart was pounding in her ears. Wasn't this what she had wanted from the first night she had met Judah? What difference did it make that he was marrying her for all the wrong reasons? What mattered was that he wanted her for his wife.

When she reached the stairs, her feet flew. She was afraid Judah would change his mind. She paused at Bandera's door, wondering whether to tell her sister, but decided against it. She would leave a note for Bandera to find in the morning.

Happiness crept into her heart. God was in his heaven tonight, because before the sun rose in the morning, she would be Judah's wife.

Judah stood beside the horses and stared into the night. He waited, counting the minutes, fearing that when Liberty had had time to think, she would refuse his offer. In truth, he did not make sure that she would be cared for, should anything happen to him. He knew, if the worst happened, his grandfather would see to Liberty if she was his wife.

A chilled wind blew off the Mississippi, and Judah huddled beneath his cloak. In the far distance he thought he heard the sound of gunfire. It increased his urgent need to marry Liberty and make sure she was safely at Bend of the River.

The front door opened, and Judah waited for Liberty to reach his side. With a smile, he helped her mount. "I am glad you accepted my offer. I feared you would not."

"I do not know why I did, Judah," she said in a small voice. "You are a very persuasive man."

He chuckled and made her a formal bow. "Behold your wedding night, Mademoiselle Liberty. The time to flee is now—if you stay, you will belong to me and I will keep you forever."

The thought of belonging to Judah made her feel warm and safe. "I have nowhere to run, Judah. It is you who has made the bad bargain. I hope you will remember that you insisted I marry you. Do you forget that I am called the 'ice princess'?"

His laughter was deep as he swung into the saddle. "Do you forget? Twice I held the ice maiden in my arms, and she thawed so completely that she burned her brand on me."

Chapter Sixteen

Judah led Liberty into the huge salon where the wedding was to take place. She stared at the canopy of fresh flowers that filled the room with their gentle scent, suspecting that Gabrielle was responsible for them.

Gabrielle, looking lovely in a pale peach gown, rushed forward to embrace her. "When Judah told me his plans this afternoon, I so hoped he would be able to persuade you to become a part of our family, my dear. You are very precious to us all."

Before Liberty could answer, Gustave bellowed out in a loud voice. "Bring her to me." He waved his cane in the air. "Let me inform her of what she is getting into by marrying this grandson of mine." The soft light in his eyes belied his gruff words. One only had to look at the rare smile that creased his face to know he was pleased about the upcoming nuptials.

Judah laughed at his grandfather. "Would you scare Liberty away before I have her safely tied to me?"

"No, I would not, you young pup, and do you know why?" Liberty stood before Gustave, and he reached out and took her hand in his. "Because she is the best thing that ever happened to you. She might just be your salvation."

Liberty was accustomed to Gustave's teasing manner, but this time she blushed prettily. She was surprised to be welcomed with such obvious approval.

"Well get on with it," Gustave said, pointing a finger at the priest who hovered near the warm fire. "I want to see my grandson married so I can go to bed and get my rest. It is much too late for an old man like me to be socializing."

When Judah removed Liberty's cloak and handed it to the downstairs maid, she looked down at her unadorned blue gown, wishing she had taken the time to change into something more suitable. She had often fantasized about becoming Judah's wife, but in those fantasies, she had always worn white satin.

As though Judah had read her mind, he smiled at Liberty encouragingly. "You would look lovely no matter what you wore. Come," he said, holding out his hand and leading her beneath the canopy of flowers. Gabrielle handed Liberty a bouquet of flowers, while Gustave looked on, his eyes shining expectantly.

Liberty caught the warm glow in Judah's eye when he smiled at her, and when his hand encased hers, she felt a thrill go through her body. As the priest spoke the words that would tie them together, Judah stared at Liberty, his heart gladdened because the woman he loved was about to become his.

The priest blessed them both, and in a deep, clear voice recited the beautiful, timeless words—cherish . . . love . . . honor. All too soon it was over, and Judah slipped a ring on Liberty's finger—she was his wife!

After they had received the final blessing from the priest, Judah gathered Liberty in a warm embrace and she was momentarily lost to everything but his nearness. His breath stirred against her ear as he spoke. "You have me tied to you now, Madame Slaughter."

"*Oui,*" she whispered, so only he could hear. "But what am I going to do with you?"

Judah laughed, and she felt warmth wash over her. A half-wicked light burned in his eyes. "I am sure we could think of something. I have several good ideas."

Judah bent his head and briefly brushed his mouth against Liberty's. When he released her, she suddenly remembered there were others in the room. Turning to her new mother-in-law, she was wrapped in a hug, while Judah received the congratulations of his grandfather and the priest.

"This is a happy day for me, Liberty. I have my son back, and you are everything I could hope for in a daughter." Gabrielle's eyes were shining with tears. "I wish your father could have been here tonight. I believe he would have given you his blessing."

"I believe he would have liked Judah, *Madame*."

"No, no, you must call me, *M'mère*." Gabrielle's eyes took on a faraway look, as if she were remembering something. "I believe that would also please Louis."

"I want to talk to my new granddaughter!" Gustave demanded, pounding his cane against the floor. "Liberty, bring me a glass of wine, and sit beside me for a moment."

Gabrielle laughed. "You had better do as he says. We in this house are all subservient to his wishes."

Several servants were hurriedly laying a table with crystal and silver, placing cake and wine in the center. Gabrielle handed Liberty two glasses of wine, then nodded in the direction of her father. "He is very fond of you, my dear. You have always been one of his favorite people. Talk with him for a moment."

As Liberty went over to the fireplace, she noticed that Judah was talking with the priest. She seated herself beside Monsieur Gustave and handed him a glass of wine.

"Tonight is a proud night for me," Gustave declared, drinking the wine in one gulp and holding his glass out for his daughter to refill. "If there were not a war going on, I would throw wide the doors of Bend of the River and we would celebrate for a week. It isn't every day one's only grandson takes a wife."

"The doctor said you could only have one glass of wine a day, Papa," Gabrielle reminded him. "This is your second glass," she said, filling it only half-full.

Gustave waved his daughter aside and turned his attention back to Liberty. "I suppose with two women living in the house, you will both make my life unbearable. I hope you will not want to put ruffles and slipcovers on the furniture."

Liberty looked troubled for a moment as her eyes sought Judah's. "I will not be living here, *Monsieur,* I cannot leave Briar Oaks at this time. There is too much work to be done."

"What's this?" the old man said, looking at his grandson. "Surely you will not allow your wife to live under the same roof as Sebastian."

Judah raised an eyebrow at his grandfather. "I appreciate your concern, Grandfather, but where my wife lives is my concern, not yours." He lifted his wineglass and smiled. "To Madame Liberty Slaughter, my wife!"

"Very well, enough has been said for now," Gustave agreed grudgingly, knowing he should not press the issue at this time. After all, he had already won a decisive battle tonight; Liberty had become Judah's wife. "Call Moses," Gustave told his daughter. "It is four hours past my bedtime."

Gabrielle laughed at Liberty. "I had better do as he says. When he has had a full night's rest, he is hard enough to live with; heaven only knows what kind of bear he will be tomorrow."

Soon the room had been cleared of family and servants, and only Judah and Liberty remained. She was sitting stiffly before the roaring fireplace, while Judah moved to sit beside her. "It seems we are alone, Liberty," he said, taking a sip of wine.

"I . . . yes. Judah, everything has happened so fast, I suppose I wasn't thinking clearly. I brought nothing to . . . sleep in. I don't even know where I am supposed to sleep."

He smiled, thinking that she appeared to be a lost little girl at the moment. "I believe it is customary for a bride to sleep with her husband." His eyes met hers and he wanted to wipe the uncertainty from them. "It is expected that we

302

will occupy the same bed, you know."

Liberty stood up and rubbed the palms of her hands together nervously. "I didn't even tell Bandera I was coming here. I left her a note, but she might be worried when she reads it in the morning."

Judah leaned back and allowed his coat to fall open. He reached up and untied his cravat, while he watched her through lowered lashes. "Liberty, come here. Sit beside me for a moment so we can talk."

Reluctantly, she dropped down onto the sofa, an arm's-length away from Judah, and waited for him to speak.

"Would you feel better if we went to Briar Oaks and spent the night?"

"I . . . no." She licked her dry lips. "That is . . . I could go home alone tonight and then . . . tomorrow—"

His voice held a hint of a smile. "No, Liberty. This is our wedding night. Is it too much to expect to spend it with my wife?"

She drew in an apprehensive breath. "I suppose it will be all right, but as I said, I did not come prepared."

He reached for her hand, stood up, and drew her along with him. "I believe there is no problem that cannot be overcome." His arm slipped around her shoulder, and he led her across the room, then down the long hall toward the stairs.

Liberty was almost giddy with excitement. The love she felt for Judah was like a pain in her heart. She stopped on the landing and glanced up at him. "Judah, I am unprepared to be a wife. I know nothing about the duties of a married woman. My mother never talked to me about the relationship between a man and a woman."

Amusement danced in his eyes. "What a good happenstance. I shall just train you myself." Then he sobered. "I remember a sassy little girl who thought man-woman relationships were amusing. Have you changed your mind?"

She raised her chin and met his eyes. "Judah, I thought I knew all the answers then. Now, I do not even know the questions, and I am . . . frightened."

His heart melted at her strangled admission, and he took her cold hand in his, slowly leading her toward his bedroom, which had been hurriedly prepared while the wedding was taking place. "Do you trust me, Liberty?"

"Oui," she said without hesitation.

"I am glad, because I hope never to do anything to cause you to change your mind." They had reached his bedroom, and he raised her hand to his lips while looking deeply into her eyes. "Nothing will happen tonight that you do not want to happen. Do you understand me, Liberty? I want to be so much more to you than just your husband. I want to be your best friend. I believe we were friends from the first night we met, don't you?"

She nodded.

His laughter was soft. "I feel like I am having a brilliant conversation with myself."

By now they were in his room, and he closed the door behind them. A single candle was burning on the bedside table, and a quick glance told Liberty that the bedcovers on the massive bed had been turned down. She vaguely assessed the furnishings, and found it to be a man's room, decorated in creams and browns.

"Well, it would seem my mother thought of everything," Judah said, picking up the pink satin gown and robe that were draped over the foot of the bed. A smile played on his lips as he looked at the provocative gown and then turned back to Liberty. "Do you think this will suffice?"

Liberty was nervously moving about the room, rearranging a vase of flowers, tilting an already straight painting that hung on the wall. She stopped when she came to the heavy cream-colored curtains, and ran her fingers over the material. *"Oui,* that will do nicely," she whispered through stiff lips.

Judah moved leisurely toward the door. "I believe it is a custom for the bridegroom to allow the bride time to make herself . . . comfortable. Suppose I give you ten minutes?"

Liberty turned her back and gazed out the window. In the far distance she could vaguely see the Mississippi. How much a part of her life that muddy river had been. She had played on its banks, boated on its waters, and eaten fish she had caught there. Tonight, for some reason, she felt like a stranger to the familiar river.

Tonight she was a stranger to herself. She had agreed to marry Judah, knowing he didn't love her. She was leaving herself open for hurt and disappointment. Whatever happened in the future, she had no one to blame but herself.

Liberty moved to the bed and picked up the pink negligée. As she ran her hands down the smooth material, her heart lightened. Her eyes fell on a small leather bag, and she opened it, discovering a brush, comb, and eau de toilette inside. Clean white bath cloths were neatly folded beside a wash basin that was filled with still warm water. Apparently Gabrielle had thought of everything.

Suddenly happiness sung in her heart. For whatever the reason, Judah had married her, and she was his wife. She hummed a French song as she stripped her clothing off and washed her body. Liberty slipped into the satin gown, loving the way it caressed her skin, and knowing she had never had anything half so nice. As she pulled on the matching robe, she pushed her feet into white satin slippers. Then she picked up the brush, released her hair from its confines, and brushed her long curls until they crackled. Liberty declined to use the *eau de toilette* since she already wore the exotic scent that Zippora had first given her on her fifteenth birthday. Having folded her clothes neatly in a stack, she placed them on a chair, wondering what to do with herself until her husband returned.

The minutes ticked away, and Liberty realized that Judah had been gone for over an hour. She now knew that for her own peace of mind, she would have to explain to him why she had tricked him the night of the masquerade ball. Absently, she sat down on the bed, but quickly changed her mind and moved over to the window.

It was a beautiful night, despite the fact that a slight wind was stirring the leaves on the magnolia trees and it had started to rain. Liberty was trying to decide how best to explain to Judah that things had just gotten out of control the night of the ball. She had not set out to trick him.

She was so caught up in her own thoughts that she didn't hear Judah return, and when his arms went around her waist, she almost jumped out of her skin.

"I am sorry to have been gone for so long. I had a caller."

"Oh?" Liberty clasped her hands together tightly, knowing it was time to tell Judah the truth. "About the night of the masquerade ball, Judah—"

He rested his chin on the top of her head. "Do you know how I first began to suspect it was you the night of the ball?"

"No. I thought I had been clever."

"Not quite. It was that wonderful scent you always wear. It smells like roses and spices on a warm spring morning. I began to question many things the other night. I also realized it was you in Zippora's cabin. Perhaps I knew all along that it was you. I am just not sure."

She whirled around to face him. "You didn't know it was me, Judah. You thought I was Bandera. I remember you called her name."

The soft candlelight made a golden halo around her silken hair. She was his, but there was so much he did not understand about the two of them. How could he explain something to her that he didn't understand himself. "Liberty, you are my wife. Let us put everything that happened before now behind us."

"I would like to, Judah. I would never have married you if I had not thought that was possible."

He gently cupped her face in his hands, and bent his head, brushing her lips with his.

Desire was on Liberty's lips as she sought his kiss, and passion burned in her veins like a raging fire. She quivered when his arms tightened around her, then he took her mouth in a burning kiss. He untied the sash of the robe and slowly allowed his hands to slide over her satin-clad hips. "I have never had worse timing in my life," he said in a deep voice, bringing her closer to his body.

"I don't know what you mean," she breathed past the loud hammering of her heart.

Holding her away from him, Judah drew in a steadying breath, trying to still his quaking heart. The caller was Étienne Banard. "I have some bad news," he groaned. "Something is about to happen, Andrew Jackson has asked to see me." His turquoise eyes held a look of regret, and he groaned. "I am sorry, Liberty, but I have to go."

She reached out her hand in fear. "Is there going to be a battle?"

"Yes, and God willing, we shall win. This is our last chance to stop the British. If they are victorious in Louisiana, the war is lost, and you will owe your allegiance to England."

Liberty fought against the panic that rose up to choke her. She would die if anything happened to Judah. She pushed the tumbled hair out of her face and met his eyes, knowing her first wifely duty was to let Judah go without recrimination. "Do you need to pack?" she asked in a small voice.

Judah pulled her to him and restsed his face against hers, breathing in the sweet scent of her, wanting to take the memory of her into battle with him. "Everything I will need is on board the *Winged Victory*." His eyes moved over her face. "I travel light when I'm on land."

She reached out a trembling hand and laid it against his cheek. He closed his eyes at her gentle touch. "There is no time to tell you how I really feel, Liberty. Étienne is waiting for me now."

"Then you had better go." She lowered her lashes so he wouldn't see the tears that were gathering in her eyes. "But I would charge you to take the greatest care of yourself, Judah." She clasped his hand, loving him in the very depths of her soul. "Do not take any unnecessary chances."

He smiled. "I seem to live a charmed life." His eyes became serious. "Liberty, Étienne says that English spies are everywhere. I want you to stay here with my mother and grandfather so I will know you are safe."

She shook her head. "I cannot do that, Judah. Do not ask it of me. It is my responsibility to look after the people that depend on me."

Judah wanted to protest, but he knew Liberty could be stubborn when her mind was set on something. "If you will get dressed, Étienne and I will see you safely to Briar Oaks," he declared.

She would have moved away, but he caught her and pulled her back. Laughter lit his eyes as he clasped her to him. "There are three hundred and sixty-five days in the year. You would have thought I could have picked a better day for a wedding, wouldn't you?"

Liberty was too worried about his safety to be amused by his light-heartedness, but she knew he would go off to war, and she would stay at home and weep for him. "I should get dressed now," she said.

Judah released her and crossed the room, knowing if he didn't put some distance between them he would not leave. "I am going to tell my mother what has occurred. I will meet you downstairs. Hurry!"

Étienne quickly kissed Liberty on the cheek, and wished

her happiness. Then Judah helped her onto her horse, and they rode away in silence. The ride to Briar Oaks was an unreal one. Everything was too quiet, as if even the elements were waiting for something earth shattering to happen. The three riders traveled speedily and urgently. When they reached Briar Oaks, the morning star was twinkling in the night sky.

While Étienne waited with the horses, Judah walked his new bride into the house to bid her farewell in private. Once inside, he pulled Liberty to him and stared at her for a long moment. "You will have a care for your safety?"

"I will, and you do the same, Judah."

He bent to kiss her tempting lips, knowing it would only make parting all the more difficult. "Don't forget, Liberty, you owe me a wedding night. When this war is over, I promise you, I intend to collect."

Before his lips could touch hers, Liberty whirled away from him and clasped the edge of the hall table so tightly that her knuckles whitened. "I will hold you to that promise," she whispered.

"Will you not kiss your husband good-by?" he asked.

With a broken sob, she ran into his outstretched arms and buried her face against his stiff cloak.

He raised her face and gently kissed away her tears. "Dare I hope that you hold me in some kind of regard, Liberty?"

"You are . . ."—a sob broker her voice—"you have been my best friend for a long time, Judah."

He softly touched her lips with his finger. "Well, that's something anyway." Placing a quick kiss on her mouth, he turned and moved out the door.

Liberty raced to the sitting room and stood at the window, watching Judah mount his horse and ride away without a backward glance. Tears gathered in her eyes and a deep loneliness pressed down on her.

Everything had happened so quickly. Little had she

known when she had gotten up that morning that before a new day dawned she would become Judah's wife, though she scarcely felt like a bride. In the back of her mind, a question nagged. Why had Judah decided to marry her?

She rested her face against the frayed blue draperies, and watched Judah until he was out of sight. "God keep you safe, my dearest love," she cried to the empty room.

December Twenty-third

Judah and Étienne were among the privileged few who had been called to Andrew Jackson's headquarters.

As he addressed the assembled men, General Jackson raised his voice and pounded his fist on the table, while his eyes spit fire. "The British are advancing along the bayous. Some are in boats, others boldly march along the riverbanks I swear no Englishman, be he private or general, will set foot in New Orleans. We shall hold them back or die trying."

The general looked at each man before he continued. "Gentlemen, this morning, the enemy advanced on Villère Plantation and captured one of our militia detachments, and in doing so, scored a tactical advantage. Furthermore, the British fleet is in a position that suggests a landing."

No one spoke, for each man realized how critical the situation had become. Jackson made a pretense of straightening papers on his desk, and Judah realized he was trying to control his emotions before continuing. "Gentlemen, I propose we hit the enemy tonight! The British are tired and our men are fresh. We will have not only the cover of darkness but also the element of surprise."

Jackson moved across the room and stood at the window, his hands clasped behind his back. When he turned, there was a grim expression on his face. "Our ship the *Carolina* is moving into position, and she will let loose a volley against the foe. That will be your signal to attack. This will also give our troops a chance to move into place. I want you all to leave now and assemble your men with great haste. Be prepared to march immediately!"

Silence ensued as each officer took his leave, but when Étienne and Judah were prepared to depart, Jackson nodded for them to remain behind.

When they were alone with him, Jackson handed Étienne a sheet of paper. "You know your friends and neighbors, Étienne. Read this proclamation from the British and tell me if you think any of your fellow Creoles will cooperate with the enemy?"

Étienne read the paper and looked at Judah. "This says that if the Creoles will cooperate and remain quiet, their properties and slaves will be respected."

"What do you think, Étienne?" Jackson pressed.

"I have to be honest with you, sir. There will be those who will not support us in this fight. I pray God, they are few in number."

"Let us hope you are right." As Jackson talked, he was buckling on his saber and making sure his pistol was loaded. "Étienne, I want you to bring your ship up behind the *Carolina* in case she needs to be reinforced. Can you manage that in so short a time?"

"Yes, sir," Étienne said, coming to attention and delivering a respectful salute. "What about Judah, sir? Does he come with me?"

"I have other plans for him. Report to your ship at once, Étienne."

Judah bowed to Étienne and watched him disappear out the door. Now that he and Jackson were alone, Judah could see the tired lines on the older man's face. For a moment, Jackson seemed to slump, then he drew in a deep breath, stood up straight and tall, and smiled.

"I have something very daring to ask of you, Captain Slaughter. I'm not sure it can be accomplished."

"You have only to ask, sir."

"Étienne tells me that you have several twenty-four pounders aboard the *Winged Victory*."

311

"Yes, sir. I have three twenty-four pounders."

"Do you think it would be possible for a man to detach those cannon, put them aboard a smaller vessel that can maneuver in the swamps, and bring them to me?"

Judah looked amazed for a moment, then he grinned. "I don't know if it can be done, sir, but I sure as hell will give it a try."

"Good, good. Find someone who knows the back ways and the swamps. It will have to be someone very clever who can get you past the British without being discovered. I don't have to tell you not to allow those cannons to fall into enemy hands. Should you be in danger of being captured, send the cannons to the bottom of the swamp — is that clear?"

"Yes, sir."

"I don't know much about such things, Judah, but it seems to me that you will need a fairly large flat-bottomed boat to maneuver in the swamps. Do you know where you can get one?"

"Yes, I believe my grandfather has such a boat, sir."

The general smiled widely. "Go to it then, Judah Slaughter. Help me keep the British out of New Orleans."

Judah was moving across the room to the door when the general called out to him. "Étienne tells me that you were just married last night. I understand you deserted your new bride to answer my summons."

Judah paused, one hand on the doorknob, and grinned. "Last night, for a fraction of a second, I did consider mutiny, sir."

Jackson looked grim. "Let's end this war quickly so I can go home to my Rachel, and you can return to your new bride."

Chapter Seventeen

Liberty had heard Sebastian returning in the early afternoon. He and Bandera had been closeted in their bedroom for hours, no doubt discussing Judah's return and what they should do about it. Liberty was glad she had recovered her note before Bandera could find it when she went downstairs that morning. Liberty dreaded the moment Bandera and Sebastian discovered that she had married Judah.

Thus far Liberty had managed to avoid Bandera, Sebastian, and his mother. Sebastian and Bandera had taken dinner in their room, and Alicia had not come down at all. Now, however, as she entered the salon, she found Bandera and Sebastian sitting on the sofa with their heads together, while Alicia dozed near the fire. When Sebastian saw Liberty, he stood up, frowning as he crossed the room to her.

"I understand that my cousin paid us a visit last night. He must not fancy his life if he is so daring in his exploits."

"You need have no concern for Judah, Sebastian," Liberty told him with the greatest satisfaction. "He has received a full pardon for the false charges that you and my sister lodged against him, and he has no reason to fear for his life."

Sebastian's face reddened in anger. "Guard your tongue, Liberty. Have a care about defending that man against your own family."

313

"If that is a threat, Sebastian, I am not impressed. Must I constantly remind you that this is my home? You cannot dictate to me here."

Sebastian frowned, and his eyes closed to slits. "How was Judah cleared? I have heard nothing about it."

Liberty shrugged. "It seems Andrew Jackson himself is responsible for Judah's pardon. You should have been here when Judah arrived last night, Sebastian. He would have told you this himself."

"I suppose he had been staying with my uncle, trying to worm his way back into his good graces?"

"Perhaps."

Bandera moved over to the fire and glanced down at her sleeping mother-in-law, wondering how Alicia could sleep through this conversation. She held her hands out to warm them as she spoke. "I have been telling Sebastian that Judah had the audacity to ask you to marry him. Sebastian agrees with me that it would be impossible for you to accept such an offer. We believe Judah wants only to hurt us through you."

Liberty walked over to the window and untied the sash, so the curtains came together. Gathering her courage, she turned to face them. "You are too late, Bandera. As of last night, I became Madame Judah Slaughter." For proof of her statement, Liberty held out her hand so Bandera and Sebastian could see her ring. "You must both give me your best wishes," she said, smiling sweetly.

Sebastian balled his hands into fists while his eyes took on a wild expression. "I will not have it!" he shouted. "Why was I not consulted on this matter?"

A deep voice spoke up from the doorway. "Because, cousin, it was none of your affair. Liberty did not require your permission."

Liberty felt her heart leap with joy as Judah smiled at her reassuringly. She had never seen him in the garb he now wore. In it, he looked every bit the sea captain in his red ruffled shirt, black britches, and soft, black leather knee boots. He gave her the merest wink before he turned his full attention back to his cousin, Sebastian.

The hatred and distrust that radiated between the two men was heavy in the room. Sebastian's face went from red to white.

"You are a trickster and an upstart, Judah," he said. "You have insinuated yourself into my life once too often, and I demand satisfaction!"

Judah's eyes were cold and deadly as he watched Sebastian. Cautiously he moved over to Liberty and placed his hand on her arm. "I would like nothing better than to oblige you, but unfortunately, I have a matter before me that takes precedence over your challenge. You can address me another day, and I will gladly meet you on the field of honor, Sebastian."

Bandera whirled around to her husband. "You fool. You have been beaten, and you just don't have the intelligence to know it. You have failed in everything you ever set out to do. I do not know why I married you!"

For a moment Judah looked at Bandera, as if seeing her for the first time. Her face was distorted with anger, her lips pulled tightly across her teeth and her eyes bulging. How could he ever have thought her desirable?

Liberty nodded toward the door, knowing Sebastian and Bandera would probably argue for hours. When they were in the hallway, Judah pulled Liberty into his arms. Neither spoke for a few moments as they stared into each other's eyes.

"How long can you stay?" she asked shyly, remembering he had promised her a wedding night.

"I have to leave shortly. Where can we go so we will not be overheard? I would not want what I am about to tell you to reach anyone else's ears."

"Have you eaten?" she asked.

"No, there wasn't time."

"Then come with me into the kitchen while I feed you, and Oralee can stand guard at the door."

"Do you trust Oralee?"

"With my life"—she smiled—" . . . or yours."

Once they reached the kitchen, and the formidable Oralee stood on the other side of the door keeping watch, Liberty placed a plate of broiled catfish and sausages before Judah.

She winced as he caught her hand. "Judah, I know it is most unconventional for the master of the house to eat in the kitchen, but this was the only place we could be sure prying ears were not listening."

"I hadn't thought of myself as the master of Briar Oaks," he said thoughtfully. "I consider myself only the master of the *Winged Victory.*"

"As my husband, you are master here, Judah. It is the law."

He smiled devilishly. "I would far rather be your master."

She ducked her head, allowing her golden hair to form a curtain around her face. She was so befuddled by his nearness, that she spoke of the first thing that came to her mind, trying to keep from throwing herself into his arms. "I apologize for the light meal, but you see, we . . . rely on what we raise on Briar Oaks or catch in the river. Food has not been plentiful lately, and there are so many to feed."

He paused with the fork halfway to his mouth. "Are things as bad as that?"

"We manage."

"I will see that you have money immediately," he said, feeling angry with himself for not realizing Liberty's desperate need.

"That is not important just now," she told him, pouring a glass of wine and setting it before him. "You said you had something to discuss with me?"

316

"Yes. I am in need of a big flat-bottomed pontoon boat. I just came from my grandfather, hoping he could supply me with one, but his is being repaired. He suggested that you might help me out."

"*Oui.* I have a pontoon boat, and you are welcome to it, but—"

"I cannot tell you why I need it. I cannot even promise to return it. All I can tell you is that it will be used in a good cause."

"It is yours without question." Her eyes sought his. "Will you be in much danger?"

"No more than I can safely avoid." He took a bite of the fish and found it tender and succulent.

Suddenly the sounds of cannon fire ripped through the night, and Liberty's face drained of color. "In heaven's name, what was that?" she cried.

Judah shoved the plate of food aside and stood up. "By, God, it's started!" His eyes blazed with an excitement Liberty did not understand. "There is nothing for you to fear. The noise you heard was just a little lady by the name of *Carolina* paying her respects to the British."

There was now urgency about Judah's manner as he walked to the window and looked toward the sound of the cannon fire, unable to see anything from his vantage point. "This is going to be a long night, Liberty," he predicted. "All could be won or lost in a matter of days."

"It sounded so near," she said, standing on her tiptoes and trying to see over his shoulder. "I cannot believe the enemy is in Louisiana and men will die tonight. Perhaps even some of my friends will die." Horror registered in her eyes as she stared at her golden-haired husband. "Perhaps even . . ."

Judah gripped her arm. "I have to leave as soon as possible, Liberty. Three of my crew members are waiting out front for me." His eyes swept her face. "I have something else to ask of you—do you know a good man

317

who is completely trustworthy and who knows the swamps well enough to avoid the British?"

"Are you going to be in danger?" she pressed.

"I live a charmed life." He touched her golden curls. "Do you know anyone who can guide me through the swamps?"

A daring plan had started to form in her mind. If Judah was going to be in danger, then she wanted to be with him. No one knew the swamps better than she. If she offered to guide Judah, he would refuse, but if she were to disguise herself so he wouldn't recognize her . . . She remembered the day she had gone fishing and had dressed like a boy. At first Judah had not recognized her.

"Oui, I know such a person, Judah. He is but a lad, but he knows the swamps better than anyone. He lives here on Briar Oaks and is a true patriot."

"Good. I apologize for imposing on you, but I seem to have no other alternative." He walked across the room. "I will be at the pier making the pontoon ready. Send the lad to me as quickly as possible." With his hand on the doorknob, he faced her. For the briefest moment his eyes seemed to caress her face. "Until later, Liberty," he said with feeling. "Wait for me to return."

As the sound of cannons echoed across the valley, and flashes of light touched the night sky like a breath of fire, Judah walked toward the river, accompanied by his men.

Liberty hurried up the stairs to the attic, hoping no one had thrown away the trousers she had abandoned after deciding to become a lady for Judah. She opened three trunks and scattered the contents over the dusty floor before she found what she was looking for.

Oralee, on Sebastian's orders, had just brought a bottle of brandy into the salon. She was standing in the doorway, and out of the corner of her eyes, she watched in amazement as a young boy came down the stairs. "I will be right back, *M'sieu,*" she told Sebastian, hurrying after

318

the intruder.

"Damn that Oralee!" Sebastian gritted out, pouring two glasses of brandy and handing one to his mother and the other to his wife. "I have two hysterical women on my hands, and Oralee can't stay to help me."

"Find out what is happening!" Bandera screamed at the top of her voice. "We will all be killed!"

"Not you, my sweet," Sebastian said harshly. "You could always entice the British to bed you instead of cutting your pretty throat."

Oralee slipped into the kitchen and grabbed the intruder by the arm. "Here, boy, what do you think you are—?" Her eyes rounded in amazement when she recognized Liberty.

"*Ma petite,* what is the meaning of this?" Her eyes moved over the baggy brown trousers and the ragged coat that had seen better days. Liberty's golden hair had been pinned to the top of her head, and she wore a wide-brimmed gray hat. "Are you out of your mind? Why are you dressed in such a disgraceful manner?"

Liberty raised her finger to her lips. "I haven't time to tell you now, Oralee. I need your help in keeping my secret. If you are asked where I am, say that I have gone to Bend of the River."

"Are you going to Bend of the River?"

"No, Oralee. It is imperative that I help Judah. No one, not even Judah, must know about this. Will you promise to keep my secret?"

The servant nodded, although her eyes were still puzzled. "I will keep your secret, but hurry. I hear M'sieu Sebastian calling me. It would never do if he were to come in here. When will you return?"

Liberty ran for the back door. "I don't know. I have to go," she called over her shoulder.

The cannon fire had ceased, and now gunfire filled the night. As Liberty raced toward the river where Judah was waiting, she could hear Bandera screaming. "We are going to die! It's the end of the world!"

Judah inspected the pontoon boat. It appeared to be seaworthy, and it would be perfect for his needs. With its flat bottom, it could easily maneuver the bayous, yet it was heavy enough to carry his cannons.

"This is a strange boat, Captain," Rojo observed, placing his foot on the deck and watching it rock back and forth. "I hope she don't sink."

"I believe you will find it fits our needs tonight. It is sturdier than it seems. This boat was built to haul crops into New Orleans and bring back supplies on the return trip." He smiled. "I hope you men are strong, because we are going to have to use the poles to maneuver it downriver and through the swamps. Part of the time we will be going against the current. That will be a new experience for us all."

When Liberty neared the boat, she feared that Judah would discover her deception, so she pulled the hat low over her forehead. She decided to speak only in Acadian French and to disguise her voice. She needn't have worried because Judah was too busy sliding the poles into the side hooks to even notice her. Three men, whom she knew were members of Judah's crew on the *Winged Victory,* were lashing barrels to the boat with ropes.

Judah spoke to her without looking up. "If you are our guide, look lively and step on board." He turned to the others and said authoritatively. "After we leave here, I want no man to speak unless necessary, because sound carries on the water. You, lad. Stand by me to navigate. I want to avoid the main river as much as possible."

Liberty pulled the warm coat about her neck and balanced herself in the front of the boat, while Judah and the other men plied the long poles to the water and moved the boat into the current. With her knowledge of the bayous and river forks, Liberty soon guided them to a little-known waterway that was almost hidden with underbrush.

An eerie quietness hung over the swamp. Only occasional gunfire could be heard in the distance as they poled through a narrow part of the bayou, where only two men were needed to maneuver the pontoon.

A sudden break in the clouds revealed ghostly cypress trees. Against the southern sky, there appeared flashes of lights and sporadic gunfire came to their ears. Judah's voice was no more than a whisper when he spoke. "I want to be out of these swamps before morning. Is that possible, lad?"

"Oui, it sounds like the gunfire is coming from around the Chalmette Plantation. I know a route that will take us past the fighting, *M'sieu."*

"Good," he said, straining his eyes in the darkness, wondering how this lad could see well enough to know where they were going with not even the stars to guide him.

When, several hours later, the boat pulled out of the swamps and onto the Mississippi, leaving the sound of fighting far behind, Judah clapped the boy on the back. "Well, done, lad. Unfortunately, the real test will be on the return journey."

"Can I ask where we are going, *M'sieu?"* Liberty questioned. "I need to know in case there is a shorter route to reach our destination."

"Our objective is straight ahead, lad. We are headed for my ship, the *Winged Victory.* You will not be needed for now. I would suggest you try to get some sleep."

Silence descended as the boat moved with the swift current. The stars disappeared behind a thick blanket of fog, and a light rain started to fall. It was cold. Liberty pulled her hat over her face to ward off the rain. She was glad she had come with Judah. No one, with the exception of herself and Zippora, knew about the hidden bayou she had guided them through tonight.

Liberty sank down and rested her head against her knees. For two nights she had not slept. Now, with the rain coming down, she closed her eyes and fell asleep. She was aware that one of the men placed his cloak about her shoulders, and she knew it was Judah.

Liberty did not know how long she slept, but she was jarred awake when the boat hit against something solid. Sleepily, she opened her eyes and realized they had reached their destination, because a huge ship loomed out of the fog.

The sound of scurrying feet could be heard as men moved across the deck of the *Winged Victory,* and someone called out. "Who goes there? Identify yourself, or get blown out of the water!"

"It's the captain, you fool," Rojo answered. "Throw down the ladder."

Helpful hands grasped Liberty, and she was aided up the rope ladder. She was fully awake now, and staring in awe about the ship. The crew snapped to attention and waited for their captain to speak. In the dim torchlight, Liberty did not miss the respect evident on the faces of the men. She was seeing a side of Judah that she had never seen before. He belongs to the sea, she thought. He was born to it.

Judah was now in command, and he spoke with the voice of authority. "Philippe, have several men detach the twenty-four pounders and load them onto the flat boat. Haste is most important."

"Aye, aye, Captain," the first mate replied. No questions were asked as the crew of the *Winged Victory* hurried to carry out their captain's orders.

Judah moved over to Liberty and nodded to the galley. "Go below and tell the cook I said he was to feed you and

322

find some dry clothes for you." Judah smiled encouragingly. "You did well tonight, lad. I regret that you will have little time to rest. Were you frightened?"

"No, *M'sieu.*"

"Good, lad. But I can almost assure you that the return journey will be far more hazardous. You are young, and if you do not wish to continue, I will understand."

"With you I am not afraid, *M'sieu.*"

"Go below now. There is no reason for you to stand out in the rain."

Liberty nodded, taking care to keep the hat pulled over her forehead. She wanted to ask Judah how long it had been since he had slept. He had pushed harder and done more than all the others. She saw the weariness in his eyes, and she wished she could take him in her arms and soothe him. Instead she moved toward the companionway, guessing that was where she would find the galley.

Liberty was hunched over the table, fast asleep, when a heavy hand fell on her shoulder. "Come alive, lad. The captain will be wanting you. It's time to leave."

Liberty looked sleepily up at the man who was Judah's first mate. "How long have I been sleeping?" she asked. Seeing that her hat had fallen off while she had slept, she met the man's eyes, and saw shock written on his face. Suddenly her face turned red, for she realized her hair had tumbled down.

"What in the hell is this?" Philippe asked, grabbing her hand and jerking her to her feet. "The captain does not know you are a girl!"

Her eyes begged him for understanding. "Please, *M'sieu,* do not tell Judah. I implore you to keep my secret. I had to disguise myself or he would never have allowed me to come with him, and he needed someone to guide him through the swamps."

Slowly Philippe's eyes lit up with understanding. "You are Liberty," he stated with growing assurance. "You are the captain's little wife!"

"*Oui,* but will you keep my secret, please, *Monsieur?* I am the only one who can help Judah."

Philippe smiled and handed Liberty her hat. "I never could say no to a beautiful woman. I think I should warn you, however, that all hell's gong to break out when the captain learns about this, *Madame.* He will find out, you know. You can't fool him for very long."

"Perhaps, but I have to chance it," she said, twisting her hair and securing it with pins, then setting the hat firmly on her head.

Philippe chuckled as he helped her poke a stray curl beneath the hat. "I can see you are going to liven up the captain's life considerably. It's easy to see why he married you. Beauty cannot be disguised."

"You have the eyes and mouth of a Frenchman, *Monsieur.*" On an impulse, Liberty reached up and kissed Philippe on the cheek. "Thank you for being such a gentleman, and thank you for keeping my secret."

Warmth was reflected in the first mate's eyes as they rested on the golden-haired beauty who had charmed him. "You had better scoot along, Madame. The captain is waiting for you, and he isn't in the best of moods." Suddenly Philippe threw back his head and laughed at the humor of the situation. "The captain isn't in the best of moods because he thinks he left his young bride so soon after the wedding."

Liberty laughed as she gave her hat a final pat. Then she went out the door and raced to the upper deck. A quick glance told her that three cannons had been loaded onto the pontoon. "Come aboard, lad," Judah called up to her. "We are ready to get underway."

Judah's attention was on the cannons as Liberty climbed down the ladder and onto the flatboat. "We are riding low in the water because of the weight of the cannons," Judah observed. "Let us hope that we don't run into rough weather and capsize. Our progress will be much slower now."

Liberty realized that she must have slept for hours, because the sun was riding high in the sky. On the horizon, dark, threatening clouds gathered, and the icy fingers of a cold wind promised to make the return trip miserable.

Judah had instructed the crew to keep the boat in the middle of the river, hoping to avoid the choppy waves. Now Liberty noticed for the first time that the *Winged Victory* was anchored in a small inlet that was well hidden from the river's main channel.

Long, tedious hours of poling passed, and they were still on the Mississippi, each man tense and fearing discovery. When the sunset streaked a blast of purple across the clouds, Liberty pointed to a quiet bayou, and with relief, the men guided the boat in that direction.

Judah glanced upward as the first raindrops began to fall. "Is the rain going to be a problem?" he asked, turning his gaze to Liberty.

"It could be, *M'sieu,* if the wind comes up. I would advise that you keep near the shore. Then, if we get into trouble, we will have a better chance of saving the cannon. About five miles ahead, the bayou narrows, and we may have problems with all this weight."

"Smart lad," Judah said, silently thanking Liberty for sending him such an able guide. His thoughts went to his young bride and he felt warm in spite of the chill wind that pelted rain into his face. He could almost picture Liberty curled up beside a warm fire, candlelight reflecting off her golden hair.

He tried to forget about the cold by remembering the many times he had been enchanted by Liberty, the minx. Every time he had been with her, she had lightened his heart and made him laugh. He must have been falling in love with her right from the beginning, though he hadn't admitted it to himself. Perhaps he hadn't allowed himself to love her at that time because she had been so young. Now he couldn't imagine life without loving Liberty.

A chuckle escaped his lips when he thought of the time he had come upon her fishing, and she had been dressed like a boy!

He smothered an oath and swung his head around to the young lad. No, he told himself. Liberty would never try to deceive him again. He would not be so easy to fool now.

He motioned for one of his men to take his pole, then moved to where the lad was huddled against one of the cannons. Suspicion ate at his mind as he dropped down on the plank seat, hoping for Liberty's sake that he was wrong.

"Have you made me look like a fool again, Liberty?" he asked in a soft voice, his eyes searching the darkness and trying to peer beneath the concealing hat.

There was a long silence before she answered. "Pardon *M'sieu?*"

He couldn't tell from the voice. It didn't sound like Liberty's, but he had to be sure. He reached out and removed the hat, and his blood flamed with anger as he watched golden hair tumble down around her shoulders. "By, God, Liberty," he whispered in an enraged voice. "Do you know what you have done? Do you have any notion of the danger you have put yourself in?"

She felt stung by his anger. "You needed me, Judah. Did you not say this was an important mission? Did I not guide you safely to your ship?"

He leaned back and stared upward, allowing the rain to cool his temper. "Must you always do this, Liberty? Do you like making a fool of me?"

"Judah, it wasn't like that. You needed a guide, and

I'm the best person for the task. I know the swamps better than anyone I know."

He thumped the brim of her hat. "Well, the harm has been done now. Put your hat back on, and hope that my men do not discover who you are. If they knew how easily you have made a fool of me, they would have very little respect for my authority."

"Judah, I did not—"

Whatever Liberty was about to say was cut off by the sound of sporadic gunfire just ahead. Before she knew what was happening, Judah roughly pushed her to the bottom of the boat and covered her body with his. The ping-ping of bullets ricocheting off the cannons could be heard.

"Get down, Rojo," Judah called out. "All of you, keep your heads down; the current is taking us right toward them."

It was hard for Liberty to breathe because Judah's body was pressing her against the bottom of the boat. "Judah," she whispered. "If we could steer to the right, there is a small bayou just ahead. I need to lift my head so I can find it for you."

"Hell, no. You are not to lift your head. You will keep it down, or you will have to fear me more than the enemy," he said in a commanding voice. "You will tell me what to look for, and I will guide the boat."

"I cannot see to guide you, if I have to keep my head down," she reasoned.

He clamped his jaw tightly together. "You will obey me in this, Liberty," he told her in a whisper. "I am going to try to get us out of trouble, but I had better not see you raise your head."

The bullets continued to fly, and Liberty held her breath, fearing Judah would be hit by one. She watched him crawl past the other three men until he was at the front of the boat. One of the men offered to help, but

Judah ordered him to remain where he was.

On his knees, Judah grasped the pole and applied pressure. They were so near the enemy that they could hear English-accented voices just ahead. Slowly, the boat moved out of the current and toward the opposite shore. Just ahead, Judah saw a fork and hoped they could reach it before the enemy reached them. He could hear the oars of several small boats splashing in the water, and he knew the enemy was in pursuit. Judah motioned for Rojo to get the other pole and help him.

"Captain," Liberty said just behind him. "If you will ease her over to your right, the current will help us along."

Judah did as Liberty advised, but still he could hear the enemy gaining on them. "That's right, *M'sieu*. You are almost there," she urged, raising her head, only to have Judah push it down again with his booted foot.

Judah could feel the boat as it caught the current. As he applied pressure to the pole, the boat moved down the narrow fork of the bayou.

"M'sieu," Liberty spoke up again. "I know a place where we can hide, one in which the British cannot find us. Just around that bend, there is a hidden cove. It is a haven for alligators, but we will be safe enough there."

Judah nodded grimly. He knew it was just a matter of minutes before the British would find the fork and be in pursuit. "Everyone to the poles," he said. "Put your backs into it, men. If we cannot outrun the enemy, we will outsmart them. Remember, if we see that we are going to be taken, the cannons will have to be sunk."

To Judah's relief, the bend loomed just ahead. He could hear the British behind them, and he knew they had found the cutoff. At last they were around the bend, and Liberty jumped to her feet. "There, Captain, see the cove just to the right?"

"That doesn't look like a cove to me, Captain," Rojo

said.

"Trust me, Captain. Behind the vines and underbrush is a perfect cove."

"Follow the lad's instructions, men. He hasn't led us wrong yet."

Minutes passed like hours as they poled the boat forward. Now they were going against the current, which made progress all the more difficult. At last the boat moved through the vines and everyone breathed a sigh of relief. There was indeed a hidden cove.

Moments later, three longboats moved swiftly past. "I count twenty men, sir," Rojo whispered. "Possibly more."

"Keep your voices down, men. We aren't out of danger. They may yet turn around and come back," Judah warned.

"They will have to come back eventually, *M'sieu*," Liberty informed them. This bayou is a dead end, leading only to marshlands and quicksand. I know a way out of here, but I doubt that they do. It is my opinion that we should remain here until they return."

"How long will that take?" Judah asked impatiently. He wanted to deliver the cannon and join the fighting. He also wanted to see that Liberty was safely out of danger.

"I would think two hours, *M'sieu*."

"Rest easy, men. It appeares we will be here for a while," Judah told them.

"Why can't we go back the way we came, sir?" one of the men wanted to know.

"We can't chance it," Judah said. "There may be others behind us. We will wait here until the danger has passed."

"But the lad said there were alligators here, Captain," Rojo said, searching the darkness, and knowing the splashes he heard along the banks must be the ugly beasts looking for a meal.

"You don't need to worry, Rojo, you are too tough for even the alligators to digest," one of the men joked, while laughing humorously. "Pity the poor alligator that sunk his teeth into you."

Silence fell across the swamps once more, while a light rain made the occupants of the boat miserable. Judah went to Liberty and wrapped his cloak around her. "I should beat you," he whispered so only she could hear.

"Would that not shock your men, Captain?" she said, noticing that some of the anger had gone out of his voice.

"Minx," he told her, wishing he dared pull her into his arms and hold her very close. She could have been killed, and the danger wasn't over yet.

"I am sorry that I—"

"Shh," he cautioned, fearing the men would hear her. "You did well, lad," he said for the others' benefit. "I doubt we could have gotten this far without your help."

Liberty basked in his praise. It was a cold, wet and miserable night, but there was nowhere else on earth Liberty wanted to be at that moment. "Then you are glad I came?" she whispered.

"We will talk about that later." Suddenly a brilliant thought came to him. "Men, it's cold and more than likely, it will get colder. Stay together for warmth and try to keep dry." He moved closer to Liberty, and she felt his warm hand slide around her back as he drew his cloak over both of them.

She was vaguely aware that the other men had pulled their cloaks over their heads and were huddled together, but she was more aware of a strong hand that moved across her shoulder and softly cupped one of her breasts. "You asked for it," he whispered against her ear. "Even now I ache for you, do you know that, Liberty?"

Oh, yes, she knew about aching and needing. Her breath caught in her throat, and she could scarcely draw it in. Judah did not speak of love, but of need and desire. At the moment, that might be all that held them together.

His hand moved down past her waist to rest against her

thigh, while he pulled the cloak over both their heads. Daringly, his hand moved between her legs, and he groaned at the warm feel of her. With a strangled cry, he found her sweet lips and smothered them with a burning kiss.

"Damn you for what you are doing to me. I have been in hell lately, Liberty. You belong to me, yet I cannot have you," he said in a tortured voice.

Liberty didn't care at that moment that there were three other people nearby. All she could think of was the man who held her in his arms and burned her lips with his passionate kiss.

Judah raised his head, trying to regain his sanity. This wasn't what he wanted for Liberty. He would not take the chance of shaming his wife before his men. "Talk to me about anything, Liberty," he whispered, a catch in his voice. "Talk to me, but do not touch me."

Liberty felt desire throb through her, and she knew she must regain control of her emotions. They were on an important mission; her feelings did not matter at the moment. She tried to speak, but could not. He was too near—so very, very near.

When her hand moved to clasp his, he flung it away, moving from her with a strangled oath. Was he crazed? he wondered. All Liberty had to do was touch him and he forgot everything else.

The heavy rain pelted him in the face and went a long way toward cooling his desire.

Chapter Eighteen

The clouds had moved away, leaving a bitter, cold night. Liberty huddled beneath Judah's damp cloak, which did little to warm her. In the hours before sunup, the British returned, just as Liberty had predicted they would, and as soon as the enemy disappeared around the bend, Liberty told Judah that they could safely move out of the cove. Cautiously at first, the men applied their poles, and the craft caught the current. Liberty moved to the front of the boat and guided them into a smaller bayou.

For four hours they fought their way through narrow passages that were choked with vines and vegetation. Rojo kept a wary eye on the alligators that often reared their ugly heads. Judah knew that the enemy was all around them, so he ordered silence.

It was past noon when Liberty guided them into a wide branch of the river and the current carried them along.

"M'sieu, you must now tell me where you want to go so I can get you there," Liberty said, still playing the part of a young boy.

"I was supposed to join General Jackson at Chalmette. I no longer hear gunfire and will have to scout out the situation before I act."

"I know where we can hide the boat. Your men can have shelter and a good meal there. Then you and I can scout out the situation, and you will know better what to do."

Judah gave her a scalding glance, but she saw defeat in his eyes. He had no choice but to do as she said.

Liberty guided them up the bayou for another hour before she motioned for them to pull over to the bank. "You must all remain here while I find out if Zippora will welcome you," she said, agilely jumping ashore.

"I'm coming with you," Judah remarked, as he, too, jumped onto the bank. "You men, look lively, and keep your guns handy. I would not like to lose you or the cannons."

Liberty made her way up the path with Judah at her side. A sideways glance told her he was staring at her, a grim expression on his face, and she knew he still hadn't forgiven her for deceiving him.

"You will give me directions on how to get to Chalmette, but you will remain here with Zippora," he said at last.

"That would not be possible, Judah. I will have to guide you through some very treacherous areas. You couldn't possibly make it on your own. There are places where we will have to walk, and you wouldn't know where to look for the quicksand or the dangerous swamp gas."

"You could draw me a map."

She stopped and looked up at him impatiently. "Understand, Judah, for better or worse, we are in this together. Neither of us is important at the moment. What matters is that you get those cannons to General Jackson. I am your only hope of doing that and you know it."

Her eyes, now the color of the sea, were swirling storm centers. He let out a disgusted oath, then motioned for her to continue. "It seems I have no choice at the moment, but we are not finished on this subject, Liberty."

By now they had reached the path where the human skull hug on the high pole. "I hope Zippora is home,"

Liberty said, hurrying her footsteps. With long strides, Judah kept pace with her.

When they reached the cabin, smoke was coming out of the chimney, and Liberty breathed a sigh of relief when she saw her friend standing in the doorway. Zippora watched them approach, a strange light in her yellow eyes. When they stood before her, she spoke first to Judah.

"So you have returned, *M'sieu*. I wondered when you would pay us a visit."

"Somehow I get the feeling that you do not wonder about anything, Zippora. I have the feeling you know all," he said, smiling at the woman who had saved his life, and had been a friend to Liberty.

She waved her hand in the air. "If I knew everything, would I be living here?"

"Zippora, I need your help," Liberty said, and the urgency in her voice drew the old woman's attention.

"What is wrong, *ma chère*? Why are you dressed as a boy?"

Liberty quickly told Zippora about their plight, and about how they had spent the night hiding from the British. "We need a place to hide the cannons, and Judah has three men who need food and rest. I will need a supply of food and the use of your skiff."

Zippora's eyes moved from Liberty to Judah. "It is done," she said with startling quickness. "I will pack you food, and you know where I keep my boat. I will send Reuben to show your men where to hide the pontoon boat, and they can rest here until you return."

Liberty reached for Zippora's hand. "Thank you for not asking questions that I cannot answer."

"A true friend never asks why, but offers help when it is needed," the wise old woman observed.

"I bless the day you became my friend, Zippora," Liberty said softly.

"I, too, bless that day, *ma petite*," Zippora told her.

Judah saw love shining in the yellow eyes that rested on Liberty, and he knew that Zippora wouldn't lift a finger to help him if it weren't for Liberty.

The bayou seemed endless as Judah plied the oar that moved the small boat along. He couldn't remember the last time he had closed his eyes in sleep. The food Zippora had provided had gone a long way toward reviving his body, if not his spirit. He and Liberty had been forced back many times by the flash of a red coat; the enemy was scattered everywhere. Thus far they had not seen one American, so they could not find out how the battle had gone the night before.

"Judah," Liberty whispered urgently. "We cannot get through this way. The British have it guarded—look to your left."

His eyes followed her direction, and he quickly paddled the boat back the way they had come, because there were enemy soldiers guarding the bank.

Liberty placed her fingers to her lips, and motioned for him to row to the shore. When the small craft bumped against the bank, she grabbed up the pack of food and water, shouldered the machete, and jumped ashore. "We must hide the boat in the swamp," she whispered. "We may need it later."

As soon as their craft was hidden among the undergrowth, Judah followed Liberty's lead. He was amazed by her ability to find her way through the swamp. She took twists and turns that would confuse the most brilliant map maker.

As the day wore on, and the afternoon sun beat down on them, Liberty felt she couldn't take another step. They had chopped and hacked their way through the rozo cane, which made a thick barrier through the swampland. The musky scent of alligator was thick in the air, and pesky insects buzzed about, sparing neither man nor beast from their sting. Trickles of perspiration rolled down Judah's face, soaking his neck and drenching his shirt.

At last Liberty stumbled and fell. Judah dropped the machete and scooped her into his arms. Sitting down on a fallen tree, he held her tightly to him. "What kind of a monster have you married that he would push you past all endurance?" he asked in a choked voice.

She closed her eyes and rested her head against his shoulder, too weary to answer. "We will rest for a while," he told her. "Will we be out of these swamps before nightfall?"

"I don't know," she said weakly. "I hadn't thought we would meet the British at every turn. If we can avoid being captured, we will come out several miles below Chalmette."

Judah felt her go limp in his arms, and he knew she could go no farther. Exhaustion had taken its toll on them both. He decided it would be wise to camp for the night, where they were.

He held her to him, while he unfolded the blanket Zippora had provided for them and spread it over the grass. Carefully, so he wouldn't awaken her, he placed Liberty on the blanket. He stared at her for a long moment, loving her in the very depths of his soul. Then he smiled. Mud was smudged on her cheek, and she looked so like the little girl he had first met.

Wearily, he lay down beside her and pulled her into his arms, certain that if the enemy came upon them, he would not have the strength to fight them off.

Liberty stirred, and her eyes fluttered open. For one breathtaking moment, she stared into turquoise eyes that seemed to shine with endless depths. She didn't know how long Judah had been watching her, but she felt self-conscious, knowing she must look a fright.

"What time is it?" she asked, upon noting that the sun had sunk low in the west. "I am so sorry I fell asleep."

He touched her cheek. "We both slept. I doubt that either of us could have gone much farther. I have decided we should rest here tonight."

She was conscious that his hand moved down her mud-streaked cheek and he softly cupped her chin, bringing her forward, within a breath of his lips. "My lovely, lovely, wife. Will you hide your beauty under the guise of a young boy?" A smile curved his lips. "Such a waste."

Liberty was trembling by the time his mouth settled on hers. He moved her trouser-clad body tightly against his, and her blood flamed when she felt the swell of his desire. The evening sounds of the swamp faded as he whispered her name in a passionate voice. She was almost mindless with need when his hand moved to her shirt front and pushed the rough material aside to reveal her satiny breasts. Dipping his head, he pressed a kiss into the valley between them.

"Not what I had in mind when I promised you a wedding night," he told her, brushing a curl from her face and looking deeply into her eyes. He was quiet for a long moment, then the ghost of a smile flickered on his lips. "I must say, Liberty, we do seem to make love in the most unusual places."

"You aren't . . . you wouldn't be considering . . . not here in the open?"

Deep, amused laughter issued from his mouth. "I believe that is exactly what I have in mind. When I am near you, all I can think about is taking you to me."

Suddenly the laughter left his eyes, and his fingers traced a pattern down her neck and across one breast. He looked up, saw the uncertainty in her eyes, and said, "I want you, Liberty. I will always want you."

Her heart cried out, for she was yearning to hear him

338

speak of love, not want. But already her body was reacting to his touch. His lips robbed her of any protest she might have made as his hands were pushing the trousers down over her hips.

Judah kissed her until she felt drained of strength, all the while he was undressing both of them. Liberty now boldly sought his lips and welcomed his thrusting tongue. She felt a painful ache start in her stomach and spread throughout her entire body. She did not heed the cool air that touched her now-naked skin.

His wonderful, magical hands slid over her breasts, then glided down her stomach to softly caress her inner thighs. She threw back her head and bit her lips as he plunged his finger into her warm softness.

Judah's heart was pounding in his ears. For the first time he was able to see Liberty as he made love to her, and it took his breath away. Her golden hair was spread across the rough blanket, and her satiny skin had taken on the silvery glow of the setting sun. Feverishly he tried to reason past the trembling of his body. Liberty made him feel so alive.

The old imitater, a mockingbird, stationed itself in a cypress tree and serenaded the lovers. Its high trilling songs intermingled with the gentle breeze. Soft grasses cushioned their bed, and the dying sunset splashed brilliant colors across the sky. From somewhere, deep in the swamp, came the haunted cry of a whippoorwill.

Liberty's breath was trapped in her lungs as Judah gently slid into her body. Both of them were so overcome with earth-shattering emotions, they did not move at first, but remained locked in a tight embrace, fitting together in perfect unison.

As Judah moved ever so slightly inside her, he felt her hot silken skin caress his throbbing manhood. A kaleidoscope of feelings dominated his mind: feelings of death and rebirth, of eternal life and wisdom, and of such a strong love that he could not speak of it.

Then savage joy tore at Judah's heart as his sensuous movements brought Liberty to him in sweet union. She clasped him to her, knowing that if she died tomorrow, she would live fully on this night. And her love for this man was so strong that she would gladly give her life for him.

A tear slid down her cheek, and Judah gently kissed it away, feeling its saltiness on his lips.

Both of them trembled as Judah plunged deeper and deeper into her softness, and Liberty moaned and dug her nails into his shoulders as tremor after tremor shook both their bodies.

Judah had never felt so satisfied when he, at last, drew Liberty's head against his shoulder. Neither of them spoke as they stared into the ebony sky and watched the stars come out one by one. Gently Judah stroked her hair.

"I feel we are the only two people on earth, Liberty. It seems, if I wanted to, I could reach up and pluck the stars right out of the sky."

She wondered what thought he was trying to convey to her. It didn't matter. She had never known such happiness. For the first time in her life, she really belonged to someone. She was Judah's wife, and there was such comfort in that thought. She dared not ask if he loved her, for the moment it was enough to know he desired her. She knew he had been as moved by their lovemaking as she had been. But was that enough on which to build a marriage? Would the day come when he would feel for her what he had felt for Bandera?

"Are you hungry?" he murmured against her ear.

"Oui."

He sat up and gathered her clothing, dumping it onto her lap. "We had better get dressed first." He chuckled deep in his throat. "I suddenly feel the cold."

They dined on dried meat, bread, and apples. Not

340

daring to light a fire, Judah pulled the blanket over them both and they enjoyed the close companionship that seemed to knit them together.

"Why did you do such a foolish thing, Liberty?" he asked at last.

She gave him a pixyish smile and asked innocently. "What foolish thing are you referring to, *M'sieu?* Marrying you?"

He hugged her to him and laughed in amusement. "That's not what I was asking, and you know it. I wanted to know why you came along with me as a guide."

"With all due modesty, I was simply the best person for the task," she said. "I believe you will have to admit I have gotten you through the enemy lines thus far."

"I am not denying that you know your way through the swamp, and I am not belittling you because you are a woman."

"What then?"

"You are my wife, and I do not fancy my wife running through the swamp, in the middle of a war, and looking like a bedraggled young boy."

Laughter bubbled up in her throat. "It was not a boy you held in your arms moments ago."

He flashed her a smile. "You little devil. You do try a man's patience. What am I to do with you?"

"I'm sure I don't know. I will probably always be a trial to you. I have that reputation. Perhaps you should treat me like the fish that are too small and throw me back." Her eyes sparkled with laughter.

"I cannot throw you back," he said, straining to pull her more tightly against him. "I seem to need you with me."

Again he was drawing her under his spell. Regardless of the hard ground and the chill night air, Liberty could not imagine a more perfect wedding night.

Later, both of them slept snuggled beneath the blanket of stars, warmed by a closeness of body and soul.

The clicking of the hammer on a gun awoke Judah. When he could focus his eyes, he found a rifle pointed at his head. "Get up real slow, mister, and don't bat an eyelash," the man with the gun warned.

Judah glanced at Liberty. She must have heard the man before he came up, because her hat was in place and she looked like a young boy again.

"Who are you?" Judah asked, coming to his feet and offering Liberty his hand so he might pull her up beside him.

Now they were joined by three other men wearing rough buckskin. Judah was almost certain they were Tennesseans, but he couldn't be sure. There was a chance they might be spies for the British.

"You ain't in no position to be asking questions, mister. It seems kind'a strange to find you sleeping out here in the swamp. Are you British or what?"

Judah decided, by the manner of their speech, that the men had to be from Jackson's troops. "No man can ever accuse me of being British," Judah stated flatly. "I am on an important mission for General Jackson."

The man with the gun let out a long stream of tobacco juice. "Now is that a fact? Well, I say you are a spy and you got lost in the swamps."

Liberty spoke up. "We are not spies. This is Captain Judah Slaughter of the *Winged Victory* and I am . . . I am his guide."

The man smiled and pulled at his beard. "This here young one's a Frenchy. Now I ain't heard tell of no Captain Slaughter. Suppose we just take you back to camp and see if you are lying."

"We will go peacefully, since that is where we were headed anyway," Judah said, reaching down and picking up the blanket.

"If you are on a mission for General Jackson, you must have met him," the man said, still suspicious.

"Yes, I have," Judah told him.

"Then, if that's so, mayhap you could tell me what color his eyes are."

"They are blue."

"Anyone could know that," one of the other men put in. "Ask him the address of Andy's headquarters. No one could know that unless he's been there."

"That's easy," Judah said, hoping he could remember. "It is on Royal Street."

"He's right. A smile spread over the men's faces. "Sorry about the rough treatment, but one can't be too careful with them English milling around everywhere. I heard tell they have a few American spies helping them."

"What is the news of last night's battle?" Judah asked. "Did we win?"

"Well, we didn't 'zackly win, and we didn't 'zackly lose. I'd say it was kind of a standoff." He patted his gun. "We introduced them British to the long rifle last night, and they ain't anxious to renew the acquaintance."

Judah smiled at the man's colorful speech. "What is our position?"

"Now that's the problem. It's one of them damned French-sounding name, like De la . . . something or the other."

"De la Ronde?" Liberty supplied.

"Yep, that's right. We got separated from our outfit last night and can't find our way out of this damned swamp. Even if you was spies, we couldn't have taken you prisoner, 'cause we don't know where we are."

Liberty laughed and started walking in the direction of the boat secured nearby. "Follow me *M'sieus,* and I will have you out of here in no time."

With four more people to take turns in rowing the boat, they soon left the swamps behind and moved down a wide bayou. Luck was with them because they did not encounter any English troops, and by noon they stepped ashore and were greeted by Jackson's army.

Judah and Liberty were immediately escorted to Andrew Jackson's headquarters. When they entered the tent, the general was bending over plans that had been spread before him. He looked up, and his eyes moved from the young boy to Judah.

"What happened to you? You look like you spent the night in the swamp."

"I did," Judah admitted, pressing Liberty down on a campstool so she would be less conspicuous. "It wasn't as easy as I thought to bring the cannons downriver. We were forced to take a back way."

"I didn't expect it would work, but I must try to acquire guns and ammunition from any source I can. Too bad you lost your cannons. We could have used them."

"Oh, the cannons are safe, sir. I can bring them to you right away."

Jackson's voice thundered out. "By, God, you did it, son. We need all the weapons we can get our hands on. For a while last night I thought all was lost. Now I realize we scored a decisive victory. Had we not struck the enemy when we did, they would have pressed their advantage and would probably be dining in New Orleans tonight."

Judah smiled down at Liberty. "I couldn't have done it without this lad, sir. He guided me through the swamps and helped me evade the British."

The general stared at the lad. "Good. Have him report to my orderly. We can use him."

Judah shook his head. "Not this lad, sir. He is going home, where he belongs."

Jackson again scanned the young boy's face with the practiced eye of an old solider. He was taken aback when he saw that this wasn't a boy at all, but a girl! "Perhaps you are right, Judah. Why don't you see h—See the lad

344

home and then report back to me as soon as possible with those cannons. We have desperate need of them."

Liberty caught the smile that etched the rough planes of Jackson's face. "Thank you for all your help, lad. We could sure use more like you."

Judah pulled Liberty to her feet and pushed her out of the tent. With long strides, he led her toward the boat. He was going to get her way from there before anything else happened.

When they were in the boat and moving with the current, Liberty tapped Judah on the back. "I will have to take you back to Zippora's cabin. You will never find it on your own."

His jaw clamped shut, and he suppressed the angry words that came to his mind. "I suppose you will have to do that. But then I want you to go home and stay."

She laughed at his anger. "General Jackson knew I was a girl."

"Yes, I know. It would seem I am the only fool around."

"Oh, I don't know," she mused. "Those Tennesseans didn't know I was a girl."

With the map Liberty had drawn for him in hand, Judah and his three crew members pulled away from shore. Liberty watched him depart, hoping he would look at her, but he didn't. How could he so easily dismiss her from his mind? she wondered. Her heart ached for him already and he wasn't even out of sight.

"Judah Slaughter has changed," Zippora observed. "It would not be easy for a man to get the better of him now."

"*Oui*. He is master of himself and of every situation he comes up against."

Zippora chuckled deep in her throat. "I do not believe

he has yet mastered you, *ma petite*."

Liberty turned worried eyes to her friend. "Zippora, Judah and I are married."

"Ah, so it has begun. I thought this might happen." Her laughter filtered through the air. "That is why his blood burns. I saw that he could not take his eyes off you."

"I wish that he loved me, Zippora. I want his love more than I have ever wanted anything."

The wise yellow eyes sparkled. "Sometimes when one is in the middle of a thing, one cannot see it clearly."

Liberty shrugged her shoulders. "Sometimes one cannot see because one does not want to."

"That is so, *ma petite.* That is so."

Liberty watched the pontoon boat disappear around the bend, wishing she could have gone with Judah. There was such an emptiness in her heart, such a loneliness, that she wanted to cry out in agony.

Zippora took Liberty's hand. "It is not long until dark. I am going to get you home so you can rest. You look ready to collapse."

Obediently, Liberty got into Zippora's boat and leaned her head back. Yes, she was weary. When Reuben scampered into the craft, Liberty made room for the boy beside her. Sleep, she needed sleep, she thought wearily. She could only imagine, how exhausted Judah must be.

When Zippora let Liberty off at the pier of Briar Oaks, she waved to her and paddled swiftly back toward the swamps. Liberty's footsteps were heavy as she made her way toward the back of the house, hoping she wouldn't meet anyone.

Oralee met her at the back door and helped her out of her coat. "I saw you coming, and am preparing a hot bath. Go to your room and strip those filthy clothes off. I will bring you something to eat." Oralee asked no questions, but there was concern in her soft brown eyes.

346

"Do not tell my sister or Sebastian that I have returned, Oralee. I am too weary to deal with them."

"They are not here, *ma chère*. Your sister cried and carried on so, M'sieu Sebastian agreed to take her and his mother into New Orleans."

"What about the fighting? How did they get past the British?"

"I do not know about such things, but I heard M'sieu Sebastian tell his mother that he had a pass for safe conduct from the British."

Liberty stared at Oralee. "How can that be?"

"I do not know."

Liberty drew in a deep breath and made her way slowly up the stairs. She was glad everyone was gone — now she wouldn't have to deal with any questions — but it nagged at the back of her mind that Sebastian had a pass from the enemy.

When she reached her bedroom, Liberty was too weary to think. She dropped down onto a chair and closed her eyes. Tomorrow would be time enough to worry about Sebastian.

Chapter Nineteen

Liberty awoke when Oralee pulled back the curtains and let the sunshine stream into the bedroom. The maid was smiling cheerfully as she placed a brightly wrapped package on the bed. "Merry Christmas, *ma chère.*"

Liberty rubbed her eyes, trying to come fully awake. "It's Christmas? How can that be? I didn't even know it."

Oralee laughed. "It happens every year on this same day. You have just been too busy to notice anything but that new husband of yours."

"Who is the package from?"

"It was brought to you by a man who called himself Philippe Cease. He said to tell you that this was from his captain."

"Oralee, I have no present to give Judah. For that matter, I have no gift to give anyone."

"That is not quite true, *ma chère.* The kitchen is filled with enough food to feed an army, and there are brightly colored bolts of material in silks, satins, and linens. Not to mention money." She dropped a leather pouch that tinkled with money into Liberty's lap. "It would seem your husband intends to take very good care of you."

Liberty's heart melted at the thought of Judah's generosity and thoughtfulness. "I wish he had come himself. Did Philippe have any message for me?" she asked hopefully. Wouldn't it be a wonderful Chrismas if they could spend it together? she thought.

"Just that M'sieu Slaughter wishes you a Merry Christmas."

Liberty threw the covers aside and moved off the bed. "Is Philippe Cease still below? I would like very much to talk to him."

"No, he said he could not stay. He and another man by the name of Rojo unloaded the packages in the kitchen and then took their leave."

Liberty pushed her disappointment aside. "I wonder what is in this box?"

"The best way to find out is to open it," Oralee suggested.

Liberty tore the brightly colored paper to shreds in her excitement. She scarcely breathed as she lifted the lid of the box, then a gasp escaped her lips as she stared at a lovely, white velvet gown and matching white satin slippers. "This is the loveliest gown I have ever seen," she exclaimed, touching the soft material. "It looks just the right size. How do you suppose Judah got it?"

"How he got it is not important. When a gentleman gives his lady a gift, she should not ask questions."

Liberty's eyes fell on something wrapped in bright blue paper at the bottom of the box. "Look, there is a note, and a smaller box."

Oralee smiled as she crossed to the door. "You read your note, and I will bring your breakfast." She paused at the door. "I almost forgot. Last night your sister, her husband, and his mother returned."

Liberty dropped down on her bed wondering what had gone wrong. "Are they downstairs yet?"

"It was very late when they returned—your sister is still in bed, but M'sieu Sebastian was up early this morning and walked down to the slave quarters."

"Whatever for?"

"Who can say why he does anything? I have never

350

known him to go to the slave quarters before." Oralee smiled, dismissing Sebastian from her mind. "If we are to have Christmas dinner, I had better go below and supervise. We have Kaki's daughter in the kitchen, and I am not sure she can cook."

Liberty was puzzled by Sebastian's actions, but she was too happy to dwell on him. She waited until Oralee closed the door behind her before she opened the note. She had never seen Judah's handwriting, and she stared at the bold script.

Merry Christmas, little one. I am sorry that we must spend our first holiday apart. I will be thinking of you and hoping that you have a joyous feast. The next time I see you, perhaps you would wear this gown for me. We will call it a belated wedding gown. The jewelry is from my mother. It was given to her by my father, on their first Christmas together. She wanted you to have it. Think of me, and I will keep you in my heart and prayers.

Love, Judah

Liberty's eyes softened, and she fell back against the pillow. What an extraordinary man she had married. There was a war going on, yet he took time to remember her at Christmas.

Liberty opened the satin-covered box and saw a gold chain nestled in a bed of black velvet. She smiled as she lifted the golden chain and found a golden pendant attached to it—a ship. Joy sang in her heart when she read the name engraved upon it: *Winged Victory.*

Laughing delightedly, she fastened the chain about her neck. She might not have Judah with her today, but she could feel his loving care and that of his family reaching out to her; she finally felt she belonged to a family.

Liberty tested the roasting goose with a fork and pronounced it tender. She smiled at the young cook, and then turned to Oralee and instructed her to see that enough food was delivered to the slave quarters so each family could have a feast. In addition, everyone was to be given enough money to purchase a new pair of shoes.

"Tut-tut, such generosity," Sebastian said, leaning against the door. "Has the hand of plenty touched you, Liberty?"

"Where is my sister?" Liberty asked, brushing past her brother-in-law as she made her way to the salon where the holly wreath had been hung.

Sebastian followed after her. "I suppose my cousin robbed Bend of the River to deliver you a feast," he said sarcastically. "He is only doing this to impress you, Liberty. You don't know his true nature."

She glared at him. "And you do?"

"I know men like him. They want only what they can get from a beautiful woman."

Liberty mumbled under her breath in vexation. By now she was so accustomed to Sebastian's irritating habits that she no longer bothered to get angry with him.

When she entered the salon, her eyes went first to the picture of her Aunt Liberty, her father's sister for whom she had been named. She had sworn, that no matter what she had to sell to keep River Oaks from going under, she would never sell her aunt's portrait.

For a moment she stood in stunned silence. The wall was blank—the picture was gone! "Where is the picture that hung on that wall?" she said in a shaky voice. Wheeling around, she faced Sebastian. "Are you responsible for this, Sebastian?"

He shrugged his shoulders and crammed his hands into his pockets. "I needed money. I found a buyer who was most generous. The Americans seem to want respectability so desperately that they are willing to acquire it through others. I can just hear this man telling his friends the woman in the portrait is a relative of his."

Hot wrath boiled up in Liberty. "You had no right to do that. It was very special to me. That was my aunt. I demand that you go immediately and get it back."

"I fear that will be impossible. You see the money is gone. I used it to settle a gambling debt. A debt of honor must always be paid."

She was so angry she didn't trust herself to speak for a moment. "You have no honor, Sebastian. You would steal from me after I gave you and your mother a home. I want you out of my house today!"

His laughter filled the room. "That will not be possible either, Liberty. You see, I have invited guests here today, and I must be here to receive them when they arrive."

"What are you talking about? What guests?"

For a moment he looked uncomfortable. His eyes shifted away from hers and he spoke in a soft voice. "I have invited the British doctors. They want to use this house to set up a hospital. I could hardly refuse."

"How dare you take it upon yourself to invite the enemy into this house. I will not allow them to set one foot in here. You must go immediately and tell them they are not welcome."

"You are a fool, Liberty." He moved closer to her, his eyes assessing her lovely face. "Do you not see the British are the superior force and they have trained soldiers. The Americans are nothing but rabble who have no idea how a gentleman fights a war. Surely you know it is wise to be on the winning side, Liberty. The English will win."

"You are a traitor, Sebastian. Get out of my house at once!"

Sinister laughter issued from his lips. "I have always loved the way your eyes sparkle when you are angry." He

353

reached out and grasped her by the shoulders. "I would do anything to please you, Liberty. If you want the British to stay away, I'll arrange it. If you want me to play your fool, you have only to say the word. Tell me what you want, and I'll do it."

"Let go of me!" she said through clenched teeth. "The only thing I want from you is that you walk out that door and never come back. You disgust me, Sebastian."

Before Liberty knew what was happening, Sebastian pulled her to him and ground his mouth against hers. She struggled and clawed at him, but he held her tightly. His lips were wet and hot. Liberty felt her stomach churn, and knew she would be sick if he didn't release her. She twisted and turned, trying to repel him, but he wouldn't release her.

"Your wife has asked for you," Oralee spoke up as she came into the room. She had seen that her mistress was in trouble, and knew of no other way to help her.

Sebastian flung Liberty away from him, and she grasped the mantel to keep from falling. She wiped her hand across her mouth, hoping to rid herself of the taste of him. Her chest was heaving as she tried to catch her breath.

"Do not ever come near me again, Sebastian. If you do Judah will kill you. Get out of this house before I have you thrown out."

"You can't order me out, Liberty." His eyes were burning with a dangerous light. "I have promised the British officers they could use this house for a hospital, and there is nothing you can do about that."

"We will just see about that," Liberty declared angrily, and she stalked out of the room, Oralee at her heels. "Oralee, go and find Delton for me. Tell him to bring several men with him. I want them to throw my brother-in-law off Briar Oaks."

Oralee's face whitened. "I cannot do that, *ma chère*. I

just discovered what M'sieu Sebastian was doing at the slave quarters this morning—he sent all the men to help the British transport their wounded here."

Liberty whirled back to Sebastian. "You will never get away with this."

He laughed. "I already have. One day you will thank me for this."

He strolled leisurely past her and moved down the hallway. "My friends will be here within the hour. I trust you will make them welcome."

Liberty pounded on her sister's bedroom door, but received no answer. In anger, she wrenched it open and stepped over the clutter and disarray to get to the window and let some fresh air into the room.

"Bandera, I want to talk to you, and you had better listen," Liberty commanded as she threw back the curtains and pushed the window open.

Bandera buried her head beneath the pillow. "Go away and let me sleep."

Liberty's eyes sparked with anger. She pulled the pillow off her sister's head and threw it across the room. "I want to talk to you, *now,* Bandera!" she stated firmly.

Bandera slowly raised her head, trying to focus her eyes in the bright sunlight that streamed into the room. She had never seen Liberty in such a state. "What is the matter with you? Are you crazed to come charging into my bedroom like some madwoman?"

Liberty's chest was heaving with anger. "Do you know what your husband has done?"

Bandera sat up and pushed her tumbled hair out of her face. *"Oui,* I do. He promised to take me and his mother into New Orleans. But instead we were forced to wait in that drafty boat while he talked with some very suspicious-looking men. Afterward, he brought us back here. I don't mind telling you, I am not happy with Sebastian. I had my heart set on going to New Orleans."

"You don't even know what I'm talking about, do you? Dear lord, Bandera, do you never think of anything save your own wants and pleasures?"

Bandera tossed her sister a scathing glance. "I never claimed to be perfect like you, Liberty. You go around with charity and goodness oozing out of your heart, and you think we will feel obligated to you because you allow us to live off your charity. Sometimes you make me sick."

Bandera's words found their mark, and Liberty realized for the first time what she must look like in her sister's eyes. Bandera was not evil; she was just weak, selfish, and easily used by others. Sebastian had promised her riches and glory, and Bandera had been willing to betray Judah to get them.

"Bandera, listen to me. Sebastian has met with the British, and told them they can use Briar Oaks as their hospital."

The color drained out of Bandera's face, and she slid out of bed, pulling on her robe. "He had no right to do that. This is not his home!"

"I want him out of here now. You go to him and tell him to pack his belongings and get out."

Bandera whirled on Liberty. "Would you throw your own sister out with nowhere to go?"

"No, I am not that cruel. You and Alicia can stay until Sebastian can provide a home for you. But I want him out of here today."

Without another word, Liberty went out the door. She was so distraught that her hands were trembling as she descended the stairs. Something about Sebastian's attitude had frightened her. When she remembered the feel of his wet mouth on hers, she experienced revulsion. She had intended to tell Bandera about Sebastian's advances to her, but had decided against it, knowing that would serve no purpose.

When Liberty reached the landing, she could hear loud voices at the front door. Her blood boiled when she saw several men wearing red uniforms at the entrance. Sebastian was talking to one of them and when he saw Liberty, he smiled.

"What is the meaning of this?" Liberty asked, facing a soldier with sergeant's stripes on his arm. "This is my house, and you are not welcome here."

The sergeant looked shocked for a moment, but quickly recovered. "Madam, we are here at your husband's invitation. He assured my captain that we could use this home for our hospital."

Liberty glared at Sebastian, who had a satisfied expression on his face. "This man is not my husband, but my brother-in-law. This is my house, and he is only a guest here. I do not condone what you are doing to my country, and I will not have you under my roof. My husband fights for the United States."

The sergeant admired the young lady's spirit and he thought she was a pretty little thing; but he had his orders, and he intended to carry them out. Taking Liberty firmly by the shoulders, he moved her aside and waved to the litter bearers, indicating that they should bring in the wounded. "I'm sorry, madam, but I have wounded, and their needs take precedence over everything else. Where would you suggest we set up our hospital?"

Sebastian stepped forward, taking command. "I believe the salon would be the best place."

Liberty froze, horror on her face, when she saw that one of the wounded was a young boy with a blood-stained bandage around his forehead. He was so young and in such pain that her heart went out to him. No matter if he was an enemy, she could not turn a wounded human being away. Was he not one of God's creatures?"

"No, the salon catches the morning sun and you would

357

have to keep the curtains closed. The ballroom would be the best place for your wounded. It is larger." Liberty brushed Sebastian aside. If the British were going to be in her home, she was going to be in charge, not Sebastian.

She walked down the hall to the back of the house, thinking how angry Judah would be when he discovered the enemy was at Briar Oaks. Suddenly, she realized the danger he would be in if he attempted to see her. She had to find a way to warn him not to come!

Liberty threw the double doors open and stepped aside. "You may use this room, Sergeant, but be warned, I do not want your men to interfere in any way with me or my family. The upstairs, and the front of the house are off limits to you. You will always use the back entrance and—"

"Excuse me for interrupting, madam, but you don't seem to understand. We are taking over your house. I would have been willing to be reasonable, but you seem to be hostile toward us. I would advise that you go to your room and stay there until the captain gets here and decides what to do with you."

"I will not!" Liberty replied, defiance flaming in her eyes. "No one tells me what to do in my house."

The sergeant smiled at her spunk as he motioned for two of his men to come forward. "Escort the lady to her room, and see that she stays there until further notice."

One of the men looked at Liberty with sympathetic eyes. "After you, madam," he told her.

Liberty caught the satisfied smile on Sebastian's face. He had gone too far this time. Something had to be done about him. He was an unfeeling animal who would do anything to get what he wanted. Holding her head high, and setting her eyes straight ahead, Liberty sailed out of the room with the two guards right behind her.

The house seemed unusually quiet. Liberty had opened her bedroom door several times, but the guard stationed beside it had motioned her back into the room. She paced about while anger ate at her mind. Yes, Sebastian has gone too far, she thought. Judah will never allow him to get away with this.

The door was thrust open, and Liberty turned to see her sister carrying a tray of food. "Merry Christmas, Liberty," Bandera said with a smile. "I hope you didn't think that we had forgotten about you. Would I forget my sweet little sister?" Sarcasm threaded her words.

Liberty went to the bed and sat down. "Surely you cannot be happy about what has taken place here today, Bandera."

Placing the tray on a table and shrugging her shoulders, Bandera turned to her sister. "Why should I care who wins in this war?" Laughter bubbled from her lips. "No, that isn't true. You see, if the English win, which Sebastian assures me they will, he believes they will give us Briar Oaks for being loyal to them." Her eyes clouded. "It isn't Bend of the River, but if the British clear the debts, Sebastian thinks we can live very comfortably here."

Liberty stared at her sister in amazement. "I always thought you were featherheaded, Bandera, but I never took you for a fool. How many promises has Sebastian made to you, and then broken? He always has these schemes, and you go along with him. The British are not going to win this war, and even if they did, they could not overturn my father's will. Why don't you use your head for a change and stop letting Sebastian do your thinking for you? Besides, Sebastian would never be able to make Briar Oaks prosper. It would take too much of his time away from gambling."

Bandera was thoughtful for a moment. "I wish *Maman* were here. She would know what was best to do."

"Bandera, listen to me, Sebastian is using you. Wake up and see for yourself."

Confusion registered in Bandera's eyes. "I don't know. I need to think."

"Bandera, you have to send Oralee to me. I need to get a message to Judah."

A smile spread over her sister's face. "Sebastian told me you would suggest something like that. It isn't me who is the fool, but you, Liberty. You think Judah is so wonderful. Do you know why he married you?"

"I don't delude myself into thinking he is dying of love for me, Bandera. We both know that Judah loves you."

Bandera's eyes narrowed. It was Liberty who was the simpleton. Bandera had seen the admiration and love in Judah's eyes when he'd looked at her sister. Jealousy burned in her heart, taking precedence over every other feeling. Finally she knew how to bring her sister tumbling off her pedestal. She was tired of feeling inferior to Liberty.

"I know why Judah married you, Liberty. It was the only way he could get his hands on Bend of the River. I happen to know that Monsieur Gustave told Judah the only way he could inherit his fortune was by marrying you. It seems the old man has always fancied you. Anyway he told Judah if he married me he would be cut out of his will."

Liberty didn't believe Bandera for a moment, but the words stung all the same. "That is just another lie spun by Sebastian. Judah does not care about Bend of the River."

"Sebastian wasn't the one who told me about Monsieur Gustave's stipulations, Liberty, because he doesn't know about it. I didn't tell him, fearing he might try to marry you himself, so he could have Bend of the River. I heard this from Judah himself. If you don't believe me, ask his grandfather. For that matter, the next time you see Judah, ask him . . . unless you are afraid to hear the truth."

Something in Bandera's eyes made Liberty believe her. No, she cried silently. Do not let this be true! She tried to smile, but did not succeed. "I cannot believe that, Bandera. Judah would never mary a woman for—"

"You admitted yourself that he didn't love you. Why else do you suppose he married you?"

Liberty had believed Judah had married her because he thought he had ruined her. Now she wasn't so sure. Doubt and pain walked hand in hand through her mind. "I won't listen to you. Sebastian has poisoned your mind, and you are beginning to think like he does."

At that moment Bandera's eyes fell on the white velvet gown that had been carefully draped over the foot of the bed. "What is this?" she asked, picking up the lovely garment and holding it up to her. "Where did you get this?"

"It is a Christmas gift from Judah," Liberty answered, only half attending to her sister. Her mind was in a turmoil. She was a prisoner in her own home, and she had just learned something very disturbing about her husband. Liberty didn't know where to turn for help. She had already decided, that if she wasn't released tomorrow, she would climb out the window tomorrow night.

Bandera smiled. "Since you cannot come downstairs and enjoy the lovely Christmas dinner with us, I think I will just borrow this gown from you."

"Do as you wish," Liberty said dully. "But I doubt it will fit you."

"It has a wide hem, and Oralee can let it out. Cheer up, little sister. You wouldn't like dining with us tonight anyway. You see, we are entertaining some of our new-found English friends. There will be two doctors, and a captain." Laughter trilled from her throat. "It's amusing when you think about it. The British will be dining on the food Judah sent to you. Do you think he would be angry if he knew he was furnishing the enemy with Christmas dinner?"

"Just leave," Liberty said, bending down and picking up the shoes that Judah had sent to her to wear with the dress, and tossing them at Bandera. "You may as well have the complete outfit. I hope your friends choke on their dinner."

"My, my, but we are vicious. *Maman* would not approve you know."

"*Maman* never approved of anything I did, Bandera. I was always a disappointment to her."

A smile played on Bandera's lips. "I know. I made sure that she saw only the worst of you. I could make her believe anything I wanted to. You wouldn't believe the things I made up about you. She was horrified that she had given birth to such a rebellious child." Bandera's eyes grew cold. "Papa always saw through my little schemes. He wasn't as easy to fool as *Maman* was."

Liberty felt the life drain out of her. She had the feeling no one cared what happened to her. "Please leave, Bandera. I no longer want to talk to you."

"It's too bad we could never be friends, Liberty. But you always thought you were superior to me — you who had the father with the aristocratic French blood, while my father was from a poor Spanish family."

Liberty sat down on a chair and stared at Bandera as if seeing her for the first time. "We could never have been friends, but it wasn't because of my father. You and I are worlds apart. There was a time when you had it all, Bandera — beauty and popularity. You could have married anyone you wanted. Look how low you have sunk by marrying Sebastian. I pity you."

"Save your pity for yourself, Liberty. You are the one who is going to need it." Bandera left and slammed the door behind her.

Liberty threw herself on the bed and lost herself in tears of misery. What was going to happen to her? What

362

was she going to do?"

The Christmas dinner Bandera had brought her remained uneaten because Liberty cried herself to sleep.

Judah looked at his first mate and his eyes narrowed with fury. "Are you sure, Philippe? Could there be no mistake?"

"I saw it with my own eyes, Captain. Me and Rojo were just pulling away from the pier at Briar Oaks, and we saw a large floating barge coming out of the mist. We rowed around the bend and watched them go ashore at Briar Oaks. There were about fifty of them, counting the walking wounded and those that were carried on a litter. I stayed long enough to find out they were setting up a hospital there."

"Did you see Liberty?"

"No, Captain, but I believe I saw a man who fit your cousin Sebastian's description. He was laughing and acting like he was great friends with the British."

"Damn." Judah clenched his fists. "I should never have allowed Liberty to go back there. I should have insisted that she go to Bend of the River and stay with my mother."

"Judging from the brief encounter I had with your wife on the *Winged Victory,* I'd say she has a mind of her own, Captain."

"Yes, she is the most stubborn, hot-tempered . . . kindhearted, adorable woman I have ever come up against."

Philippe threw up his hands. "Save me from men who are in love. I never thought to see the day you would give up the free and easy life to concentrate on one woman, Captain. I know several ladies who will not be too happy about that turn of events."

Judah fixed his first mate with a disagreeable glance. "I

363

have no time for your little jests, Philippe. I have to know what is going on at Briar Oaks."

"I don't see how you are going to do that. The place is crawling with the enemy and is a veritable fortress, with guards posted about fifty yards apart."

Philippe was surprised to see the smile on his captain's face. "I know someone who can get past the guards and they wouldn't dare challenge her," Judah said. "No one would dare challenge Zippora."

"Are you referring to that old woman you told me about, the one with the yellow eyes?" Philippe asked.

"Yes. I believe you and I will just pay a little visit to her this afternoon."

"Are you sure you can find her place? You said it was deep in the swamps."

Judah laughed and clapped his friend on the back. "I have a map Liberty drew for me." He sobered, and his jaw came together in a stubborn line.

"No one had better touch Liberty. If they do, they will answer to me."

Chapter Twenty

A strange noise caught Liberty's attention, and moving to the window, she pushed the draperies aside. At first she was too stunned to feel rage. It appeared that one of the British soldiers was in the magnolia tree outside her window, and he was cutting off the branches!

Liberty pushed open the window, and called down to him. "Who gave you permission to cut my tree? I insist that you stop this instant."

The young soldier smiled at the pretty young woman. "I'm sorry, madam. I am just following orders."

"Who gave the order for my tree to be butchered?"

He smiled sheepishly. "I am sorry, madam. I was told, that if you asked, I was to say that your sister informed the colonel that you have often used this tree to leave your bedroom. The colonel ordered it trimmed back so you couldn't reach it."

Liberty was so angry that she could not find her voice, but anyway she realized nothing would be gained by arguing with the man. He was only carrying out orders. It was Bandera who drew her anger. How could her own sister betray her?

Liberty watched as the big overhanging branch that grew next to her window splintered and fell to the ground. She couldn't understand why the British officer would want to keep her a prisoner in her room.

There had been only the sound of intermittent gunfire all day, and Liberty did not know what was happening. For all she knew, the war might have been lost.

A knock on the door caused Liberty to start. "Come in," she called out, hoping it would be Oralee, because she yearned for a familiar face. Instead, when the door was pushed open, she saw the young soldier who had been sawing the limbs off her tree.

"Begging your pardon, Mrs. Slaughter, but Colonel Newman would like to see you downstairs right away."

"If he wants to see me, let him come to me," Liberty said, raising her chin haughtily. She was not in the least happy about being summoned in her own home.

The young man smiled at her, and his eyes looked kindly into hers. "Ma'am, if you wouldn't mind a suggestion, you should do as Colonel Newman says. He's in a position to make things a lot easier for you . . . or more difficult, if you know what I mean."

Liberty picked up her shawl and pulled it around her shoulders. She would very much like to keep her pride and demand that the colonel come to her, but the truth of the matter was, at this point, she would do almost anything to get out of this room. "It would seem I have little choice. Lead the way," she said.

As they descended the stairs, Liberty asked, "What news of the war, *Monsieur?*"

"I don't believe I'll be giving away any secrets if I tell you it's a stand-off, Mrs. Slaughter."

At least that is something, she thought. The war has not been won, but it isn't lost either.

Colonel Graham Newman was a man in his early thirties, and already he was a seasoned veteran, having served in two campaigns — one in France, and now here in this godforsaken country, called America. Nothing had prepared him for the kind of war the Americans waged; they called it Indian warfare. The Americans could strike

366

anywhere and anytime, leaving their enemies confused and bleeding, and they disappeared as quickly as they had come. They seemed to do their best fighting at night, a fact the British had been forced to adjust to.

He shuffled the papers on his desk and leaned back, closing his eyes for a moment, trying not to think about the loneliness that weighed on his shoulders. He had been away from England too long, and he yearned for his home. Soon it would be spring, and the roses in his mother's garden would be in full bloom.

Aside from the many problems which had plagued Colonel Newman, there was the lady of the house to deal with. If her sister and her brother-in-law were to be believed, the lady had two heads and breathed fire. If the lady was indeed the wife of Judah Slaughter, the notorious pirate who had preyed on British shipping and British naval vessels, it was a stroke of luck that she had fallen into his hands.

The Admiralty would give much to get their hands on Judah Slaughter. He was responsible for the sinking of the *Royal George*, the capture of the *Freemont*, and the seizure of Admiral Sills and his crew. Word had come from headquarters that Colonel Newman was to use the lady, in any way he felt necessary, to obtain Admiral Sills's freedom.

Newman's eyes dimmed. It was distasteful to him to use a woman. But he was a professional soldier, and he would do what he must to help win this war. He could always hope the woman was a simpleton so he could easily maneuver her to his best advantage. Perhaps he could induce her to write a frantic note that might bring her husband to her rescue. Newman would like nothing better than to catch Captain Judah Slaughter in a trap. The man that captured the notorious captain would gain great recognition.

The door was pushed open, and Colonel Newman caught a flurry of pink and a flash of golden hair. He sat up straight, as a lovely young woman advanced toward him, anger burning in her glorious, blue eyes. He was stunned as he waited for the beautiful vision to speak, wondering if she was real or if he had conjured her up out of his loneliness.

"I assume I am addressing Colonel Newman," Liberty said, raising her chin and glaring at him even as she wondered why he was staring at her so strangely.

Her French accent was as lovely as she was. If this was the lady of the house, she did not fit her relatives' descriptions. She was barely more than a child. Perhaps there was some mistake.

He stood and bowed to her politely. "I am Colonel Graham Newman, at your service, Mrs. Slaughter."

"I am surprised you know my name, Colonel. I had thought myself all but forgotten by the intruders who occupy my home."

"You will excuse me, ma'am, but I arrived late last night. I did not learn about your detention until that time." He smiled, thinking to win her confidence with kindness. "As you can see, I made you my first order of the day."

"That is not quite true, Colonel. Your first order of the day was to cut the branches off my magnolia tree. I demand to know the reason you think you can come into my home and treat it as if it were your own?"

He was enchanted by the way her eyes changed color when she became incensed. "Alas, Mrs. Slaughter, war makes warlords of us all. I like the idea of forcefully using your house no less than you do. No one as lovely as you should be forced to remain in her room. We would all enjoy your company at dinner tonight."

Liberty was not appeased. The colonel had pretty

manners, but she was not one to be won over by charm. "I do not desire to dine with you. May I assume I am still free to choose with whom I dine?"

"Indeed, the choice is yours, but I would hope you would reconsider. It will all be quite proper, if that is your concern. Your sister and her husband will be dining with me as well."

She looked at him through veiled silky lashes. "That is just another reason for me to decline. I have no wish to be at the same table with Bandera and Sebastian."

"But I assumed that your sister—"

"Do not assume anything where my sister is concerned, *Monsieur*. However, I have no intention of discussing my private family matters with you."

He seated himself at the desk and waved her to a chair. Liberty ignored his gesture, choosing to stand instead. "If you do not wish to dine with me, what can I do for you?"

"You can vacate my house."

"Aside from that?"

"You could always remove the guard from in front of my door."

He smiled. "After seeing you, I believe I will leave him there for your own protection. You are far too lovely to be left unguarded with so many men in the house."

"Is that meant to be amusing?"

The smile left his lips, and he leaned forward, thinking the direct approach was the best way to proceed. "Tell me about your husband, Mrs. Slaughter."

"I would be glad to, Colonel. My husband is an American, who, like thousands of his countrymen, resents your trespassing on land that does not belong to you."

Instead of being angry, Colonel Newman was further intrigued. "You French, in Louisiana, must be more than confused as to what country you belong to since it has changed hands so many times."

369

"We belong to ourselves, and we have the right to choose who will represent us." Her eyes flashed like blue ice. "I would like to stand here chatting with you, Colonel, but I have better things to do with my time."

"Such as returning to your room?"

"Is that an ultimatum?"

"That depends. If I allow you free access to the house and grounds, will you give me your word that you will not try to send word to your husband?" Colonel Newman thought he was being very clever. He wanted Judah Slaughter to find out his wife was being held against her will. But it must be handled in such a way that Captain Slaughter wouldn't suspect a trap. After seeing the lovely Liberty, Colonel Newman had very little doubt that Slaughter would come for his wife if he thought she was being detained.

Liberty was quiet for a moment as she pondered his words. If she told him she would not try to see Judah, would he let her out of her room? No, she could not lie to gain her freedom. She would do everything in her power to try to get in touch with Judah.

"I am sorry, Colonel. I cannot promise you that. I will do everything in my power to contact my husband."

"You see my problem then?"

"If that is all you have to say, I wish to return to my room. I have no desire to talk to you any longer."

Liberty had already started across the room when he called out to her. "Wait. I have another matter to discuss with you. I have been pestered all morning by some strange women who says her name is Zippora. She refuses to leave until she sees you. I am told she has camped on the front steps and hasn't budged since early this morning. Your brother-in-law informs me that she is some kind of a witch, but I doubt that. Would you like to see her?"

Liberty spun around. *"Oui,* I would like very much to

see her, Colonel. Zippora is a good friend of mine."

"An odd friendship," he mumbled under his breath. Standing up, he flashed her a smile. "If you will agree to see the woman in my presence, I will allow her to come in."

"I would much rather see Zippora alone in my room. I am not accustomed to having my conversations overheard by a complete stranger."

He chuckled and moved to the door. "I understand how you feel, but I must insist that you remain here with me. I would not like you to pass on any information to her that might be used against us by the Americans."

"Zippora hardly has Andrew Jackson's ear," Liberty argued.

"That may be true, but I'm not sure she hasn't Judah Slaughter's."

Liberty thought it better not to press the issue. It was enough to know she was not alone and that Zippora had not forgotten her.

As Colonel Newman spoke to the orderly who stood just outside the door, Liberty went to the bookshelf and pulled out a volume and casually turned the pages. She didn't want the colonel to know how anxious she was to see Zippora. She had a feeling the man was up to something, but she didn't know what it could be.

When the door opened and Liberty saw that dear face, she dropped the book and ran across the room to be held in Zippora's comforting arms. She had forgotten to act with restraint. "I am so glad to see you," she cried, letting her emotions pour out. "I have never felt so alone."

"I have been trying to see you all day, but they wouldn't let me. I see you are very pale and have lost weight. Have you been mistreated in any way?"

"I have not been physically harmed, if that is what you are asking, but I have been confined to my room like a common criminal."

Zippora turned her yellow eyes on Colonel Newman. "Hey, *Anglais,* I will take *Ma'dame* away with me today. It is not seemly for a young lady of delicate upbringing to be confined with so many soldiers in the house."

Colonel Newman seated himself at the desk, and studied the old woman intently. Picking up the feather pen, he rolled it between his fingers. "I think not . . . Zippora. Mrs. Slaughter will continue her stay with us."

It went against everything Colonel Newman believed in to say the next words. "I find Mrs. Slaughter a very attractive woman. I have only begun to enjoy her company. Who can say? I may decide to send her to England. I am sure she would make a fitting trade for some of our prisoners." Colonel Newman knew the British government would never hold a woman hostage for any reason. He could only hope that Mrs. Slaughter was unaware of that fact.

Zippora's yellow eyes took on a strange glow as she stared at the Englishman. "It is a dangerous game you play, *Anglais. Ma'dame*'s husband will never allow that to happen."

That was what Colonel Newman was counting on. He stood up, eying both women. He placed the pen down and crossed to the door. "Just to show you that I am a gentleman, I will leave the room and allow the two of you to have a few moments of privacy."

Zippora's eyes followed the man. She frowned and turned to Liberty when he closed the door behind him. "There is something not right here. That man is up to something. Do you know what he is trying to accomplish?"

"Like you, I know he is up to something. But I cannot yet see what it is. I cannot be of any importance to the British government. I do not even know why he keeps me confined to my room. I begin to think it might have something do with Judah."

"I believe you could be right, *ma petite*. The word is out that Judah Slaughter is a hero. He sunk one *Anglais* ship and captured another. It is even whispered that he captured a high-ranking admiral. I believe this man knows that and plays games with you because he wants something."

"Oui, but what does he want, Zippora?"

The old woman chuckled and picked up the pen that had been so conveniently placed at their disposal. "I believe it is intended that you should write your husband a note and I should deliver it to him. However clever the *Anglais* thinks he is, we will be even more clever."

Liberty took the pen and smiled at Zippora. "I believe I am beginning to understand too. They want me to beg Judah to come for me, and then they will be waiting for him." She lowered her voice. "I would just hate to disappoint the man—shall I write Judah a note?"

Liberty had no sooner handed the note to Zippora than the door opened and the colonel entered. He pretended not to see Zippora push the note into the bodice of her gown, but his eyes swept the desk and saw that the pen had been moved. With a self-satisfied smile, he spoke to Liberty.

"I fear your friend must leave now. As soon as my aide returns, he will escort you back to your bedroom."

Liberty hugged Zippora, and the old woman whispered in her ear. "Have courage, little one. Judah Slaughter is a clever man. He will find a way to get you out of here."

When Zippora left, Liberty again experienced the heavy loneliness. She walked over to the window and watched Zippora make her way down to the river. She was aware that the colonel had come up behind her, but she did not acknowledge his presence. He, too, was watching Zippora's departure.

The old woman untied her skiff and got inside. As the boat caught the current, it disappeared around the bend to be lost from sight.

Liberty turned to find a gratified smile on Colonel Newman's face. "I trust your little note will bring your husband to the rescue in due time."

"What makes you think I wrote my husband a note, Colonel?" she asked, pretending innocence.

The colonel walked to the desk and picked up the pen. "I know you wrote your husband a note, Mrs. Slaughter. It will do you no good to deny it."

Liberty stalled for time, knowing that each precious moment meant Zippora was farther out of reach of the colonel's men. "What are you implying?" she wanted to know, still playing the part he expected her to play.

His self-satisfied laugh grated on her ears. "You think me a fool, Mrs. Slaughter, but it is you who are the fool this time. I purposely left the room to allow you time to write your husband a note." His eyes held a hint of superiority. "Did you beg your husband to rescue you?"

Liberty knew that Zippora was already far beyond the colonel's reach. "You have found me out, *Monsieur*. I do not know what ever made me think I could fool you."

He smiled indulgently. "Do not feel too bad, Madame Slaughter. I set a trap for you, and you fell into it. There is no shame in being outwitted by a man of experience."

"Why did you not try to keep me from getting in touch with my husband, Colonel?"

"Your husband has been a thorn in our side for some time now. Lately he has become bold in his raids on our ships. When he comes to rescue you, he will be walking into a trap, because we will be waiting for him."

Laughter danced in Liberty's eyes. "I am sorry to disappoint you, Colonel, but my husband will not be coming for me. You see, he has never been accused of being a fool."

Colonel Newman watched her closely. "I would be willing to wager he will come."

"Then you would lose, *Monsieur,* because my note was not an appeal for help; it was a warning to Judah that you were setting a trap for him and that he must not come anywhere near Briar Oaks."

Colonel Newman's neck turned red, and the color soon spread to his face. He rushed across the room and called out to his orderly. "Get to the boats and stop the old woman that just left. I want that note she is carrying!"

Liberty swept past him. "I will just go to my room, Colonel. It has been a most trying day . . . for fools."

He stared after her as she climbed the stairs. By God, she was some woman. She had been aware of what he had been trying to do. Amused laughter met Liberty's ears, and she turned back to see the colonel's eyes dancing with mirth. He gave her a sweeping bow. "You have won the day, Mrs. Slaughter. I pray the American men are not as clever as their women. If so, we are done for."

Andrew Jackson's camp was buzzing with activity. Men were coming and going as they prepared for battle.

Zippora had been directed to Judah's tent, and she now waited for him to finish Liberty's note before she spoke. "I do not believe Liberty is being mistreated in any way. She will be fine as long as the *Anglais* keep Sebastian and Bandera away from her. Liberty tells me that her sister and brother-in-law believe the *Anglais* will give them Briar Oaks if they win the war."

Judah's jaw clamped together in anger. "I will not have her remain under that roof one more night. I don't trust Sebastian or Bandera."

"I believe the *Anglais* will protect Liberty. She is too valuable to them to let any harm come to her. I, too, share your concern for her where Bandera and Sebastian are concerned."

"Damn, I was a fool to let her go back there. I tried to

get her to stay with my mother, but she insisted on returning to Briar Oaks."

"Liberty can be stubborn when she wants her way. I am sure the colonel found that out after I left," Zippora said, smiling.

A grin touched Judah's lips as he thought of the clever way Liberty and Zippora had dealt with the Englishman. "I would like to have seen the man's face when he learned that you and Liberty tricked him." Suddenly a troubled thought came to him and the smile left his face. "I hope it didn't make him angry enough to punish Liberty."

"No, he was a gentleman. I read in his eyes that his business was very distasteful to him. However, like you, I believe that the sooner we get Liberty away from Sebastian, the better. He is touched with greed and a thirst for power, and one never knows what he might do."

Judah glanced down at Liberty's note, folded it, and poked it into his pocket. "Tomorrow night, I will go after her. I believe I can come up with a plan, but I will need your help."

"I will help you, Judah Slaughter. You have only to tell me what to do."

"Once again I am indebted to you, Zippora. I do not know what good angel put you in my path, but you have saved my skin more than once."

Zippora smiled. "The good angel is Liberty." She went out of the tent and Judah followed her. "I will await word from you tomorrow," she told him.

"I will come for you at sundown."

He watched her walk away holding herself straight and tall. To some, Zippora might be a frightening figure, but to him she was a guardian angel.

The night winds blowing through the tree branches caused eerie shadows to dance across the window. Liberty

376

lay in bed, staring at the ceiling. Today, as the colonel had talked of Judah's daring adventures, she had realized how little she really knew about the man she had married.

She got out of bed and moved to the window, her feet noiseless against the cold floor. Glancing out, she knew there was no way she could escape through the tree now that the branches had been cut back. Judah was out there somewhere and she hoped he would heed her warning and not attempt to rescue her. She did not want to see him end up a prisoner of the English.

Sebastian lit a cigar and watched the smoke fan out about his head. "I wonder if you have overestimated my sister-in-law, Colonel Newman. Liberty is not as clever as you seem to think she is."

"I believe it is you who underestimate Mrs. Slaughter. She knew from the beginning that I was playing a game with her today. In underestimating her, I lost the chance to get my hands on her husband."

"Knowing Judah as I do, I would not discount the possibility that he may yet try to rescue Liberty."

"I am very aware of that. I have two guards posted below, watching her bedroom window, and no one can get past the men who guard the house."

"Any word on the war, Colonel? Do you know where Jackson is?"

Colonel Newman looked at the foppish man who sat across from him. He had little liking for Sebastian Montesquieu, but the Creole had been very useful to him. "It is said that Jackson is held up at a place called Chalmette, getting ready for a hard push. Since the ground is too wet for trenches, the Americans are building mud walls."

Sebastian laughed scornfully. "Do they think the mud will hold back your armies? I can see you are dealing with imbeciles. It is but a matter of time before you march triumphantly into New Orleans."

Colonel Newman took a sip of his wine and glanced around the book-lined room. What a showplace it must have been at one time. "How little you know the Americans if you believe that. I admit they have fought several disastrous battles in this war, but that was before General Jackson was put in charge. The man is a genius at strategy." Newman took a puff on his cigar before he continued. "I heard an interesting story about him. It is said that he blames us for the death of his mother and two brothers. What we are facing here is a man with a personal vendetta—that's the most dangerous kind of man."

Sebastian stubbed out his cigar. "I wonder if you would allow me to see my sister-in-law. My wife is concerned about her, and I would like to report firsthand that she is not suffering from her confinement."

"It is not my impression that the two sisters have a high regard for one another."

"As you saw from your visit with her today, Liberty can be willful and strong-minded. Bandera is of a gentler nature, and the two of them often quarrel. But nonetheless, Bandera worries about Liberty."

Having met both sisters, Colonel Newman favored Liberty's open honesty to her sister's secretiveness. "I will allow your wife to visit her sister tomorrow . . . if your wife is still concerned about her welfare." He had been told that Mrs. Montesquieu had not thus far inquired about her sister's well-being.

Sebastian shifted his eyes and stared at the toe of his boot. "But I thought if I could see—"

"I consider the matter closed," Colonel Newman snapped, rising to his feet. "Since the hour is late, I am sure your sister-in-law is in bed. I suggest we both seek our own beds. In the event that Judah Slaughter comes to rescue his wife, rest assured that we will be ready for him."

Later, as Sebastian paused at his bedroom door, he glanced down the hall to where the guard was posted at Liberty's door. He thought of her, lying soft and lovely in her bed, and he felt an ache deep inside. Why did she always torment him? He wanted her, and one day he would have her, just as he would one day have Bend of the River.

Sebastian now knew the one way to get even with Judah was through Liberty. But at the moment, with her under the protection of Colonel Newman, he could not get to her any easier than Judah could. . . .

Chapter Twenty-one

January 6, 1814

For over a week Judah and Zippora had attempted to rescue Liberty, but Briar Oaks had become an armed fortress. Over twenty guards patrolled the grounds, and up to now, it had been impossible for Judah to get close to the house.

"It's tonight or never, Zippora," Judah whispered, plying the oar to the water. "With this fog, we just may succeed."

Zippora brought the boat in close to the riverbank, while Judah checked his pistol to make sure it was loaded. "We are fortunate that the mist is so heavy, Judah Slaughter," she whispered. "It will be impossible for the guards to see you, and that will work to your advantage."

"You are an amazing woman, Zippora. I'm not even sure I can find the house in this mist, yet you were able to find your way down the river."

Zippora pulled her hood over her head and huddled in the bow of her small boat. "You must have a care when I put you ashore. Keep to the trees on your left, and the path will lead you to Liberty's bedroom. Do you remember which window I told you to look for?"

Judah was grim-faced. "I hope so. I would sure be out of luck if I ended up in the wrong bedroom."

The boat bumped against the bank, and Judah shouldered the rope and stepped ashore. He listened for a moment to see if there were any guards nearby. Hearing nothing, he moved up the embankment.

Zippora followed him to the first tree. "I will wait here for you, *M'sieu*. You must hurry and return before the mist clears."

"If I am not back in an hour and a half, it will mean I ran into trouble, and you must leave immediately. Is that understood?"

"I hear you," she said, feeling the cold mist against her face. "I scouted the area yesterday and discovered there are five guards at the front of the house. They are no more than fifty paces apart, so have a care. There is also a man that walks the pier. It is best to avoid that area completely."

"Wish me luck," Judah said, staring into the total darkness ahead and wondering if he would be able to find Liberty, let alone rescue her.

"Luck will be with you. You must use your wits, but you have the courage of a lion, Judah Slaughter."

His dark cloak swirled out about him as he turned and moved away, soon to be swallowed up by the eerie darkness.

Unable to sleep, Liberty threw the covers back and made her way to the window. It was past midnight and she stared out at a mist so thick she couldn't even see the tree that stood outside her window. Once in a while she would hear the voice of a British sentry calling out to report his position.

A chill passed through Liberty's body, and she shivered and pulled her shawl about her for warmth. Would this nightmare never end? She was desperate for news of the war, but no one would tell her anything. There had been cannon fire for the past two days, now even that had stopped. Two warring forces had come together, so why was it so silent?

She was desperately alone. She hadn't seen a friendly face since the Zippora had come to visit. Had everyone forgotten she existed?

A tear made its way down her cheek. Perhaps it was good to have all this time to think about her marriage to Judah. If he had married her just to get his hands on Bend of the River, it was her own fault. She had gone into marriage knowing that Judah did not love her.

"Oh, but I do love him so desperately," she cried out, burying her head in her arms and giving in to total melancholy. "I just wish I knew where he was, and if he is safe." Liberty had half-expected Judah to make an attempt to rescue her. In some part of her mind she felt sad because he had not at least tried.

"Fool," she said to herself. "Didn't you ask him to stay away? Do you want him to be captured?" A tear made a trail down her cheek. "I must really be getting desperate— I am starting to talk to myself."

Judah carefully placed one booted foot in front of the other, knowing any sound would be magnified in the darkness. He had hardly gone twenty paces when he heard someone coming toward him. Quickly, he flattened himself against a tree trunk and pulled his cape about him.

The guard paused an arm's-length away from Judah and stood as if listening for something. Judah's senses became alert, and he was prepared to strike in case the man discovered his presence. He gripped the handle of his pistol, and then decided that if he fired his gun, the shot would alert the other guards and his chances of rescuing Liberty would be lost. He would have to take the man on in hand-to-hand combat.

Judah was ready to spring when the guard turned on his heel and moved out of sight. Judah breathed a sigh of relief, and waited until the man's footsteps faded into the distance before he continued toward the house.

He ducked from one tree to another until the house loomed out of the mist before him. Then his eyes sought the window that would be Liberty's. Cautiously he walked to the tree just below it, and he assessed the situation. There was no way he could get to Liberty without using the rope. He grabbed a branch and swung himself into the tree, just in time to avoid the sentry that walked by.

The English soldier paused in his duty, and propped his rifle against the tree trunk. Minutes passed, and the man still didn't move. Judah became irritated, for precious time was passing. He had to rescue Liberty before the mist cleared. They would have no chance at all when the morning sun burned it away.

Liberty had fallen asleep curled up on the window ledge. She awoke with a start; a sudden noise had shaken her out of her sleep. She listened for a moment, but there was no sound. Cold and stiff, she stood up and tried to restore circulation to her legs.

A sound, like someone throwing pebbles against her window, caught her attention. She listened until it came again. Someone was outside her window. Pressing her face against the frosted pane, she could see nothing. She had convinced herself that she must have imagined the whole thing, when she heard it again.

Liberty slowly opened the window, and before she could react, a dark shrouded figure swooped inside, knocking her to the floor and landing on top of her. Immediately enfolded in a dark cape, Liberty fought to get free. But a man's hand clamped over her mouth, and panic rose up inside her. She pushed against the strong hand that seemed to cut off her breathing.

"Have no fear, my lady wife," a beloved voice whispered in her ear. "I have come to get you out of here. I am going to take my hand away from your mouth now, but do not make a sound," he cautioned.

"Judah," she whispered as he scooped her up in his arms and held her tightly against his broad chest. Joy threaded her words. "You came for me."

He pressed his cheek to hers, and tightened his arms about her. "Did you think I would not? Surely you knew I would never allow you to become anyone's prisoner." He smiled. ". . . Except mine."

Her heart sung with happiness because he had come for her, yet she feared for the man she loved. "Judah did you not get my note warning you not to come? Do you not know you are in danger?"

His lips brushed against hers and he laughed softly. *"Madame,* do you not know your husband is accused of being a pirate who thinks nothing of danger?"

"Judah, be serious. You are in peril here. You must leave immediately."

He set Liberty on her feet. "I will not leave without you. Dress quickly. I had to deal with one of your guards below. I fear he will regain consciousness at any moment and alert the house."

Liberty's hands fumbled, she was in such haste to get dressed. Pulling on her gown, she felt Judah's hands at her back, tying the bow at the neck. "I would rather be undressing you," he whispered against her ear, sending shivers of delight to dance down her spine.

She reached up to place her hand on his, but Judah had already moved across the room to look out the window. Liberty gathered up her cloak and pulled it around her.

"Come on," he called to her, as he tested the rope he

had tied in the branches of the tree. "We must leave now. It sounds like the changing of the guard. Hurry!"

Liberty flew into his strong arms, and to her surprise, he threw her across his shoulder. She hardly had time to gasp in surprise, before they went flying through the air and he landed softly on the sturdy tree branch.

Judah set her down beside him and caught her about the waist to steady her. "So far, so good," he laughed. "Now you must clutch me around the neck, and I will descend the rope. Are you frightened?"

"No, not with you."

"Good girl," he said, feeling great pride in his wife. He had known many women who would have been hysterical under similar circumstances, yet not once did Liberty express fear or doubt. She did not hesitate to follow his every command without question.

Her hands went around his neck, and he lowered them both down the rope. Judah could hear the moaning of the man he had knocked unconscious. He knew they had to hurry. When his feet touched the ground, he pulled Liberty behind the tree.

He realized that it was long past the hour and a half Zippora was supposed to wait for him. If she had followed his instructions, she would be gone by now, and their chances of escaping were very slim.

Judah clasped Liberty's hand. "Do you feel up to running?" he asked urgently.

"*Oui,*" she said, lifting her gown. "I can run very fast when the need arises."

Their feet seemed to fly as they headed in the direction of the river. Behind them, Liberty heard a voice calling out. "Intruder on the premises! Sound the alarm! Sound the alarm!"

They ran and ran until Liberty felt that her lungs were going to burst from lack of air. Her legs would no longer hold her and she slipped. She would have fallen to the ground had Judah not grabbed her. Without breaking his stride, he swung her into his arms and continued toward the river. He was hoping Zippora would meet them when they got there.

The mist was beginning to clear, and the first rosy glow of morning touched the Eastern horizon. Several shots rang out, and then bullets were whizzing all about them. Judah jumped behind a tree, listened to the sound of running footsteps. "Pray we have a boat when we reach the river, Liberty," he said, clasping her to him. He took a deep breath and bounded down the embankment, his black cape flying behind him.

"Over here," Zippora called out. "Hurry!"

Judah seemed to sail through the air as he leaped off the embankment and landed softly in the boat. When the small craft stopped rocking, he deposited Liberty in the rear, and pushed her head down. "Keep low," he cautioned. He then picked up an oar and helped Zippora row, knowing they must get out of range of the British guns.

Bullets whistled past them as several soldiers gathered at the river's edge. Others were ordered into boats and were soon in pursuit.

Zippora only laughed. "The *Anglais* would be wiser to stay on land. In no time at all they will be hopelessly lost in the mist. We are safe from them now. Besides I took advantage of the time while I was waiting. Those boats will not remain afloat for long."

Liberty drew in a deep breath. Her heart felt light as she hugged her cape about her. Judah did care about her. Had he not risked his life to rescue her tonight?

As the sound of English voices faded behind them, they caught the current and headed downriver.

"Where are we going," Liberty asked, when they moved past the bayou that would take them to Zippora's cabin. Not that she cared. It was enough to be free.

"I am going to take you where you will be safely out of British hands, and where they will not find you," Judah told her.

"You cannot take her to Bend of the River," Zippora said, leaning back and allowing Judah to do the rowing. "It is surrounded by the *Anglais*. They might capture her again."

"I know," Judah said, allowing the current to sweep them downriver. "I am taking her to the *Winged Victory*. You should stay aboard with her, Zippora."

"No, I will return home. I am in no danger."

By the time the mist had cleared, they had passed the enemy position and were approaching Colonel Jackson's headquarters at Chalmette. Judah rowed ashore and helped Zippora and Liberty to disembark.

Liberty looked from her husband to her dear friend Zippora. "How can I say thank you?" she asked, tears shining in her eyes. "I am most grateful to both of you."

Judah flashed her a smile, and Zippora turned away to climb back into her boat. "I have no time to listen to this," she said in a gruff voice, but Liberty saw that her eyes were shining with happiness. She watched the old woman pull away from shore and paddle to the middle of the river. Liberty raised her hand to wave good-by, and Zippora acknowledged her with the merest nod of her head.

"That is an amazing woman," Judah observed. "I wager there is not another like her anywhere in this world."

Liberty nodded in agreement.

Judah's eyes were warm as they rested on her face. "Are you tired, little one?"

"A little."

"Come, I will have Philippe escort you to my ship. You can rest when you get there." Taking her arm, he led her through the camp.

Disappointment showed in her eyes. "Will you not be

388

coming with me?"

"I am afraid not. Like many of my countrymen, I am committed here, Liberty. The English want New Orleans, and they know they have to go through us to get it."

For the first time Liberty noticed the activity going on around her. Walls built of mud ran along a deep canal. Fence posts had been driven into the ground to reinforce the rampart, and artillery was placed behind it at strategic points. Some men were drilling, while others were cleaning their rifles. A few slept on the cold ground, and Liberty suspected they must have been on night duty. There was tension in the air, a premonition of things to come.

For the first time Liberty felt the horrors of war. Men were preparing to fight, to kill one another. Perhaps blood would be spilled on the very ground where she now stood.

"Come away with me, Judah," she said, in a moment of weakness, looking at him with pleading eyes. "Please do not stay here."

"I cannot, Liberty, and I do not believe you really want me to. Could you respect a man who would turn his back on his duty?"

"I . . . no. It's just that—."

"I know," he said, smiling down at her. "You haven't had anyone to look after you since your father died. It's only normal that you would be concerned about the only stability in your life, which at the moment happens to be me."

Liberty looked at him strangely. "Was that the way Judah thought she felt about him, as someone she could depend upon?"

"Judah, you are my husband."

His eyes moved across her face. "I haven't forgotten, Liberty."

Suddenly she was terrified for him. Suppose he was

wounded, or even killed, in battle? "Judah, what will really happen here?" she asked.

"I won't lie to you, little one. There will be a battle such as we have never known before." He glanced about him at Jackson's strange-looking army. The British know they will have to go through us to get to New Orleans, but we intend to stop them here—we have to!"

Liberty's eyes came to life with flames of patriotism. "I wish I were a man. I would stand beside you and fight to the bitter end." She turned to him, her eyes expectant. "I don't suppose you would allow me to stay?"

He smiled and shook his head. "No, I will not. And none of your tricks either. You are going where you will be out of the line of danger."

"Will you have the fire power of the *Carolina* when the battle starts?" she asked, remembering the ship had helped Colonel Jackson in the last battle.

"No, she was set afire by the British. We saved some of her guns, however. They are mounted and ready to fire. Her crew members hope to get their revenge."

"What of the cannons that we brought through the swamps?"

"They are primed and ready. My gunners from the *Winged Victory* will man them when the battle commences."

By now they had reached a tent, and Judah led Liberty inside. There she saw Philippe and several other men she recognized from the *Winged Victory*.

"Gentlemen, I would like to present to you my wife, Liberty Slaughter. Liberty, this is Rojo. Philippe you already know. James Brent, Robert Massey, and George Cummings. The others are either in camp or downriver guarding the ship."

Each man quickly removed his hat and faced Liberty with shining eyes. Philippe appointed himself as spokesman. "Madame Slaughter, we are indeed honored to be presented to you. We stand ready to help you in any way we can."

The others shook their heads in agreement, except Rojo. He stared into clear blue eyes and lost his heart. Surely she was the most beautiful creature he had ever seen. "The captain is a most fortunate man, *Señora*. I have never seen anyone more pretty," he blurted out, provoking rib gouging and snickers from some of the other crew members.

Judah looked at each man through lowered lashes, which brought immediate silence. "Philippe, choose three men and escort Madame Slaughter to the *Winged Victory*. You can send the others back, but I want you to remain with my wife until further notice."

"Aye, aye, sir," Philippe answered. "Are there any other instructions?"

"Yes." Judah lowered his voice. "Should the war go against us, you are to get my mother, and my grandfather if he will go with you. Then I want you to take the *Winged Victory* to Boston. Is that understood?"

"Aye, Captain." There was a grave look on the first mate's face, because he usually went into battle with his captain. The two men shook hands. "God keep you, Captain," Philippe said.

Liberty felt a sob building up deep inside her. How could she walk away from the man she loved, knowing she might never see him again. She tried to think of Colonel Jackson's wife, Rachel, and how hard it must have been for her to send her husband off to war—but it didn't help. She held her back straight and refused to cry in front of Judah's men. She would show everyone what it meant to be Judah Slaughter's wife.

Judah took Liberty's arm and led her back toward the river, while the four men escorting her followed, just out of earshot. Neither of them spoke until they reached the longboat, then Liberty turned to her husband. "Take care of yourself," she said bravely.

"I shall. You will be well cared for, Liberty. Philippe will guard you with his life. I trust him completely, I hope you will too."

"*Oui,* of course." She clutched his shirt front and gazed into his eyes. "You will not take any unnecessary chances, will you?"

He smiled. "You have my word, I will not."

She drew in a ragged breath, wishing he would take her in his strong arms and assure her that they would soon be together. The wind ruffled her golden hair, and he smoothed it down with his hand. He touched his finger to his lips and then pressed it gently to hers. "We will be together again soon, little one . . . soon."

Liberty turned away, knowing she could no longer hold the tears back. Judah helped her into the boat, and the others climbed in after her, taking up the oars. She refused to look back at Judah until the boat had moved a safe distance downstream.

When Liberty could trust herself to turn, Judah was too far away for her to see his expression, but he raised his hand to her and she waved back. She wished she dare ask Philippe to turn the boat around and take her back. What would she do if anything happened to Judah? She hadn't had the chance to tell him she loved him.

She pulled her hood over her head so it would hide her face from the others. Only then did she allow the tears to flow freely. Soon they rounded a bend, and she could no longer see her husband. The men must have known what she was feeling, because no one spoke. The only sounds that could be heard were the distant singing of a mockingbird and the swish of oars as they sliced through the water.

Sebastian slammed his fist down on the desk and

winced in pain. "What imbecile allowed Judah Slaughter to come into this house and spirit Liberty away right under our noses?"

Colonel Newman smiled. "Since I am in charge here, I suppose you could say I was that imbecile."

Sebastian cleared his throat. "I did not mean to imply that you were at fault, Colonel. I was referring to the guards who were on duty last night. They were careless and unprofessional. I demand that they be reprimanded."

"You are in no position to demand anything. And since you are not a military man, how would you know what was professional and what wasn't?"

Sebastian chose to ignore the insult. He realized he had spoken rashly. The one thing he did not want to do was turn Colonel Newman against him. The man was in a position to help him get his hands on Briar Oaks, maybe even Bend of the River.

"I have to hand it to Slaughter," Colonel Newman stated, admiration threading his voice. "He took us completely by surprise. I wouldn't have thought any man could have navigated in that heavy fog and mist last night."

Bandera had been sitting near the fire, trying to keep warm. She got up and crossed to her husband. "What is to be done to recover my sister, Colonel? Have you sent men to search for her and bring her back?"

"I don't mean to sound indelicate, Mrs. Montesquieu, but I no longer have an interest in your sister. I admit it would have been nice to capture Judah Slaughter, but since that did not happen, we still have a war to fight."

"Does it not bother you that my cousin made fools of us all?" Sebastian wanted to know. "I would think, if for no other reason, you would want to retake Liberty to redeem your honor, Colonel."

Colonel Newman laughed aloud. "My honor was never at stake. Judah Slaughter is the one who redeemed *his*

393

honor last night. We held someone who belonged to him, and he took her back against impossible odds. I would have attempted the same had I been in his place."

Sebastian stared at the colonel in astonishment. "If I did not know better, I would think you admire my cousin."

"I do admire him. He has courage beyond that of most men. I'd bet you are not even aware of some of his exploits at sea."

"No, nor do I want to know about them," Sebastian said pettishly. "I do not admire his kind."

Bandera tapped her shoe against the floor in vexation. "I see that old witch Zippora's hand in this. Only she could have guided Judah here last night." She turned her eyes on the colonel and flashed him a smile. "Surely you are going to help us get my sister back. We cannot leave her in the clutches of that pirate Judah Slaughter."

Colonel Newman's mouth tightened into a firm line. He had been in close contact with Bandera and Sebastian since Christmas. It was all he could do to stay in the same room with them. "Your concern for your sister is very touching. But I believe she would rather be in the hands of her husband than locked in her bedroom. I have been astounded that you never asked me to release your sister from her confinement, *Madame*. Indeed, I was told that you did not once ask to see her." A devilish smile lit the colonel's gray eyes. "At least your husband showed enough concern to ask to be admitted to her room on several occasions."

Bandera's eyes flamed with jealousy as she whirled on Sebastian. "You never told me you had tried to get in to see Liberty."

He waved her aside. "It was not important."

"You can't get it through your head that my sister despises you, can you, Sebastian? If she would give you a second glance, you would be on your knees to her. You should have married Liberty instead of me."

Colonel Newman walked out of the room, closing the door behind him and thinking he would take a stroll on the grounds, get a breath of fresh air. For his part, he decided the lovely Liberty Slaughter was just where she ought to be. She certainly had no friends in this house.

"I salute you, Captain Slaughter," he said under his breath. "Well done."

Chapter Twenty-two

January 8, 1814

It was just daylight when the British fired a rocket into the air. That rocket was quickly followed by another and still another. This was their signal to attack, and was hastily answered by volleys from the Americans who were dug in behind the mud ramparts, their guns primed and ready.

Across the river valley, in New Orleans and points beyond, the whole earth seemed to tremble as two warring factions came together in a life-and-death struggle. Wild creatures fled as man pitted his strength against his fellowman.

Gaps were blasted in the American lines by enemy artillery, but were quickly filled with fresh troops as the enemy marched within musket range.

To the advancing British, the American line looked like a continual wall of fire because the American soldiers stood four deep behind the protective wall. One soldier would fire his gun, step back to reload, and be replaced by another. The sequence was repeated over and over.

Nonetheless the never-ending line of British soldiers marched forward, fell, and died. They kept coming at the Americans, with guns blasting and flags waving.

Twenty-five minutes of continual firing, of ripping

apart their offense, passed before the advancing British withdrew from the line of fire.

As the day wore on, filled with British advances and retreats, it soon became clear that the Americans were triumphant. A brave, but sorely wounded army finally retreated in defeat.

Judah picked up the tattered American flag that had fallen near him, and waved it in the air, while patriotic voices cried out in unison. Then Jackson rode among his troops, speaking words of encouragement.

When the report came in later, it was hard to believe there had only been seven Americans killed and six wounded. The British had suffered a far greater loss; their dead and dying littered the battlefield.

Liberty stood on the deck of the *Winged Victory*, listening to the sounds of battle in the distance. She could see nothing but an occasional puff of smoke that drifted through the air to disappear among the clouds that hung low in to the sky. Yet cannon fire shook the earth and rumbled like distant thunder.

She was horrified by the fighting. She wanted to cover her head and pretend it was not happening. She closed her eyes tightly, and prayed with all her might that Judah would not be among the casualties. All day she stood at the railing, searching, waiting, hoping for Judah's return.

It was not yet afternoon when the big guns fell silent, and an ominous feeling of unreality settled over the land. Philippe tried to get Liberty to go below and rest, but she would not give up her vigil, weary though she was. She was determined to wait for some word of her husband.

Liberty thought only in terms of the human lives that were being sacrificed. When night fell, she still stood on deck, unable to leave until she had heard some word from the battlefield. An hour passed, and then another; and still she waited.

Philippe brought her a tray of food, but she couldn't eat it. "I am sorry you had to stay with me, Philippe. I know you wanted to be with Judah today."

The first mate's eyes held an earnest light. "The captain paid me a very great honor today, *Madame.* He entrusted his most valued treasure to me when he placed you in my keeping. That means a great deal to me."

Liberty could find no appropriate words to say, so she and Philippe stood silently together, waiting and listening for the small-arms fire to cease. Finally, just before dusk, the firing did stop and a deathly quiet hung over the land. Liberty held her breath, wondering what the silence meant. Exhausted and frightened, she refused to go below and rest as Philippe suggested. She kept watching for the approach of a small craft, hoping for word of Judah.

It was almost midnight when Philippe's keen ears picked up the sound of a small boat rowing toward them. He pushed Liberty behind him, as the craft bumped against the *Winged Victory.*

"Ahoy, you aboard, I have news of the battle."

Philippe recognized Rojo's voice and threw the ladder down to him. As soon as Rojo was on deck, Liberty rushed to him. "Tell us your news," she cried, trying to read his face in the half light of the one torch Philippe held in his hand.

"It is a victory! We did not let the British break through our lines. We held them back. General Jackson believes the war is all but over. America has won!"

Liberty felt her body tremble. "What news of my husband?" she asked, almost afraid to hear.

"The captain is a brave man. As always, he was in the middle of the heaviest fighting. Even though he is not an infantryman, today he fought as if born to be one, *Señora.*"

"He . . . is unharmed?"

"The captain did not even get a scratch, *Señora*," Rojo assured her.

Liberty reached out her hand to Philippe for support as she felt herself falling, and for the first time in her young life, she fainted.

Philippe quickly handed Rojo the torch, then gently lifted her in his arms and carried her toward the captain's cabin, while a concerned Rojo followed. The mate laid her on the bed, bent down beside her, and patted her hand. "*Madame,* are you all right?" Philippe asked with concern.

Slowly Liberty's eyes fluttered open. For a moment she wondered where she was. Then she remembered Judah was unharmed! She smiled sheepishly at Philippe, who had such a look of distress on his face. Rojo was hovering behind Philippe, his face drawn up in a worried frown.

"I am fine," she assured them both. "It is more embarrassing than anything else. I promise you, I have never before fainted."

"No need to be ashamed, *Madame*. It is no wonder you fainted, because you had nothing to eat all day. If I bring you a tray with something special that the cook has made for you, will you try to get it down?"

She smiled. "*Oui*, I feel like I could eat my weight in food, Philippe. This is a glorious time to be alive." She glanced at Rojo. "Did my husband send word to me as to when I should expect him?"

"*No, Señora.* I was to tell you to remain here on the *Winged Victory* until otherwise notified."

Philippe saw the disappointment on Liberty's face. "Let us leave and allow *Madame* privacy." He turned to her at the door. "I will bring you something to eat."

Liberty, deep in thought, was hardly aware that the two men had left. If the war was drawing to a close, then everything in her life would be coming into focus, and she would have to deal with the many problems that faced

400

her. Most pressing was her dilemma over what to do about Sebastian and Bandera. They must be made to leave Briar Oaks, she knew that, as she knew that Judah would demand satisfaction from Sebastian!

Another thought came to her; she would now have to face some truths about Judah. Could he have married her just to get back at Bandera as her sister, had suggested? Liberty would not allow herself to believe that Judah had married her only to get his hands on Bend of the River. She could not admit that might be true, because if it were, Judah's motives had not been that different from Sebastian's. No, Judah was no more like Sebastian . . . than she was like Bandera.

Liberty looked at the cabin for the first time. It was paneled in dark wood. Besides the bed, there were green leather chairs, a desk, and several bookshelves containing books, charts, and maps. Her senses were filled with the aroma of leather and sea air. Liberty had a feeling that she was intruding. This was Judah's world and she had only been invited into a small corner of his domain.

She moved to the bookshelves where maps and charts were stacked. Absently she removed a map, unrolled it, and traced the different coastlines with her finger. She noticed that a circle had been drawn around one of the islands.

In response to a rap on the door, Liberty called out to bid whoever it was to enter. A smiling Philippe appeared and placed a tray of food on the desk.

"Do you think Judah will mind if I look at his maps, Philippe?" she asked in a troubled voice, thinking she should have asked before she took out the map.

He glanced down at the map Liberty was studying, and smiled. "No, he would not mind. I see you are interested in the West Indies." He pointed to the circle on the map. "That's Martinique. I suspect as soon as this war cools down the captain will be taking you there."

"Martinique. I have never heard Judah speak of it."

"Perhaps I spoke out of turn. It could be that the captain wants to surprise you. Please forget I mentioned it and eat your dinner so you can renew your strength."

She smiled at the way Philippe treated her. He spoke to her much as her father would have. He was growing dearer to her every time she met him. She rolled the map up, then placed it back on the shelf. "The map will be our little secret," she said, smiling brightly.

Philippe was charmed by his captain's lady. Every moment he spent in her company made him more aware of why Judah had married her. She was exceptional. Not only beautiful, but kind and thoughtful as well. A real lady, she was, with winning ways and a genuine smile.

Philippe held the chair for her, then waited to see if she would eat. When she picked up the fork and speared a piece of chicken, he was satisfied and he left to attend to his duties.

Liberty surprised herself by cleaning her plate. She felt safe and more secure than she had felt in a long time. Weary, she stripped down to her petticoat and climbed into Judah's bed. Here, among the things he loved, Liberty felt close to her husband. Her body sank into the soft downy mattress which enveloped her like a caress, and she was soon asleep, lulled by the soft, swaying motion of the *Winged Victory*.

Liberty stirred and opened her eyes. It was dark in the cabin, and she couldn't see anything, but she had the feeling someone was in the room with her.

"Have no fear, it is me," Judah said reassuringly. "I tried not to awaken you since Philippe told me you needed your rest."

Excitement flowed through Liberty. She was alone with her husband, and his deep voice stirred flaming desire to

402

life within her.

"Do you mind a bed partner?" he asked, bending down and placing a quick kiss on her lips.

"I . . . no, of course not." How could she mind being in bed with her husband when she had yearned for his touch for so long?

Judah pulled the covers aside and slid in beside her. He allowed her no time to think, but pulled her body against his. "You feel so good," he murmured, as he pressed against her body molding it to his. "In the thick of the battle today, thoughts of holding you like this kept me going."

Liberty suspected that Judah was a master of pretty words, that he always told a woman what she wanted to hear. At the moment it did not matter. A sigh escaped her lips when he smoothly removed her undergarments. His breathing was deep as he allowed his hands to glide sensuously across her naked flesh. Softly they caressed her breasts, cupping, circling, driving her out of her mind. When he bent his head to take a swollen nipple between his lips, she could feel the warm heat from his mouth. Meanwhile his wonderful hands were working magic all over her body. Her skin seemed to tingle everywhere he touched her.

The pounding of her heart sounded loud in her ears, and when his mouth sought hers, his drugging kiss made the earth spin. Liberty clung to Judah as if he were her life line. Her body seemed to belong more to him than to her, because he controlled her every move.

"I ache for you, little one. I need you desperately. Do you know what it felt like to board my ship tonight, knowing you would be here?"

"No," she whispered through trembling lips. She only knew that he was stamping his ownership on her body, and she would belong to him forever.

Judah could not wait any longer. His flesh cried out for

this woman. He gently pulled her beneath him and parted her thighs, and her body arched to meet his glorious thrust. His searing entry was made easier by the moistness of her.

Judah was powerful and strong, yet with Liberty, he was gentle. He took her slowly and easily, filling her body and filling every empty void in her life. He was everything a young girl could ever hope for in her hero, and more — so much more.

As their bodies moved together in perfect unison, Judah's hot breath fanned her lips. "Kiss me," he whispered. "Help me forget the things I witnessed today."

Liberty heard his cry and took his head between her hands, guiding his lips down to her mouth. She would help him forget the men he had seen die. She would give him so much of herself that he would be unable to think about anything else.

Judah's body trembled as her soft hands moved down his spine to clamp his waist. The sweet aroma of her was in his heart, embedded in his brain, filling his mind and his being. She had the power to make him a beggar if she but knew it. A groan escaped his lips as she arched her hips, taking him further inside her. It was bliss, it was seething excitement. Rigid pulsating fire emptied from his body into hers, filling her with the life-giving miracle.

For a moment everything stopped. There was no life outside this room, there were no feelings outside what they were feeling. They were suspended in time, carried away by a feeling every man and woman hope to find, but few ever do. Wave after wave of sensuous feelings bonded them together. They were two halves that became a whole. It had been so perfect — a thing of beauty and unreality.

When Judah could speak past the lump in his throat, his voice was husky in her ear. "You are mine, Liberty. You always have been, you always will be."

How could he know? she wondered. Could he have

guessed that she had loved him from that very first night they met? *"Oui,"* she said, against his lips. "I am your wife."

Suddenly, just having her for his wife was not enough—Judah needed to hear her say she loved him. He rolled over and clasped her to his manly chest. "Liberty, how do you feel about me?" He hoped she would say that she loved him. He was tense as he waited for her reply.

Liberty longed to confess her love, but she could not. She had been hurt too many times by the people she loved. How could she tell Judah she loved him, knowing he loved her sister? There were two things she didn't want from Judah, pity and disgust. If she admitted her love for him, it might bring out both.

"I am most grateful to you, Judah. I did not get a chance to thank you properly for the Christmas presents and—"

He cut off her words as he jerked her against him. He wanted to hear her speak of love, not gratitude. Perhaps it was too soon to expect her to have the same deep feelings he had. She was so young yet. If he were patient, and proceeded slowly to court her affections, she might learn to love him. They had not had the chance to spend much time together. They must get to know one another better.

Liberty softly touched his golden hair, wondering why he had become so silent and withdrawn. She loved the way he held her in his strong arms; it gave her a feeling of belonging. She loved him so desperately, she wondered if she could keep him from finding out how much she cared for him.

"I have a surprise that I think will please you, Liberty," Judah said, resting his face against hers. "At least I hope it will please you."

She nestled her head against the crook of his arm and snuggled as close to him as she could get. "I like surprises—good surprises."

He laughed deep in his throat. She could be so adorable that she melted his heart. "What would you say if I told you I was taking you to a beautiful tropical island with me?"

Joy surged through her. "Oh, Judah, that would make me so happy. I would so love to be on an island with you."

He traced her lips with his finger. "Would you, love?"

"Oh, *oui* . . . but can I just leave like this—I mean without letting anyone know?"

He chuckled. "You are my wife, who else would you like to tell?"

"I . . . your mother and grandfather."

"I have already informed them. They both wish us a happy voyage. As a matter of fact my mother knew you would be needing a few things so she packed a bag for you. She hopes you will not mind wearing some of her gowns. When we arrive at our destination you can buy whatever you desire."

"Your mother is always so kind," Liberty said, still having misgivings about just sailing away and leaving her responsibilities behind. "But I do not feel right about leaving Briar Oaks. There is so much to do."

"All you have to do for the next few months is be young and carefree . . . and keep me happy." Judah could not tell Liberty that he was taking her away because he feared for her safety. She had been used as a pawn to trap him; he couldn't take a chance on that happening again. When General Jackson had asked Judah to go on this mission for him, Judah had known he could not leave Liberty at the mercy of others.

Happiness warmed her heart as she nestled her cheek against his. "When do we leave?"

"With the morning tide."

Liberty was confused. "But the war—the British?"

"The war is all but over, Liberty. Jackson scored a tremendous victory today. All that remains is the mopping up, and they don't need me for that."

"Why are you leaving now?"

"General Jackson has asked a favor of me and I could hardly refuse." His eyes darkened. "Besides, this is my chance to settle an old score for my father."

"Is it anything you can talk about?"

"Not to any extent. I have given my word that what I do will be a secret."

"It is dangerous isn't it?"

Judah smiled. "The only danger I see for me . . . is you."

"I am serious."

"So am I."

Sensing that Judah did not want to talk about his mission, she changed the subject. "I am glad you are taking me with you."

His hand slid over her soft shoulder. He dared not tell her that he was taking her with him because he didn't trust Sebastian not to harm her if he left her behind. He could not even chance leaving her with his grandfather, for he feared Sebastian would find a way to get at her.

"Will the war be over when we return?" she inquired, absently winding a strand of his golden hair around her finger.

He drew in a deep breath. "I hope so, Liberty. I saw things today that I want to forget. I never thought I would say this, but I admire and respect the English for the way they fought. They came at us out of the mist, and they kept coming even though our men kept cutting them down. They stepped over the dead bodies of their own and still kept coming. I have never before seen, nor do I ever expect to see, such bravery. They had to know they were going to die."

Liberty clasped him to her as if he were a child who

needed comforting. He was so brave and daring that it was hard to think of him having any weaknesses. She knew tomorrow he would have pushed his troubled thoughts aside, but tonight he needed her.

"Judah, I suppose many good men were killed today on both sides. That is war, and it will continue to be so as long as one man covets what another man has."

He smiled. Already the pain of the day was beginning to fade from his mind as he was caught in her web of warmth. "So young and so wise," he murmured, moving his mouth across her face and finding her velvety-soft lips.

Judah slid his hands through her silken hair, and Liberty's blood rushed through her. Then, as his hands moved over her naked flesh, she wondered if she would always feel this earth-shattering desire each time he touched her.

As if he had read her mind, he said, "I die inside when I am near you and cannot touch you, Liberty. My body aches to possess you. Never keep yourself from me." His whispered words were threaded with agony.

Liberty closed her eyes, not fully understanding what he needed from her. She sighed as she allowed her sense of touch to take over her being. Judah might not love her, but he had to recognize how perfectly their bodies complemented one another—he had to.

Liberty had been at sea for three weeks and she had loved every moment she'd spent aboard the *Winged Victory*. She relished the feel of the rolling deck under her feet, the invigorating aroma of salty air.

Her days were spent learning about the ship and what made it work; the crew was only too happy to explain their duties to her. Sometimes she would go below and help Ira, the cook, or just lie in the captain's cabin, reading one of Judah's books. Several times Judah had allowed her to take the wheel, and he was teaching her some shipboard terms.

Liberty gloried in the feeling of power she got from turning the wheel at a spoken command from Judah. She could see now why men went to sea; nothing could match the exhilaration of being master of one's own fate.

Liberty was even beginning to believe her father had been right when he had said she would one day bloom into a flower. Under Judah's gentle guidance, she was indeed blooming and becoming pretty.

While her days were spent in happy pursuit of new adventures and in learning, her nights were spent in total bliss. Judah, the patient lover, introduced her to joys of the body and the spirit that she had never dreamed existed. When she lay in his arms after he had made passionate love to her, she wished they could sail on forever and never reach land. As long as they were on the *Winged Victory*, Judah belonged to her.

The *Winged Victory* had now reached the West Indies. Her voyage had been blessed with bright sunny days and star-kissed nights. As she sailed past several small islands, Liberty tried to guess which of them was Martinique. Apparently none, because the ship sailed on, and there was no sign that she would weigh anchor.

Liberty stood on the deck, glorying in the beauty of the sunset. The sun's dying rays, cast against the ocean, turned the whitecapped water a sparkling golden color, and the snow-white sails of the ship billowed atop a dark wine-colored sea. At that moment the hull of the ship lurched upward, as if in a dramatic attempt to touch the sun.

Liberty's eyes moved over the *Winged Victory*, loving every inch of her, from the top of her sails to the companionway that led below. Every man on deck had a duty to perform, and each took his task seriously. Liberty had learned that the crewmen were equally committed to having fun when they were off duty. They danced and lifted their voices in song. Now, however, the sailmaker was mending a torn sail, two men were lashing down the cannons, and Philippe was taking wind readings.

Judah stood at the wheel, his legs widespread and his eyes staring straight ahead. The gentle wind ruffled his golden hair. Since the weather was so warm, his sleeves were rolled up, revealing his bronzed, muscular arms. His white shirt, open at the neck, exposed the golden hair on his chest, and Liberty's heart leapt when he turned his turquoise eyes on her and smiled with a promise of things to come.

She opened her arms wide and turned her face to the heavens, embracing the dying sun and wishing this day would never end. Her heart was so filled with happiness that she couldn't imagine being anyone but herself. She pitied any woman who did not have Judah for her husband.

"Land ho!" came the cry from atop the crow's nest. "Home port dead ahead."

Liberty's eyes excitedly moved to the west, where she saw an island that appeared to be a huge green emerald sparkling in the sun. She turned to Philippe who had just come up beside her. "Did he say 'home port,' Philippe? I assumed Boston was still home port to the *Winged Victory*."

"No, not since Judah's cousin had the authorities looking for him."

"Oh, *oui*, of course. Judah has still told me very little about this island."

Philippe smiled, loving the childlike shine in her eyes. He bowed gracefully to her. "May I offer my services, *Madame?* What would you like to know?"

410

"Everything."

Philippe's laughter reached Judah's ears, and Judah smiled, appreciating the close relationship that had developed between his first mate and his wife. Philippe kept a protective eye on Liberty.

"I will try to cover as much as I can in the limited time we have before we anchor," Philippe replied. "With all due modesty, however, I admit to being very informed about this island."

"What crops does she produce?" Liberty asked, for she was a planter's daughter.

"Ah, demon rum is her chief export. It is made from sugar cane that is produced here. Besides that, there are coffee, cocoa, cinnamon, and mahogany."

"I'm impressed. Tell me about the terrain."

"You will find it ranges from salty, barren land to rocky, mountainous terrain, and even arid rain forest."

"Tell me where we are going?" she pressed.

"Oh, no *Madame*. If the captain has not told you about that, he must want to surprise you. Therefore, I will not be a party to ruining his surprise."

As the *Winged Victory* drew nearer to Martinique, Liberty feasted her eyes on the breathtaking scene. The island appeared to be sleeping lazily in the sun. From its rock-strewn shores arose spectacular mountains — volcanoes. In the distance she could see palm trees and lush green vegetation.

She expected Judah to drop anchor, but instead he skirted this side of the island and made for the west side. While he stood at the helm to navigate due to the tricky tide, Philippe remained at Liberty's side and directed her attention to points of interest. "You will find Martinique as French as New Orleans, *Madame*," he said. "The Creole girls are very beautiful here." His eyes danced merrily. "I have always found French women most beautiful."

Liberty's laughter was musical. "I am sure that would

411

have nothing to do with the fact that you are French, would it, Philippe?"

"Perhaps . . . perhaps it would have a great deal to do with it," he admitted.

"Are you from France, Philippe?"

"*Oui, Paris.*"

"Do you ever want to go back?"

"No. I have all a man could want in life. If I had stayed at home, I would have become a cobbler, and I'd never have known the adventures I have experienced aboard the *Winged Victory.* I am a contented man."

"But you must have family still living in Paris."

"I have a brother and a sister. My sister lives in Boston, while my brother, Pierre, is the captain's foreman here on Martinique."

Liberty looked up at her husband, who was issuing orders which were speedily obeyed. "Some men were born to the sea, weren't they, Philippe?"

He followed her eyes. "If you are talking about the captain, don't be too sure. I believe a gentle hand could keep him on land and make him like it."

Her eyes were wide and apprehensive. "Do you really believe that?"

"If I did not, I would not have said it," Philippe assured her. Gently taking her chin, he turned her to face the quiet cove the *Winged Victory* was now entering. "You are home, *Madame.*"

Liberty watched in amazement as brown-skinned natives dove into the water and swam to meet the ship. She laughed delightedly when they did tricks in the water to amuse those aboard.

"Who are they?" Liberty asked Philippe.

"They work for the captain," he informed her.

"Are they slaves?"

"No, the captain does not approve of slavery, and there is no slavery on this island."

"Oh," she said, not really understanding. There were some fifty heads bobbing in the water. Why would Judah need so many men to work for him? Her eyes followed the path that led up the grassy slope, and she caught her breath at what she saw. The house that dominated the small cove looked very much like many of the plantation homes of Louisiana. It was built of white rock and had galleries all the way around the first and second floors. Belvederes topped the roof to give panoramic views of the surrounding countryside and the harbor.

Her eyes sought Judah's, and he smiled down at her. She took a step toward him and another. Then, forgetting where she was, and that there were many pairs of eyes watching them, Liberty ran up the quarter-deck and threw herself into Judah's arms. "It is beautiful, so beautiful," she cried.

He laughed delightedly as he hugged her to him. "Welcome home, my lady wife," he told her.

Chapter Twenty-three

Sebastian glanced around the elegant salon of the Purple Peacock, without really hearing the sound of babbling voices. This had once been the favorite gambling establishment for the young Frenchmen of New Orleans. Now Sebastian hardly recognized anyone. Since the American victory over the English, the place had become overrun with the American rabble. Creoles now sought their pleasures where they would not have to be under the same roof with the ungentlemanly Americans.

Sebastian leaned into the table and lifted his glass to his lips. He still frequented the Purple Peacock, because he had found it easy to take money from the Americans. They seemed to fancy gambling with a real Creole, and he had been only too happy to oblige them.

Sebastian had bitterness in his heart, and a need for revenge still burned inside his gut. Everything he had ever wanted was now lost to him. He had talked with his attorney that day and had learned that Bandera had no chance of inheriting Briar Oaks, even if Liberty were to die. The plantation would go to Judah because he was her husband.

Raw smoldering anger dominated Sebastian's every thought. It was not fair that Judah had everything and he was left with nothing. His lip curled in contempt when he thought of Bandera. Too late he had discovered that no one ever possessed Bandera. She was shallow and self-centered—a real bore when it came to intelligent conversation. And she was even more boring in bed, never seeming to acquire new tricks from her varied lovers.

Sebastian's eyes sparked with desire as he thought of the beautiful, desirable Liberty. She was everything a man could want in a wife. He imagined the heights a man could reach if he were to possess her. Yes, Judah had it all, and Sebastian had been left with nothing—nothing! Sebastian knew his days at Briar Oaks were numbered. He would have to be gone before Judah returned, because his cousin would demand satisfaction from him. Sebastian had no intention of facing Judah over a dueling pistol.

Suddenly, Sebastian's attention was drawn to the stairs, and his eyes widened in admiration of the beautiful, auburn-haired woman who had just entered. She appeared to be in deep conversation with a gentleman who looked vaguely familiar. The pair turned to look at Sebastian, and then the man left and the woman descended the stairs with such grace that she seemed to float on air. Sebastian decided that she must be new in town, because he had never seen her before. He watched her pensively look around the room, and then to his surprise, she walked in his direction. As she approached Sebastian's table, he saw that she was not as young as he had first thought, but beautiful nonetheless.

Her eyes darted nervously over his face, and then down to her clutched hands. He saw her distress, and he rose to his feet to offer her a bow and a smile. *"Mademoiselle,* how can I be of assistance to you?"

Adriane Pierce had been apprehensive about approaching Sebastian, and she was relieved to find him to be responsive to her. "My name is Adriane Pierce. You were pointed out to me as Mister Montesquieu, Judah Slaughter's cousin, sir. I wonder if I might sit and talk to you for just a moment? I promise I will not take up much of your time."

Sebastian was at his most charming. "I can assure you that my time is yours. Please be seated."

He held a chair for her, and she sat down; then he snapped his fingers to summon a waiter. Sebastian gave his order in French, and, when the waiter departed, turned his attention back to Adriane Pierce. "So you are a friend of my cousin, Judah? Did you come here from Boston?"

"Yes, I arrived only yesterday. No one seems to be able to tell me where I can find Judah. The proprietor of the inn where I am staying was kind enough to point you out to me. He said you might be able to help me—I am desperate!"

Sebastian smiled inwardly. He didn't have to be told that Adriane Pierce was, or had been, Judah's mistress back in Boston. The lady didn't seem to know Judah was married, or she did not care. "Have you heard nothing from my cousin, *Mademoiselle?*"

"No, nothing. Not since he left Boston three years ago. Several months back, I heard indirectly from his mother, and it seemed she didn't know where Judah was either. I fear he may have met with some terrible fate. I could not go on not knowing what had happened to him . . . and I could hardly contact his mother."

Sebastian saw the anguish in Adriane's eyes, and he leaned forward, placing his hand on hers. "Let me put your mind at rest. Judah has come to no harm. In fact my wife heard from a friend only yesterday that Judah is in Martinique."

Relief showed on Adriane's face as she shook her head. "Where is Martinique?" Her clipped Boston accent massacred the French name.

"It is an island in the East Indies."

"Oh, I see."

"We expect him to be away for some time."

"I wonder if it would be proper . . . no, I could never consider going to this island to see Judah."

Sebastian was trying to think of a way to turn this meeting to his best advantage. This lovely charmer just might be the tool he needed to lay another trap for his cousin, but this time he would have to proceed very carefully. Sebastian did not want to make mistakes that would again give Judah the advantage. Apparently Adriane had not heard that Judah had taken a wife. His eyes gleamed brightly as he began to spin his lies.

"Adriane Pierce," he said thoughtfully. "I have heard Judah speak of you often." He smiled and released her hand. "He is very fond of you, you know?" Adriane Pierce would help him destroy Judah!

"I do not delude myself about that, Mister Montesquieu. If Judah cared anything about me, he would surely have gotten in touch with me before three years had passed."

"I happen to know he would welcome you with an open heart. How would you like to travel with me to Martinique?"

Adriane looked at him suspiciously. "I do not know what you think of me, Mister Montesquieu, but I do not go off with gentlemen I do not know."

"Oh, no, no, *Mademoiselle,* you misunderstand me. I am a happily married man. It is just that my cousin has been most unhappy lately. I believe you could bring joy to him again."

Sebastian's lies made Adriane's eyes sparkle. "Do you really think so?"

"Indeed I do." He lowered his eyes and stared at the large diamond on her finger. "Of course, it will cost a great deal of money, and I am not a wealthy man."

"Mister Montesquieu, I am a singer by trade, and I have never wanted for money." She stood up, her elation

418

evident. "How can I thank you for your kindness? You have given me new hope." Adriane had never been able to forget Judah. No other man had fulfilled her as a woman, and she could not wait to be reunited with him.

Sebastian came to his feet and took her hand, raising it to his lips and softly kissing the tips of her fingers. "I always like to see a lovely woman smile."

"I must be off so I can make arrangements right away. Thank you again for your kindness, Mister Montesquieu."

Sebastian felt a plan forming in his mind, a plan that might help rid him of Judah for all time. He would strip Briar Oaks to the bare walls to get money for passage to Martinique. "As it happens, *Mademoiselle*. I have been wanting to see Judah, myself. I believe I will go to Martinique with you, so you will have an escort."

"But your wife—"

His eyes narrowed to slits. "My wife has the same feeling for my cousin that I do. We both would do all in our power to see that he has all he deserves."

Liberty discovered that the house had just recently been built and that Philippe's brother, Pierre, had sparsely furnished it just prior to their arrival. As she moved from room to room, making notations on what furniture was needed, she felt she was doing something to please Judah. He had asked her to furnish the house as she saw fit, and had assured her that money was no object. She had decided on lemon yellow walls in the dining room, and a mahogany table and buffet, made by the local furniture makers, would add just the right touch.

Liberty was bent over the paper, making notations, when Judah came up behind her and planted a kiss on her neck. She turned to him and a happy smile lit her eyes. "I did not expect you home so soon."

419

"I have been thinking about you all day, Liberty. I came home to see if you were also thinking about me, and I find you busy, not missing me in the least."

"I always miss you when you are away."

Judah stood before her, not as the sea captain but as lord of the manor, a plantation owner. He had so many different sides to his personality, and Liberty was fascinated by them all. His golden hair was slightly windblown, and he wore a white shirt, tan trousers, and brown English riding boots. When his sun-browned hand covered hers she melted against him.

He smiled down at her and thought how adorable she looked with an ink smudge on her cheek. "Are you putting my house in order, Mistress Slaughter?"

"I am attempting it. I do hope you will like what I am doing."

He saw the uncertainty in her eyes. "If you are satisfied with it, I know I will like it," he assured her.

"Do you not think we should talk over the details so you can tell me if there is something you don't like?"

"No, the house is your domain. I leave it all in your capable hands. I have something else on my mind."

Liberty smiled up at him in amazement. "It is the middle of the day!"

His laughter was warm as he gathered her close. "No, that is not what I had in mind at the moment." He arched an eyebrow at her. "However, it might not be such a bad idea." A devilish glow lit his turquoise eyes, and a smile played on his lips.

Liberty's face flamed red, and she buried it against his chest. But Judah lifted her face and placed a kiss on the tip of her nose. "How would you like to go exploring with me today?"

"I would love it. When can we leave?"

"You go upstairs and get into your riding habit, and I will have Hayman prepare us a basket of food." Staring into her seemingly bottomless eyes, Judah resisted the urge to take her upstairs to their bedroom. "Hurry, Madame Slaughter, you are wasting time, and keeping the horses waiting."

As Liberty's horse followed Judah's down the steep rocky trail, she had a magnificent view of the countryside. The bluest sky she had ever seen hung above an equally blue sea, and puffy white clouds floated lazily overhead. While below a bower of wildflowers marked the landscape with vivid colors as if an artist's hand had painted them there. The air was crisp and clean, scented with the mixed aroma of hibiscus and wild orchids, but Liberty could see fields laid out in orderly furrows, a testament to man's intrusion on nature's world. This touch took something away from the wild beauty and serenity of this island paradise.

Judah had reached the bottom of the incline, and was waiting for Liberty to join him. When her horse drew even with his, she caught her breath at the beauty that met her eyes. They were in a cove, surrounded by the high rock formations that cut it off from the rest of the world. The only access to it the way they had come, or by sea. A lovely lagoon shimmered in the sunlight, and wild orchids grew everywhere, their scent dominating the air.

Her eyes were shining as she gazed at her husband. "Oh, Judah, this is the most perfect place on earth. I can almost imagine that we are the only two people left on earth. Who owns this land?"

Judah found joy in viewing life through his wife's eyes. She had such a zest for living, she found beauty where it was overlooked by others. Judah could remember the heavy feeling of loneliness he had experienced the first time he had come upon this grotto. Now, with Liberty beside him, it felt like a paradise.

"This land belongs to you, Liberty. I give it to you as a wedding gift." Her eyes danced with joy as her delighted laughter mingled with the gentle sea breeze.

Before Judah could dismount and help Liberty from her horse, she had slid off the animal's back and was running toward the lagoon. Raising her arms to the sky, Liberty appeared to embrace the day. Judah came up behind her and slid his arms about her waist, loving her with all his heart.

"I am delighted to see joy on your face, Liberty," he murmured. "The little girl I first met had such sad eyes. I always wanted to be the one to bring you happiness."

Liberty looked up at him, her eyes softened by his words. "I never knew you felt that way, Judah. I thought you viewed me as a troublesome child."

He swung her around and rested his arms on her shoulders. "Someday I will tell you how I really felt about you. Are you happy, little one?"

Joy sparked in her blue eyes. "Oh, *oui,* Judah. I have never been this happy before. I belong to someone, and someone belongs to me."

Judah's heart ached at her admission. As he rested his chin on the top of her head, he closed her eyes. Could this mean she was beginning to love him? He took her chin and raised her head so she had to meet his eyes. "I am finding out it takes very little to make you happy, little one. Would that it will always be this easy to bring joy to your heart."

She could have told him that having him near her was all the joy she needed at the moment. Instead she asked. "How many women can boast that they were given a beautiful paradise for a wedding present?"

For one wild, breathtaking moment, they stood staring into each other's eyes, and Liberty was lost in depths of turquoise blue! He was pulling her to him, tugging at her heart, demanding that she yield. Judah found himself wishing Liberty would give herself to him completely. He knew when he held her in his arms at night she always held some part of herself back. Suspended in time, two tortured souls reached out to each other.

Just when Liberty thought she could not stand it any longer, Judah smiled at her. A wisp of hair blew across her face, and he tucked it behind her ear before he grasped her shoulders and brought her up on tiptoe. "If we are alone here, perhaps we should take full advantage of the situation," Judah suggested in a deep voice.

When his lips settled on Liberty's, she was lost. As he lifted her in his arms and carried her behind a clump of flowering bushes, she shivered with delight. Gently he laid her down on the soft green grass, while his eyes caressed her face.

"Judah, suppose someone were to come upon us?" she asked, although more aware of the look in his eyes than the threat of any would-be intruder.

His smile was rakish. "No one will come here," he assured her, while his hands moved up her leg, pushing her skirt to her waist. "You are so warm and alive," he said, pressing his mouth against the pulsebeat in her throat. When his hands moved between her legs, his touch was sweet and gentle.

When he moved over her, she felt that an eternity passed before he slipped into her quivering warmth. Liberty stared into his face, trying to guess what he was thinking and feeling, but his long sweeping lashes covered the glow in his eyes. Still, she could see by his expression that he was moved by their coming together, and she knew the trembling of his body came from touching her.

As he moved forward inside her, his eyes opened, and she caught a glimpse of such intense longing it almost took her breath away. "Liberty . . ." he whispered in an agonized voice.

Liberty did not know what he might have said, because

his lips covered hers in a burning kiss. He touched her hair and then his hand slid down to rest against her arched neck.

A fire ignited within their bodies, its flames leaping higher and higher, until they were both consumed by a passion swept so strong neither of them could stop it. Amid lovely wild orchids, that resembled brightly colored butterflies, Judah took Liberty to his body, and she surrendered to him completely.

Liberty stared into the passion-laced eyes of her husband, and had to close her eyes against the bright glow she saw there. She hugged him to her, knowing there was a part of him that reached out to her. They never spoke of love, but their eyes spoke of wild, unbridled desire . . . and then fulfilment.

Liberty's head was against Judah's shoulder as her heartbeat returned to normal. Glancing at his face, she saw his eyes were closed. At that moment, she wished she knew what he was thinking, but as always, his mind was closed to her.

She suddenly felt that none of this was real and that she had been living in a fool's paradise, trying to forget the real world that beckoned to her. This paradise did not really belong to her — Briar Oaks belonged to her.

"What is the matter?" Judah inquired, catching the troubled look in her eyes.

"I was just thinking about Briar Oaks," she admitted. "I am going to have to go back soon, Judah. You must know I have to."

He rolled to his feet and helped her stand. She could not read his thoughts, but she heard his deep intake of breath. "As soon as I fulfill a promise I made, I will take you back, Liberty. When the time comes, you will not have to face Sebastian alone. I will be beside you." He smiled and took her hand. "How would you like to go for a swim in the lagoon?"

424

"But—"

"No buts, little one. You can swim, can't you?"

"*Oui,* of course."

Liberty pulled back from him as he gave her a devilish smile. "Do you come peaceably, or do I carry you?"

"Judah, no!"

His laughter filled the air as he lifted her over his shoulder and ran toward the lagoon. She tried to wriggle out of his arms when she saw that he was going to jump in the water, but was unsuccessful. Cool water closed over her head as Judah slipped her around and molded her to his body. Then his mouth closed over hers in a burning kiss that carried them both to the surface. Liberty became a part of the earth and sky, as Judah deepened the kiss.

Liberty felt him lift her onto the bank, and he hovered over her, his golden hair dripping water in her face and a slight smile on his lips. "The next time I ask you to go for a swim with me, I suggest you listen."

She giggled and rolled away from him. "You have ruined my riding habit."

"It does not matter, I will buy you dozens of riding habits. I will shower you with gowns and jewels that will make you the envy of every woman who sees you."

She extended her hand to him. "Your wedding ring and the ring Zippora gave me are all the jewels I will ever need."

He stood, and pulled her to her feet. "I have a jewel in you, little one. I don't know when I have spent a day I enjoyed more than this one."

Liberty agreed with him; this had been a perfect day. Nonetheless, she was in a more sober mood as, while their clothing dried, she and Judah ate the picnic lunch Hayman had prepared for them. Later, as they rode along the beach, the incoming tide moving in and out as their horses kicked up a spray of sparkling white sand, the laughter returned to her eyes and her spirits soared. For a while Judah and Liberty were two young people without a care in the world, and Judah became even more enchanted with his beautiful little wife.

They remained in their paradise when the moon rose over the ocean, casting its silvery light against the moon tide. It was a day Liberty would never forget; a day that had shown her yet, another of Judah's many faces. On this day she had met Judah the carefree lover, and she thought she loved him the most.

Just when Liberty thought her heart would burst from all the happiness she had experienced that day, Judah lifted her from her horse and carried her back to their secret cove. On a bed of orchids, his wonderful hands worked magic on her body, and again they scaled the heights of ecstasy.

"The end to a perfect day," he whispered in her ear. "You have taught me how to have fun and to really see the beauty of life, Liberty. That is something I have rarely had time for."

She brushed a fragrant orchid against his lips, realizing the great responsibilities that had weighed heavily on his shoulders. She wished she could always make him laugh as he had today. But Judah was a man driven by some hidden need, and he would never find complete happiness until he had resolved whatever was preying on his mind.

As they rode back to the house, a bright moon lighting their way, Liberty was still under the influence of their many hours together. There were stars in her eyes as Judah lifted her from her horse, holding her longer, and closer to his body, than was necessary.

"I had fun today, Liberty," he said, finally setting her on her feet.

"It was the nicest day I have ever had," she told him, her eyes shining earnestly.

Judah was about to say something more, when Philippe spoke to him from the shadows of the front gallery. "I

426

have been waiting for you, Captain. We have problems with the *Winged Victory,* and I thought you would want to know." The first mate turned to Liberty and smiled at her. "Begging your pardon, *Madame."*

She smiled at him. "How are you, Philippe? I don't get to see much of you anymore."

"I am just fine, *Madame.* I have been kept busy modifying the *Winged Victory.* We are going to need all the speed we can get out of her for the task that lies ahead."

Judah took Liberty's arm and led her toward the front door. "I will just see that Liberty is settled in for the night, then I'll join you, Philippe."

When they were inside the house, Judah looked at Liberty apologetically. "I am sorry this came up. Don't look for me tonight."

She hid her disappointment. "What did Philippe mean, that you needed speed for the task ahead of you? What task?"

"Liberty, I told you that General Jackson asked me to do something for him. This is unofficial, and I cannot really talk about it, but there is a pirate by the name of Abdul Ismar who is causing no end of grief to American shipping. His latest venture was to capture an American naval captain—Blackburn—his wife, and two daughters. I will be making an attempt to rescue them. I hope you will understand that I have been wanting to meet Abdul Ismar for a very long time. He is the man who killed my father."

"Oui, I do understand, Judah." Her eyes searched his. "I can see that you have to go after the man."

"Abdul Ismar is the worst of the Barbary pirates, Liberty. I am told that he sells women into . . . slavery. I fear for Captain Blackburn's wife and daughters if they are not rescued."

Liberty shuddered. "This will be very dangerous for you, will it not?"

427

His eyes danced as if he mocked the thought of danger. "I once told you that I live a charmed life."

"I do not suppose you will allow me to go with you?"

Judah frowned. "No, that would be impossible." Without another word, he turned to the door. "If I don't return tomorrow, do not be distressed. Time is getting short, and I will stay with the *Winged Victory* until she is ready."

Liberty didn't move for some time after Judah had gone. Then with a heavy sigh, she walked down the hallway and up the stairs to her room. She would always cherish the hours they had spent together that day. She shivered, thinking it might be the last time they would laugh as they had, for she feared for Judah, knowing he would have no thought of his own safety when he came up against the man who murdered his father.

She didn't bother lighting the candle as she removed her clothing and slipped into her nightgown. And in the dark, she stood at the window watching the activity aboard the *Winged Victory* and dreading the moment when the ship would be ready to sail.

Liberty remembered what her father had once told her, that every man must at some time in his life stand up for what he believed in, or walk the path of cowardice. Judah was a strong man with many convictions. He would always face bravely whatever came his way. Liberty knew he was afraid of no man, and that frightened her very much. She could not love him if he were less than he was, but at times she did wish he was just a simple planter.

She breathed in the fragrant night air. "Rest easy, my love," she whispered. "I pray that one day soon you will find peace and contentment."

Chapter Twenty-four

Liberty had spent the last week working on the house. She tried to keep busy so she wouldn't feel lonely and restless, but there were days when she missed Briar Oaks, though she tried not to speculate on what was happening at home.

She lovingly selected materials and furnishings that would make this house a home of which Judah could be proud. And she had selected china, crystal, and silver—even the pots and pans for the kitchen, as well as the household linens, the rugs, and the draperies. Some of the furniture would be made on the island, but most of it had to be ordered directly from France. Liberty was finding out that Judah was a very wealthy man, and that he wanted only quality furnishings in his island home.

As Liberty came in from the garden where she had been supervising the planting, she could hear a bird singing in the wild-orchid tree at the front of the house.

Hayman, the cinnamon-skinned houseboy, bowed to her. "Perhaps *Ma'dame* would like for me to bring her something cool to drink. You could sit in the shade of the gallery; there is a slight breeze stirring today," he suggested.

"*Oui,* that would be nice, Hayman. I would also like you to contact a local carpenter and ask him to attend me tomorrow. I want him to build shelves in the upstairs hallway. Also inform him that I would like the bookshelves in the library to be made of the finest mahogany."

"I will do as you say, *Ma'dame*. I have put Mam'zelle Pierce in the only other bedroom with a bed; is that satisfactory with you?"

"I was not aware that we had a guest. Who is Mam'zelle Pierce?" Liberty asked, thinking the woman might be the wife of one of the Judah's men.

"I do not know, *Ma'dame*. She told me she was an old friend from Boston and was expected."

Liberty smiled, thinking this might be a friend of Gabrielle's. "Extend my invitation to Mam'zelle Pierce, and tell her I would be honored if she would join me on the gallery for refreshments."

Liberty wandered outside and stood gazing at the lush green countryside. Since the house was set high on the mountain, she could see for miles in every direction. To the east she could see men working in the fields, and just below, the *Winged Victory* was riding at anchor, her white billowing sails kissing the clear blue sky.

"It will not work, whoever you are." The feminine voice came from the doorway. "There has never been a house big enough to support two mistresses."

Liberty turned, expecting to see a woman the age of Judah's mother. The smile left her face when she saw a beauty no more than ten years her senior. The woman wore a pale blue gown that complimented her rosy complexion. She was tall and slender, and her movements were graceful. Her heart-shaped face and the dimple in her chin added to her beauty.

Thinking the woman had a wonderful sense of humor, Liberty smiled at her. "I trust you found your room comfortable?" she said, still not sure how to welcome their guest. "Had I knows beforehand of your arrival, I would have had your room prepared. I hope you will forgive the confusion; you see we are just furnishing the house."

Adriane Pierce stared at the lovely young Creole girl.

430

Judah had replaced her with a mere child! Adriane had dreamed of this reunion all the way across the sea, and she certainly had not envisioned a beautiful young girl spoiling it for her.

"I don't know who you are, but I would suggest you pack your bags and get out immediately," Adriane said, moving to the railing and glancing down at the *Winged Victory*. "I have been Judah's mistress since long before you snipped off your baby curls. If you entertain any notion that you can replace me in his affections, you would do well to forget it."

Liberty gasped in disbelief as she stared at the brazen woman. "Surely you jest? I know Judah's friends have a wonderful sense of humor, but they would never do this to me. I find this situation tasteless and not in the least humorous."

Adriane stared into soft blue eyes framed with golden lashes. Upon closer inspection she saw that this young woman was an exceptional beauty—just the kind that would draw a man's attention. "I assure you I would never jest about anything so serious. I am asking you to leave so there will not be a scene when Judah arrives."

Liberty raised her chin and glared at the newcomer. It was still difficult for her to believe this was actually happening. "If anyone leaves, it will be you. Judah will not be happy when he comes home and finds you here, *Mademoiselle*."

"Will he not? I have come a long way, and I do not intend to have my reunion with Judah spoiled by a baby-faced child," Adriane retorted. "Judah always hated scenes, you know."

Adriane removed her hat and patted her hair into place before facing Liberty again. "When he comes home, I will tell him you said farewell. I'm sure he will understand."

It had always taken a great deal to make Liberty angry, but this woman seemed to have found the means to push her past anger. Never had she known a woman to so brazenly flaunt the fact that she was a man's mistress. Not even Bandera had been so bold. Liberty was angry with Adriane, but she was furious at Judah. Her eyes were blazing as she faced her adversary.

"I have no intention of leaving, *Mademoiselle*. I am sure you can find your way back to Boston, or wherever it is you came from." Liberty entered the house, hoping to put an end to the conversation, but Adriane followed her into the parlor.

The older woman laughed deep in her throat while she seated herself on a chair. "No, that's not the way it is going to be. You will go to the village, back to your mama, or wherever you came from. For years now I have watched pretty girls trying to insinuate themselves into Judah's life, but he always returns to me." Her eyes narrowed, and she spoke the words Sebastian had instructed her to say. "You do not stand a chance with him while I'm here. You see, Judah asked me to join him—he was afraid he would be bored."

"Judah did not ask you to come here, he wouldn't."

Adriane did not answer, but merely smiled, while looking down her nose at Liberty as if she were a bothersome child.

Liberty was so angry that tears filled her eyes. She would not believe that Judah had sent for this woman. No, he would never do that. Surely there had been some mistake. "I do not believe you, *Mademoiselle*."

"Believe what you will . . . or you can wait to hear the truth from Judah himself, Adriane responded."

Liberty had never been one to give up a fight, and she wasn't going to give in. "Will you leave now, or shall I have Hayman show you the door, *Mademoiselle?*"

"That is not very sensible. I am being kind when I tell you that you are young and pretty," Adriane offered generously. "There will be many men tripping over themselves to get to you, but Judah won't be one of them."

At that moment Hayman entered the room. His eyes moved to Adriane and then to Liberty. "This came for you, *Ma'dame.* A boy handed it to me and then left."

Liberty was glad for the interruption so she could have time to think. Her hands tremblied as she took the note from Hayman, then nodded for him to leave the room. Her eyes blurred as she read the message.

> Liberty, I have word from your sister. She is gravely ill and has been asking for you. If you want to hear more about her condition, you can find me at the Trade Wind Inn.

There was no signature. Liberty shook her head in confusion. Had the whole world gone crazy today? She glanced at Adriane, knowing she would have to wait until later to deal with this woman. Right now, she had to find out about her sister.

Liberty placed the note on the table and turned to face Adriane. "I will be going into the village, *Mademoiselle,* and will be away most of the afternoon. I hope that you have the good judgment to be gone before I return. If you do not, I will have you thrown out."

Liberty squared her shoulders, and swept out of the room without a backward glance. In the hallway, she almost bumped into Hayman. From the look of concern and confusion on his face, Liberty realized that he must have overheard the conversation between her and Adriane Pierce.

"Did I do something wrong, *Ma'dame?* The *Mam'zelle* said that she was expected. I did not know that — "

"That does not matter, Hayman. Have the carriage brought around to the front. I will be going into town."

"But, *Ma'dame,* the master will be most distressed if you leave. You stay here, and I will see that the *Mam'zelle* leaves. She will not bother you again."

"Hayman," Liberty said, speaking sharply to him, "I told you to have a carriage brought around to the front. Do it now." She was sorry for the hurt she saw in Hayman's eyes, but she did not intend to stand in the hall and discuss something of such a delicate nature with a servant. Nonetheless as her anger reached its zenith, she told herself that poor Hayman wasn't to blame this situation was Judah's fault.

"Do not be concerned on my account. I hold you blameless in all this," she assured Hayman in a kinder voice.

"But, *Ma'dame—*"

Liberty turned away and climbed the stairs. She had to get to the village and find out about Bandera. There was no love between them, but they were sisters, and for that reason alone, Liberty could not bring herself to wish Bandera ill.

Liberty made it to her room before the tears fell. She knew that Adriane Pierce was, or had been, Judah's mistress, and it wounded her deeply. Angrily she brushed the tears away. Judah would have some explaining to do. Always before when she was hurt or troubled, Liberty had gone into the swamp to talk to Zippora. But she was no longer a child; she was a woman in love with her husband, and she would fight for him!

She picked up her bonnet and placed it on her head. When she heard the carriage pull up to the front of the house, she dashed down the stairs, hoping she would not encounter Adriane Pierce. If the woman was still in the house when she returned, then she would deal with her.

Judah had been aboard the *Winged Victory* all day, supervising the loading of supplies. Kegs of explosives were stowed below decks in readiness for the hazardous

434

venture ahead. Since the crew had not been to sea in some weeks, they were anxious to set sail.

Judah had come home to tell Liberty that he would be sailing on the morning tide. As he climbed the path to the house, he thought it was strange that only the parlor was lit and the rest of the house was in darkness. He hurried up the steps, thinking it strange that Hayman did not meet him at the door.

On entering the hallway, Judah stopped short when he saw Adriane Pierce standing in the doorway that led to the parlor. Confusion knitted his brow, and his eyes narrowed in disbelief.

"What, in God's name, are you doing here, Adriane? Where is Liberty?"

"Not a pretty greeting, Judah." Her lips pursed into a pout. "I was told you would be happy to see me." Adriane saw no welcome in Judah's eyes.

He pushed past her, and his eyes scanned the parlor. There was no sign of Liberty, so he turned back to Adriane, anger smoldering in his eyes. "You had better have a very good reason for being here," he declared.

"Judah, I do not understand. I was led to believe that you would welcome me. Otherwise, I would never have come."

"Where is Liberty?"

Adriane was beginning to realize that Sebastian Montesquieu had lied to her when he had said Judah would be glad to see her—but why? "Your little house guest has gone." Adriane's eyes narrowed spitefully. "I thought you went for more sophisticated women, Judah. This one is hardly old enough to be weaned away from her mamma."

"Did you tell her about you and me?" he asked in a demanding voice.

"Yes. I told her I was your mistress. Why shouldn't I? What are a few truths between mistresses."

Judah's eyes were cold with contempt, and they looked

right through Adriane. She shivered as he pushed her away and rushed to the hallway. "Liberty, where are you?" he called. "Liberty!"

As he spun around to face a now-befuddled Adriane, Judah addressed her in a harsh whisper. "Where is my wife?"

The color drained from Adriane's face and she gripped the doorknob to keep her balance. "Your wife! No, Judah, no! I didn't know . . . please forgive me. I did not know that she was your wife. Your cousin told me you would be glad to see me. He even told me you wanted to get rid of the woman who was staying with you, that I should tell her to leave."

"Where is she?" Judah had spoken softly, but his turquoise eyes were burning with anger.

Tears moistened Adriane's as she drew herself up with as much dignity as she could. "It seems I have been the object of a cruel jest, Judah. Can you ever forgive me? I would never have come, had I known you were married."

Judah did not feel inclined to forgive Adriane at the moment, though he suspected that Sebastian had perpetrated the whole incident. He had known Adriane long enough to realize she would never have flaunted their past relationship in front of anyone. "I assume you met my cousin Sebastian and he put you up to this?"

"Yes, but I don't understand why he would use me to hurt your wife. Your cousin assured me you had told him you wanted to see me again."

"I never discussed you with Sebastian. You should have known that."

She reached out to him. "Judah, forgive me. As we were sailing to Martinique, your cousin assured me you had been miserable without me. How could I have known he was just using me?"

Judah's heart stopped beating, and fear for Liberty gripped him. "Did you say Sebastian sailed here with you?"

"Yes, he did. He told me to come on out here and he would join us tonight. I believed him."

"Where is Liberty?" he asked, fear nagging at his brain.

"She received a note and rushed off. I believe she said she was going to the village," Adriane whispered. Her eyes implored Judah to understand. "Judah, you must believe that I would never have come here if I had known you were married."

"Where is Hayman?" he asked, too fearful for Liberty's safety to hear what Adriane was saying.

"I . . . he drove your . . . wife into the village."

"How long ago was that?"

"I don't know. Perhaps three hours." Adriane moved into the parlor, picked up the note Liberty had left there, and handed it to Judah. "When she got this message she seemed to be in a hurry to leave. Perhaps if you read—"

Judah grabbed the note and quickly scanned it. His eyes were wild as he crumpled it in his fist. "My God, it is from Sebastian—he has Liberty!" He quickly turned to Adriane and roughly grabbed her by the shoulders. "You had better give me some answers—and quickly. If my cousin has harmed one hair on Liberty's head, you will answer to me."

Adriane was in a state of confusion. "Why would your cousin want to harm your wife? That does not make any sense, Judah."

"You are either an innocent victim or a clever accomplice. Either way, you are going to give me some answers, Adriane."

At that moment Hayman's voice drew their attention. *"M'sieu,* come quickly. The mistress has been forcibly taken away. I tried to stop them but . . . there were too many of them. I followed them to a ship called the *Sea Serpent."* Hayman collapsed onto the floor and Judah bent down to him. There were cuts and bruises all over his face.

Judah sprang into action. "Adriane, I do not know at this moment if you are friend or foe, but I am trusting you to go to the *Winged Victory* and tell Philippe to have her ready to sail immediately. Have the ship's doctor come back here and tend to Hayman. Hurry!"

Adriane glanced into Judah's beautiful eyes and saw unbearable pain. He was desperately in love with his wife, and she was sorry that she had been used to hurt him. "I have always been your friend, Judah. Do what you must to find your wife. I will see that Philippe gets your message."

Judah felt as if he had been delivered a mortal blow. The *Sea Serpent* belonged to the worst pirate to sail the Caribbean. He closed his eyes, fearing what Liberty's fate would be in the hands of Abdul Ismar. He realized that Sebastian had found the way to hurt him most—Liberty.

Urgency was in his step as he raced from the house to saddle his horse. All the while he was praying that he would reach Liberty before Sebastian did her any harm!

Liberty pulled her bonnet over her forehead as Hayman helped her from the buggy. The Trade Wind Inn was a crumbling old limestone building that had known better days. The women leaning in its doorway were dressed in soiled, ill-kept gowns. They looked at Liberty suspiciously, while children wearing tattered clothing played in the filthy street. Liberty raised her handkerchief to her nose, trying not to breathe in the stench. As she glanced about the dark narrow streets, she shivered.

"Ma'dame, you should not be here. This is a bad place filled with cutthroats and pirates. Even the authorities will not come here." Hayman looked about him nervously. "Let me take you away. The master would not approve, and he will be angry with me for bringing you

here."

Liberty took a hesitant step toward the inn. She did not know who had sent her the note about Bandera, but it had to be someone who knew them both. Confused by the meeting with Judah's mistress, she was now frantic about Bandera. She had to find out about her sister.

"I have no intention of going home until I have completed my business here. You may come in and wait with me," Liberty said, acting far braver than she felt at the moment.

The common room of the inn was dimly lit, and smelled of stale rum and unwashed bodies. As Liberty's eyes adjusted to the poor light she resisted the urge to bolt for the door. More than a dozen unsavory-looking men occupied the tables. With their dark, swarthy faces, they were exactly the types Liberty had always envisioned pirates to be. She realized that every eye was trained on her, which made her even more nervous.

A plump woman with stringy black hair approached. As she wiped her hands on a soiled white apron, her glance revealed her contempt for the well-bred Liberty. "If you be Liberty Slaughter, they want you up them stairs," she said with an undefinable accent.

Liberty smoothed her leather gloves over her fingers. "I do not intend to go up those stairs, *Madame*. Please inform the person who wishes to see me that I will be waiting for him by my carriage."

The woman placed her hands on her hips, and gave Liberty a scathing glance. "I am not here to do your bidding, you fancy piece. If you want a message delivered, do it yourself." With that, she turned away, leaving Liberty to stare after her.

Amid several hoots and suggestive remarks, Liberty felt Hayman's hand on her arm. "We will go now *Ma'dame?*"

"No . . . I have to go up those stairs." She moved back into the shadows so the leering men could not see her.

"Will you come with me, Hayman?"

"*Oui, Ma'dame.* If you are determined to do this thing, I will not allow you to go alone."

The boards creaked as Liberty ascended the stairs. Every eye in the common room was trained on her, and she had to keep reminding herself that she was doing this for Bandera.

At the top of the stairs all was in dark except for the light that streamed out of an open doorway at the end of the long corridor. "I do not feel good about this, *Ma'dame,*" Hayman said, moving closer to Liberty, so he could protect her if need be.

"We will not enter the room, and we will leave as soon as I have the information I came for," she assured him.

Liberty felt, rather than heard, the men who came out of the shadows and grabbed her and Hayman from behind. A scream escaped from her, and she struggled to free herself. Hayman was fighting with his assailants, but Liberty saw him knocked to the floor and he did not rise.

Suddenly, a gloved hand was clamped over Liberty's nose and mouth, shutting off her breathing. Then something came down hard on her head, and she felt herself falling into oblivion. Just before she lost consciousness, she heard a familiar voice that sent chills down her spine.

"Bring her in here, and don't hurt her," Sebastian ordered. "We will gag her before taking her aboard."

Liberty awoke to the swaying motion of a ship, and it took her several seconds to remember what had happened. Her eyes roved over the cabin, and she sat up quickly when she saw Sebastian smiling at her. His foot was propped on a chair, and he was slapping his leather gloves against his thigh.

"So, you have come back to us. Welcome aboard the *Sea Serpent.*"

Liberty slowly stood up on shaky legs. She was frightened, but she didn't want Sebastian to know it. "What do you think you are doing, Sebastian? Where is Hayman?" she demanded.

"All in good time, Liberty. First of all, I want you to meet Captain Abdul Ismar. Captain, my sister-in-law, Liberty Slaughter. Did I not tell you she was beautiful?"

Liberty's mind was still groggy, but she recognized the captain's name. Abdul Ismar was the pirate that had killed Judah's father and had kidnapped the American ship captain and his family! She stared at the man's swarthy skin and dark eyes. She had thought he would be much older, but very little gray laced his dark hair and mustache. He was dressed in red leather boots and trousers, and looked every bit the pirate he was. As his dark eyes moved over Liberty, a smile played on his thick lips.

"You were right, my friend. She is a rare jewel. I will gladly pay the price you asked."

Liberty could feel the hair on the back of her neck stand on end. "Sebastian, what is the meaning of this? You had better take me ashore at once!"

"Alas, *ma chère,* I cannot do that. You see, my friend here has plans for you." Sebastian crossed the cabin and stared down into her face. "What a pity, Liberty. It could have been so different if only you had shown me the slightest kindness."

She was revolted by his nearness. When he reached for her hand, she clasped both of them behind her. "I never liked you, Sebastian. Your uncle and I could always see through you; we knew your real character."

Sebastian's face reddened, and he drew back his hand to strike Liberty, but it was caught and held fast by Captain Ismar. "No, no. Do not damage the merchandise. My buyers would not appreciate any bruises on her pretty face."

Liberty felt all the life drain out of her. She looked

from Sebastian to Captain Ismar. "You cannot mean that you are going to . . . No, it cannot be!"

A slow smile curled Sebastian's lips. "You catch on quickly, *ma chère*. The good captain here belongs to the Barbary pirate brotherhood. He will see that you are placed in good hands." Sebastian grasped Liberty's chin and made her look into his eyes. "Who knows, with your beauty you may end up in some sultan's harem."

Liberty spun away from Sebastian. "Do not put your filthy hands on me again, Sebastian. You are more barbaric than your pirate friend. Judah will kill you for this."

"I expect him to try. Oh, Judah will come after you all right, because we have left a trail he can easily follow. But that will be his undoing. My friend here has long fancied himself the captain of the *Winged Victory*. He wants to see my cousin hanging from her yardarm."

Liberty shook her head. "Judah will not fall into any of your traps. He is much too intelligent for that."

"Ah, yes, under normal circumstances," Captain Ismar agreed. "But Judah Slaughter will not be thinking clearly. He will be thinking with his heart and not with his head. That is when he will lose the advantage and I will have him. There are many who would like to see the end of Judah Slaughter."

Liberty's heart ached at the thought of Judah falling into the hands of his father's murderer. "Sebastian, do not do this," she pleaded, trying to reach a part of him that was not corrupt. "You and Judah have the same blood running in your veins. He is your cousin!"

Sebastian nodded. "Exactly. Being of the same blood, he has cost me everything I have ever wanted."

Liberty saw the evil in Sebastian's eyes, and she knew it was pointless to try and reason with him. She would have to pray that Judah would know this was a trap and not be caught in it. "Bandera is not ill at all, is she, Sebastian?

You sent the note to lure me to the inn."

"Clever girl."

"How is Hayman?"

Sebastian shrugged. "He suffered a few bruises. I made sure he would be able to tell Judah what had happened to you. Actually, the whole thing was rather cleverly thought out."

Liberty took a hesitant step toward the open door, hoping she could make a dash for freedom. "It was you who sent Adriane Pierce to see Judah."

"Another stroke of genius. Poor Adriane was so in love with my cousin, she would have done anything to see him. She did not know I was using her."

Captain Ismar saw Liberty's intention and moved to stand at the door. Liberty took a deep breath, trying not to panic. She could hear the peal of a church bell not far away, and she realized they were still in port. She would try to keep Sebastian and the captain talking long enough for Judah to find her.

"I know what the captain has to gain by kidnapping me, but I do not know what you have to gain, Sebastian. As much as my sister dislikes me, she would not agree to what you have in mind for me."

"Bandera will always agree with anything that will gain her wealth. You see, Liberty, with you and Judah dead, I will at least inherit Briar Oaks, if not Bend of the River."

"I do not know why you would want Briar Oaks. It is about to go under because of the debts."

"I know someone who is willing to pay a good price for it."

"Briar Oaks will never belong to you, Sebastain. If I am declared dead, it will go to Judah."

He smiled. *"Oui,* but who will it go to upon Judah's death, *ma chère?"*

Liberty's eyes widened in horror as she saw his evil plan for the first time. ". . . In that case Bandera . . . will

443

inherit," she choked out.

Sebastian worked his hands into his gloves. "I have managed to solve all my problems with a single stroke, *ma chère*. You will have to excuse me now. I must board a ship sailing to New Orleans."

Silently, Liberty watched Sebastian step to the cabin door. "We all have our crosses to bear, Liberty. Mine will be knowing I will never see your lovely face again." For a moment his eyes swept her face. "I love you, you know. I think I always have."

Liberty stared at him in disbelief. "If this is love, Sebastian, I would not want to see how you hate."

"The hate I have for Judah is stronger than any other emotion I might have. I will be glad when he learns that I have at last got the better of him."

"You will never get the best of Judah, Sebastian." Liberty turned her back on him, knowing that, for her, all was lost. She dared not dwell on what her fate would be at the hands of this pirate. She heard the door shut and spun around to find she was alone. Panic seized her, and she ran to the door and pounded on it. Only silence met her ears.

Liberty leaned her head against the door and allowed tears to fall freely down her cheeks. Why had she gone to the inn today? She had not been thinking clearly or she would have realized it was a trap. Now her foolishness might cost Judah his life.

She felt the ship break away from the pier and move with the tide. Then she sank to her knees and buried her head in her hands. She knew in her heart that Judah would come for her. She had foolishly set in motion the wheels that would bring destruction to them both!

Chapter Twenty-five

Judah stood at the helm of the ship, staring straight ahead. His turquoise eyes were cold with anger, and the line of his jaw tightened. If the owner of the Trade Wind Inn had been telling the truth, and Judah had no reason to believe otherwise, Liberty was in the hands of Abdul Ismar, his father's murderer!

For the first time in his life, Judah had the bitter, acid taste of fear in his mouth—fear that Ismar would harm Liberty before he could save her. The pirate had seven hours' head start on Judah. It was doubtful that Judah could catch him before he reached Tripoli.

Philippe stood at Judah's side, sharing his captain's concern for Liberty. The first mate glanced up at the dozen men who had climbed the masts, and then at an equal number who had formed a bucket brigade, preparing to wet down the sails.

"The men are standing by for your order, Captain," he stated.

Judah allowed his eyes to move over the waiting crew. The process of wetting the sails was very simple, and he wondered why it wasn't practiced more often. The theory was that when the sails were wet they held breeze better, thus allowing the ship to gain several knots. Judah was desperate to shorten the distance between the *Winged Victory* and the *Sea Serpent*.

"Issue the order to commence, Philippe. I do not want one dry thread on the sails."

Philippe yelled down to Rojo. "Step lively. Wet the sails!"

The first bucket was lowered into the churning sea. When it was full, Rojo pulled it up by the rope, and passed it down the line. He then lowered another bucket, and another. The men worked fast and silently, knowing their captain was on a desperate mission. Each of them wanted to reach the pirate before the captain's lovely wife was harmed.

The water splashed on the canvas, some falling onto the deck and filling the crew's nostrils with its salty aroma. In no time at all, the sails became heavier, and responded by catching the stiff breeze. All afternoon buckets of water were run up the masts to the men waiting to splash them on the sails. By nightfall Judah knew he had gained on the *Sea Serpent*. He expected to sight her sails early the next morning.

Liberty huddled on the bed, her eyes wide with fright. Every time she heard approaching footsteps, she would cringe. For three days she had been locked in the cabin, seeing only the silent man who brought her food twice a day. Now she heard a key grate in the door, and she pressed her back to the wall as Abdul Ismar entered.

The man gave Liberty a long searching glance before he approached her. Then he picked up a chair, and straddled it. "I can see that you are looking pale. I am told you have not eaten." His dark eyes moved over her with such intensity that she could almost read his dark thoughts. He feared that if she became ill, he would not be able to sell her at the slave market.

"I will not eat your food," she told him, her eyes flashing defiantly and her chin rising stubbornly. She was frightened, but she did not want this man to know.

His eyes narrowed, and he stroked his beard. "You must tell me what food you prefer, and I will have my cook prepare it for you. I cannot get money for a sickly woman." His eyes raked her face and then her body.

"You can go to the devil," she declared, pressing her back against the wall, frightened of what he might have in mind for her.

His laughter sounded sinister. "If you fear you will lose your virtue with me, you can put that fear aside. I have never had any interest in a reluctant woman. I do not relish having a woman cry and wail in my bed. Still, you are an unusual beauty. I should have no trouble getting a high price for you."

"I know about you and how you sell women to the highest bidder, *Monsieur*. I had heard that you kidnapped an American sea captain and his whole family. No doubt you have already disposed of the man's wife and daughters."

His lips thinned in a smile. "You are speaking of Captain Blackburn. I have not yet found a buyer for the two Blackburn daughters, but I shall."

Liberty was very frightened, but she thought if she kept Abdul talking that might draw his attention away from her. "Do you hold the Blackburns captive in Tripoli? Are you taking me to Tripoli?"

He flicked the lace at Liberty's collar, and she pulled away from him. "I am taking you to Tripoli . . . but the Blackburns are in Martinique. I tell you this because you will have no means of passing the word to anyone else. You may be surprised to learn that the Blackburn family is being held in the basement of the Trade Wind Inn."

Her breasts were rising and falling with her heavy breathing. Liberty could not stand to be in the same room with the man. "You are a monster."

Abdul Ismar gripped her chin, and stared into her face. "And you are exceedingly lovely."

Liberty batted his hand away and scooted off the bed. "Do not ever touch me again, *Monsieur*. You are a heathen and a barbarian."

Abdul's laughter startled her. He stood up, and swept her a bow. "I am glad to see that you have not lost the fire that flamed in your eyes." He walked to the door, and smiled at her. "I will send fruit and sweets to you. Let us hope you will eat. You may want to keep your strength up so you can witness the battle between myself and your husband. Captain Slaughter's sails were sighted about an hour ago. It is an inspiration to see how he hastens to meet his death."

Liberty clasped her hands behind her. She did not want Abdul to see how badly they trembled. "The man who can beat my husband in a fair fight has not yet been born. You should prepare to meet your end, *Monsieur*."

"Ah, but you see, pretty lady, my salvation rests on the fact that I will not play fair. I will always remember this as the day I captured the famous Judah Slaughter."

Liberty turned her back, no longer wanting to talk to the man. She hoped he had not seen the fear in her eyes. Judah was sailing into a trap, and it was her fault.

Liberty did not hear the sound of Abdul's soft, Moroccan leather boots as he crossed the cabin to her. She jumped, and spun around when he touched her arm.

Abdul held his hands palm up to show he meant her no harm. "I merely wanted to point out your husband's ship. Come and see it for yourself."

Abdul pointed at the scuttle, through which bright sunlight streamed into the cabin. "Look well on the *Winged Victory*, Madame Slaughter, for she will soon be mine."

Liberty stood on tiptoe and glanced at the white sails that appeared against the blue horizon. For a moment joy sang in her heart at the thought that Judah was so near. Then she realized that he was sailing into danger and her heart ached. "Will you spare my husband's life?" she asked, turning to look beseechingly up at the captain.

"If he cooperates I will not take his life. It will be a

great triumph for me to march through the streets of Tripoli, displaying Judah Slaughter as my prisoner. Knowing the proud man he is, I do not think he would like that. He would probably rather face death than disgrace."

"Why do you hate my husband? What has he ever done to you?"

Abdul stared at Liberty in amazement. "I do not hate Judah Slaughter. If anything, I admire him. It is said he is the greatest captain of his time. Will I not be praised and admired if I capture such a man?"

Liberty turned her eyes back to the triangular sails of the *Winged Victory*. Even now the gap between the two ships was becoming less, and Liberty wished she had some way to warn Judah of the danger he faced. "Perhaps, Captain, my husband will be the victor today. If he is as great as you say, he may know you have set a trap for him."

Abdul's dark eyes flashed. "That is true, beautiful lady. This will be a contest between your husband and myself. Before sunset one of us will be victorious. I wonder which one of us it will be?"

"You will be the loser, Captain. My husband will see you dead."

Abdul smiled and shrugged his shoulders. "It may be as you say, but I will find no shame in dying at the sword of Judah Slaughter." He bowed to her once more and crossed the cabin. "I will send food to you, which I will expect you to eat."

Liberty watched Abdul disappear out the door. He was right; this battle would be a contest between him and Judah, and one of them would lose. Please, she silently pleaded, do not let it be Judah.

Judah lightly turned the *Winged Victory* into the wind to slow her. "There is something amiss here, Philippe.

449

Abdul Ismar has lowered his canvases as if he wants us to catch up with him. What do you make of it?"

Philippe focused the eyeglass on the pirate ship, *Sea Serpent*. "I see a lot of activity on deck, Captain. They are loading their cannons. Like you said, they appear to want us to catch them."

"Let's do the unexpected then. Let the sails run loose. We will force them to make the first move. Ready cannons."

Philippe passed the captain's orders on to the crew. If any man thought his captain's decision strange, he did not say so. As always, Judah's orders were obeyed without question.

Abdul Ismar walked the deck, watching the wind ripple the slack canvas on the *Winged Victory*. His dark eyes raked the sky, and then he looked back at his adversary. "They must have been hit by a sudden wind squall," Abdul said to his second in command.

"I believe it is a trick, Captain. I believe that Judah Slaughter wants us to lose our nerve so we will make a mistake. Or, perhaps the American captain is a coward and does not fancy a fight."

"No, Judah Slaughter is no coward, but he is a slippery bastard. I have heard it said that when he is outgunned by an enemy, his astuteness and valor carry him through to victory. I believe he does not fire because he fears his wife will be hit." Abdul stroked his beard. "Yes, that must be the reason. I do not believe he will fire on us at all. He lies out of range of our cannons, thinking to wait us out. Turn the ship into the wind and raise the sails. We will offer him a target that he cannot resist. I want to see just how far he can be pushed."

Philippe glanced at Judah. "Watch him, he's coming in close, Captain."

"As quietly and inconspicuously as possible, raise the

cannon barrels," Judah called down to his men. "Let the *Sea Serpent* make the first pass without firing. I have a strong suspicion she will make a second pass, and even a third. Hold your nerve, she is testing us."

"What if they fire a broadside, Captain?" Philippe asked.

"I don't think they will. I believe Captain Ismar fancies the *Winged Victory* for himself. He thinks to win in hand-to-hand combat, thus saving damage to the ship."

The *Sea Serpent* passed so close that she sprayed sea water onto the deck of the *Winged Victory*. Judah smiled at Captain Ismar, who stood at the helm, and gave him a bold salute.

"Hold your fire, men," Judah cautioned. "Steady, steady. Wave to them—act friendly."

Rojo glanced up at his captain as if he had finally lost his reason in wanting them to smile at the enemy. Having no liking for the pirates, the most Rojo could manage was a scowl.

"Do not despair, men," Judah called out. "You will get your chance. We will give them a few surprises on the second pass. Look lively, she is coming about."

Judah watched the oncoming ship with a smile on his lips. "Philippe, pass among the men and tell them to aim the cannon high. I want to hit the masts and nothing else. I do not want a shot going astray and injuring Liberty."

Philippe grinned. "Aye, aye, Captain. We will put the masts right in their laps."

Liberty could see nothing from her vantage point. Standing on her tiptoes, she almost lost her balance when the *Sea Serpent* came about. Finally, as the ship turned leeward, she caught a glimpse of the *Winged Victory,* and she wondered why her sails were running lose. What was Judah doing? Was he going to give up without a fight?

The cabin door opened, and Captain Ismar strolled in,

a wide smile on his face. "It would seem your husband wants to offer me the *Winged Victory* as a gift. He offers no resistance for fear of harming you. I had expected a glorious battle from Judah Slaughter. Apparently it took his love for a woman to bring about his destruction. What a pity."

Liberty felt tears in her eyes. Captain Ismar was mistaken; Judah had not come because of his love for her. He had planned on facing Abdul Ismar in battle anyway. Her capture had merely advanced the time of the fight. "You have not won yet, Captain. Judah will never surrender the *Winged Victory* to you without a fight."

Abdul was so certain of victory, he had come below to gloat before Judah Slaughter's wife. "Will he not surrender? I have made a pass in front of his nose and he holds his fire. I am about to pass in front of him a second time. When I meet him on the third pass, I will cut him down with cannon fire. If any men are left on board after that, I will place them in irons."

"You said you wanted Judah alive," Liberty reminded the pirate.

"Perhaps I will still spare his life. It is something I will think on. I see no glory in capturing a man who will not even fight."

Kaboom! The loud explosion rocked the *Sea Serpent*. The ship shuddered and groaned, and Liberty was thrown to the floor while Captain Ismar grabbed onto a chair, trying to steady himself. His face was drained of color, and his eyes were wild as he heard the sounds of splintering wood.

"That bastard!" Abdul Ismar shouted, running to the door just as another explosion rocked the ship. "That tricky bastard."

Liberty crawled over to the bed and pulled herself up onto it. By now, the sound of cannon fire filled the air and the *Sea Serpent* rocked drunkenly as the two ships

452

came together in a grinding clash. Liberty clamped her hands over her ears, not wanting to hear the sounds of men in pain and agony. The exploding cannon fire soon gave way to crackling pistol shots. Liberty realized that the crew of the *Winged Victory* had boarded the *Sea Serpent,* and both crews were now engaged in hand-to-hand combat. For what seemed like an eternity she lay trembling on the bed, too fearful to move.

Moving across the deck of the *Sea Serpent,* Judah finally faced the man he had sworn to kill. Eyes blazing, he crossed swords with the pirate. In Judah's heart, hatred burned. This man had killed his father and taken his wife captive. "If you are a religious man, Captain Ismar, I would suggest you make peace with a higher power. I am about to end your miserable life."

"You will try, Judah Slaughter, but I do not think you will succeed," Abdul bragged.

"Before I end your life, I want you to know why you must die," Judah said, slicing through the air with his rapier.

Ismar made a thrust, which Judah easily side-stepped. "You do not have to tell me. I know it is your wife that I have below in my cabin."

"My wife is only part of why you must die today, Captain Ismar. You see, I am also here to settle an old debt."

Abdul thrust again, but Judah's rapier caught and held the pirate's blade. "What old debt? I know of nothing I have done to you."

Judah's blade sliced through the air and the point rested against Abdul's throat. "Many years ago, you killed my father. I want you to remember this as you die."

Abdul dropped his sword and stared at Judah, knowing he had been outsmarted in every way. "I do not remember your father. I have killed many men. How can I be expected to remember them all?"

Judah's eyes burned into the pirate's. "If you cannot remember my father, think of my wife. You will die for both deeds!"

Before Judah could make his final thrust, the mast above him groaned and swayed. He glanced up, and saw that the battered spar was about to come tumbling down. With a wide leap he made it out of the way, but the luckless Captain Ismar was pinned beneath the broken mast. Judah did not have to examine the man to know he had not long to live.

Liberty pulled on the door, but it would not budge. She then paced the floor, wishing she knew what was happening on deck.

Suddenly the door was thrust open and Judah stood before her. Liberty stared at the bloodstained blade in his hand, evidence that he had cut his way through the enemy to get to her. She reached out her hand to him, unable to force words from her throbbing throat.

Judah's eyes came to rest on Liberty's face. He witnessed momentary hesitation, then joy and relief before he moved to her and gathered her in his arms.

Liberty threw her arms around her husband, loving the strength that flowed through him to her. "You are alive," she cried, burying her face against his neck. "I was so afraid you would be killed and it would have been my fault."

She felt Judah tense. He waited for her to raise her head and look into his eyes. "Were you hurt in any way. Did that bastard touch you?"

"No, Judah, I was not harmed. I was just frightened. He was going to . . . to sell me . . . to—"

"Do not think about it, Liberty. You are safe now." Judah picked her up in his arms, and held her to him for a long moment. Then he silently made his way out the door and up the companionway.

Once on deck, Liberty closed her eyes against the ghastly sights and sounds that surrounded her. The *Sea Serpent*'s three masts had been shattered, and men lay under their weight, either dead or dying. Judah's arms tightened around Liberty. He wished he could spare her the sight of men dying.

He stepped over debris, and was about to leap onto the deck of the *Winged Victory,* when a weak voice called out to him. "Judah Slaughter, help me. Be merciful and put me out of my pain."

Judah glanced down at Captain Ismar, a grim expression on his face. "You deserve nothing from me."

Liberty shuddered when she saw that Abdul was pinned beneath a splintered mast and blood was trickling out of the corner of his mouth. She raised her head, stared in disbelief at her husband. This was a side of Judah she had never seen. How could he be so heartless? Pity softened her heart, and she wriggled out of Judah's arms. Moving quickly across the deck, Liberty picked up a dipper of water, then knelt down beside the dying man. Despite Judah's protest, she raised Abdul's head and gave him a drink.

"Judah Slaughter," Abdul whispered in a pain-dulled voice. "You are a most fortunate man to have this . . . angel for a wife. You have won . . . you are the better . . ." Captain Abdul Ismar's eyes darkened, and his head fell sideways in death.

Liberty could only stare in horror at the death mask that descended over Abdul's face. Judah muttered an oath, and picked Liberty up in his arms. She could feel the anger in him as he jumped across the rail, and landed on the deck of the *Winged Victory*.

A shout went up from the *Winged Victory*'s crew as Judah placed Liberty on her feet. Joy was on the faces of the men who had just performed a daring rescue. Liberty's heart reached out to every one of them, as tears ran freely down her cheeks.

"Thank you all," she said, looking at each dear face, and receiving smiles of adoration in return.

When Liberty saw Philippe, she ran to him, and was quickly enclosed in a hug. "We are glad to have you back," he said in a gruff voice. "I know I speak for all of us when I tell you how glad we are that you are safe, *Madame.*"

Liberty moved out of the circle of Philippe's arms when she saw the scowl on her husband's face. "How many of our men were injured or killed?" she asked, looking around to see who might be missing.

"Not a one, *Madame,*" Philippe assured her. "Unless you count the dunking Rojo got when he missed the rail and fell into the sea. He almost missed the whole battle. By the time he got onto the deck of the *Sea Serpent,* the battle was over and most of the prisoners had been rounded up and placed below in chains."

This brought laughter from the rest of the crew and a mumbled oath from Rojo.

"Philippe, if you can be spared to attend to your duty," Judah said acidly, "you can come about, and fire shots into the *Sea Serpent.* Send her to the bottom of the sea."

Philippe cleared his throat. "Aye, aye, Captain. Men, look sharp we still have work to do."

Judah took Liberty by the hand and led her down the companionway. By the time they reached his cabin, she saw the anger burning in his eyes. "Must you flaunt yourself in front of my men?" he asked angrily. "I could not believe you gave comfort to Abdul Ismar. Did you make him fall in love with you too."

"Judah . . . I . . . no. That is not fair. I never . . . I wouldn't do that." Hurt showed in her blue eyes. "How can you even suggest that I—"

He broke in, his voice sharp. "I will expect you to

remain below until we reach our destination. Now, that we have come this far, we must proceed to Tripoli and try to rescue the Blackburn family."

Liberty was hurt and angry. She raised her chin and gave him a haughty glance. "The Blackburns are not in Tripoli. Captain Ismar told me that they were being kept at the Trade Wind Inn, at Martinique."

Judah's eyes narrowed with jealousy. "How did you come by that little piece of information? Did you charm it out of the pirate?"

"No, I did not. He was so sure you would not be able to rescue me that he volunteered the information."

At that very moment, the sound of cannon fire ripped through the air, followed by a splintering of wood and a loud explosion. Liberty knew that the *Sea Serpent* would soon rest in in a watery grave. She shuddered, thinking how differently this day could have ended.

Still hurt and confused by Judah's attitude, she went to the bed and sat down. She could feel his eyes on her, but she refused to look at him.

"I trust you will heed my advice and remain in this cabin," he said.

At last she gave him a scorching glance. "I would not dream of disobeying. I thank you for the rescue, Judah. I do not thank you for your cruel words. You treat me like a wayward child when I am your wife."

"I am very aware that you are my wife, Liberty. I could hardly forget that."

"Perhaps if I were your mistress, I would get more courtesy from you," she said in an angry voice.

Their eyes locked in mental combat. Liberty did not flinch or lower her eyes. All Judah really wanted to do was take her in his arms and hold her close to his heart. He realized he had been acting like a jealous fool.

He took a hesitant step toward her, but when she looked away from him, he felt a chill in his heart. "I will not disturb you tonight, *Madame*."

"I am sure you would rather spend your time with Adriane Pierce. It is a pity you had to interrupt your little reunion with her to rescue your wife."

Judah's jaw tightened, and his turquoise eyes burned with green flames. Without another word he turned, and left a confused Liberty, wondering why he had acted as if he despised her. She lay back on the bed wishing Judah would come back.

For the three days that it took to reach Martinique, Liberty remained in Judah's cabin. In that time, her husband did not visit her, and her pride would not allow her to ask to see him. Finally Philippe came to the cabin to escort Liberty ashore.

A clear blue sky welcomed the *Winged Victory* back to Martinique, but Liberty did not see Judah as she crossed the deck of the ship, and climbed down the rope ladder. The first mate accompanied her to the house and left her in the hands of a smiling Hayman. Adriane Pierce was gone, but then Liberty knew she would be. Judah was not so foolish as to keep her under the same roof with his wife.

After Liberty had eaten cool sliced melon and drunk a cup of tea, she felt more like herself. She stood on the front gallery and gazed down at the *Winged Victory*. There was a lot of activity on deck. She watched several men leave the ship, armed with guns and swords, and she knew they were going to the Trade Wind Inn to rescue the Blackburn family.

Liberty went to her bedroom. She was exhausted because she had not slept in several nights, and she only intended to lie across her bed for a short rest. Instantly, her eyes fluttered shut, however, and she soon fell into a deep sleep.

She was awakened by someone shaking her shoulder.

"Ma'dame," Hayman said, stepping back a respectable distance. "Philippe Cease is below with orders to take you to the ship. I am to tell you that you should pack your belongings because you will be going home."

Still under the druglike influence of sleep, Liberty went downstairs to find Philippe waiting for her. "The captain told me to inform you that you would be sharing his cabin with Madame Blackburn and her two daughters. He hopes this will meet with your approval," Philippe said.

"Then you managed to rescue the Blackburn family?"

"Oui, there was nothing to it. The captain told the man who owns the inn to deliver the Blackburns to us immediately."

"You met with no resistance?"

"None. The man was only to glad to comply. You see he had a dozen guns pointed at his head." Philippe laughed. "As a matter of fact, he could not wait to have the Blackburns off his hands. Especially when he heard Captain Ismar was dead."

When Liberty turned to the houseboy who had served her so well, she held out her hand to him. "I will miss you, Hayman. You have done your duty well."

His dark eyes glowed as he shook her hand. "It was a pleasure to look after *Ma'dame.*"

"I know you will look after the house. Perhaps I will see you again before too long."

Hayman nodded. "It is a big responsibility to keep things in order. I will see that the house is kept nice for your return, *Ma'dame.*"

Philippe smiled down at Liberty. "Are you glad to be going home?"

"Yes. It will be good to see Briar Oaks."

Philippe led her out of the house, and Liberty was settled in the buggy before she spoke. "Philippe, will Adriane Pierce be sailing on the *Winged Victory* with us?"

The first mate met Liberty's eyes. "No. The captain put her on a ship for Boston."

As the carriage moved away, Liberty waved to Hayman, who looked like a lost soul standing all alone. She wondered if she would ever see him or Martinique again.

When she boarded the *Winged Victory,* she noted that Judah was at the helm of the ship, but he spared her no more than a quick glance. With her chin held high and her back straight, Liberty made her way down the companionway.

When she entered the cabin, she saw that three cots had been set up. Silently she looked at Madame Blackburn and her two daughters. The mother was plump with graying hair and a ready smile. One of the daughters was only a child, about ten years of age. The other daughter was very pretty, with glorious red hair and soft white skin, and obviously in her early teens.

"You must be Liberty Slaughter," the woman said. "I am sorry you will be forced to share your cabin with us, but we have little choice in the matter. I cannot tell you how much we owe your husband for rescuing us from those horrible men. We thought we would never draw another free breath."

Liberty smiled at her. "I am sure my husband was only too glad help you. Since we are going to be sharing this cabin, I suggest we introduce ourselves by our first names. I am called Liberty by my friends."

Mrs. Blackburn nodded to her youngest. "This is Charity, and her sister is Hope. My name is Faith."

"How very clever," Liberty observed. "Faith, Hope, and Charity."

The oldest daughter seated herself on Judah's bed and smiled up at Liberty. "This is *his* bed," she said with a sigh. "You are so fortunate to have such a brave and handsome husband, Mrs. Slaughter. I may try to steal him from you."

The girl's mother gasped and looked embarrassed. "Hope, how can you say such things after all Captain Slaughter has done for us."

Liberty's eyes met Hope's and she saw the smile that lingered there. Somehow it reminded her of Bandera. "Do not scold your daughter, *Madame*. Judah is accustomed to ladies throwing themselves at him."

Liberty saw Hope's eyes narrow, and she smiled at the girl. "I am sure Judah will be amused by your daughter's attentions, *Madame*." Liberty was weary of scheming women who tried to get Judah's attention. In her present mood, she would gladly hand him over to any one of them.

"I beg you to forgive my daughter's bad manners, Mrs. Slaughter. She really means no harm. She is just young and flirtatious."

Again Liberty looked into Hope's eyes. This mother and daughter reminded her of her own mother and Bandera. She did not relish the thought of being cooped up with them all the way back to New Orleans. "All is forgiven if you will instruct your daughter to remove herself from my bed, and seek her own cot."

Liberty knew she was not being very gracious, but she was fresh out of patience. Right then, all she wanted to do was get home to Briar Oaks. She could not wait to see Sebastian's face when he discovered she had not met some terrible fate at the hands of Abdul Ismar.

Chapter Twenty-six

On their journey to New Orleans the passengers and crew of the *Winged Victory* had been blessed with two weeks of golden sunshiny days and star-studded nights.

Judah now stood at the helm and watched his wife take a turn around the deck with the youngest Blackburn girl. He yearned to feel the touch of Liberty's soft skin, he dreamed of kissing her sweet lips until she begged for mercy, he ached to possess her body, to hold her to him so she would know she belonged to him alone.

Judah could not blame Liberty for her anger toward him. He had done everything wrong. Instead of confessing his happiness at having her safely back with him, after he had rescued her from Abdul Ismar he had acted the jealous fool. Instead of telling her how much he loved her and ached for her, he had been cold to her. Judah knew Liberty still wondered about his relationship with Adriane Pierce. He wondered how he would explain to her that Adriane was a part of his past and now meant nothing to him.

Judah watched the older Blackburn girl make her way up the steps of the quarter-deck toward him. She was an obvious flirt, and she irritated him.

"Good afternoon, Captain Slaughter. I hope you do not mind if I watch you for a while?" She batted her eyes coquettishly. "I am fascinated by this ship . . . and her captain."

He watched her face beam with pleasure as he looked at her. "You are welcome to watch as long as your mother or father are with you. I do not recommend that you come to the quarter-deck unescorted."

Hope moved closer to Judah, and it was no accident that her arm brushed against his. "Why, Captain, would I not be safe with you?" Again she batted her eyes, a habit that was beginning to annoy Judah.

"Let us just say that it is not wise for you to come here, Miss Blackburn."

She boldly slid her hand through his arm. "Will you not call me Hope?"

"No, I will not, Miss Blackburn." Judah glanced down and saw Liberty watching him. He issued a silent oath, knowing what the situation must look like from a distance. In irritation he glared at his wife for making him feel guilty when he was not.

Hope Blackburn licked her lips and lowered her lashes. "Would you want to ravish me if you found me alone, Captain?"

Judah pried her hand from his arm. "I am not in the habit of ravishing silly little girls, Miss Blackburn. And why should I? If you have seen my wife, you know she is everything a man could want in a woman. She has beauty, kindness, and most of all, she knows how to conduct herself like a lady, a virtue that I prize above all others."

A flood of color stained the young girl's cheeks. "I . . . am sorry, sir," she stammered. "It is just that you are so brave and strong . . . I believe you are the most wonderful man I have ever met. I did not mean any disrespect."

Judah saw the tear that slid down Hope's cheek, and he spoke to her more kindly. "I thank you for the compliment, but I have no interest in any woman other than my wife. You are a lovely young girl and do not need to flirt with an old married man."

Hope's eyes sparkled. "Do you really think I am pretty?"

"I do."

"Am I as beautiful as your wife?"

Judah smiled, and his eyes moved to Liberty, who was gazing out to sea. He knew she was unhappy because Hope Blackburn was showing him so much attention. "In my eyes, Miss Blackburn, no one is as lovely as my wife. You see, I look at her with the eyes of love, and it is hard for me to find one flaw in her."

"Does she know how fortunate she is, Captain?"

His laughter was deep. "I certainly hope I can convince her of that, Miss Blackburn. Now run along and do not again come up here without an escort."

The young girl nodded her head, and moved slowly down the steps. She just knew she would die from unrequited love for this strong man who had given his heart to his unworthy wife.

Liberty was seething on the inside. Judah had not once come near her since they had left Martinique, yet he seemed to encourage Hope Blackburn's attentions. In the last few months she'd had nothing but trouble with men. First there was Judah, then Sebastian and Abdul. For her part, all men could just go to the devil. In her mood she wanted no part of any of them.

"You must not mind my sister, Liberty," Charity Blackburn said softly. "Mama says she is too pretty for her own good. I wish I could be pretty like her."

Liberty looked down at the little face with the soft gray eyes, at the unruly brown hair; and she felt an ache in her heart. This girl reminded her so much of herself when she was growing up that she wanted to comfort her. "I know you will not believe this, Charity, but you will one day be prettier than your sister."

Liberty saw Mrs. Blackburn approaching, but Charity had not. Liberty knew if she never did another useful thing in her life, she would save this girl from the heartache she had lived through as a child.

The young girl shook her head sadly. "Mama says I will never be pretty and I suspect she is right."

Liberty drew in a deep breath. Taking Charity's hand in hers, she knelt down beside her. "Listen to me—hear and remember. I know what you are feeling. Once I, too, stood in the shadow of a beautiful sister. You will one day grow up, and I hope you will forget the hurt you have felt because of your mother and sister."

The young girl's eyes rounded in wonder. "You could never have been anything but beautiful."

Liberty stared right at Mrs. Blackburn, knowing Charity did not realize that her mother was standing right behind her. "I can assure you I was very homely as a child, a fact that my mother and sister never failed to point out to me. I cannot understand anyone who dwells on something so artificial as facial beauty, while overlooking the inner beauty of a child. Such people do not realize the hurt they are inflicting, hurt that will last a lifetime."

"I do not blame my mother, Liberty. She cannot help it if she loves my sister better. How can she love someone as ugly as I am?"

Liberty watched Charity's mother go down on her knees, and gather her daughter into her arms. With tears in her eyes, Faith Blackburn spoke. "My dearest child, how could I have been so heartless. I did not realize what I was doing to you until just now." Her tear-bright eyes met Liberty's. "How can I make it up to her?"

"I believe you have already started to do that," Liberty said, moving away to leave mother and daughter alone. She wondered how different her life would have been if someone had made her mother understand the harm she had done her two daughters. For the first time, Liberty realized that Bandera had been the one most harmed by their mother's attitude. Perhaps it was too late for her, but she hoped the Blackburn sisters had a wiser mother.

It was a quiet night, and the *Winged Victory* sailed smoothly over the waves. Faith Blackburn was brushing Charity's hair, while Hope flipped through one of Judah's books. Liberty watched the mother lovingly kiss her younger daughter's forehead. The older woman caught Liberty's eye, and mouthed the words, "Thank you."

When a rap came at the door, Liberty opened it to find Philippe smiling at her. "Good evening, ladies," he said politely, removing his cap and tucking it under his arm. "I have come to steal your hostess away from you. Her husband wants to see her."

Liberty gathered up her shawl, and placed it around her shoulders. As Philippe held the door for her, she swept past him, anger flaming in her eyes. When they were out of earshot of the cabin, Liberty turned to the first mate. "How dare Judah send for me, summon me before him like a lowly servant. Would it ever have occurred to him to come for me himself?"

Philippe chuckled. "He would have come himself, but to tell the truth, he's a bit put off by the older Blackburn daughter. She is always pestering him, and he wants to avoid her."

As they ascended the companionway, Liberty felt the cool night breeze on her face. There was no moon, so it was very dark. "You will find the captain waiting for you at the helm, *Madame*. I will bid you a good night." With those words Philippe moved into the shadows and disappeared down the companionway.

Liberty slowly made her way up to the quarter-deck. It was always reserved for the captain and first mate, and the common sailor was not welcome there unless invited. Furious, Liberty wondered if Judah had invited Hope

467

Blackburn onto the quarter-deck. The girl had certainly been there often enough.

"Thank you for coming, Liberty," he said, as she stopped beside him. "I would not have blamed you if you had declined my invitation."

It was too dark to see his face clearly; he was no more than a vague shadow. "I could hardly do that, Judah. Whatever my faults, I would never embarrass you in front of others by refusing."

"Yes, I counted on the fact that your manners are always impeccable."

Liberty was so near Judah that she could feel the heat from his body. For one crazy moment she wanted to melt against him, to have him hold her in his arms. "What did you wish to see me about?" she asked, stepping back to put some distance between them.

Judah could smell the fresh clean fragrance that she always wore. His head was reeling from her nearness, and he felt desire flame to life inside him. He tried to ignore the ache that cried out to be eased by her.

"I wanted to tell you that we should be arriving at New Orleans tomorrow. I believe we should talk about a few things, Liberty."

"I have nothing to say to you, Judah. I am going home to Briar Oaks as soon as I can."

He was quiet for a moment. "I cannot allow you to do that, Liberty. When you face Sebastian, I will be beside you. I don't need to warn you he is dangerous."

"I am not afraid of Sebastian. Briar Oaks is my home, and I do not need you to help me defend it."

"Oh, really?" he said in a biting tone. "I suppose you didn't need my help when you were held captive by the English at Briar Oaks? And how well did you handle Sebastian in Martinique without my help?"

"Is that all you have to talk about, Judah? I am really very tired and I planned to go to bed early."

468

"Liberty," he said, reaching out and taking her trembling hand in his. "We have a great deal to talk about. I just don't know where to start."

"I do not want to hear anything you have to say, Judah. We should never have been married. We are all wrong for one another." Her words were like a dagger in her own heart. She squeezed her eyes tightly together, glad that it was too dark for Judah to see her tears.

"Liberty, there are many things that have been wrong between us and I don't know how to explain them away."

"Do you not know how to explain why your mistress *Adriane Pierce,* ordered me out of your house? Can you not explain why Charity Blackburn is always hanging onto you, Judah?"

He began to massage her hand, and slowly he pulled her closer to him. "Dare I hope that you are jealous?"

"I believe humiliated is a more accurate description. If these past weeks are any indication of what life with you is going to be like, I can well do without it. I will never again stand by and play second fiddle to someone, Judah. My girlhood was spent in the shadow of my sister, and I did not feel good about myself. I can promise you, no one will ever again make me feel unloved. I . . . do not want to be your wife."

"Liberty, I hope you don't mean that."

"I do mean it."

"I suppose you think you would have been better off if you had married one of your Creole gentlemen?" he bit out.

"Perhaps."

"I am well aware that you are exceedingly lovely and had many admirers. If you are trying to make me jealous, you have succeeded."

"No, Judah, that was not my intention. I do not play games. You have me mixed up with my sister."

He dropped her hand. "If you no longer want to be my

wife, that is my misfortune, Liberty. In trying to do the right thing by you, it seems I did everything wrong. What do you want of me? Tell me so I might know," he said softly. "What do you want me to be?"

"I have never asked anything of you, Judah. I married you, knowing you did not love me. Perhaps if you had been able to marry the woman you loved, you would now be happy. I just don't know anymore."

Judah stared at her in wonderment. How could she be so mistaken? How could she not know that he loved her beyond all reason. He couldn't lose her. He had to make her love him. "Liberty, we have so much to talk about, but now is not the time. When we anchor I have to make sure the Blackburns are put on a ship for Philadelphia, and I want you to go to Bend of the River. As soon as I am able, I will come to you. Give me a chance to explain my feelings before you decide anything."

A chill wind ruffled Liberty's hair, and she pulled her shawl tightly about her shoulders. "You will know where to find me if you want to talk, Judah. You have always known where to find me."

The muscles in his body tensed as she turned and walked away. Judah wanted to go after her and declare his love, but instead he listened to her footsteps fade into silence. He raised his head to the dark sky, knowing that if he couldn't have Liberty, nothing had any meaning for him. She was his heart—she was his life. The night's biting chill now reached the very depth of his being. The sun would not shine so brightly, nor would the birds singly so sweetly when he was without Liberty's smile.

Judah cursed himself for a fool. If he wasn't careful he would become just like all the weak-minded men he had always despised, and forever be writing poetry to his ladylove.

When the *Winged Victory* anchored in New Orleans, Liberty had said good bye to the Blackburns with little regret. Judah was nowhere to be seen when she boarded the longboat with Philippe and four other crew members. As it moved swiftly through the current of the Mississippi, Liberty felt as if she had been away for a lifetime. It would be hard to pick up where she had left off.

As the longboat moved past Chalmette where the battle had taken place between the Americans and the British, she saw the scars on the land. Trees had been splintered and the earth had deep gaping holes. Perhaps Chalmette should stand as a monument to remind man of how destructive his battles were.

Philippe pointed to the battlefield. "We have just about come full circle, *Madame*. One wonders if we have gained any knowledge from all this. I wonder, was it worth it?"

"Some will say it was, Philippe. Perhaps this war had to be fought to make way for peace. I pray it is the last battle that will ever be fought on American soil."

"So do I."

"Will you . . . will Judah be going back to sea?"

Philippe stared at her for a moment. "Didn't he tell you?"

"No, we have hardly had a chance to talk."

Philippe lowered his voice so only Liberty could hear him. "When you see him again the two of you can work out your problems."

Liberty smiled. Philippe had become so dear to her; she would miss him when he left. "I know a ship captain's life is at sea. I would not be at all surprised if Judah decided to take the Blackburns to Philadelphia himself."

"Look, there is Bend of the River just ahead," Philippe observed, glad to end the conversation. He wondered why Judah had not told Liberty his plans.

When the boat was secured to the pier, Philippe helped Liberty ashore. Already the buggy was making its way toward the pier to take her to the big house. "The captain sent a man early this morning to tell his mother to expect you. I have no doubt they have been watching the river for you all morning." He tipped his hat. "I'd best be getting back, *Madame*. The captain told me not to linger."

She reached out her hand. "Will I see you again, Philippe?"

He took her small hand in his. "Not for a long time, *Madame*. I will be sailing within the week."

"I will miss you, my dear, dear friend," she said, fighting tears.

"There is not a one of us that will not miss your sweet smile, *Madame*," Philippe declared in a gruff voice that was threaded with emotion. When he released her hand, he quickly hopped into the boat, and Liberty waved to him and the other crew members. She couldn't bring herself to leave until they disappeared around the bend. Some of her happiest moments had been spent aboard the *Winged Victory*.

As the buggy drew to a halt beside Liberty, a smiling Biff leaped down and loaded her trunks into the back seat. After he had helped her into the buggy, she arranged her skirt and then glanced at the big house. "Take the side road, Biff, I will not be stopping off at Bend of the River—I am going home."

"But, *Madame*, I was told to bring you to the house."

"When you get back, you can explain to Monsieur Gustave that I had something important to do—something that would not wait."

"Yes, *Madame*," Biff said obediently.

Bandera was lounging near the fire when Oralee burst into the sitting room. "It's Liberty. She's come home!" the excited woman declared.

472

"Liberty is dead, Oralee," Bandera said dully. "I do not appreciate your jest — it is in the poorest taste."

"It is the truth. I didn't believe it either, but I saw her with my own eyes."

Bandera slowly stood up, not daring to believe that her little sister still lived. She had found, to her surprise, that she had grieved for weeks when Sebastian had told her that Liberty had drowned at sea. Now she was afraid to believe that Liberty was alive, lest it be a mistake. "Show me my sister, Oralee. When I see her face, then I will know she is alive."

As Liberty got out of the buggy and slowly walked up the steps, a heavy loneliness descended on her, and she couldn't shake it — not even when Oralee came bursting out of the door and grabbed her in a tight hug. "We was told you were dead, *ma chère*," she cried, forgetting to be formal. "Praise the good Lord, you are alive!"

Liberty looked past Oralee to the ghost-white face of her sister. *"Oui,* I am alive." She moved past Oralee and stood before Bandera. "What? No regrets at seeing that I still live, dearest sister?"

Bandera stood as if turned to stone, but for the single tear that rolled down her cheek. "I cannot believe it. I had thought myself alone in the world, with no one to care for me. Now you are home, and you will make everything all right."

Liberty stared in disbelief at her sister. "You change your loyalties so quickly, I can never keep up with you. I suppose I should be grateful that the British have vacated my house so you and Sebastian will not have me locked in my room."

"It was wrong of me to side with Sebastian against my own sister, Liberty. I know that now. I wish there were some way I could make it up to you. Perhaps your coming home will give me a chance to make amends for the way I treated you in the past."

473

Liberty had never before seen her sister in this mood. But she had often been fooled into believing Bandera had changed, only to find that was not the case, so she was not taken in by this newly found sisterly love. "Where are your husband and Alicia, Bandera? I have a few things to say to all three of you. If I have you all together, that will save me the trouble of repeating myself."

"I suppose you haven't heard. Alicia was drowned in the river three days ago. It was the strangest thing. She never went near the river, because she was deathly afraid of it. Yet, Sebastian found her floating face down under the pier. He swears it was that old witch, Zippora, who was responsible."

"If Alicia is dead, it is not Zippora's fault. If anyone was a witch, it was Sebastian's mother."

Bandera shook her head. "You have become hard, Liberty. There was a time when you had charity in your heart for everyone, but that no longer seems to be the case."

"I had to become strong to survive, Bandera. Your husband has tried to rid the world of me, but he has failed. Now that I am home, I will expect you and Sebastian to vacate the house."

"I don't blame you. Neither Sebastian nor I deserve any charity from you. I am sorry to tell you that he has stripped the house of everything but the barest necessities. He has even sold all the slaves. Nothing remains but Oralee and a half-empty house."

"No, he could not have sold all the slaves," Liberty said with a catch in her voice. "I made a promise to Delton that he and his family would never be sold or separated. Surely Sebastian would not take it upon himself to sell what belongs to me."

"It was awful," Bandera said, placing a shaky hand to her brow. "Delton was crying and begging Sebastian not to break up his family, saying you promised never to

474

separate them."

Liberty had never known such fury. "I'll tell you what you can do, Bandera, if you are really as penitent as you claim. Find out who purchased Delton and his family and then tell Sebastian he has until tomorrow morning to get them back or I will have the authorities throw him in jail. I will, Bandera, I swear it."

Sebastian chose that moment to come out of the house. "Well said, Liberty. It gladdens my heart to see that you are still with us."

It was all Liberty could do to stand there and look at Sebastian. Her hatred for him was so strong that it almost choked her. "Did you tell my sister that you had me sold to a pirate who was going to resell me to the highest bidder in Tripoli?"

Bandera swung around to face her husband. "No, he did not tell me that. He said that you and Judah had been lost at sea."

"Tell my sister the truth, Sebastian. Tell her how you schemed and plotted to get your hands on Briar Oaks," Liberty demanded.

Sebastian's smile was malignant, and his eyes took on a smoky haze. "I keep trying to be rid of you and my cousin, but you keep turning up." He reached down and removed a dagger from the tip of his boot. "Perhaps I made the mistake of leaving others to do the work for me. This time I will do it myself, so there will be no mistake."

Oralee, seeing what Sebastian was going to do, made a dive at him, but he side-stepped her and struck her hard across the face. She crumpled at his feet.

"How dare you," Liberty said, more concerned for the injured servant than for her own safety. She ran to Oralee and dropped down beside her, lifting her head. Oralee's breath was warm on Liberty's hand so Liberty knew she was merely unconscious.

475

She raised her eyes to Sebastian, and they were dancing with blazing anger. "You have a lot to answer for, Sebastian. I am going to have the authorities lock you away so you cannot hurt anyone else!"

Laughter spilled from Sebastian's lips. "You will not be alive long enough to do anything, Liberty. This time I will see that you are dead."

Liberty watched with horror as he aimed the dagger at her. "I am very good with the dagger, Liberty. I can split a leaf from a tree at fifty paces."

Bandera looked from her husband to her sister. "No, do not hurt Liberty!" she cried, running forward, just as Sebastian threw the dagger.

Liberty screamed as Bandera thrust herself between her sister and dagger. She watched in stunned horror as the knife entered Bandera's body! A red stain covered the front of her sister's gown, and she reached out to Liberty, then whispered in a pitiful voice. "I tried to make . . it up . . up to . . ."

As Bandera collapsed into Liberty's arms, Liberty tried to hold onto her, but Bandera's body was limp and she slid to the ground, carrying Liberty with her.

Liberty did not know how much she had loved her sister until she saw her lying dead at her feet. Kneeling down beside Bandera, she gently removed the dagger from her sister's chest, while staring into blank eyes. She pressed her hands over the wound, frantically trying to stop the flow of blood that now stained her own gown. Blinded by tears, she realized it was futile—her sister was dead!

Hatred burned in Liberty's eyes as she looked up at Sebastian. "You have killed her!" she cried, horror in her voice. "You will pay for this, Sebastian."

Sebastian had been silently staring from Liberty to Bandera, stunned because he had killed his own wife. Now he whirled on Liberty. "You and Judah have robbed

476

me of everything, Liberty. You will soon join your sister in death."

Liberty watched Sebastian pull a derringer out of his breast pocket, knowing she was alone with a man determined to end her life! There was no one to help her. She took a step backward, aware that Sebastian was beyond reason. If only she could make it to the river and into a boat, she might be able to escape from him.

She took another step backward, while Sebastian watched her suspiciously. "You cannot get away from me this time, Liberty. How beautiful you will be in death. Then you will belong to me alone, and no one can ever take you away from me."

Liberty had never been so frightened in her life. She turned and ran toward the river knowing Sebastian would not be satisfied until she was dead.

She was not aware that a strong wind had begun to blow off the Mississippi, or that dark clouds, boiling like an angry sea, had dipped down over her. She ran as fast as she could, but she could hear Sebastian gaining on her. Is this the way my life is going to end? she wondered desperately.

A sudden pain shot through Liberty's side, and she stumbled and fell to the ground. With her golden hair blowing across her face, she raised her head to see that Sebastian was bearing down on her.

Judah jumped from his horse and ran down the hill toward Liberty. He saw her trip and fall at the same time he saw Sebastian raise his derringer and take aim. Judah was too far away, and he knew he could never reach Liberty in time to save her. He reached out his hand and cried into the wind. "Help her! Dear Lord, please help my love."

Judah's eyes were drawn to the river's edge, and he saw

Zippora with her arms raised over her head. He was too far away to hear what she was saying, but he could hear her shouting some kind of chant.

Sebastian had aimed his gun at Liberty's head, and eyes closed, she was waiting for the impact of the bullet. Liberty saw neither Judah nor Zippora, nor did she see Sebastian pause and stare at the old woman with fear in his eyes.

The wind whipped Zippora's hair and plastered her gown to her thin frame. Her gnarled hands reached into the heavens as she cried out. "Let the hand of revenge strike the spawn of the devil. Let him return from whence he came."

Judah was running toward Liberty, when a bolt of lightning split the sky. Its jagged edges danced in the air, then pierced Sebastian like an avenging spear. His agonized screams made Liberty look up. She was horrified by what she saw—Sebastian seemed to glow as electricity, from the lightning bolt, jolted throughout his body.

Liberty felt herself go limp, and she was soon lost in the soft, trouble-free world of unconsciousness. Judah scooped her up in his arms and examined her for wounds. He did not know that the blood which covered her gown, and come from her sister. Finding no injury, he held her tightly to him.

Zippora appeared at his side and looked into Liberty's face. "She is unconscious. Perhaps it is better that way. Take her away from this scene of death, Judah Slaughter."

Judah looked into the old woman's strange yellow eyes. "I do not know if you are a devil or an angel—I am not even sure that my eyes have not been deceiving me—but I thank you for saving Liberty's life just now."

The old woman chuckled. "If I saved her, it is up to you to make her happy."

Judah smiled at the old woman. "I would be afraid to do otherwise with you around. I would hate to face the

478

consequences."

"You have nothing to fear from me. Just keep the little one safe. She will need all your love and strength in the weeks ahead."

Judah lifted Liberty in his arms, and was about to walk away when his eyes fell on Sebastian's body, which was still smoldering. The stench was unbearable, that of burning flesh. Judah spoke to the old woman. "Zippora, did you do what I think you did?"

She looked at him innocently. "What do you think I did?"

"Never mind. I don't even want to know. I will send someone over from Bend of the River to deal with this."

Zippora watched as the tall, handsome Judah Slaughter mounted his horse, his precious burden in his arms. "It is going to be all right, Liberty. That man loves you so much he will help you forget all about the sorrow of this day," she said quietly.

Then, without a backward glance, Zippora made her way to the river and got into her skiff. As she paddled toward the swamps, the clouds rolled away and the winds calmed, the sun shone down on the river, and birds sang sweetly in the nearby trees.

Chapter Twenty-seven

For five days Liberty lay in a bed, thinking and feeling nothing. She was aware of shadowy forms that moved about the room, administering to her needs, but she had lost touch with reality. Perhaps she just did not want to remember, knowing she would feel pain if she did.

One morning she awoke to hear the birds singing in the tree outside her window, and to realize she was at Bend of the River, not Briar Oaks. With each passing day Liberty grew stronger. And at last the day came when she felt well enough to sit up in bed and take some nourishment on her own.

Liberty stared at the curtains that were stirred by the soft breeze blowing through the open window. She had just bathed herself, and she was reclining on the bed, garbed in a fresh white nightgown. She plucked at the lace on the sleeve of her gown while Gabrielle arranged a vase of bright-colored flowers and then set them on a night table close to her.

Judah's mother smiled down at her lovely daughter-in-law. "Liberty, I see that you are well on the way to recovery. Do you feel like seeing Judah? I have been hard pressed to keep him away from you so you could rest."

Liberty felt the muscles in her body tense. She had known this moment would come, and she dreaded it; for she feared Judah would tell her he no longer wanted to be married to her. "I had thought Judah might have sailed away on the *Winged Victory*."

"No, he has been here the whole time you were ill. As a matter of fact, it was he who sat up with you at night in case you needed someone." Gabrielle fluffed up Liberty's pillow, then sat down beside her to brush her hair. "You had nightmares and had to have someone with you around the clock. Do you remember that?"

"No, I don't remember."

"Perhaps that is a blessing."

Gabrielle finished brushing Liberty's hair and tied it back with a pink ribbon. "Now you look lovely."

"Gabrielle, I am sorry to have been so much trouble."

"Nonsense. You gave me the chance to take care of my new daughter. You could never be trouble to those of us who love you." She kissed Liberty's cheek. "I am going to go out now, and I will send Judah up to see you."

Liberty felt trapped, for she knew there was no way she could avoid seeing Judah. Would he be angry with her because she had disobeyed him and gone to Briar Oaks alone?

Moments later he entered the room, but his face was a mask, revealing none of his feelings. Liberty's eyes followed him as he strode to the window and stared out. How handsome he looked in his buff trousers and black boots. His blue cutaway coat was open to reveal an even lighter blue shirt.

His eyes rested on her face, and he thought how like a little girl she looked. "I am glad to see you are feeling better, Liberty. We have been very concerned about you."

"I seem to have lost any recollection of some of what happened at Briar Oaks, Judah. Will you fill in the missing pieces for me?"

He pulled up a chair, and sat down beside her. "As you already know, Oralee is none the worse for her ordeal. However, your sister and Sebastian are both dead. They were both buried here at Bend of the River."

Tears came to Liberty's eyes, and she whispered, "At last Bandera is at Bend of the River where she always wanted to be."

Judah wanted to pull Liberty into his arms and assure her that this sadness would pass, but he didn't. All he could do was watch her as she raised her face to him. "Are you angry with me for going to Briar Oaks, Judah?"

"I should be, but I could never stay angry with you. After you left the ship, I decided to make sure that you were safely at Bend of the River. I was not in the least surprised to find that you had gone to Briar Oaks. When I got there, Sebastian was holding a gun on you. The rest I am sure you will learn in time. Right now you have enough grief to deal with."

Liberty met his eyes. "What about you, Judah? Are you . . . did you grieve because Bandera is . . . dead?"

He looked at her, a puzzled expression on his face. "I am sorry only that her passing causes you pain. She was not a good sister to you, Liberty. Oralee has told me how difficult it was for you to grow up in that house with your mother and sister. I never suspected you had been through such hell."

His eyes held so much kindness, that Liberty felt her heart swell with love for him. "The past is dead, and I suppose it should be put in its proper place. I will try to remember only the good things about Bandera. She . . . died saving my life."

Judah reached out and gripped her hand. "Yes, do remember that, Liberty."

"Everyone has been so kind to me." She looked into his beautiful eyes. "I want to thank you for all you have done. I am told that you sat by my bed at night."

Judah reached up and touched her pale cheek. "I did no more for you than you did for me when I was in Zippora's cabin." His eyes danced with mirth when he remembered her coming to him as his lover. "Well, perhaps I did not do quite all that you did for me."

Her cheeks flamed and she ducked her head. "Judah, I never thought of myself as a weak female who would faint, but it seems I have turned into one."

"I wouldn't worry about it. You have been through a lot lately. Try to rest and regain your strength."

"I am strong now, Judah. I want to get out of this bed, but your mother insists that I remain one more day."

"I can see that you are stronger. Perhaps between the two of us, we can convince her to allow you to get up this afternoon. Would you like that?"

"Yes, very much."

His eyes moved across her shining hair to rest on her upturned nose. "I want to tell you a few things that may put your mind at rest. First of all, I did not send for Adriane Pierce, Liberty. She would never have come to the house had she known that you were my wife. Sebastian used her to hurt you."

"You and she were very close, weren't you?"

"I will not lie to you, Liberty. At one time we were more than friends."

"She was very beautiful. Did you love her?"

"No, Liberty, there was never love between us. At least not on my part. And now I want to clear up any misunderstanding there might have been about Hope Blackburn. To me she was just a bothersome child. I spent most of my time telling her how wonderful you were. I had no feelings for her one way or the other. She was certainly not my ideal woman."

"What is your ideal woman?"

His smile was radiant. "My ideal woman, is a precocious, golden-haired, blue-eyed minx by the name of Liberty Slaughter."

She leaned back against her pillow, too afraid to believe what he was telling her. "You do not have to be kind to me, Judah. As far as Adriane Pierce is concerned, I realize you would not have brought your mistress into our home. And I know you would not have flirted openly with Hope Blackburn."

"Liberty, I am glad you realize this. There is no woman in my life save yourself." He smiled down at her. "Now, to move on to a safer subject. Oralee told me how upset you were because your slaves had been sold. With her help, we found them all, and they are now back at Briar Oaks. Also, I have paid off all your father's debts, and at this time I am buying back as many of your treasures as I can find. Oralee seemed to think you would be particularly pleased to learn that I had located the portrait of your Aunt Liberty."

Welling tears burned Liberty's eyes. "There are no words to express my gratitude to you, Judah," she said, wiping the tears away. "I am most grateful to you for your kindness. I don't know how I will ever repay you."

"I didn't do it for kindness, Liberty. My motives were not nearly so noble. I wanted to weaken your defenses."

"What defenses?"

He crossed his long legs and rested a sun-browned hand against his boot. "The defenses you have built between you and me, Liberty. The ones that stand between us like a wall."

"There is no wall between us."

"Is there not?"

"I . . . perhaps there is."

His golden hair was streaked by the sunlight that filtered through the open window, and she was mesmerized by his handsomeness. She tried to avoid his eyes, but he grabbed her head between his hands and made her look at him.

"While were were on the *Winged Victory*, I told you that we needed to talk, Liberty. Do you feel up to it now?"

"I . . . yes, I suppose." She had no idea what he wanted to say to her, but she prayed he hadn't taken her threats seriously when she had said she did not want to be married to him. She couldn't imagine not being his wife. Even if he did not love her, she still wanted to stay with him.

"I once asked what you want of me, Liberty."

"Yes, I remember."

"Have you thought about it? Do you have an answer for me?"

She stared at him in confusion. "I don't know what you mean, Judah."

"It is very simple, Liberty." He looked deeply into her eyes. "If I can keep you with me, I will do anything—be anything—you want me to be. You have only to tell me what you want, and if it is within my power, it is yours."

Liberty felt a sob building in her throat. Had she just heard correctly? Was Judah saying that he wanted her? She was blinded by tears as she shook her head, still not understanding. "Please explain what you mean," she choked out.

"What do I have to do to make you love me, Liberty? Do you want me to be your jester and make you laugh? Would you rather I be your gallant, and drop to my knees whenever you enter a room? How about an adoring lover? I would court and woo you every day, Liberty. I can be all these things for you, if it will make you love me. Tell me what you want of me? I love you so desperately that I don't know how to handle the emotions I am feeling. You see, I have never been in love before and it has me thoroughly confused."

Liberty felt as if her breathing had stopped. She stared at Judah, thinking she must have misunderstood. She was afraid to believe he loved her. "But you loved . . . Bandera," she said in confusion.

"No. I was infatuated with her for a few weeks, and

thought it was love. I realize now what a puny emotion it was compared with the earth-shattering feelings I have for you, Liberty."

"Judah, there is something else I have to ask you. Did your grandfather offer you Bend of the River if you would marry me?"

"He did, but that was not why I married you. I married you because I couldn't live without you."

Tears ran down Liberty's face, and she reached out her hand to him. "I cannot believe you love me, Judah. Please do not say it if it is not true."

His hand trembled as he touched her lips. "How can I joke about a love so strong that I cannot even catch my breath when you are near me?" His eyes were shining with unshed tears. "I had thought to put some distance between us until you decided how you felt about me, but I realized that no matter how far I ran, I could never get you out of my mind."

Liberty saw uncertainty and pain in his glorious eyes. She took his hand and laced her fingers through it. "How could you not know that I loved you even as a child, Judah? I lost my heart to you the first night I met you." Tears now flowed, unchecked, down her face. "I love you so much, how could you not know?" She pressed her cheek to his, then raised her head to stare into his eyes. "My dearest, dearest love, you asked me what I want you to be. Never be anything other than what you are. You are everything a man should be. You have been kind and patient with me. You have slain all my dragons. You are the man I fell in love with on a summer night, so long ago."

His arms went around her like two iron bands, and he buried his face in her fragrant hair. "I cannot believe that you return my love, Liberty. I don't deserve to have you love me, but I am damned glad you do," he said, some of his arrogance returning.

She raised her face to his. "You are mine, Judah Slaughter. You always have been mine." As she tossed her golden mane, her eyes danced with happiness. "Although, I didn't know it until a few moments ago," she added.

"Minx," he said, moving onto the bed and pulling her into his arms. "I have something else to tell you. I think it will explain why you fainted—and why my mother has been so protective of your health."

"Am I ill?"

Judah smiled, and his whole face lit up with happiness. "The doctor says I am going to be a father, and that makes me extremely happy."

Liberty stared at him in disbelief, while her hand stole down to cover his, where it rested on her flat stomach. "Is the doctor sure?"

"Yes."

Laughter escaped her lips. "I cannot believe it. Me, a mother—and you . . . a father," she said in awe. "Oh, Judah, how can I stand all the joy you have brought to my life?"

"You deserve every happiness, my little one. I want to cherish you and fill your life with joy."

Her brow furrowed. "This is a strange marriage we have, Judah. I always thought it was the woman who told the man she was going to have his baby."

He held her tightly against him. "There is nothing ordinary about us, Liberty. Ours is a rare and beautiful love." He chuckled. "Since I have known you, you have had me in a spin and right in the palm of your hand."

Her eyes were bright with tears. "Just think, Judah, we are going to have a baby."

"Yes, my dearest heart. Just wait until Philippe hears the good news. He will be happy for us."

"Where is Philippe?"

"He sailed to Europe with a load of sugar cane."

"Why did you not sail with the *Winged Victory?*"

488

"Philippe is her captain now. My grandfather is happy that I have decided to settle down and raise crops and children."

Liberty tossed her pillow in the air and moved onto his lap. "I like the part about raising children."

Judah stared into blue eyes that were alive with love. "The doctor said if we were very careful I could make love to you."

Liberty sighed as her husband's lips settled on hers, in a kiss that started softly and sweetly, but soon became passionate, so passionate it made the blood race through her body. As Judah drew her to him, his hands moved up her neck to cup her face.

"My mind is on fire," he murmured in her ear. "Perhaps we will both stay in bed today."

"Judah, we have come a long way to find the happiness that could have been ours from that first meeting."

He tangled his hands in her hair and brought her lips close to his, so that his warm breath touched her skin. "Our lives and dreams have been magically spun on a silvery sea of moon tide."

Epilogue

It was a crisp sunny afternoon, awash with brilliant fall colors. Judah approached the house, noticing that a buggy was drawn up to the front door. He smiled to himself, for he knew his grandfather had been inviting friends and neighbors to Bend of the River so he could show off his new great-grandson.

On entering the house, Judah walked past the salon, where his mother and grandfather were entertaining their guests. He went through the study, and out onto the back veranda. The now familiar voices of the matronly gossips, Madame Dancy and Madame Pessac, reached Judah's ears as he went down the five steps that took him into the garden.

"What a fortunate child," Madame Dancy observed, staring at the golden-haired baby. "Just think, he will be heir not only of Bend of the River and Briar Oaks, but I hear Monsieur Slaughter owns a huge plantation in Martinique."

"Yes, and I believe this is by far the handsomest baby I have seen in a long time," her friend said.

"Naturally. How could the child be anything else with Liberty as his mother?"

"Well, his father is handsome," Madame Pessac stated.

"I can remember a time when you thought Judah Slaughter was uncivilized," her friend reminded her.

"And so did you," Madame Pessac snapped.

"I was wrong, and I admit it. Like everyone else, I now know that Sebastian and Bandera had us all fooled. Imagine them conspiring to discredit Monsieur Slaughter."

Judah smiled as the matrons' conversation drifted out to him. It seemed he had finally been accepted by the *crème de la crème*.

Gustave made his way to the cradle and stared down at the sleeping child. "Your grandson has done you proud, Gustave," Madame Dancy said. "We were just remarking on how beautiful this child is."

Gustave's voice softened with pride. "I will have to agree with you. My great-grandson is an exceptional child."

Gabrielle moved forward, and tucked the satin coverlet across her grandson's legs. She smiled at her father, and linked her arm through his. "A child brings such joy to a home. I hope Judah and Liberty fill this house with children," she said happily.

Gustave's eyes sparkled. "I wouldn't mind a girl or two," he offered generously. "But I insist on more great-grandsons to carry on the . . . the . . ."

Gabrielle laughed warmly. "To carry on the Slaughter name, Papa?"

Gustave nodded his head, and a rare smile thinned his lips. "Slaughter is a respectable American name." With one last glance at his great-grandson, he crossed the room. "I'll leave you ladies to watch over the child. It is time for my treatment."

Madame Dancy looked at Gabrielle. "What treatment is your father referring to?"

"Do you know Zippora?" Gabrielle asked.

"Yes, she's the witch isn't she."

Gabrielle laughed in amusement. "I do not believe she is a witch, but she has certainly improved my father's

492

health. She lives here on Bend of the River, you know. Liberty insisted that Judah build a house down by the river for Zippora and her grandson."

"Do you really believe that Zippora has improved your father's health?" Madame Pessac asked with wide-eyed interest.

"My father swears by her cures."

"I believe I will pay a call on her before I leave. I have had this misery in my back. Perhaps she can do something for me."

"You will have to wait your turn," Gabrielle said, lifting the baby in her arms, and kissing his soft cheek. "You see, Zippora has become very popular, and many of our friends seek her cure."

Judah felt contentment wash over him. Now that he had a son, he realized why his grandfather had such a deep love for the land. Land was everlasting, something he could pass on to his child.

Judah's eyes moved over the garden until he saw Liberty. His heart was filled with love for his golden-haired wife as he walked toward her.

Liberty moved down the garden path feeling the warm sun on her face. When she saw Judah coming toward her, her footsteps quickened. His turquoise eyes spoke to her of love, and her heart raced within her.

Judah enfolded Liberty in his arms, and as she clung to him, warmth filled his heart for Liberty's sweetness filled his whole being.

Between the two of them, there was no need for words as they walked, arm in arm, toward the house. The sun shone down on their world, and there was eternal love and contentment in their hearts.

THE ECSTASY SERIES
by Janelle Taylor

SAVAGE ECSTASY (Pub. date 8/1/81)   (0824, $3.50)

DEFIANT ECSTASY (Pub. date 2/1/82)   (0931, $3.50)

FORBIDDEN ECSTASY (Pub. date 7/1/82) (1014, $3.50)

BRAZEN ECSTASY (Pub. date 3/1/83)   (1133, $3.50)

TENDER ECSTASY (Pub. date 6/1/83)   (1212, $3.75)

STOLEN ECSTASY (Pub. date 9/1/85)   (1621, $3.95)

Plus other bestsellers by Janelle:

GOLDEN TORMENT (Pub. date 2/1/84)   (1323, $3.75)

LOVE ME WITH FURY (Pub. date 9/1/83) (1248, $3.75)

FIRST LOVE, WILD LOVE
(Pub. date 10/1/84)   (1431, $3.75)

SAVAGE CONQUEST (Pub. date 2/1/85)   (1533, $3.75)

DESTINY'S TEMPTRESS
(Pub. date 2/1/86)   (1761, $3.95)

SWEET SAVAGE HEART
(Pub. date 10/1/86)   (1900, $3.95)

*Available wherever paperbacks are sold, or order direct from the
Publisher. Send cover price plus 50¢ per copy for mailing and
handling to Zebra Books, Dept. 2182, 475 Park Avenue South,
New York, N.Y. 10016. Residents of New York, New Jersey and
Pennsylvania must include sales tax. DO NOT SEND CASH.*